Danuta

Danuta Reah lives in Sheffield with her artist husband. She currently works as an education consultant and as a university lecturer in English Language.

She is a fan of comics and graphic novels, and is interested in the relationship between popular fiction, folklore and anthropology. She is a published cartoonist and writes textbooks on English Language and Linguistics.

Only Darkness is her first novel. Her second, *Silent Playgrounds,* is available in hardcover from Collins Crime.

BY THE SAME AUTHOR

Silent Playgrounds

DANUTA REAH

ONLY DARKNESS

To Patricia

memories of RCAT!

with best wishes

Danuta Reah

HarperCollins*Publishers*

This novel is entirely a work of fiction. The names, characters
and incidents portrayed in it are the work of the author's
imagination. Any resemblance to actual persons, living or
dead, events or localities is entirely coincidental.

HarperCollins*Publishers*
77–85 Fulham Palace Road,
Hammersmith, London W6 8JB

The HarperCollins website address is:
www.fireandwater.com

This paperback edition 2000

First published in Great Britain by
HarperCollins*Publishers* 1999

Copyright © Danuta Reah 1999

Danuta Reah asserts the moral right to
be identified as the author of this work

ISBN 978-0-00-741383-6

All rights reserved. No part of this publication may be
reproduced, stored in a retrieval system, or transmitted,
in any form or by any means, electronic, mechanical,
photocopying, recording or otherwise, without the prior
permission of the publishers.

This book is sold subject to the condition that it shall not,
by way of trade or otherwise, be lent, re-sold, hired out or
otherwise circulated without the publisher's prior consent
in any form of binding or cover other than that in which it
is published and without a similar condition including this
condition being imposed on the subsequent purchaser.

Mixed Sources
Product group from well-managed
forests and other controlled sources
www.fsc.org Cert no. SW-COC-001806
© 1996 Forest Stewardship Council

FSC is a non-profit international organisation established to promote the
responsible management of the world's forests. Products carrying the FSC
label are independently certified to assure consumers that they come
from forests that are managed to meet the social, economic and
ecological needs of present and future generations.

Find out more about HarperCollins and the environment at
www.harpercollins.co.uk/green

For my mother, Margaret Kot, who died
before this manuscript was accepted for
publication.

ACKNOWLEDGEMENTS

With many thanks to the people who gave me help and advice when I was writing this book, particularly to the e-mail writers' group: Sue, Penny and Jenn for their constructive criticism; to Janet, Jennifer and Kathryn for their support; to Detective Chief Inspector Steve Hicks for his advice about police procedure – where I've got it wrong, it was where I didn't follow that advice; and, of course, to Ken and Alex. (Alex – particular thanks for allowing me to borrow Buttercup. I hereby return her.)

People who are familiar with South Yorkshire will recognize that Moreham is closely based on Rotherham. I hope that the inhabitants of that historic town will forgive me for the liberties I have taken with their geography. People who know Rotherham will also recognize that City College campus is based on the campus of Rotherham College of Arts and Technology, before its refurbishment. No other reference to this establishment is intended.

...... *all my light drawn in to shed*
Only darkness on the living, only darkness on the dead

from 'The Death of the PWD Man', *Tony Harrison*

1

It was a Thursday in December, the night that Debbie saw the killer.

She had just finished her evening class and was on her way out of the college. It was late – about nine-thirty. The students had kept her talking after the class was finished, and by the time she had dumped her books in the staff room and grabbed her coat, Les Walker was standing in the entrance lobby waiting to lock up after her.

He jingled his keys as she approached and tapped his watch meaningfully. 'Not got a home to go to?'

'Doesn't seem much point now,' she said, looking at her watch in response to his gesture. 'Sorry. Are you on again first thing?' Debbie hated keeping people waiting. 'Have I stopped you from going home?'

Les shook his head. He didn't seem too put out. 'No, it's gone ten by the time we're finished here. Got to check all the rooms on the top yet.'

He opened the heavy entrance door. A gust of wind pushed it in against him, and a spatter of rain hit the floor. 'Wild night,' he observed. 'Got your car in the top car park? We've not locked it yet.'

'No.' Debbie looked apprehensively at the shiny dark of the pavement. 'I'm on the train.'

'You be careful then.' Les was serious now. 'Remember those girls . . .'

Thanks, Les, I needed that. 'That was way over outside Doncaster.'

'Not got him yet. He'll do it again. That kind of nutter, he'll keep on till he's caught. They want hanging, doing something

1

like that, I'll tell you . . .'

The sound of feet on the steps outside silenced him, and Rob Neave, the security officer, pushed his way through the door. His hair was plastered to his face with the rain, and water was dripping from his jacket. 'Finished over here?' he said to Les. He acknowledged Debbie with a nod.

'Just got the top floor to do.' As Rob Neave had overall control of the day-to-day running of the building, and a reputation as a bit of a new broom, the caretakers were wary of him. 'Just seeing Debbie out. I was telling her . . .'

The wind gusted again, and the sound of a window swinging back against its hinges stopped him. He looked at Debbie. 'You be careful, now.' He disappeared up the stairs, leaving her with Rob Neave.

She finished fastening her briefcase and looked towards the door. 'I'd better be off,' she said uncertainly as the wind sent rain spattering across the windows.

'Are you in the top car park? The lights are out. I'll walk across with you.' The car park, late in the evening, was dark and deserted.

'It's OK,' she said. 'Thanks. But I'm on the train.'

He looked at her thoughtfully. She was aware that her mac was only showerproof and her shoes were lightweight for this kind of weather. *It was fine this morning!* She pulled out her umbrella, and he shook his head and laughed. He held the door open for her and watched her down the steps as she struggled to open her umbrella against the wind, then he closed the door, leaving her to the mercy of the storm.

And it was a storm. The rain was drenching, and the wind carried it round, up, under her umbrella, driving against her, freezing her face as she tried to pull the collar of her coat around her. She hurried down the hill towards the station. She was later than usual, but there was a chance the bad weather might have delayed her train and she had some hope of catching it. If not, she was in for a half-hour wait on a freezing platform. There was a small waiting room, with seats and a wall heater, but it was always locked when the last of the station staff left at nine.

She reached the main road and waited for the lights. It was raining too hard to see clearly if any cars were coming. The air smelt unusually clean. Normally, there was a miasma of car fumes at this junction, but the rain seemed to have cleaned them away. The green man lit up, and she hurried across the road, towards the bridge. She might just do it. As she crossed the bridge, she could hear the river rushing against the narrow banks, swollen by the rain.

Another gust of wind caught her, and she heard the sound of glass shattering. Some insurance jobs tomorrow, she thought, reminding herself to check for fallen roof tiles in the morning. She splashed through the puddle outside the station, and was under cover.

The ticket office was a blank face requesting her to buy her ticket on the train. The screen showing arrivals was a black and white blur – another storm victim. She began to run towards the platform in case her train was in. She hurried down the covered ramp, and then, seeing that there was no train on the platform, slowed down. Had she missed it, or was it late?

The platform was empty, and she began to realize that there was something wrong with the light. It was yellow and flickering, not bright enough. The shadows in the corners were larger and darker, and the waiting room was black. She tried the door. Locked. The opposite platform – the only other platform – was in darkness, and the fair-haired young woman who sometimes shared Debbie's evening wait on the other side of the rails wasn't there. There was no one there, so the Doncaster train must have gone.

I didn't mean to think about Doncaster.

The wind caught the platform sign and sent it rattling on its chain against the pipe work. The rain splashed on the rails, and then stopped. The light flickered again, the strange, yellow light, and then there was silence.

Uneasy, Debbie stood at the edge of the platform looking to see if the train was coming. Her feet crunched in something. She looked down. Glass, broken glass. She remembered the noise of glass breaking as she came over the bridge, and looked round. Up. The glass over the light was broken, and

3

the tube was hanging loose, giving off that dull, flickering light.

That wasn't the wind. Someone broke that. Someone broke that just as I crossed the bridge. No one came out of the station.

She looked back up the ramp towards the only exit. Her mouth went dry. Someone was standing there at the top of the ramp, not moving, just looking towards her on the platform. She couldn't see him – it must be a him, he was so big – clearly. The light was behind him. Her sensible brain said, *It's a passenger, don't be stupid,* but the hairs were standing up on her arms, and her heart was thumping. The figure began to move towards her down the ramp.

There's no way out!

Just then, the sound of the train came up the track. She waited in suspense for its lights in the dark. Her legs felt shaky and she wanted to grab the train door as it went past her, slowing. She pressed the door-open button without waiting for the light, and when the door finally slid open almost fell into the carriage. Then she felt like a fool, and looked out of the window to see what her alarming fellow passenger was doing.

But there was nobody there.

By the time Debbie got home, it was late. She closed her umbrella, shaking it as she did so, and hurried down the passage that led on to the back of the row of small terraced houses. She went in through the kitchen, dumping her coat and umbrella behind the back door, and quickly through to the living room, turned on the gas fire and stood there for a few minutes soaking up the heat. Debbie's dream was to come back to a warm and welcoming house, but she didn't have central heating yet, and Debbie couldn't see when she would be able to afford it. The salary of a young further-education lecturer didn't allow for luxuries.

The room was starting to warm up now. Debbie looked round it with some pride. She'd bought the house eighteen months ago. It had been, in estate agents' jargon, in need of modernization. She hadn't been able to afford rent and a mortgage, so she lived in the house, keeping one room more or less habitable, while the rewiring, plumbing and plastering went on around her. Now it was gradually starting to look the way she wanted it to, and this room was almost finished. Fitted carpets had been beyond her pocket but her mother had offered her the Persian rug from the little-used front room of the house Debbie had grown up in. Debbie accepted the rug, sanded, varnished and sealed the boards herself, and the rug glowed in the middle of the floor. She had changed her mind about a fitted carpet when she had seen how it looked. There was very little furniture in the small room – two easy chairs and a polished table in between. Bookshelves ran up each side of the chimney breast. There were pictures on the walls – a drawing of the woods outside Goldthorpe, and a framed poster for the Monet exhibition that Debbie had seen at the Royal Academy a few years ago. The only other ornaments were a group of photographs on the table.

The photographs were strictly family – her father with a younger Debbie, looking proudly at his daughter as she smiled toothily and waved a trophy. What was that for? The junior swimming gala? Her mother looking unaccustomedly serious in her Open University graduation gown. She'd insisted on having an official photograph taken. *I've waited long enough for this*, she'd told Debbie and her husband. A later picture of her father, taken about a year before he died.

The cat flap sounded its snick-snack rattle, and Debbie's cat came urgently into the room, tail up, with breathless mews of excitement. She picked it up and went into the kitchen, looking for the tin opener. The cat nibbled her ear and clawed impatiently at her shoulder. She put it on the floor, where it wove in and out between her feet, tripping her up as she filled a dish with food. When the dish was on the floor, the cat single-mindedly put its head down and ate. Debbie hadn't meant to get a cat. She was out a lot, she needed to go away, it just wasn't convenient, but when a bedraggled kitten had turned up cowering behind the old shed in the garden, she couldn't turn it away. It had taken her a week to coax the little animal closer and nearly a week more before she could touch it. After that it began to come in the house. Two weeks later, it was turning its nose up at cheap cat food and ambushing

Debbie's ankles as she went past. She called it Buttercup, because of its yellow tabby coat.

She remembered her wet mac in the kitchen, so she took it into the hall and hung it on a hook. If it didn't dry in time, she'd just have to wear her jacket tomorrow. She was reluctant to sit down and be quiet. Usually after an evening class, she spent maybe half an hour just winding down, having a glass of wine or maybe a beer, listening to music; and then she would take another glass of wine into the bathroom and run a hot deep bath – setting the water heater to come on early on Thursdays was one of her extravagances – then lie there sipping wine and relaxing. When she felt sleepy, she went to bed, and usually fell asleep in minutes, not waking again until the alarm went off at eight.

She poured herself a glass of wine, went back into the living room and sat down in front of the fire. The memory of that encounter at the station lingered and she couldn't settle. When she closed her eyes, she could see that strange light. The drumming of the rain on her window became the drumming of the rain on the station canopy. The figure on the platform began to walk towards her and her legs were heavy and she couldn't move. She tried to call out but her voice was too weak to make any sound. She looked for the train coming in, but the line was gone and a fast-flowing river, smooth and dangerous, ran beside her. She looked at the ground and the river was running underneath her feet. The thin lattice she was standing on began to crumble away. The dark figure was behind her, but she couldn't see it.

She jerked awake in the chair, the image shattering, the rushing of the river becoming the hiss of the gas fire. It was time she was in bed.

Early next morning, in the small hours, after the storm had blown itself out, a freight train taking a load of scrap from Leeds to Sheffield slowed a bit as the train approached the junction near Rawmarsh, in response to the signal. As it speeded up again beyond the junction, the driver noticed something slumped against a post by the rails. It could have

6

been a sack of rubbish. He radioed through and the call went to the local police to investigate.

'Where exactly did he say?' Kevin Naylor walked along the track side and shone his torch along the line towards the bridge. The railway was particularly inaccessible here, and they'd had to bump the car along a muddy bridle path and walk to the bridge.

'Just beyond the junction.' His partner, Cath Hill, was fed up. It was cold and wet and she didn't want to push through the thick undergrowth alongside the track in search of somebody's dumped rubbish. They'd been heading back for a break when the call had come through. She poked around in the bushes. 'Enough condoms here to start a factory. It's along the line, he was coming through the junction, he said. He hadn't stopped but he'd slowed right down, so it's probably not too far along. He said something about a post. Let's get this done and get back to the car.'

As they walked back along the line, playing their torches ahead, the light from the steelworks faded behind them. Cath shone her torch against the bushes. The wet leaves glistened back at her, but the light hardly penetrated the shadows in the thick foliage. Gravel crunched underfoot, and something rustled and moved in the undergrowth. She shone her torch at the sound, but it wasn't repeated. The wind was getting up again, and Cath had to brace herself as it rattled the leaves, releasing a sudden spatter of rain water. Ahead was a cutting where the track ran into darkness. Cath didn't fancy going into that narrow space without knowing what was ahead. The hairs on her arms were beginning to rise, and she looked back along the track to make sure she wasn't alone.

She shone her torch through the gully, playing the light up and down the wet stone. She could see the post now, just beyond the far end, and, yes, there was something bulky lying against it. Her fatigue had gone, and she felt apprehension tightening her stomach. Her senses sharpened. She called to Kevin who was shining his torch into the undergrowth further back along the line. He started in her direction. Cath walked towards the post. She didn't hurry now because she knew what was there. In the torchlight she could already see fair hair, and as she got nearer she could see the woman's face oddly shadowed, her eyes great pools of darkness. She moved up to the woman and crouched down in front of her, shining the torch directly into her face.

'Oh Christ, oh shit!' She pulled the torch back as Kevin's shone over her shoulder. She heard his exclamation as he turned away. The lower half of the woman's face was covered with black tape that had made it appear shadowed from a distance. Her eyes were – not there. She stared at them from bloody sockets, her head held back against the post by the wire twisted tight around her neck.

Rob Neave turned over in bed, woken up by his radio. Half past five, just time for the shipping forecast and *Farming Today*. He usually woke at this time, early shift or not, and either listened to the radio as he got up, or lay in bed listening as the shipping forecast became the farming programme, and then *Today*. The farmers were worrying about pigs again this morning. He was getting to be an expert on pigs – the price of pork, anyway. He'd never seen a real pig in his life.

He decided to go in for the seven-thirty start again. There wasn't too much to be at home for, and if he didn't have to go to work, he found it hard to get out of bed at all. Didn't seem much point really. He hadn't got in until gone ten the night before, listened to some music, drunk a couple of beers. It had been a long day, so he'd made himself something to eat and gone to bed. Sleep hadn't come easily. He'd turned on the radio in the end and listened through close-down and then the *World Service*.

He was coming out of the shower, towelling himself when he caught the end of the first news bulletin . . . *The body of a woman was found on railway lines early this morning in South Yorkshire. A police spokesman commented that it is too early to say how the woman had died. Three women have been killed in the South Yorkshire region in the past eighteen months and their bodies left on or near railway tracks . . .*

He listened to the end of the bulletin which just recapped on the killings, but gave no more information about the dead

8

woman. He could see Deborah Sykes in her light mac, struggling to hold her umbrella straight as she had disappeared into
the storm the night before. He decided to leave breakfast, and
started pulling his clothes on, looking round for his keys and
cash. Ten minutes later he was braking for the first set of
lights that held him on red in the middle of an empty road.

2

City College, Moreham, is so called because it stands in the centre of the town, five minutes' walk from the train and bus stations, and just a stone's throw from the fine medieval church and the chapel on the bridge. The college buildings display a selection of twentieth-century architecture. The North building, the most modern, nearly twenty years old, presents a face of smoked glass to the world; its entrance is hard to find and the casual visitor can get lost in a confusing maze of corridors. The Moore building, the middle sibling, is a box of glass windows and concrete, nearly forty years old, and shabby and depressing. Inside, it is more comfortable. On the other side of the road stands the oldest, and the most beautiful despite its run-down appearance, the Broome building, an elegant art-deco construction with an oak door in its curving facade. Its windows watch you like eyes.

Debbie had overslept, and had arrived at the station two minutes before a train was leaving. She usually read the paper on the journey, but as she hadn't had time to buy one, she stared out of the window instead. The track side was overgrown with weeds and the high walls were covered with graffiti – mostly incomprehensible and, to the uninformed eye, indistinguishable, tags, and the occasional word. *Joke* was written in letters about two feet high across a wall covered and over-covered in spray paint. When Debbie had been at college, the graffiti had been political: anti-government slogans, ANC slogans, comments about the Gulf War, even some left over from the bitter miners' strike – *Coal not dole, Thatcher out, Save our pits.* Now it seemed to be tagging, a meaningless cry of, *I'm here!* or the inevitable, *Fuck you, Wogs stink, Irish scum.*

The train ran on through the industrial East End of Sheffield where the skeletons of the great steelworks were gradually disappearing and the streets and houses looked decayed and defeated. The toy-town dome of Meadowhall shopping centre stood among sprawling acres of car parks, already full. People struggled off the train, other people got on. They looked anxious and tense. The bridge that took the shoppers over the road was seething with people. *To the shopping*, a sign said. *Joke* . . . The train pulled out, past some tumbledown buildings, through areas of green where the canal ran sluggish and black close to the line. *Fisto* was spray-painted on a stone building, and again on a derelict shed. It looked quite decorative. The spire of Moreham church came into view, and Debbie picked up her bag as the familiar platform ran past her window.

The college day was in full swing when she pushed her way through the crowd of students on the steps leading into the Broome building. The day was fine after the storm of the night before, but cold. The steps served as an informal coffee bar, meeting place and, since the college management implemented a no-smoking policy, a smoking room for students and staff. It didn't make a particularly attractive venue, as a busy road ran between the buildings, and conversation was interrupted by the noise of cars, and buses pulling away from the stop outside the main entrance. The air always smelt dirty, particularly on cold, still days.

Debbie nodded to Trish Allen, a psychology lecturer and hardened smoker, who was continuing her class through the coffee break with a small group of students, all huddled in a companionable, smoky ring. She saw the lanky figure of Sarah Peterson, one of her A-level students, standing uncertainly in the entrance, drawing awkwardly on a cigarette. Debbie greeted Sarah as she went past and received a quick, eyes-averted smile. She felt tempted to go back out and join the group on the steps, spend ten minutes talking to another human being – something she hadn't done since nine-thirty the previous night, but she pushed through the double doors into the dark, high-ceilinged corridor beyond.

One of the first people she saw as she pushed through

the doors was Rob Neave coming down the stairs towards her, heading out of the building. He stopped when he saw her. 'Get wet last night?' he asked. Debbie nodded and he laughed. She began to feel more cheerful.

'There was something I wanted to ask you about,' she said. 'I had a bit of bother last night, during my class.'

'OK. I'm on my way to a meeting now.' He pulled an eloquent face. 'But I'm free later. I'll come along to your staff room – four-thirtyish?' He directed a smile at her that made her feel pleasantly buoyant, and she turned towards her staff room. Chatting with Rob Neave was one of the grains of sugar in the otherwise worthy muesli of Debbie's working life.

The lie on Debbie's timetable was that Friday morning was her morning off, as payback for her evening class. The lie on her contract was that she worked a thirty-five-hour week. She was usually at her desk by ten on Friday mornings, catching up with her marking and the never-ending paperwork that was now a feature of the job.

She let herself into the small room she shared with Louise Hatfield, who was in charge of the English section which, these days, meant her and Debbie, and the changing faces of part-time staff who were employed through an agency. When Debbie had started at City, the English section had consisted of five members of staff, but financial crises and falling student numbers had led to a series of early retirements, and now there were just Louise and Debbie. 'There goes my empire,' Louise had remarked to Debbie at the end of last term. 'Our days are numbered too. You mark my words, girl.'

Debbie had been hoping that Louise would be in the staff room, but the locked door told her that she must still be teaching – so no one to talk to. She began to sift through the pile of mail on her desk. She was tired. When she'd gone to bed, she hadn't been able to sleep, and had lain awake listening to the radio until gone three. Now she was at her desk, she couldn't concentrate. She wanted to talk to someone about the odd scene at the station the previous night, laugh about it to get rid of the lingering feeling of – what? – dread? – that the silent figure had evoked.

Don't be stupid. It was nothing.

She sighed and turned over the pile of post that had arrived on her desk that morning. Most of it was circulars and advertising from companies selling textbooks and training. Bin the lot. There were a couple of memos, one from the principal about an audit of class registers, and one from the union about the ever present threat of redundancy.

Debbie ran her hand through her hair, worried. She felt vulnerable. She wasn't sure how she would manage if she lost her job. There was no point in thinking about it for the moment. She had other things on her mind – like marking. She pulled her work folder towards her, and tried to pin back a lock of hair that had freed itself from its confinement of combs. The disturbance brought the whole lot down round her shoulders, and she irritably pulled it back off her face and wound a rubber band round to hold it. Fifteen A-level essays to mark, and about thirty GCSE pieces. She picked up the first one and started reading.

She wasn't even halfway through at twelve-thirty when hunger drove her over to the canteen in the Moore building.

Fridays usually weren't too busy in the canteen. Most students didn't have classes on a Friday afternoon, and a lot of those that did 'wagged' it. Debbie collected a mixed salad from the salad bar, struggled with her conscience and got a side order of chips, and looked around for somewhere to sit.

'Hey, Debbie!' Tim Godber, media studies lecturer, journalist *manqué* and at one time a lover of Debbie's, was waving her over.

'Hi, Tim.' Debbie was wary. She'd been very attracted at one time, but once they had fallen into bed together after a departmental party, he'd turned into a game player who'd tried to control and manipulate her through different hoops via charm and indifference, and Debbie was nowadays more put off than interested. They'd gone out for drinks together a couple of weekends ago, and again ended up in Debbie's bed, but she'd told herself the next morning that that was the last time.

He pushed his hair back from his forehead and moved his

empty tray to make space at the table for her. 'How are you, sweetheart?'

'I'm not your sweetheart.' Debbie had learnt to be brisk. 'And I'm fine. How are you, lover boy?'

'I'm not your lover boy, and I'm fine too.' Tim no longer found it necessary to charm Debbie. They chatted in a desultory way as they ate, exchanging gossip from their different staff rooms. Debbie was fielding an invitation for a drink, when there was a flurry of discord from the coffee bar at the far side of the canteen, shouts and the sound of breaking china – *breaking glass* – that meant either horseplay or a fight. She got up from the table to see what was happening, though she had no intention of doing anything about it. Some of the young male students could be quite intimidating. Someone seemed to be dealing with it anyway. The shouting had died down. Rob Neave was talking to a group of students over where the trouble had been.

Tim, who had no more desire than Debbie to get involved in student fights, looked relieved, but continued to watch the situation with interest. 'Machismo fascismo,' he said, 'wins out every time.' Debbie looked at him. 'Your friend the ex-policeman. The one laying down the law over there.'

He did look a bit authoritarian, actually, but Debbie was damned if she was going to agree with Tim about it. She liked Rob Neave. 'I don't think he's laying down the law. Why should he be doing that? He's just sorting them out. Is he an ex-policeman?' Debbie thought that she ought to have known it.

Tim knew everything. It was partly his journalist's love of gossip, and partly his connections at the local newspaper. 'That's his job. Security, antivandalism, keep the buggers down. You remember that business with the lift last term?'

Debbie shook her head. Tim's story gradually came out about how some students at the end of last term had vandalized one of the lifts in the Moore building so badly they'd jammed it, trapping themselves inside. When they pushed the alarm button and summoned a rescue party, Neave, working the situation out, had delayed the rescue for two hours, claiming they couldn't get the lift moving. The caretakers had stood around outside the lift, threatening to light a fire in the shaft. By the time the pair were released, they were pretty subdued, and the college authorities, faced with a bill for the lift repair, weren't in any mood to listen to complaints. Debbie laughed as he got to the end of the story. Tim was a good raconteur. 'Anyway,' he went on, 'the railway strangler has struck again.'

'What?' Debbie dropped her fork.

'Didn't you hear? It's been all over the radio this morning. It'll be in the paper as well, I should think. They found a body on the line last night.'

Debbie felt cold. 'Where? When last night? Who was it?'

'On the way to Mexborough, I think. They haven't given a name and they haven't said it's him again, but it must be.' He picked up one of Debbie's chips and ate it. 'You'll get fat.' He ate another.

'Not at this rate. Look, Tim, this woman, she wasn't killed in Moreham, at the station, was she?'

'Don't know, shouldn't think so for a minute.' He began to look at her more closely. 'Why? Come on, tell me.'

Debbie found herself telling him about her encounter at the station last night, and the way the strange figure had made her feel. 'He looked sort of, well, dangerous,' she finished, lamely. 'It's nothing.'

'No, go on, it's interesting.' She had his attention now, and he plied her with questions she couldn't answer. Had she really heard the sound of breaking glass coming from the station? Not from anywhere else? What did he look like? Was she sure he didn't catch the train?

'Perhaps you saw him – the strangler,' he said, half seriously.

'Rubbish! If it was over at Mexborough it can't have been anything to do with what I saw.' Debbie was annoyed because she felt uneasy.

'It's the next stop up the line.'

She thought about it, and then saw what time it was. 'Oh, God, I've got to go. I'm teaching in five minutes.'

Tim smiled at her encouragingly, and as she left was getting out a notebook and pen. 'I'll just stay here and get some work done. It's quieter than in our staff room. See you later.'

As she left the canteen, she saw Rob Neave leaning against the wall watching the students with a conspicuously bleak expression. He caught Debbie's eye and winked. As she went past him, he said, 'It'll be nearer five than four-thirty. Is that OK?'

'Yes, it won't take long. It's nothing much.'

He looked sceptical. 'Your last *nothing much* took half my budget,' he said, referring to the time when Louise and Debbie had decided to take advantage of the fact that the college had actually appointed someone with responsibility for security. They'd campaigned for better lighting in some of the isolated parts of the campus, assuming that the boyish face and easy charm of the new appointee meant he would be a pushover. He'd proved to be a tough negotiator, who was, fortunately, on their side. They'd got their lighting.

Debbie noticed as she looked more closely at him that he was tired and drawn. She wondered if he was another person who'd had a sleepless night. She almost told him about her experience at the station. She felt in need of expert advice.

Debbie's Friday afternoon A-level class distracted her and she forgot, for the moment, about the incident at the station. The students were studying 'The Rime of the Ancient Mariner', and making heavy weather of it. Debbie had asked them to think about the lines: *God save thee, ancient Mariner!/From fiends that plague thee thus!/Why look'st thou so?' With my cross-bow/ I shot the Albatross.* Why, she had asked them, did the mariner shoot the albatross that had brought good luck to the ship? Somehow, the discussion had got hijacked into an animal rights argument that was interesting, but not what Debbie wanted them to do.

'Anyway, it's cruel,' said Sarah Peterson, who had been following the discussion closely. Debbie sighed. Sarah rarely contributed, but it was typical that when she did it was with the wrong end of the stick securely in her hands. She could see Leanne Ferris, one of the brighter members of the group, about to deliver a sharp rebuttal, and she pulled them back to the poem, and began to work them around to thinking about a less literal interpretation. She saw Sarah diligently writing down the points she was making.

Sarah was Debbie's particular concern that year, a different kind of student from Leanne. Leanne, quick-minded and confident about her own ideas, would sail through anything the exam system threw at her, as long as Debbie could persuade her to do a bit of work. Sarah worked very hard, but didn't understand. She had no confidence in her own ideas and opinions, so she wanted someone – Debbie in this case – to tell her what she should think. She didn't want to know why the answers were correct, what they meant or what the implications were. She just wanted the answers, as her palpable puzzlement when answers weren't offered made clear.

After the class, Sarah waited until the others had gone, and then asked rather diffidently if there was time to discuss her last essay. 'The one I did on *Othello*. I didn't get a very good mark.' She rummaged in her bag and produced the essay which looked rather crumpled, and a can of Coke. 'I've got to go straight to work,' she said apologetically, gesturing at the can. Sarah, like a lot of students at City, could only afford to stay at college by working. She had a job at a pub on the outskirts of Moreham.

They discussed the essay, or at least, Debbie did, while Sarah wrote things down. 'Have another go at it,' Debbie suggested. 'Once you've got one good essay, it gives you a model for others. Let me have it on Monday, OK?'

'Thanks, Debbie.' Sarah smiled and briefly met Debbie's eyes before hurrying out. Debbie collected her things and headed back to her room.

When she got there, Rob Neave was leaning on the windowsill beside her desk, flicking through the pages of one of her books – a collection of Auden's poems. He usually showed some interest in her books, though she sometimes found it hard to tell if he really meant it. His face could be difficult to read. He looked up as she came in. 'Deborah.' He was one of the few people who used her full name. 'So what's this *nothing much* problem?'

'Do you want a coffee? There was something else as well,

actually.' He declined the coffee, as she knew he would. He'd made some pointed comments in the past about the standard of the coffee that she and Louise drank. He waited as Debbie got herself a drink, idly turning the pages of the Auden.

She remembered the last time she'd talked to him about poetry. He'd picked up a copy of *The Waste Land* from where it was lying on Debbie's desk. What had this got to do, he'd wanted to know, with the lives most of the students led? 'A lot,' Debbie had retorted. And was it going to help them with what they really needed in their lives – a way to make a decent living? 'It teaches them how to think.' Debbie wasn't giving anything away to anyone about the value of studying literature. He'd argued the point good-naturedly for a bit longer and she'd wondered at the end of it if he'd been winding her up.

'You can borrow that, if you want.' She was surprised when he said he would. 'I thought you didn't see any point in poetry,' she said.

'I didn't say that.' He was still turning the pages, but not really reading.

Aware that it sounded a bit blunt, Debbie asked, 'Is it right that you used to be in the police?'

He looked at her. 'Who's been talking to you? Yes, for ten years.' He didn't seem to mind her question, but something told her not to ask any more.

'Let me show you this.' She took the book out of his hands, and started leafing through it. 'This one. That end bit there.' She was looking at the lines towards the end of 'The Shield of Achilles', the bit about the ragged urchin in the weed-choked field. *That girls are raped, that two boys knife a third/ were axioms to him, who'd never heard/ Of any world where promises were kept/ Or one could weep because another wept.* He read it through and looked at her, waiting. 'Didn't you meet that boy a hundred times when you were in the police force?'

He was still reading the lines. 'Yes, you see them all the time.'

'That's what I meant. Poetry has a lot to do with their lives.'

He grinned, acknowledging both the point, and the fact

18

that she wasn't prepared to let the argument go. 'OK, but you can romanticize as well.'

'I don't think that romanticizes. It calls raping and killing axioms.' She was standing close to him as they read the lines, and she was aware of the warmth coming from him, the smell of a laundered shirt, the faint smell of sweat.

He nodded, but cut the topic off. 'Right. What's the problem.' He listened while Debbie outlined the concerns that she had working in Room B110 at night, where the curtainless windows, brightly lit, looked out on to the street and gave any passer-by a clear view of who was – and who wasn't – in there. She told him about some trouble she'd had with youths in the street the night before. He looked at her – 'Why didn't you report it at the time?' – making a sudden switch from friendly to official. She had seen him use this device to wrong-foot people, and now it derailed her.

'There wasn't anyone around to report it to,' she protested, sounding defensive in her own ears.

He thought for a moment and seemed to make a conscious effort to move back into a more relaxed stance. 'I know there's still a problem with security in the evenings. You could do with mobile phones really, the teaching staff.' He gave her a quick smile. 'But that'd be the rest of my budget.' After he'd made some notes, he said, 'What was the other thing?'

'Oh, well . . .' Debbie was a bit uncertain now, unsure of his reception, but he leant back against the wall and waited, so she told him about her encounter at the station. He listened in silence. 'Should I tell the police?' she said.

'Yes. Next question.'

'Do you think it had anything to do with the murder?' Debbie tried to keep the anxiety out of her voice, but something must have come through, because he narrowed his eyes and his face went serious.

'I've no idea, Deborah. You'll have to tell them and let them work it out. Why don't you bring your car when you're working late?'

'Because I haven't got one. I don't drive.'

He looked exasperated, but Louise turned up before he could say anything, and the conversation turned to more general college matters. After a few minutes he left, promising to get back to Debbie about Room B110.

Louise was packing a pile of marking into her briefcase. 'A bit of leisure activity,' she added, seeing Debbie look at it. 'Doing anything interesting this weekend?'

Debbie felt low. 'I hate weekends. I'm not going anywhere, I haven't got anyone to go with and even if I did I've got so much work I couldn't anyway.'

'Fancy a drink this evening?' As Debbie accepted Louise's invitation, she thought that the older woman must have seen how down she looked. Debbie, the youngest lecturer in the English and humanities team, was usually known as the most cheerful, having, as Louise pointed out, a lot more energy than the others, 'and the chance of a future that will get you out of this dump.' They agreed to meet later at Louise's house. Louise didn't like pubs much, and Debbie felt like a quiet evening.

Rob Neave was home in his flat, listening to music and letting his mind drift. Maybe things were getting better. They didn't seem to be getting any worse. The flat was tiny, a bedsitter, really, but called a flat because it was self-contained. He had a small kitchen and a bathroom to call his own, and that was all he'd wanted at the time. He'd taken the first offer on the house he used to share with Angie, the first offer that would cover the mortgage. All he'd taken from the house were his stereo and some pictures. He'd bought everything else he needed – a bed, a chair, carpets, curtains, a cooker. It was all he could manage to do, to find a new place to live, a new job.

The evening stretched in front of him, bleak and empty. He could go out – but where and why? He could stay in, read, listen to music, like he'd done for the past countless number of evenings. He wondered about giving Lynne a ring, going over to her place, talking a bit of police shop, picking up the gossip, spending a couple of hours in her bed. It would be a distraction, something to do. Though she'd probably be busy at this short notice.

Maybe it was time to move on. Staying here, everything

was a reminder. Places he went to, people he saw. He'd found a letter waiting when he got in, from an ex-colleague, Pete Morton. Morton had gone into the security business up in Newcastle, Neave's childhood city. He'd written to ask if Neave was interested in joining him. *There's a load of work here*, Morton had written. *I'm starting to turn stuff down*. Neave thought seriously about the offer, about going back to Newcastle. He needed to get away.

Applying for the job at City College had been part of getting away. He didn't know anyone there, and no one knew him. The job had looked interesting as well. The place was wide open, equipment was walking out through the front door, the buildings were being vandalized and staff and bona fide students were starting to feel intimidated. It had been a challenge he'd enjoyed, imposing a system on to the anarchic world of post-sixteen education. It had given him something to think about, but he'd done as much as he could there.

He knew he wasn't particularly liked. It didn't worry him. He had the capacity to get on well with people, inspire trust – it had been an asset in his last job, but he didn't need it now. His face in repose looked boyish and good-humoured, and his eyes, despite – or perhaps because of – the lines under them that seemed to be a permanent feature now, tended to look as though he smiled a lot. When people found out he wasn't the easy-going person he seemed, they resented it. But he got results.

He thought about his conversation with Deborah Sykes that afternoon. He remembered his first meeting with her. She'd been banging her head against the brick wall of management, trying to get a perfectly reasonable request for decent lighting implemented. The response had been to agree in principle and postpone action *until the budget allowed* – i.e. indefinitely. He'd played traitor on that one, and helped her get it through. She, and then Louise, her sharp-tongued boss, had become his first supporters in the place. He enjoyed their company, and had taken to dropping into their room to talk to them.

He'd fired Debbie's evangelical instincts when they'd had some kind of argument about books, about the value of poetry, and she'd started lending him things she wanted him to read. Typical bloody teacher. He smiled. He liked Debbie, and he'd been relieved when he'd seen her come through the college entrance that morning. His mind wandered. He could picture her now, not very tall – her head had just reached his shoulder when she stood beside him this afternoon. She kept her black hair firmly pulled back and held in a knot with pins and combs, and it had smelled clean and sweet. He tried to picture it curling down round her pale, pretty face and over those small, high tits . . . He shook himself awake, pushed that line of thought out of his mind – *you don't need that* – and picked up the book she'd lent him, turning the pages back to the poem she'd pointed out . . . *were axioms to him, who'd never heard/ Of any world where promises were kept/ Or one could weep because another wept.*

She was right, he'd known them, the empty-eyed children who didn't seem to know – or to care – what or why their lives meant to themselves or anyone. And maybe it was him, too.

He read on through some of the other poems, and found more words that spoke to him – *the glacier knocks in the cupboard, the desert sighs in the bed* . . . He even found that 'Stop all the Clocks' poem from the last film he'd seen with Angie. He couldn't read that. It had made Angie cry, and it would make him cry now, if he could cry, if he wanted to cry.

'The thing is,' Debbie said, pouring herself another glass of wine. 'Sorry, did you want one? The thing is, I like being on my own and I don't – if you see what I mean. When things are going OK it's great, but when you've got something on your mind, you haven't got anyone to talk to.' She stood up, feeling the wine she'd drunk, and got another bottle out of her bag. 'I bought a red. Is that all right?' She had arrived about eight-thirty, and they'd spent the first hour talking about work, students, and drinking a bit too quickly.

'Yes, fine. I dunno about all this talking it over.' Louise had been married for twelve years and sometimes envied Debbie her freedom. 'Dan only has conversations with the television these days. What problems? Want to talk about it?'

22

'Oh, it's complicated. A bit of it's Tim, I suppose.'

'Tim Godber? He's always a problem. I wish he'd go and be a proper journalist and stop wasting my time.' Louise had to organize curriculum and timetables, and thought that Tim didn't take his teaching work seriously. 'What's your problem with Tim?'

'Well, we had a bit of a fling and I wish we hadn't. There's something a bit creepy about him.'

'Is he giving you any hassle?' Louise's voice sharpened.

'No, oh no, nothing like that. I just wish, I don't know, that I'd kept away from him, really . . .'

'Did you enjoy it at the time?' Louise refilled her glass and raised an eyebrow at Debbie.

'Well, OK, yes, I did.'

'Well then.' Louise dismissed the problem. 'Was that all? That's worrying you, I mean? You've been quiet all day.'

'Louise?'

'Still here, still listening.'

'You know Rob Neave?'

'The security man? Yes. What about him? You haven't joined the Rob Neave fan club, have you?'

'Is there one?'

'Oh, I think so. I wouldn't kick him out of bed. Mind you, I wouldn't kick Tim Godber out of bed either, if that was all I had to put up with from him.'

'Someone told me he used to be in the police.' Debbie had been curious about Rob for a while, but this was the first opportunity she'd had to ask questions.

'Neave? That's right. I don't know much about it, though.'

'Why did he leave, do you know?'

'No, some kind of personal crisis, I think. Something to do with his marriage? I don't know any more, though someone said he was drinking a lot before he came to City.' Louise was looking at Debbie speculatively. 'Be careful,' she said.

Debbie wanted to leave the subject now. She hadn't known he was married. If he still was. She went on, quickly, and rather addled by the wine, to tell Louise about the man at the station. Louise listened quietly until Debbie had finished.

23

'And he, Rob Neave, said to go to the police. I can't see how it could be to do with the killing, but . . .'

Louise was her efficient work self now. 'Wait until tomorrow, then see what's in the paper. If it is one of those killings, go and tell them. If it isn't, then you've no need to worry. And I wouldn't tell anyone else. You don't want it all over the college.'

'I've already told Tim.'

Louise's eyebrow lifted again. 'Bad idea,' was all she said.

They'd moved quickly since finding the body. The men searching the embankment by the line had found a handbag discarded in the grass. A purse was still in there, intact, containing £30, a debit card, a credit card for a chain store, some miscellaneous receipts and other pieces of paper that were being checked to see if they gave any information about the woman's movements in the weeks and days before she died. It seemed certain that this had belonged to the dead woman, as there was a brand-new travel pass with a photograph, and though her face was brutally changed, it looked very like – the same mass of fair hair, the small features. Mick Berryman, the senior investigating officer, had looked at the photo for a moment, then said, 'Has anyone checked out this address?'

Now he was looking at the scene-of-crime photographs, with Julie Fyfe's sightless face staring at him from the track side, half masked by the tape over her mouth, the thin cord embedded in the bruising round her neck. He looked at the initial report from the pathologist: . . . hands secured by tape round the wrists . . . cuts to the hands . . . numerous cuts, bruises and abrasions to the body . . . injuries to both eyes . . . He hadn't been prepared to commit himself any further at that stage. Had she been raped? *Damage to the genital area made that a possibility but he couldn't say until after doing a postmortem.* Were her injuries pre- or postmortem? *Impossible to say without further examination.* What kind of maniac dumped mutilated, dead women by railway lines? *More your field than mine.*

'OK.' Berryman looked at the team who were working on the strangler killings. 'It isn't officially confirmed yet, but we all know – we've got another one.' He pinned the

24

photograph up on the board, and ran through the known facts about this killing. 'Young woman, twenties found' – he indicated on the map – 'here, just outside Rawmarsh, near the junction. Injuries to the eyes. Mouth and wrists taped. Bruising to the neck, general damage, probable sexual assault. What else?' Berryman could see Lynne Jordan, a DS who had been involved with the team since the first murder, checking back through her notebook.

'First week of the month,' she said, flicking over a page. 'That's different. The others have all been in the last week. Poor visibility – the moon was well into its last quarter. A rainy night – it was fine when Kate and Mandy disappeared.'

'Any thoughts about that, Lynne? Anyone?'

'The rain – if it's as heavy as it was last night – that makes our job more difficult,' Lynne said. 'A lot of evidence could just get washed away. On the other hand, it makes it more likely that he'll leave marks. Footprints, tyre tracks.'

Berryman nodded. The problem was, the killer had left them nothing like that so far, except for one set of fingerprints, on the handbag of the first victim.

'How could he know? If he's planning ahead.' That was Steve McCarthy, also a DS who had, like Lynne Jordan, been on the team since the beginning. He was looking at Jordan with some hostility. 'What about broken glass?'

'The light above the post was smashed. How recently we don't yet know. They're looking for glass on the body.'

'Timing.' That was Lynne again. 'We thought his interval might be getting shorter. We've got a seven-month gap, a six-month gap, but now we've got eight months.' She shrugged. She didn't know what to do with the information. They wanted a pattern, not randomness.

'Show us on the calendar, Lynne.' Berryman believed in visual presentation of information.

Lynne went over to the calendar that was pinned to the wall next to the display board. 'The first killing, right, was at the end of March. That was Lisa. Seven months later, we get Kate. Last week in October. Six months after that, Mandy is killed, last week in April. That looks too much like a pattern to ignore. We expected the next one at the end of September, but nothing happened. Until now. Now we get one in the first week of December. Why the change?' There was a murmur of interest, a shifting, around the room.

'Or was it just coincidence?' That was Steve McCarthy again. Berryman scowled. Steve and Lynne tended to contradict each other's ideas. He thought he'd been lucky at the beginning to have both of them on his team, because they were both good, skilled detectives. When the killer struck again, and again, he'd kept them working close to the centre as he coordinated the massive team that was now working on this investigation. He was beginning to wonder if this had been wise. They couldn't seem to work together. He moved on to the next point.

'How did he get her to Rawmarsh?' Berryman tapped his pointer on the map. 'If he grabbed her in a car, why leave her there? There's no road runs close to where he dumped her. If he grabbed her at the station, how did he move her up the line?'

'Took her on a train?' Dave West, facetious. There was a stir of laughter around the room, lightening the atmosphere. West, a young DC on Lynne Jordan's team, was dealing with this case early in his career. Some detectives never had to deal with a random killer, or the horrors of a sadistic sex killer.

Berryman treated it as a serious suggestion. If there was a way . . . 'Tell me how he gets a dead woman on the train without anyone noticing, and how he gets the train to drop them off between stations, and I'll give that one some serious thought.' He waited to see if anyone else had anything to say on that point.

'Emergency stop – communication cord?' McCarthy's face indicated that he saw the flaws in this, but was putting it forward anyway. Berryman shook his head. They'd thought of that. No train on that line had had an unscheduled stop that evening.

'It's the same . . .'

'Kate Claremont . . .'

McCarthy and Jordan started together. Berryman looked at Lynne. She said, 'It's the same problem we've got with Kate. She was dumped on the line away from the road.

26

There's a footpath, but I wouldn't want to carry someone – dead or alive – all that way. How did he get her there?' She was only voicing a problem they'd discussed before. No one had anything to add.

Berryman felt weary at the thought of the work ahead. They'd done it all before, the house-to-house, tracking down the people who'd last seen the victim, talking to the relatives. It had got them nowhere, so far. OK, they needed her identity confirming, they needed to find her next of kin – who was missing her now? They needed to find out where she was going the night she died, who she'd seen in the days, weeks or even months before she died. They needed to know if she was just a random victim in the wrong place at the wrong time, or if she was carefully selected, chosen by the killer because something had drawn him to her. They needed to know this about all the victims, and they had so little to go on. Four women: Lisa, Kate, Mandy – and now Julie? It seemed it couldn't be any other way, and he felt as though he'd let them down, each one more than the last. And the next one and the next one?

3

Saturday morning's paper confirmed to Debbie that the dead woman was indeed a victim of the railway strangler. Debbie looked at the photograph of the woman who'd died, then read the article. The police put out the usual advice about women being careful, not going out alone after dark, etc., etc. She read through the article again, trying to find anything that might link the murder to the station, but as Tim had said, the body had been found several miles up the line at Rawmarsh. She looked again at the photograph of Julie Fyfe, twenty-four, younger than Debbie, and dead. She was laughing in the picture, at someone off camera to her left, fair hair tumbling rather glamorously round a small-featured face. Debbie looked for a long time, then she took some pieces of paper from beside her phone, and held them round the face in the picture, trying to see it with the hair pulled back into an elegant, business style. That cold feeling was coming back again now, because the face looking back at her could be, might be, no, *was* the face of the woman, the woman she'd seen so many Thursday nights, the woman who waited on the opposite platform for the Doncaster train.

Cover her face. Mine eyes dazzle. She died young.

There was a phone number in the paper, and after several attempts she got through. The officer she spoke to seemed quite calm about what she had to say, which was a relief, but asked her if she could come in to talk to them in more detail. He wanted her to do that as soon as possible, which made that cold feeling stronger. 'Can you make it today?' he'd said. Debbie decided to go that morning. She wanted to exorcize the whole experience, and be reassured by the indifference

28

of the police that she had seen nothing and knew nothing. She didn't want to think about the implications of anything else, but she couldn't stop. If it had been . . . him, then had she, Debbie, missed lying dead on the tracks by minutes? Had talking to Les Walker and Rob Neave saved her life? And cost Julie Fyfe hers?

The man who took her statement was pleasant, polite and not as reassuring as she had hoped. He asked her a lot of questions, some about the appearance of the man, though Debbie could tell him very little, and some questions were the same ones that Tim had asked her, coming back again and again to the broken light. 'I just don't know,' Debbie said in the end. 'At the time it seemed to come from the station, but I didn't really think about it until I saw the glass. I just assumed, I suppose.'

'That's OK, Miss Sykes. Now just tell me again – you don't think the man got on your train.'

'I'm certain he didn't.'

'OK, and you're sure you've never seen him before?'

'I'm not certain, I couldn't see him well enough, but I didn't recognize him from what I did see. I don't think I've ever seen him before.'

'I'd like you to talk to our artist, see if you can put together any kind of picture of this man' – he waved aside her objections – 'just a general impression if that's all you can manage.' He asked her some questions about the woman on the opposite platform, without either confirming or denying this was the murder victim, and some questions about her own Thursday night routine. He thanked her for coming in, but Debbie was still uneasy. 'Do you think it was him?' She wanted him to reassure her that it was nothing, nothing at all.

'I don't know, Miss Sykes. Leave it with us. It may not be relevant, but we need this information to find that out. You did the right thing coming in. By the way, we'd appreciate it if you didn't talk to anyone about this.'

'I've already talked to one or two people – I was worried.'

'Well, if you could just avoid discussing it from now on . . .'

* * *

29

At the Saturday briefing, Berryman and his team went over the preliminary results of the postmortem on Julie Fyfe. It was the same as the others. Nothing that pointed directly to the killer, no hair, no fingerprints, no blood, no other fluids, no footprints. 'Fuck-all,' Berryman told them. What evidence there may have been had been washed away by the torrential rain. The ground underneath her body was as wet as the surrounding area, which suggested that she'd been dumped after the worst of the storm was over, but she was wet through with rain. She'd been outside for the storm.

What they did have, told them that she had almost certainly been killed by the same man. Death was by strangulation using some kind of smooth fabric, but whatever had been used had moved several times round the woman's neck. The wire had been used after she was dead. The pathologist thought that the killer may have used partial strangulation as a means to subdue her, before he actually killed her. There was evidence of sexual assault – vaginal and anal bruising and laceration, a lot of internal damage. 'He's using a tool other than his tool,' the pathologist had told Berryman. 'Something thin and sharp, pointed. She would have bled to death if he hadn't strangled her.' The injuries to the eyes were caused by gouging – probably manual. 'He was wearing gloves. Look for bloodstains on gloves,' Berryman told his team. The general bruising and laceration was most probably caused by dragging of the – unconscious?, and later dead – woman along the ground. The lack of bruising and bleeding from some of these injuries suggested they were postmortem. There was possible impact injury, as though, after death, she had fallen heavily. Some gravel had been retrieved from the cuts. There was glass on the body. It was Lynne Jordan, the only woman on the team, who asked which of the other injuries were pre- or postmortem. Berryman couldn't reassure. The sexual assault was carried out while the woman was alive. The other injuries? 'Around the time of death,' was all the information the pathologist could give them.

'Did the glass come from the broken lights at Moreham station?' That was Lynne again. Berryman shook his head. The glass came from the broken light near where the body

30

had been dumped. There was no guarantee that Julie had gone to Moreham station, though it was probable that she had done so. They still hadn't been able to trace her beyond the time she left work. Though the team had made extensive enquiries, no one had been found who had been on that route at the relevant time.

'We've got one statement that just came in,' Berryman said. 'It relates to the crucial time – shortly after nine-thirty. This woman says that the station was deserted, except for one person, a man, who was behaving a bit oddly. I don't have to tell you, we need to track him down. I'm still hoping for a car as well. There must have been cars going that way.' Berryman took a deep breath. 'OK. Let's run through everything we've got. Let's see what we're missing here. He might be a lucky bastard, but he can't do this and leave us nothing. There's something we're missing.'

That evening found Mick Berryman still at his desk. He'd been woken up at four the previous morning by the call from the station reporting Cath Hill's find. He probably wasn't going to see his kids today, nor his wife, for that matter. His family was on the back burner until this enquiry was over – if it ever was. He was going over some of the earlier statements, and was looking at the information that had come in from that teacher this morning. Could be nothing, or it could be something very important. It could be their first sighting of the killer. If only they could establish where Julie had been when she was taken. They'd searched the station at Moreham, but there was nothing much to see. Unless forensics came through with something. They needed to track her movements. He began to make notes.

She'd left work at nine-twenty, as usual for a Thursday. That had been easy to establish. She'd almost certainly walked to the station, despite the bad weather. It only took five minutes. She hadn't called a taxi and there wasn't a bus. Could she have accepted a lift? The people who worked with her were pretty certain: not Julie, she was far too careful, only with someone she knew. (And how often was it someone they knew, someone they trusted?) It was no distance to the

31

station, anyway, she'd almost definitely gone there. But her train had been cancelled. She would probably have seen that on the screen as she arrived, but it had also been displayed on the platform screen. Could she have caught an earlier train? No, the earlier one had left over half an hour before, at eight-thirty-three, and yes, it had been running on time. So what had she done? Had she decided to wait for the next train? That seemed unlikely as it was over forty minutes before the next train was due. She would surely have gone for a bus or a taxi. Was she so broke she couldn't afford to? Or so tight-fisted? He made some notes and thought on.

She hadn't been at the station at nine-forty, according to the statement Deborah Sykes had given. So – leaves work at nine-twenty, at the station by, what, between nine-twenty-five and nine-thirty. By nine-forty, she had gone. He reached for Deborah Sykes's statement again. Who'd taken it? McCarthy. Everything should be there. Right. No one had come out of the station as the Sykes woman had come in. She hadn't passed anyone on her way to the station. If Julie had left the station as soon as she saw the first display screen, she would almost certainly not have been on the road by the time Deborah Sykes came past. If she'd gone down to the platform before seeing her train was cancelled, then Deborah should have seen her walking back. He needed some more timings. He needed to know how long she'd been in that station.

Lynne Jordan was on the train to Sheffield. She'd taken to using the train when time permitted. Like most of her colleagues, she knew the roads of the area so well she could drive them with her eyes shut, predict the level of traffic for any time of day, say which roads the joy-riders were likely to choose to career their purloined cars around, tyres screeching as they performed their antics. But she didn't know the trains. When the team pored over the maps, when they looked at the places the victims had been found, she saw pieces of landscape, not a seamless whole.

Today, she had made a mistake. She was spending an evening in Sheffield, and it had seemed a golden opportunity. But of course, by the time she got on the train, it was dark.

It was after eight-thirty, and the line outside the carriage window was invisible. She contented herself with getting a feel for her fellow travellers. There was a young man behind her, whose Walkman leaked a penetrating metallic beat. Somewhere further back in the carriage, there was someone with a loud and persistent sniff. A group of youths had piled on to the train at Meadowhall, shouting and nudging each other, sprawling over the seats, shoving their heavy trainers on to the upholstery. They brought the distinctive smell of young male into the carriage with them.

Lynne tried to see out of the window. The interior of the carriage reflected darkly back. She could see the empty crisp packet that lay on her table, the pool of liquid spilled from a soft drink container. She held her hands up to shadow her eyes. She could see light glinting off the tracks. She put her face closer to the window, then recoiled as something flashed past so close it seemed about to hit her.

They were passing a train. It wasn't another passenger train – it seemed to consist of low, flat trucks with piles of long thin objects strapped to them. Her train slowed briefly, and she realized the other train was stationary, or moving very slowly. She saw the lights and tunnel ahead that meant they were nearly into Sheffield. The train came to a standstill. The freight train crawled past. She sighed and looked at her watch. She was going to be late.

Debbie came home from the police station as worried as she had been before she went, maybe a bit more worried. Talking to the police made it seem more real, that maybe she had seen the killer. Going out and getting drunk seemed like a very good idea.

So that night she went clubbing. She called Fiona, a university friend who was trying to make a career as a jazz musician and singer, but Fiona had a gig that night. 'Try Brian,' she suggested, naming the third member of their trio from student days. Brian was free, and so were some of the others, so Debbie enlisted them for a night out. She drank too much, danced a lot, drunkenly snogged Brian in the dark shadows of the club, and then later even more drunkenly snogged

33

a beautiful stranger who appeared and then disappeared through the gaps in her memory. Her friends took her home and steered her through the front door. She must have got herself to bed, because she was there, alone, when she woke up the next morning with her head throbbing, her stomach heaving and her shoes still on. And nothing was any better.

The music is loud and invasive, and he purses his lips with judicious annoyance, then closes his window. He likes to keep the window open because there is a slightly sweet, sickly smell in the room that, he must admit, he finds a bit unpleasant. He can still hear the music, though not so loudly. The young man in the basement flat downstairs has no consideration for others. He really doesn't approve of that. He decided that morning to let himself have the day off, but already he's getting a bit restless. He's the sort of person who likes to be doing things. He wonders if he deserves an hour with his trains — he has been working very hard, after all. Yes.

He pulls down the loft ladder, the loft being the feature that made the house so attractive to him when he looked at it. It was worth all the noise and disturbance he had to put up with by letting rooms. And after all, it wasn't the worst kind of noise and disturbance. No one paid any attention to him. Everyone left everyone else alone. That was the way he'd been brought up by his mother, to approve of things like that. Live and let live.

The loft is truly magnificent. The roof is high above his head. The floor joists have been boarded over so that he can walk around without fear of putting his foot through the ceiling of his room below. He wired it himself so that he has all the power he needs, but no heating. He doesn't need heating up here. But there is a small freezer in one corner, and a computer in another. He has all the facilities he needs. What is even better is its size. It stretches over the whole roof area of the house, and, as he found out one day, has access to the roof space of the house next door. The house next door is the first one of a block of three terraces, each one just like his, that have been converted into flats. It is a very simple matter to crawl through, and then climb out on to the fire escape at the back. No one notices one more person using those stairs that serve for every flat in the block.

He turns on the light that hangs from the roof joist — just a bare bulb, no need for anything fancy – and looks with some pleasure at his railway. He's tried to make it as realistic as possible, to include the other landscape features, the hills, the river, the canal way. When he planned it, he decided to use n-gauge track so that the layout didn't become too big – even so, it's a close thing. He gets his map out. Even though it isn't a working day, there's no harm, surely, in just looking. After all, he needs to start planning another hunt.

4

The story appeared in the local paper that Monday: 'I SAW THE FACE OF THE STRANGLER' the headline declaimed, above a photograph of Debbie. The article, which was on the third page, was part of a big spread about the murders the paper ran that day. Details of the victims were given again, some quotes from the bereaved relatives and comment from the police. An editorial chided the investigation team – more in sorrow than in anger, it was true. *Everyone knows the difficulties of the task these men and women face, and the* Standard *does not underestimate these. But the women of South Yorkshire are entitled to travel freely without fear* . . . The article about Debbie began: *Teacher Debra Sykes, 26, had a chilling encounter the night the Strangler struck. The attractive brunette told our reporter, 'I just knew there was something wrong. There was something terribly wrong at the station that night.'* The article went on to give the basic details of Debbie's story, including the broken lights, and the way the man had apparently tried to approach her. The police were quoted as saying that they were aware of the story but had no reason at present to think that Ms Sykes's experience had anything to do with the killing. The quote rather implied that Debbie was a bit of an attention seeker. There was also an appeal for the man at the station to come forward *'so that we can eliminate him from our enquiries.'* The article had a by-line: Tim Godber.

The first that Debbie heard about the article was Monday morning, when she was teaching her second-year A-level group again. Leanne Ferris, unusually prompt, dumped her bag on her desk, opened a can of Coke and said, 'We want to hear about the murderer. Go on, tell us.' Debbie looked blank. Leanne dived into her bag, and after a few seconds rummaging, pulled out a copy of the paper. 'They're doing a big thing about the Strangler, so I got it. Look.' She showed Debbie the article, and the others crowded round.

'It's a good picture, Debbie.' That was Sarah, with her usual capacity for focusing first on the least important issue. Or maybe to Sarah that was the most important – to look nice if she appeared in the local paper. Debbie recognized the photograph. It had been taken at the staff party in July. In the original, she and Tim had been together. This one was cropped, so she was alone, smiling up at someone who wasn't there. She didn't know if she was more angry or upset. She played down both the article and her reaction to it for the students, much to their disappointment.

'Did he look really scary, you know, mad?' Leanne's eyes were bright with eager curiosity.

'Look,' Debbie began, firmly. 'No one even knows . . .'

'Did you see the body?' That was Adam, aficionado of video nasties.

'No one knows . . .' Debbie tried again.

'Were you scared?' That was Sarah.

'Listen.' Debbie's voice was louder than she'd intended. She got a moment's silence. 'Listen. There's no reason to think that the person I saw was the killer. No one knows. I just talked to the police and I don't want to talk about it any more.'

'Didn't he chase you then? With a knife?' That was Leanne again.

'Oh, come on, Leanne, it doesn't even *say* that there. Now I'd just like to . . .'

'He cuts their eyes out,' Leanne said with relish to the rest of the group.

Adam chipped in. 'He doesn't use a knife. Not at first. He strangles them.'

'Oh, trust you to know that!' That was Rachel, more level-headed than Leanne, quieter. 'Look, Debbie says she doesn't want to talk about it. Let's drop it. Have you marked our essays, Debbie? Did I get an A?'

The session dragged on from there.

Debbie was angry, and she was worried. She left the class-room quickly when the morning was over, ignoring requests from the cohort of poor attenders, including Leanne and Adam, that she go over the new assignment again. 'I'm sorry, I haven't got time,' she said, and then felt guilty. In the staff room, in response to Louise's interrogative look, she said, 'I didn't talk to them.'

'I thought you didn't,' was all Louise said.

The rest of the day she seemed to be saying over and over – I didn't see the Strangler, I *didn't* talk to the paper, I don't want to talk about it now. She got a memo from one of the vice-principals asking her why she had given an interview to a local paper without clearing it with the college management, and wasted her coffee break trying to make contact with someone to explain – not that they'd believe her. She looked out for Rob Neave, so that she could explain to him what had happened – she wasn't sure why she felt that was important, only that it seemed to be – but he was nowhere around. 'He's working off site today,' Andrea, the clerical officer for that section, told her when she asked. She didn't see Tim Godber until she was leaving at five. He was unapologetic.

It was a legitimate interview; Debbie should make it clear if she was talking off the record and what was she making all the fuss about? He'd only written what she had told him.

Debbie left college that day in the mood she'd often left school when she was a child, particularly that bad year when two of her classmates – once her friends – had decided to gang up on her. 'We don't want *you*,' Tracy would say, putting her arm through Donna's; and, 'Nobody play with Deborah Sykes, her mum's a witch!' they'd tell the others. She couldn't remember now what had started the campaign, or what had ended it, but she could still remember how miserable it had made her feel. She often thought that the saying, *Sticks and stones may break your bones but words can never hurt you* was one of the most stupid ones she'd ever heard.

As she walked through the town centre, she couldn't shake off a feeling of foreboding. It was as if she was being watched by malicious eyes. She had felt exposed in the college, as though people were looking at her, talking about her, but now the feeling chilled her as it followed her through the streets to the station, until she managed to shake it off in the anonymous brightness of the train.

When she finally got home, the phone was ringing. She waited for a minute to see if it would stop, and when it didn't, she answered it. 'Deborah Sykes speaking.' Silence. 'Hello?' she said. There was no reply, and then the phone was put down. She tried 1471, but no number was recorded.

Sarah was combing her hair in front of the mirror in the students' cloakroom, prior to going home. She could smell the smoke from Leanne's cigarette as Leanne and Rachel chatted over a cubicle door. Sarah stared into the mirror, and wondered if her face was too fat. She was thinking about Nick. Was she attractive enough? When she looked in the mirror she thought she was, but sometimes she caught sight of herself unexpectedly and saw someone frighteningly plain. She was seeing him on Friday. She put away her comb, anxiously looking at her reflection.

'. . . essay title?'

'Sorry?' Her hand jerked a bit. Leanne was beside her, energetically back-combing her hair.

'Have you written down that essay title?' Leanne bundled her hair up on top of her head. 'Look out, world,' she said. She usually relied on other people to keep her up to date with assignments. 'Are you coming to Adam's party on Friday?'

Sarah felt the usual pang of exclusion. 'He didn't ask me,' she said.

Leanne was applying colour to her eyes. 'You don't listen, do you? He asked everybody in the group. You can come with me and Raich if you want.'

Sarah was cautious. Leanne made her nervous. 'I can't, thanks,' she said. 'I'm seeing Nick.'

'Bring him.' Leanne fastened a clip into her hair. Sarah bit her fingernail. Nick could be difficult with other people. He didn't like students.

'OK, I'll ask him,' she said, not meaning to. 'Thanks.'

'Don't ask him, tell him,' said Leanne, running the tap over

39

her cigarette end and discarding it in the basin. 'See you.' She and Rachel left.

Sarah went back to her contemplation of the mirror. Now Leanne would want to know why she wasn't there on Friday. She couldn't say that Nick didn't want to go. They wouldn't ask her again. Maybe she should suggest it to him. It was the kind of thing he liked, though Sarah preferred quieter places where her soft voice wouldn't be drowned out by loud music and shouting. Maybe if they did that they wouldn't have an argument. She ran a tentative hand over the bruise hidden by the scarf on her neck.

Mick Berryman's mind shut down on him. He needed a break. The clock on the wall said six, but it hadn't been altered since the clocks went back weeks ago. He'd been at it for over ten hours. He could go home, put his feet up, but he decided to go over to the Grindstone for an hour or so. He needed a drink and he needed some quiet.

The pub, like most of the pubs in Moreham centre in the early evening, was almost empty. There were a couple of old men at a table in the corner, and a solitary drinker at the bar, reading a paper. As he crossed the room, he realized that the man at the bar was Rob Neave, and slowed his pace for a moment.

It was eighteen months now since Neave had left the force. He'd been one of the most talented officers in the division, following Berryman up the promotions ladder. They'd worked together, and they'd spent a lot of time at this bar. They'd made a good team. He couldn't understand why Neave had left what had been a promising career, getting his promotion to DI six months before he gave it all up. But after Angie, Neave had gone to pieces. His colleagues had rallied round in support, looked after him, got him drunk – not that he'd needed any help with that at the time. Finally, Berryman had advised him to go on sick leave and get some help, even though that would put a blight on his promotion prospects. But Neave wasn't interested.

'The fact is,' he'd told Berryman, 'I just don't give a bugger about any of it any more. I just want out.' Berryman was beginning to understand that feeling now, though he hadn't been able to understand it then, the same way he'd never been able to understand Neave's obsession with Angie – oh, pretty, he'd give you that, but weird. He couldn't have stood it for a week.

He hadn't seen Neave for nearly six months. Claire had had a go at him – 'Why don't you ask Rob round for an evening? We'll feed him up, have a few beers, it might cheer him up.' Claire had developed a soft spot for his ex-colleague. He'd phoned, but the offer had been declined, as Berryman had known it would be. Without the job, they had lost their common ground. He went up to the bar. 'Want another one in there?'

Then he couldn't think of anything to say. Berryman had been with Neave when he and Angie first met, and it had been Berryman who had seen him at the end. She stood between them like an unspoken ghost.

Neave looked pleased to see him, but turned down the offer of a drink. He still had almost a pint in his glass and it looked as if he had been spinning it out for a while. They exchanged bits and pieces of news, the talk halting and awkward. Looking around for topics, Berryman glanced at the paper Neave had been reading when he came into the pub. It was the *Moreham Standard*. It was open at the two-page spread about the Strangler.

Berryman groaned. It had got in the way of his thoughts all afternoon. The police should be doing this, the police aren't doing this, Christ, what did they expect? Magic? Neave glanced at him, saw what he was looking at and gave him a sympathetic grin. 'Giving you a hard time,' he said, rather than asked.

'They want my balls on a plate,' Berryman said gloomily.

'Yeah. Then Mystic Meg could gaze into them and give you the answers.' Neave looked at the paper again. 'Is it right? You've got nothing?'

Berryman decided to talk. He knew he could trust Neave to keep his mouth shut. 'This bastard really knows what he's doing,' he said, after a moment. 'He's not made many mistakes. We're getting nowhere. Four of them now, and we've got nothing.'

'Nothing? You must have something. He's got to leave something behind.'

'Oh, we've got stuff that'll help when we catch him. *If* we catch him. We've got lines of enquiry we haven't used up yet, but we've got nothing to tell us who he is. It'll be a Yorkshire Ripper thing again. He'll do it once too often and we'll have him. This kind of thing doesn't help. It just gets people panicked, and it puts out information I don't want putting out.' He tapped the article headlined, *I saw the face of the Strangler*. 'That's rubbish. It's just speculation. Stupid bitch.'

Neave looked at the article. 'He works at the college,' he said, indicating the name of the writer. 'She probably forgot he was a journalist when she talked to him. She was worried about it. She asked me what she should do.' He intercepted Berryman's look and grinned again. 'I told her to talk to you lot. I didn't tell her to sell her story.' He thought about it for a moment. 'You're worried about it though. Was it him she saw?'

'I don't fucking know. Whole of South fucking Yorkshire knows, but I don't.'

But the fact was, Berryman *was* worried by Debbie's story. 'One thing we've got is that we know where he picked up the first one, Lisa Griffin. He left her by the track just outside Mexborough station. That's where she was headed for, and we had witnesses who put her there. He's learned something since then. We don't know where he killed the others. They were dumped on the line away from any stations. There were two things we found – fingerprints we can't account for, on her bag. I'm not saying they're the killer's, but they're there. Also, broken glass. We don't know why. He'd taken the lights out on the platform near where we found Lisa. We found broken glass on the others as well. Kate, Kate Claremont, there was glass in her hair. And there were bits of glass caught in Mandy's dress.'

Neave looked off into space, his eyes half closed. 'Is it lights he doesn't like, or is it glass? Reflections? Does he need the glass? Does he use it on them?'

Berryman went over the old ground again. They didn't know, they could only guess. 'The glass isn't the kind that breaks into shards. It doesn't look like a weapon. He seems to be funny about lights. He smashes them, but he isn't consistent.' He saw Neave's question forming. 'We don't know. It could be a convenience thing, pure and simple, but it's there.' He sighed and emptied his glass. Neave signalled to the barman.

'How does he pick them up?' he asked.

'Good question,' Berryman said. 'And one we'd like the answer to.' They didn't know where he'd picked them up, where he'd taken them or where he'd killed them. They knew what he'd done to them though. 'This last one, for instance, Julie, she was last seen leaving work on Broomegate. She never got home. He must have got her shortly after she was last seen, but the time of death was probably around midnight. If he picked her up on the street, someone should have seen it. There were enough cars around. If he picked her up in the station, how did he get her to bloody Rawmarsh? If he's using a car, he's got to get her out of the station and then he's still got to get her down to the line – no road where we found her. *Someone* must have seen *something*, but no one's come forward.'

'Apart from.' Neave indicated the photo in the paper.

Berryman scowled. 'We need to talk to her again. We need to be sure that Julie wasn't at the station. We need to find this man, whoever he is. *He* might have seen something.'

'But it could be your man?' Neave didn't wait for an answer. 'So how does he find them?' His glass was now empty. He shook his head as the other man gestured to ask if he wanted another. He had that narrow-eyed intent look that Berryman remembered from earlier days.

'We're working on it,' he said. The general feeling of the men working the investigation was that the killer chose his victims at random – waited till he saw a likely-looking one, then struck. Berryman wasn't so sure. 'I've got a bit of a feeling about it. Lisa's little girl, she's only five, she kept talking about *the ugly man* – and Mandy's mum said that Mandy had been getting some funny phone calls. Mind you, she said that was down to Mandy's boyfriend. I don't know. It doesn't add up to much. We've looked into it, and there's nothing there you can put your finger on. I've got Lynne Jordan's team working on it now. You know Lynne?' Neave made a noncommittal noise. 'The boyfriend admits he made "one or two" calls. It's not just that, though. It's too neat the way he lifts them. He always manages to do it without a witness. He's got to know about them to do that. No, my money says he plans it well ahead.'

It was gone ten when they left the pub. Berryman headed for his car and Neave turned towards the river and his flat. Outside the pub, he zipped up his jacket and thrust his hands deep into his pockets. Winter had the town in its grip now. The air was icy and the pavement sparkled with frost. The centre was deserted as usual – just a few kids rode their skateboards around the pedestrianized shopping area, a small group of adolescents huddled together outside the local burger joint. His footsteps echoed as he walked through the pedestrian precinct towards the river. The wind cut between the buildings and blew bits of rubbish around on the ground and up into the air. An empty can rattled its way down the street as if in pursuit of the lighter burger cartons and chip wrappings. A twenty-minute walk and he'd be home. He was glad he didn't have to watch over his shoulder, to be wary of every empty alleyway. He thought of Deborah walking through the town centre alone.

Berryman's mind drifted back to the past. Angie. He and Neave had been working over in Sheffield at the time. There had been some attacks on women in the university district. A young woman had reported a prowler and they were following it up. The house was a typical student house, a terrace with an uncared-for frontage, and ragged curtains up in the bay window. The young man who opened the door gave them a hostile stare as they announced themselves, then called over his shoulder, 'Angie!' He pushed past them on his way out. Neave gave Berryman a look – *give the little shit a hard time?* – but they let him go. Putting the frighteners on a cocky young man wasn't what they were here for.

44

A young woman was coming down the stairs, tying the belt of a flimsy dressing gown round her waist. Her hair was wet, and she was carrying a towel. She looked surprised to see them. 'I thought . . .' They were obviously not who she was expecting to see.

Berryman took over. He always played the hard man, a part he was well suited to with his heavy jaw and thick eyebrows. Neave would stay back, quietly, looking sympathetic and friendly. It established a useful relationship if it was needed for later, though it didn't particularly reflect the way they actually were, Berryman thought. He was a bit of a soft touch, unlike Neave. He introduced himself, showing her his identification. 'We're here about this man you reported.' She had phoned in, and later told the patrol officer that a man had been peering in through the ground-floor windows late at night. Berryman didn't doubt it, if she always went around dressed like that. Her gown was made of some silky material that kept sliding off her shoulders, and where her wet hair dripped on to it, it clung and lost its opacity.

He tried to catch Neave's eye as the woman took them into the downstairs front room, but all he met was an expression of blank amazement. He looked as if he'd been hit by a car he hadn't seen coming. Berryman grinned. He didn't often see Neave rattled.

The room was a tip. There were papers all over the floor, and books. Two empty cups occupied the rug in front of the fire. The walls were a confusion of colour from pictures, posters, photographs, hangings all tacked up at random. In one corner there was a music stand and a violin case on the floor beside it. There was a bed under the window with a patterned cover thrown over it. The woman sat down on the rug, briefly revealing the inside of a white thigh, and gestured towards the bed. 'I'm a bit short of chairs. Please sit down.' Berryman sat himself gingerly on the bed. He didn't like mess and he didn't like women who couldn't keep a place clean. Neave remained standing and leant his arm on the mantelpiece. The woman began to towel her hair in front of the fire, the towel providing some of the concealment that the dressing gown failed to do.

'Right, Miss . . .' Berryman checked his notes. 'Kerridge. What can you tell us about this man? Just start from the beginning and tell us what you can remember.' It didn't sound like the same man – it sounded like the Peeping Tom they'd had problems with in the past. He wound the interview up quickly, asked her if she'd be prepared to make a statement and look at some photographs. As they left, he was conscious that Neave had been a silent spectator throughout. He tried a ribald comment on the woman's dress or lack of it, but got a monosyllabic response. Neave could be a moody bastard.

He didn't say anything to Berryman about seeing the woman again, but three weeks later she had moved into his flat, and two years after that, just after Flora was born, they were married.

They were all young, under twenty-five. Lisa was the oldest at nearly twenty-five, Kate was just twenty, killed within a month of her birthday, Mandy was twenty-one and Julie was twenty-four. Their lives had some similarities, some differences. Lisa was married, had been for three years. Her young husband had been given a hard time by the investigating team when her mutilated body had been found on the line near Mexborough station. She had a little girl, Karen, five years old. Kate and Mandy were both single and had no children. Kate got out and about – the Warehouse, pubs with comedy evenings, concerts at the Arena, the students' union, the Leadmill. Lived in a shared house with three other students. Lots of boyfriends, no one special. They'd talked to them all. Nothing. Mandy was quieter, lived with her parents, had a little mongrel bitch, had been engaged for a couple of months but had just finished with her boyfriend. They'd given him a hard time, too, but there was nothing they could pin on him. Julie, they still had to find out more about Julie. She was single, lived alone, apparently had no children but they didn't have much more information yet. Lisa worked part time as a secretary, Kate was a politics student, active in the students' union, Mandy was a clerk for the local council and Julie was a PA. Her company had just won a Small Business of the Year Award before she was killed.

Lynne Jordan went through the details of the victims again, looking for that elusive something that linked them together. It was there, and she was missing it. She looked at the photographs the families had supplied. Lisa was dark-haired, attractive. She was smiling at the camera and doing an exaggerated glamour pose. She looked young, happy, confident. Kate was more serious, dark-haired again, strong features, well-defined brows. This picture had been taken when she was campaigning for the student union presidency. Attractive, but in a different way from Lisa's vivacious femininity. Mandy had fair hair, a light brown often called mousy. She smiled rather tensely and artificially at the camera. A plain woman, if the picture was right. *She doesn't take a good photo, our Amanda,* her mother had said sadly. *We had a lovely one for the engagement announcement. We put it in the paper.* Julie was blonde, fine-boned, lovely. She smiled confidently at the camera, a young woman at ease with her looks.

Their dead faces stared back from the board in the room where Berryman's team was based; and from another wall, in another place.

He keeps the photographs on a board just by the entrance to his loft. He likes doorways, entrances, spaces that are neither one place nor the other. In the doorway, on the threshold, there is a place that is nowhere. It is a place where it is easier for him to be his real self. It is a dangerous place – some people protect themselves from it by hanging charms above the door, or protect their loved ones by carrying them across it. It isn't dangerous for him, he lives in this space. He doesn't need any charms. He can't keep his souvenirs on the threshold, but he likes to see his pictures as he climbs from one world into another.

The trains are rattling around the tracks, running to time, running like clockwork. At eight-thirty-two, a train pulls into Goldthorpe station, another pulls out of Sheffield on its way to Barnsley, another on its way to Hull, calling at Meadowhall, Moreham Central, Mexborough, Conisbrough, all the way to the end of the line. Signals change, points move, freight trains rush through stations without stopping, slow and stop at signals. At night, the landscape is illuminated with points of light – lights at the stations, lights where the roads run near to the track – but there are dark places too where the track runs through unlit expanses, the trains briefly lighting up the night and vanishing, leaving silence behind them.

The Christmas shoppers are out in force now. They crowd the stations. An InterCity express thunders through the small station at Meadowhall, as the tannoy warns travellers to stand back from the edge as a fast train is approaching. These places are dangerous. A station is a first step across the threshold. A train is a doorway. The train is the doorway, with its exit miles, maybe hundreds of miles, away. The threshold ends at the destination. But things can happen in places that are no places, places that are doorways hundreds of miles long. Such places are dangerous.

He can't settle. He needs to do something. He looks at the paper again. He frowns. When he first saw it, he'd been quite upset. They were saying, they were implying, that he'd made a mistake, and he hadn't made a mistake at all. It was all a matter of timing. He knew the other Thursday woman would be there. He'd arranged it so that he was gone by the time she arrived. Of course he'd had to go back. He needed to check that he hadn't left anything behind. He liked to prolong, to savour the moment, to delay just a little. He'd had the forethought to make sure that the light was dim on the other platform. He would have done something about her if he'd needed to. In fact, he can see that it might all be working out for the best. He gets his scissors out and carefully cuts around the photograph. This is the first time he's had a such good photograph of before. The others are most unsatisfactory. The photographs of after are better. If you want a job doing well . . .

He knows why he can't settle. He's been given the sign. He needs to hunt again, and time is getting short. This one is a good one. She goes to places where he can hunt, he knows that already. After all, he's been watching. Carefully, he tapes the photograph to his notice board in the loft, and looks at it for a moment. Then he takes a Stanley knife and, using a fresh blade, cuts first one eye, then the other from the picture. Then he pushes a pin through the place where the mouth is. This one speaks and he doesn't much care for what it says.

5

Tuesday morning, Debbie, who had woken up at about half past five and had been unable to get back to sleep, caught the seven-twenty train and was actually in college by quarter to eight. She had planned to spend an hour catching up on her marking, but as she sat at her desk sipping a cup of bitter coffee, she realized that she wasn't going to be able to concentrate. Right. Something else then. She had her GCSE English class at nine that morning. They'd been looking at ghost stories – it was a topic Debbie always did at Christmas, and she was trying to get them to write stories of their own. They had trouble with writing horror, because the model from their own experience of books and film was fantasy based and excessively violent. The idea that their own world of the everyday could be far more horrific was alien to them. Debbie decided that today she would show them ghosts.

The Broome building offered an excellent venue for a ghost story. Debbie went roaming, trying to remember the best stories, find the best places. The high-ceilinged corridors were shadowy, brown, grey and black, the brighter colours on the paintwork long since worn off. Ghosts could easily walk here. Debbie went on up the stairs to the top corridor – there was a story here – and began a narrative in her head in which someone was standing where she was standing, her back against the window, watching through the crazed glass in the swing doors, the shadow of *something* stalking her, knowing she was trapped in a dead end with no way out but the eighty-foot drop through the window behind her.

Footsteps beyond the doors brought her back to earth – the sound was heavy and solid. A man, then. She peered back down the corridor into the shadows, and saw a shape loom against the glass. The door opened, and Les came through, carrying a bunch of keys. He looked at Debbie.

'Morning,' he said. Should she explain what she was doing? He didn't seem curious, but he must have wondered. As he came towards her, she said, 'I was just looking at those places that you tell the stories about, you know, the ghosts.'

'Not me.' Les looked dour. 'It'll be one of those young ones telling you a lot of nonsense. I've worked here near on forty year, and I've never seen any ghosts.'

'But they're good stories. I was trying to remember that one that was supposed to have happened one Christmas – I'm sure it was you that told me.'

'Oh, you mean the footsteps on the long staircase.' Les seemed reluctant to tell the story at first, but Debbie had remembered it as soon as he mentioned the staircase.

The long staircase was originally a fire escape. It ran in a spiral down the inside of a tower-like structure built at the point where the corridors ended. An external fire escape now served the building. The doors that led on to the long staircase were nailed up and had been since before Debbie started work at the college. The only way on to it now was through the IT resource centre. At the back of the room was the old fire exit with a push-bar handle. Students no longer used the long staircase which led out into the lane behind the college, and now it was mostly used for storage. It was dark even on the sunniest day.

The story that Les was telling was about a caretaker who had gone down the staircase one night to check that the outside door was locked. He went down the stairs and checked the door. He didn't check anything else, because there was nothing else to check. As he was climbing back up the staircase, slowly, because it was late and he wasn't a young man, there was a sudden draught, the door above him slammed shut and the light went out. He stopped, because it gave him a shock to be suddenly in the dark, then went on, a bit more quickly now. It was cold and somehow unpleasant, at night, on the stairs, in the dark. Then he stopped again. Down below him, on the stairs he'd just climbed, he could hear something, something that sounded like footsteps coming lightly and quickly up the stairs behind him, from where there had been nothing but an empty staircase and a locked door. He didn't wait. He ran as quickly as he could in the dark, up the last two flights to the door that was hard to open from the inside. As he struggled with it, he could hear the footsteps getting closer and moving more quickly as they came towards his landing. He managed to get the door open, was through it and had it shut and bolted behind him more quickly than he thought was possible. He was leaning against the door getting his breath when something struck it with such force he was knocked to the ground. But nothing was ever found on the staircase to account for it.

When Debbie had first heard the story of the footsteps that came from nowhere, pursuing their victim in the dark, the hairs had stood up on her arms. That would be an excellent story to tell the students. She could take them on to the stairs, show them.

The double doors were pushed open, making them both jump, and Les fumbled with his key ring as Rob Neave came into view. 'On the warpath today,' he muttered.

Neave saw Debbie, and made some attempt to hide his irritation. 'I want you down with the delivery van,' he said to Les. 'Get Dave or someone to open these rooms and for Christ's sake don't take all day.' His face was white and he looked ill, as if he had a serious hangover. Debbie remembered what Louise had told her the other evening.

'That was my fault,' she apologized for Les. 'I was getting him to tell me his ghost story.'

Neave looked at her with a faint smile and shook his head when she asked him if he knew it, so she told him the story she'd just heard from Les. He didn't seem too impressed. 'You don't believe all that, do you?'

'Of course not, but it's a good story. Don't you think so?'

He smiled properly this time, and she felt a small sense of triumph. 'No, I just see Les coming up the stairs with his head tucked under his arm.' She laughed, and then he said, 'I need a word with you. Will you be in your room around five?'

* * *

51

The ghost tour of the Broome building went down very well. Debbie wondered, only half facetiously, if she should suggest it to the college marketing forum as a money spinner. Despite the success of her class, she felt uneasy. That feeling of foreboding was back, and she was glad that the college was bustling with pre-Christmas activity. She felt better in the crowded corridors. As soon as she was on her own she had that feeling of eyes on her, a sense of cold and menace. She cursed Tim, and she cursed herself for thinking about ghost stories – especially college ones.

It didn't help when, at coffee break, her head of department summoned her to his office to discuss the newspaper article. Peter Davis listened to her explanation, but his concluding, 'Well, we'll let it go this time but don't let it happen again,' served to fire up her anger. It was hard to pull her mind away from it and concentrate on her class. Anyway, she missed coffee.

At lunchtime there was a union meeting. City College was in trouble. Falling student numbers and financial constraints meant that the college was losing money, and the college management were planning cuts. The union was fighting for its members' jobs, but the staff were divided and undecided. The meetings were usually acrimonious or inconclusive.

The room was filling up as Debbie arrived. She'd meant to give herself time to buy a sandwich before the meeting started, but she'd stayed behind to talk to two of the students, and had had to come straight along. She saw Tim Godber indicating an empty seat next to him, but ignored him – *Why is Tim trying to be friendly again?* – and found a seat at the other side of the room. The news was all bad. City College was running more deeply into debt, and the management were looking for savings in the staffing budget. Nervously, Debbie thought about her overdraft and the money she needed each month just to pay the mortgage.

She had to leave before the meeting was over, and go straight to the classroom for her afternoon session with another GCSE group. They were a particularly lively group – standard euphemism, Debbie thought, for difficult and obnoxious – and she didn't feel up to controlling them through a trip round the building. No ghost tour, then. She decided to read them some ghost stories instead, and try to get them writing that way. They enjoyed the stories and contributed some of their own – mostly plots from videos, but there were one or two local stories that were interesting, and Debbie got them to record those on to audio tape, after they'd giggled and messed about. The students stopped cooperating when it came to writing, though, and dealing with the disruption, the constant demands for attention, requests for pens and paper tried her patience almost to breaking. By the end of the afternoon she had a headache and was too exhausted to feel hungry, even though she hadn't eaten since she left the house that morning.

When Rob Neave got to the staff room it was gone quarter past five. Debbie was sitting in her chair drinking coffee and eating chocolate. She offered a piece to him. 'What is it about teachers and chocolate?' he said, turning her offer down.

'This' – she waved the chocolate bar – 'is because I haven't had anything since breakfast.' He still looked tired, she noticed, as if he'd had as little sleep as she'd had these past few nights, but he looked better than he had in the morning, more like himself. She wanted to say something about this, but she couldn't think of any way to say it that didn't sound like an intrusion. 'Have you heard about the cuts?' she asked instead.

He had but didn't seem too concerned. 'I'm not planning a long stay here, anyway.'

Debbie wondered when he planned to leave. The place would be duller without him. 'You said you wanted to see me about something, didn't you?'

He seemed unsure of himself, which was unusual. 'That thing at the station. I've been talking to some people,' he said, choosing his words carefully, 'and it's possible you did see something important that night . . .' He was watching her closely now. Debbie put down her chocolate bar. She wasn't hungry any more. 'It's a long shot,' he said. 'They'll want to talk to you again, I think. Just – be a bit careful. Don't use the train on your late nights.'

'Is this official?' Debbie tried hard to keep her voice calm.

'No, it's just advice. From me, not them.'

'I need a drink.' Debbie plucked up her courage. 'Come and have a beer or something – if you're free.'

He looked at his watch and hesitated. She thought he was going to refuse, but he said, 'I've just got some stuff to see to in the office. Where are you going? Across the road? I'll see you in half an hour.'

Suddenly elated, Debbie packed her work into her briefcase and sorted her mail into the out tray. As she was leaving the room, the phone rang, and it was a bit more than half an hour before she was walking through the door of the Grindstone into the smell of beer and old smoke, and saw Neave leaning on the bar, talking to the landlord.

He bought the first round, bringing the drinks over to a table, and dropping a packet of salted peanuts in front of her. 'You need to get something inside you,' he said, pushing his chair away from the table as he sat down, and hooking his foot over the rung of another. Debbie felt shy, as though she didn't know what to say to him in this new context, but he didn't seem to notice anything, and talked casually about the pub and how it had been the place where the police used to drink, when he was in the force. 'More crimes got solved at this bar than at the station,' was how he put it. He seemed more relaxed in this atmosphere, and Debbie asked him a bit about his life in the police force. He made her laugh with some stories of the things he'd seen and the people he'd met, and then he asked her about herself, moving on to her parents, her childhood, her current life and her plans for the future.

Debbie found herself talking about her father, something she didn't often do. 'He was a miner,' she said. 'It was in the family, kind of thing. His father was a miner as well. He used to spoil me rotten.' Rob sat there quietly, watching her as she talked. 'He couldn't cope when they closed the pits down. He got paid off, but he couldn't get another job. He used to hate the way the people down at the job centres talked to him.' She paused. She wasn't sure about the next bit.

'What happened?' He was sitting close to her, listening.

'He died . . . It's some time now.' But Debbie could remember what it felt like, believing he hadn't cared enough, thinking that he had chosen to leave them. She still felt angry about it. She wanted to change the subject. She realized that, though they'd been talking for a while, she still knew very little about Rob.

'You're not local, are you?' she asked.

He shook his head. 'I've lived round here for years, but no, I was born in North Shields. Lived in Newcastle while I was growing up.'

'What brought you to Moreham?' It seemed a strange place to come, to Debbie.

'Nothing. I came to Sheffield to work.' He still seemed relaxed, but Debbie was aware that he was stonewalling her questions, that he didn't want to talk about himself.

She tried another tack. 'You said you weren't planning to stay at City. Where next?'

He was looking round the room, watching the other drinkers at the bar. 'Nothing planned. But City has only ever been a temporary thing. You ought to be thinking about moving on as well. It's no place to get stuck.'

'I like it.' Debbie recognized his ploy to turn the conversation back to her. 'I like the students and I like the work. I am looking for something else though – but only because of what's happening.' She tried again. 'Would you go to another college, or what?'

He laughed. 'No, I'm not planning a career in college security. I don't know yet, something. Do you want another drink?'

'My round.' Debbie reached for her purse and found it contained her travel pass and fifty pence. She went red. 'Oh, God, I ask you for a drink and I haven't got a penny on me.'

He thought it was funny. 'I'll ask you next time I'm broke. Don't worry, Deborah. Come on, what do you want. I'm buying.'

'OK, thanks, I'll have the same again. But next time . . .'

When he came back from the bar he smoothly took charge of the conversation again. 'Your father wasn't an old man, was he?'

Debbie shook her head. 'He was fifty-five when he died.' She thought Rob was watching her, but he was looking across towards the bar, frowning slightly, as though he was thinking something over.

'What is it that makes you so angry about it?' His question was so unexpected that she felt winded. The response was forced out of her before she had time to think about his right to ask it.

'Everything. All of them.' She felt her face flush. 'He thought it was his fault, you see. He was a pit deputy and he thought he should have joined the strike.' She looked at Rob, uncertain whether to go on. 'It wasn't his fault. He voted to strike. He was Catholic,' Debbie explained. 'His mother's family were deep-dyed Irish Catholics. So he felt guilty.' She thought about it again. 'They just threw them out, made them feel useless. Oh, there was good redundancy, but Dad didn't want that, he wanted his job, he was proud of it.'

He leant towards her, his arms on the table. 'And what happened?'

'Nothing happened. He got cancer. Lung cancer. He'd had a cough for a while. But he wouldn't do anything about it. We could tell, me and Mum, that he wasn't well, but he just didn't seem bothered. By the time they found it he was too far gone.' She sighed. It had been an awful death.

'You were his only daughter?'

'His only child.' Debbie smiled. 'He wasn't a practising Catholic by the time he met Mum. That was something else he felt guilty about.' She shook her head. 'It's not something I really understand.'

'No. It's not something I know much about.' That was the first personal comment he'd volunteered.

She told him something about the stories her father used to tell about the priests and nuns, and her Aunt Caitlin's house in County Cork with its holy pictures and statues.

'You didn't get all that?' he asked.

Debbie shook her head. 'Like I said, he'd given up Catholicism by the time he met Mum. She wouldn't have had any truck with it anyway. It was something that happened when he was a teenager. His sister, she was only a baby, she died. She was

56

only about three months old, and she hadn't been baptized. She'd been ill. My grandmother, apparently she believed that the baby wouldn't go to heaven because it hadn't been baptized, and she was just destroyed. My father said that he realized then he didn't believe a word of it any more.'

He went on watching her after she'd finished, unnervingly silent until she saw that he hadn't been paying attention, was thinking about something else. His face looked tense, distant. He shook his head. 'Sorry,' he said, 'I just thought of something.' He checked his watch. 'I've got to go.' She felt a stab of disappointment. His glass was empty. He waited while she finished her drink. 'Are you on the train?' Debbie nodded. 'I'll walk down as far as the bridge with you. I'm going that way. When's your next train?'

A bit fazed by the sudden change, Debbie scrabbled in her bag and checked her timetable. 'It's in ten minutes.'

It was nearly seven as they left the pub, and the town centre was quiet. A cold wind was blowing now, buffeting against the buildings, pulling Debbie's hair out of its pins and combs and whipping it against her face. They didn't talk as they walked towards the river. The station lights came into view, and they stopped at the crossing. 'I go this way,' he said. He looked over towards the station. There were people going in. It looked quite busy. 'Will you be OK from here?'

'Yes, fine.' Debbie checked her watch. 'I'm early.' She had nearly seven minutes before the train arrived, assuming it was running on time. She looked at him. The wind had blown his hair about and he'd turned his collar up against the cold. His face was half in shadow. She shivered.

'You're frozen,' he said. 'There's no warmth in that.' He touched the collar of her mac. 'Here.' He unwound the scarf he was wearing from under his coat and wrapped it round her neck. His good humour seemed to be back. He caught hold of one of the tendrils of her hair that had escaped from its confinement and tucked it behind her ear. They looked at each other in silence for a moment, then he said, 'You'd better get that train.' He waited as she crossed the road, then turned and walked away towards the river. She could hear her train on the line. She hurried to the station entrance, and an hour later she was standing in her kitchen, feeling unaccountably depressed.

She ought to eat something. The two beers she'd had with Rob had gone to her head. She wandered round the kitchen, opening cupboards. Buttercup yarped insistently at her feet. 'I've fed you,' Debbie told the little cat, and, picking her up, took her to the cat dish. Buttercup spurned the food with a burying motion, and hurried back to the kitchen after Debbie, mewing.

Some pasta, some wizened mushrooms, some eggs and some onions were the results of Debbie's trawl. A mushroom omelette, then. She put some oil to heat in the frying pan, and stirred the eggs in a dish. She washed the mushrooms and chopped them, deciding to fry them in butter as she deserved a treat. The mushrooms were cooking, and she was just pouring the eggs into the pan when the phone rang. Shit. She was tempted to leave it, but she couldn't stand a ringing phone. She was always convinced it was something serious on the other end. As soon as she picked it up, it stopped. She banged it down in frustration, and it started again. She picked it up and again it stopped. She waited a moment, then just as she was about to pick up the receiver to try 1471, the phone rang a third time. She grabbed it and waited. A voice she recognized well at the other end said, 'Debbie?'

'Mum!' She was relieved. 'Are you having phone trouble again?' Gina Sykes had been supplied with a series of jinxed phones by an increasingly apologetic and baffled phone company. The most recent one had behaved itself until, apparently, now.

'No. Should I have? After all the trouble I've had . . .' And she rattled off into the long story about inefficient operators and astronomical phone bills. Then she said, 'Now, love, I'm phoning about that article in the *Standard*. Why didn't you tell me about it? It's a bit much when I'm terrified for my daughter nearly a week too late.'

Debbie sighed. She'd been hoping, rather unrealistically, that her mother wouldn't see the article, as she rarely read the local paper. She explained what had happened, and, feeling a bit guilty for not having said anything to her mother about

58

the whole business in the first place, she told her about the interview with the police, and a slightly edited account of Rob Neave's opinion.

'Well, you pay heed to that,' Gina advised her. 'It's what your dad would have said as well. Listen, Debbie, I'm going up to the grave on Saturday, taking some flowers. Do you want to come too?'

Of course! It was her father's birthday on Saturday. Debbie, who never remembered birthdays – sometimes including her own – had always relied on her mother to remind her, so she could send her father a card and a present. Now it seemed she needed to be reminded about anniversaries. She felt guilty. 'Of course I will,' she said, trying to remember if she'd made any arrangements for the weekend. 'Shall I try and make it over on Friday night? If I'm not too busy. I could stay Saturday as well.' Though her mother was only a few stops up the line, Debbie didn't see as much of her as either of them would like. Debbie's work schedule got in the way, and Gina's job, though part time, occupied irregular hours.

After some more desultory conversation, Debbie rang off, and stood by the phone, looking at the photo on the table, her and her father displaying that trophy so proudly. Had her mother been trying to get through or not? Or was there someone else trying to phone her? A smell of burning brought her back, and she rushed to the kitchen to be confronted by pans full of burnt eggs and blackened mushrooms. She scraped the eggs on to a saucer and offered them to Buttercup, who crouched down intently to eat them. She dumped both pans in a sink full of water, angrily ripped a crust off the end of the loaf and ate it dry. It was stale.

Midnight, and again, Neave couldn't sleep. He drank some beer, listened to some music, read for a while, but he couldn't get his head to be still. It was all there, just waiting. The smallest thing brought it back. Angie.

The children's home where he'd spent most of his childhood had been run by people with very traditional views – no political correctness there. Boys were encouraged to boys' activities and girls to girls'. He hadn't minded this, except for the book with the pictures in. 'What are you reading that for?' Marlisse used to say. 'You don't want to read that. You're a boy,' and she'd substitute a sports book or an adventure book that she considered more suitable.

But the book with the pictures fascinated him and he went back to it again and again. All the pictures were mysterious, with watery, twisting colours that suggested unseen things lurking in the shadows on the page. The pictures were all supposed to be of fairies and elves – which is why Marlisse thought it wasn't a boy's book – but these weren't pretty little children with big eyes and gauzy wings. Some of them were twisted, ugly and strange, and some of them were wild and dangerous. There was one picture that he couldn't get out of his mind. In the background of this picture, a figure was half concealed behind some flowers. She had red-gold hair and an expression of glee on a face that had a wild, pinched beauty. He had been in love with her – whatever she was. They had had adventures together where he'd saved her from dungeons, and enemy soldiers, and high mountains and dark caves. She had been a companion in some of the loneliest times. He hadn't thought about the picture for years, and had certainly never expected to see it again, until she'd run lightly down the stairs in that dressing gown and looked at him with surprise.

He could see Berryman watching her as she knelt in front of the fire. He'd watched her as well. She'd known, and had casually moved the towel that she was using to dry her hair to obscure Berryman's view. But she had known he could still see her from his position by the mantelpiece, and had sparkled her eyes briefly in his direction. She was playing a dangerous game, and he liked that.

He waited until the end of that shift. It was nearly seven before he left the station. He turned down Berryman's suggestion of a drink. He had two days free now, and he and Berryman had plans for them, involving a couple of women they'd met the week before and invited over to his flat Saturday night; but first he decided to go back. He wasn't quite sure what he was going to say – *More questions? Forgot to ask . . . ?* He'd wing it when the time came. He parked outside the shabby terrace. It was getting dark now. He tried out one or two phrases – *Sorry to disturb you again, could you just go over* . . . but it wasn't how he expected.

He knocked at the door. He could hear music coming from the downstairs room, which stopped as he knocked the second time. She opened the door and looked at him, then she smiled and invited him in. She took him into the room they'd been in earlier and she made some kind of gesture, of welcome, he wasn't sure. She was dressed now, wearing something that seemed to consist of scarves and swirls, a confusion of shadow colours. Her hair, now it was dry, curled on to her shoulders a vivid red-gold. He couldn't stop looking at her.

The violin was out of its case, propped up next to the music stand. 'I was just practising,' she said. 'I've nearly finished. You don't mind waiting?' She picked up the instrument again, smiled briefly at him, and then became intent as she played. He watched the way her body bent and danced with the music, as though she was part of it. She was unselfconscious. He had given himself the right to watch her last time, this time she had given him the right. When she finished the piece she was playing, he asked her about the music. He'd never heard anything like it before. She picked up the violin again and played him pieces as she was talking about them. Then she showed him how to draw the bow across the strings and after a couple of tortured cat sounds, he produced a high, clear note.

His interest aroused her enthusiasm. She pulled out some books of songs that he had forgotten he knew, and made him sing, harmonizing her clear soprano with his tenor, but he didn't have the technique to do that for long, and they ended up laughing and breathless. Then they talked, sitting in front of the fire. He was good at getting information out of people, he could question them gently, expertly until they told him far more than they intended, but this time he let her draw him out, talked about things he'd rarely talked about before, until she knew as much about him as he knew about her. There was no rush, no hurry.

It must have been three in the morning before they were

talked out, and she lay down on the bed. She looked tired. The shadows under her eyes were violet. She reached out her arms in invitation, and he stretched himself out beside her, running his fingers down her face and across her mouth.

Afterwards she asked him, 'Did you come back for anything special?'

'This,' he said, with absolute honesty, holding her tightly, feeling her shaking as she laughed. Dangerous games.

They hardly left her room that weekend. She was alone in the house – her fellow lodgers had all gone away. When Sunday evening and work loomed, he had to go. It wasn't like it usually was, the insincere promises – *Bye, give you a ring, see you later*. It was as if he had a barbed hook in his flesh, except it didn't hurt, unless he tried to pull away.

It wasn't until afterwards, in the sudden, shocking silence after she was gone, that he realized they'd been playing a far more dangerous game. He couldn't go back. He was left like the survivor of a shipwreck washed up on some remote and rocky island, and there was no way back, and no way forward.

6

Midnight. Debbie jerked awake. Her heart was hammering as though she'd had a shock. Breaking glass . . . a dream? When Debbie was small, she used to have a recurring nightmare. She was chased through her familiar house by giants, giants that moved slowly but relentlessly, their faces distorted and flattened. She ran, her legs heavy and slow, towards the deep wells and shafts she had to climb down to escape, but at the bottom of each there was something sinister and dangerous – sometimes a large screw turning like a giant engine, sometimes fast-flowing but dark and silent water; sometimes a black gliding shape that drifted soundlessly past. As she lay in bed now, she realized she had been dreaming. A giant had been chasing her.

She looked at the green digits on the clock radio and groaned. She'd been so tired she'd gone to bed at ten, tried reading, but her eyes had started to close so she'd turned the light off and drifted to sleep. Now she was wide awake. She turned over and tried to pull her pillow round to support her head. That wasn't right. She tried another position and an itch in the small of her back disturbed her. She turned on to her back and stared at the ceiling.

The window was a black rectangle in the darkness. She watched it. Was there something moving out there beyond the sill? She thought she could see shadows. She could hear a faint scraping noise, outside. A kind of crunching, like footsteps on gravel, slow stealthy footsteps like someone trying to make no sound at all. *Don't be stupid, it's just your imagination!* She hadn't closed the curtain. Slowly, she sat up, pulling the quilt around her against the cold. God, it was freezing. Wrapped in the quilt, she got out of bed and, pressed to the wall, peered out of the window. Blackness. There was something wrong, something odd, something out of place. She couldn't tell what it was at first, then she realized that the streetlight that shone over the fence into her back garden wasn't lit. The small back yard was a pool of night. She couldn't hear the sound any more. She strained her ears, listening. Nothing. She opened her bedroom door very quietly. Still nothing. She realized she didn't want to go downstairs, into the dark, and she didn't want to turn the lights on and let anyone know that she was there.

She went back to bed, and lay there in the silence as the shadows moved outside her window, and the rectangle gradually lightened, and she fell asleep.

When Debbie left the house the next morning, rushing because she had overslept, she saw Jill, her neighbour, talking to Mr Fenton whose house backed on to the gennel from the other side. 'Morning, Debbie,' Jill called. Debbie waved.

Mr Fenton hurried over. 'Bloody vandals, excuse my French, love,' he said. Mr Fenton took a grandfatherly interest in Debbie. 'Look at that light,' he said in disgust. Debbie looked up at the streetlight. It had been smashed, the glass scattered over the ground. 'I heard it breaking,' he said, 'but I just thought it was kids breaking bottles again. I came out this morning to clear up, and there it was.' He shook his head. Debbie didn't have time to get into a long conversation, particularly not one that was going to be about what Mr Fenton had and hadn't fought the war for, so she explained she was in a hurry and left him with Jill. She thought he had a point, though.

The early light of a winter morning is starting to lift the shadows. The shapes are becoming clearer as the darkness recedes. The loft keeps the night for longer. It is not easy, planning a hunt. It takes time, dedication, strength. For a moment, he feels cold, lost, and he moves over to his railway, studying the tracks, the tunnels, the maze — his hunting ground. While the shadows are still there, he remembers. He remembers the dark places, the muffled breaths, tight, laboured. He remembers the waiting, the knowing . . . Her eyes will shine in

*the dark place, shiny tracks on her face. He remembers gleamings
in the moonlight, soft breath, going, gone . . .*

*He crosses the loft to where the overalls hang, carefully placed
on the row of hooks on the wall. Four of them. And a new one,
on the next hook. The cold feeling is mixed with a tension now, an
excitement, a stirring in his groin. He wraps his arms round one
of the overalls, burying his face in it, breathing in the smell that
has gone sour and tainted, like the rest. He remembers, rubbing his
stiffness against the stains.*

She didn't tell Detective Sergeant McCarthy about her broken
night, of course, when she went to the police station that
afternoon. The day hadn't started well. She had missed her
train and arrived in the college just in time to go straight into
her first class. She felt jangled and disorientated. She wanted
to say to the students, 'I'm too tired to do this now. Can we
do it later?' At coffee break, there was a note on her desk,
asking her to phone DS McCarthy at Moreham police station.
He wanted to see her as soon as possible, and he was free that
lunchtime. She wasn't hungry, anyway.

She was bracing herself for another inquisition about the
article, but he didn't mention it at first, and she thought
maybe she would get away with it. Instead, he asked her
about the Thursday-evening encounter, going over and over
the details, clearly trying to work out what she had seen, what
she had imagined, what she had not been able to see. He was a
tall man with fair hair and unfriendly blue eyes, and she found
him intimidating. He was trying to push her into giving him
definite answers to his questions, and there was very little
she could be sure about. She hadn't seen the woman she
often saw on the opposite platform; no, she didn't see her
every week, but she'd been there for the past three or four
weeks.

She didn't know if the woman used the train every Thursday. She'd usually been there last term, but Debbie hadn't
been at the station in the evenings over the summer – there
were no classes. Evening classes had started again at the end
of September. She'd certainly seen the woman since then,
and she'd certainly been at the station for the past few weeks

– three? Four? She couldn't be sure. Yes, she waited on the platform; no, the rain wouldn't make any difference, the platform was sheltered; no, she couldn't be certain she wasn't waiting on the ramp or the bridge, she hadn't looked; *yes*, she had seen a man; no, she couldn't identify him. Over and over it they went, until at last he said, 'Thank you, Miss Sykes, you've been very helpful.' Meaning, 'You haven't given me much I can work on here.'

He did talk about the article then, about how it was unwise, how she shouldn't have talked to anybody, about the undesirability of having a high profile when a killer such as this was on the streets, about being careful and about telling them at once if she had any reason to think anyone was watching her. Debbie felt an impotent anger at having to explain and excuse her own actions. She hadn't done anything!

She left, feeling wrung out and exhausted.

Debbie stayed at her desk until after five, then packed some work into her briefcase to finish at home. It weighed a ton, and as she came to the stairs, she pushed the button for the lift, in case it was already there. She heard a distant clang, and decided not to wait, but headed down the stairs to the basement exit.

She heard the lift clunk to a halt as she hurried down the stairs. She should have waited for it. Then she heard it moving on down towards the basement. Someone must have called it from below. She looked at her watch – five-thirty. She might just make it in time for the next train. She heard the lift doors open below her as she hurried down the last flight of stairs.

It was dark. Someone had turned the lights off, and she didn't know where the switches were. The open lift doors illuminated the bottom of the stairwell, but the corridor to the exit was in blackness. She felt uneasy in the darkness, and hurried round the corner to the doors. As she reached them, she had a sudden sense of someone behind her, close. She spun round but there was no one there, just the dim shadows. The clang of the lift doors made her jump, and she heard the lift hum into life.

She pushed through the doors and into the alley, where

the light of the streetlamp calmed her nerves. Her talk with DS McCarthy had turned her into a wreck. Debbie took a deep breath, looked round her at the groups of people walking down the alley, the lights from the shop windows, open late now for Christmas, and telling herself firmly that everything was normal, she walked briskly to the station.

It was Thursday again, her long day. Debbie had a class from nine till twelve-fifteen, a tutorial group from one-thirty till three and her evening class at six. At the beginning of the term, Peter Davis had tried to put a nine o'clock class on her timetable for Friday morning, but Louise had put her foot down and after some heated discussion he had agreed that Debbie could have her half-day in lieu on Friday morning *for the moment*. '"For the moment", my arse,' Louise said. 'He's not pulling a stunt like that and he knows it. Just let me know if you have any hassle.' College rumour had it that Peter Davis used to count his testicles after a meeting with Louise. Debbie was glad to have her on the same side.

She was tired. Term had run for thirteen weeks without a break, and there was still a week to go before the Christmas break. The students were starting to get tired as well, which made them less responsive, more inclined to complain, miss classes, leave work undone. She decided that she'd take her evening class on the ghost tour. She'd check with Sheila, the IT receptionist, that the room would be open so she could take her students on to the long staircase. It would be particularly spooky at night. They'd enjoy that. Then next week, the last class of the term, they could have a kind of Christmas party, and watch a film – did she have a good ghost story in her video collection? She must remember to book a video.

So much to do. She had half an hour before her class started so she could get some marking done. Had she got all her handouts ready for her first class? Her mind felt woolly and unfocused, and the vague depression that had started two days ago was still with her. As she walked along the corridor to her class, she felt that now familiar sense of menace, so strongly that she turned round sharply to see who was behind her, but there were only a few students on their

67

way to classes, and one of the caretakers at the far end of the corridor, checking the fire escape door.

Her lethargy lasted through her morning class, and on into the afternoon. She was trying to get her tutorial group to start thinking about their university entrance. The students, who still had one more year at college, couldn't see the urgency, but Debbie knew from past experience that if they didn't get started now, there would be a terrible rush next September. 'You may not care,' she said, 'but I'm going to be the one picking up the pieces and I can tell you now that I'm not picking up the pieces for anyone who hasn't put in the time this year.'

They were neither impressed nor convinced.

Her energy came back a bit by the time her evening class started. The idea of the ghost tour had been a good one. Even the most disaffected, the eye-raisers, the lip-curlers, became enthusiastic about this assignment. 'Writing horror,' Debbie told them, 'isn't just about writing a lot of gore. I know' – she held up a hand to silence some objections – 'some writers write excellent gore. What I'm saying is you don't have to, and if you aren't a very experienced writer, it's difficult to write convincingly. Let the readers' imagination work. Let them frighten themselves.' She read them an extract from Shirley Jackson's novel, *The Haunting of Hill House*, the passage where two women huddle in a locked room listening to something not human pounding on the doors in a deserted corridor, and feeling for entry to the room where the women are trapped: *. . . The little sticky sounds moved on around the door frame and then, as though a fury caught whatever was outside, the crashing came again and Theodora saw the wood of the door tremble and shake, and the door move against its hinges . . .* They listened with the intentness of real interest until Debbie finished reading.

'That's crap, that,' volunteered Shawn. 'You want to see that bit from *Scream* when –'

'Not films,' Yvonne said. 'I think that was great, that, Debbie, it was really . . .'

'What *did* come through the door?' That was Nargus.

'What do you think?' Debbie was enjoying herself. There was a confused mixture of voices as each one tried to think of

68

something horrible enough, and disagreed with each other's suggestions. 'So you see,' Debbie said, 'everyone thinks something different was on the other side of the door. Shirley Jackson never tells you, because what you can imagine is much worse than anything else. She just describes what happens and you do the rest.'

'That's crap, that . . .' But Shawn's voice lacked conviction now, and Debbie felt she'd got them into the right mood for the ghost tour. She took them to the locations she'd got stories for, trailed part of the way by one of the caretakers, one she didn't know, who concealed his interest by studying fire hoses and testing the doors of empty rooms. When they got to the highlight, the long staircase, she led them through the IT suite to the old fire door, and pushed the bar down to open it. The door opened on to a landing halfway up the staircase. The spiral stairs ran up into shadows and down into shadows, illuminated by a single light. She took them up to the top, and showed them how the doors, one on each landing, were firmly nailed shut. Then she took them down to the bottom, to show them the door leading out on to the lane that ran behind the building. She put her briefcase on the floor and turned the handle of the outside door to demonstrate that it was bolted and that no one could get in. Then she told them the story.

'. . . coming up the steps behind him.' Debbie finished to a satisfactory silence. Then there was a hubbub of questions, interest, appreciation. They went back to the classroom, and she set up the assignment. 'For next week, please, a first draft of a ghost story, set in a place you know well. I want you to convince me, and I want you to frighten me. OK?'

Just before nine, as she shut down the computer, Sarah Peterson noticed the man in the blue overalls – again! She'd stayed on at college to finish her essay before the deadline. Tomorrow evening was Adam's party, so she was going to have to work an extra shift at the pub this weekend. Tony, the landlord, had been a bit funny with her when she'd asked for Friday evening off, and she felt guilty about letting him down.

The man in the blue overalls – she frowned, thinking. She'd

seen him twice before, when she'd been looking for Debbie. She hadn't wanted Debbie to know she was waiting for her, so she'd been keeping in the background, and each time, he'd been there. She'd hardly noticed him at first, and then – when there was nobody around, apart from her – suddenly he'd been there. He made her feel – wrong, uneasy.

And now . . . there he was again. She stayed at the screen of her computer, peering over the top. He was going across to the old fire door. He turned and Sarah ducked behind her screen. She looked round the room. She was the last student. There was just the receptionist tidying up at the desk. Sarah moved round her table, and headed towards the door the man had just gone through. She was going to see what he was up to, just peek round the door, when the receptionist's voice interrupted her, making her jump guiltily. 'What are you doing? It's after nine. You'll have to leave now, the caretakers will be locking up soon.'

Nine o'clock came and went. The class meandered out, discussing the evening, asking Debbie questions, checking on the requirements of the work. Once again, it was late when she came out, and the caretakers were locking up. She hurried to the staff room and then realized that she didn't have her briefcase. Where was it? Could it wait till tomorrow? Oh God, it had her purse and her keys in. Then she had a sudden picture, *oh, no* . . . of her putting the case down near the bottom of the spiral stairs.

She rushed back to the main entrance where Les was shuffling around with a window pole. 'Les!'

'What do you want, love?'

'I've left something upstairs, I'll be a few minutes, OK?'

'Don't worry. We've not finished on top floor yet.'

'Right. Great. I'll just get it.' She ran upstairs, and pushed open the doors of the IT suite. The room was unlit, silent and empty. She turned on the light at the far end, and crossed through the pools of shadow to the fire door. It opened, and she peered into the darkness uneasily. She tried the light switch, but the light wasn't working. She had a feeling she'd turned it off at the bottom of the stairs earlier in the evening.

Oh, well. There was enough light from the open door. She nerved herself, then went cautiously down the stairs.

The bottom of the stairs were in darkness. There was a strange smell down there she hadn't noticed earlier, stale and fetid. She groped around the wall for the light switch, but when she found it, it didn't work. Her bag would be over by the wall. She felt her way across, was reaching to find it, when a sudden draught swirled round her and the door two landings up closed with a crash.

Debbie was plunged into complete darkness. At first she was just surprised, then her heart began to hammer, and she was terrified. She tried to run back up the stairs, but tripped and fell on the first step, scraping her shin on the stone. The sudden pain brought tears to her eyes, and she stopped, breathing deeply, calming herself. The smell seemed to be stronger now.

It's OK, it's OK, the wind blew the door shut. You can open it again. Don't be frightened by your own stupid ghost stories.

She climbed the stairs more slowly now, a faint light from the grimed-up window helping her to see a little. There was no light on the landing, but she reached out for the door, feeling over it for a handle. None. Of course, it was for getting out, not getting in. She pushed against it, but it wouldn't budge. She was trapped. Les knew where she was – no, he just knew she'd gone upstairs. He might not even realize she hadn't come down again and left. She felt her mouth go dry and her heart begin to beat fast again.

Stop it, calm down. Bottom line is you spend the night on these steps.

She took a deep breath, and called. Nothing. Her voice had a muffled sound that made her remember how thick the door was. She yelled again, and banged on the door. Still nothing. She could try going up the staircase and calling there. If Les was on the top floor, he might hear her. Then she realized. She could unbolt the bottom door, get out that way. She was just feeling with her foot for the first step of the flight down, when she froze.

Down below her, in the dark, down below her where there was nothing but the locked door, she heard a sound.

71

'Hello?' Her whisper echoed round the stairwell. There was only silence, then she heard it again, a faint scraping noise. She kept quite still, staring into the dark until colours danced in front of her eyes. She felt cold. Another sound like, *please not*, like a footstep down in the darkness below her. She was suddenly convinced that something, no, someone, was coming quietly but deliberately up the steps towards her. The blood pounded in her ears and she made a dive for the next flight, falling again but not feeling the pain this time.

Not up. There's no way out!

Now she couldn't mistake it. There were footsteps on the stairs below her and that awful smell was in her nostrils. She pounded on the door, shouting to drown the sound more than anything else. She wanted to shut her eyes, bury her head, just wait until it was over. There was no one to hear her. She didn't know if she was afraid of the supernatural or the real. She felt a gust of cold air blow over her and knew that whatever was coming towards her meant her harm.

Then the door to the IT suite opened and she fell through it against the person who had opened it, grabbing on to him, trying to press her head into him, to hide herself from the thing on the stairs.

'Deborah! Come on, Deborah, it's OK, you're all right, I heard you, you're OK.' It was Rob Neave holding her, trying to calm her down.

'Oh, God, Rob, there's someone down there, I heard someone down there!' He pushed her away from him at once and went to the door.

'I can't see anything. Are you sure . . .'

'Rob, I know, I heard it, please believe me.' It was important, very important that he believed her. He had a torch attached to his belt and he went through the door, shining its inadequate light in front of him. Debbie followed. He shone it up and down the stairwell, but there was nothing there. He went down the steps into the darkness, as Debbie watched the light of his torch. He said something more to himself than her, then came up again more quickly, carrying her briefcase. His expression was unreadable.

'There's no one there now,' he said, and made a quick

gesture to silence her protest, 'but I think someone was. The door at the bottom – the bolts are drawn.' Debbie's legs began to tremble so much she thought she was going to fall over. He said something she couldn't catch, his voice sounding impatient, but he put his arms round her until the shaking stopped. She pressed her face into him, breathing in the warm smell of him, the cotton of his shirt, his skin. 'OK?' he asked. She nodded and he let her go, steadying her with his hands on her arms. 'Right, I've locked the door. Do you want to tell anyone? The police?' She shook her head. He looked at her. He seemed watchful, tense.

'It was probably nothing, my imagination, I don't know, I just don't want any more . . .' She heard tears coming into her voice and stopped. He slipped his arms round her again and pulled her face against him. 'It's OK, Deborah, you're OK.' He seemed more aware of how frightened she had been and was gentler now, stroking her hair, soothing, saying, 'It's OK . . . it's OK,' until she felt herself relax.

She straightened up and wiped her face with her hands, pushed the loosened combs back into her hair, feeling dishevelled and confused. She swallowed and found her voice. 'I think I've missed my train.' That wasn't what she meant to say. 'I mean . . . thanks for . . .'

'Don't worry about that. I can take you back.' He was looking at her, concerned. 'You need a drink.' He hesitated as though he was thinking something through. 'I should put in a report about this.' He looked at Debbie again. 'It'll keep. Whoever it was will be miles away by now. Have you got your things?'

Debbie gestured to her briefcase. Her mac was squashed into the top. 'Yes,' she said. Then, 'Rob? That drink? I don't think I could face the Grindstone . . .' The pub could be crowded and noisy this late, she knew.

'No. I know somewhere quieter.' He looked at her for a moment. 'Come on.'

He drove her to a pub by the river. It was small, shabby and run down, but quiet. She didn't want to talk at first and sat quietly letting the drink unwind her. He seemed to know how she was feeling and wandered easily through a range of topics

73

that didn't require much response from her, and gradually she felt herself relaxing. The events of earlier began to fade from her mind and when she found herself laughing at something he said she decided she had recovered. She owed him a drink from their visit to the Grindstone, and he'd already bought a round, so she asked him if he wanted another. He checked his watch. 'Do you need to be home at any particular time?'

'No.' She pictured the black windows of her house. 'There's only the cat waiting.' Then she thought again about the black windows, and the empty passageway leading to the back of her house and it came racing back into her mind – the dark stairs, the sound of footsteps, quiet but clear in the shadows below her, the way she had been trapped. The warmth seemed to drain out of her and her hand shook as she took a quick swallow of her drink. She looked up and met his eyes. He didn't look away, but lifted his hand towards her and, after a moment of hesitation ran his fingers down her face and round the back of her neck, twining them in the tendrils of hair that hung there. Debbie's face felt warm and she had trouble finding the rhythm of her breathing. 'You don't have to be on your own,' he said. He leaned forward and touched his mouth lightly against hers, giving her time to draw back, if she wanted to. 'You can come back with me.'

Friday morning, Debbie sat at her desk staring at nothing, trying to let the thoughts in her head settle into some rational focus. She had already been on the receiving end of Louise's waspishness for forgetting the marks list she'd promised to bring in at the end of the week. She'd found her keys slung carelessly on her desk. She must have left them there last night. Debbie thought that if she'd known the keys were still on her desk she might not have gone down the long staircase in search of her briefcase. She could have managed without her purse until this morning. Maybe it would have been better. This morning . . . Louise was asking her something and she brought her attention back. 'What? Sorry?'

'I *said*, have you got the A1's first set of essay marks? I also said, "Do you want to borrow a million pounds?" Either way I didn't get through.' Louise's voice was sharp.

'Sorry.' Debbie shook her head to clear it, knowing she wasn't responding properly. Louise gave her a look and returned to her notes.

Last night . . .

His flat was just across the road. He didn't say anything as he let her in, ushering her into the small room – narrow bed against one wall, shelves with books and some sound equipment, a chair, cushions on the floor, gas fire turned low. He switched on a table lamp, poured her a glass of whisky and put some music on – beautiful, melodic music that was surprisingly joyful. He wasn't, she realized, someone she associated with joy. There wasn't any need to say anything then. He watched her as she swallowed the whisky nervously. She looked at him, but he didn't look away, kept his eyes on hers, watching.

He came over to where she was standing, and took the glass out of her hand. He unbuttoned her blouse and she let it slide down her arms to the floor. She unfastened her skirt, and let it fall round her feet, slid off her shoes and stockings. He put his hands round her waist and kissed her open mouth. She could taste the whisky on his tongue. The rough cloth of his shirt and the cord of his trousers pressed against her skin. She could feel his erection. He ran his hands down her back, hooking his fingers in the top of her pants and pushing them down. She let them drop to the floor, stepped out of them and kicked them away.

He lifted her on to the bed, and undressed in the shadowed light, watching her all the time. She felt a nervous excitement in her stomach, the beat of her pulse in her throat. He lay down beside her, putting his hands behind her head to release her hair from the pins and combs that held it. It tumbled down round her face and over her shoulders. He was confident, knowing, and she relinquished control to him. He was unhurried as if they had all the time there was. She lost herself. He could see it in her face and whispered, 'Come on, Debs, that's right, that's good.' He put his arms round her, stroking her, prolonging the moment.

Later, he got them more whisky, and they leaned back against the pillows, listening to music. Debbie drifted into a doze against his shoulder. Later still, they stood under the shower together, and he laughed as the water ran down her face and into her mouth. He gave her a dressing gown and towelled her hair in front of the fire, letting it stream through his fingers as it dried. He pushed her down on to the cushions, his hands finding the knot in the dressing gown cord.

After, he said, 'Do you want to stay? I can still take you home if you want.'

'I want to stay.' They drank more whisky, then she felt hungry so he got them some bread and cheese.

'I didn't cater for a guest,' he said.

The bed was small, but she fell into a dreamless sleep beside him. She woke up in the night, three-thirty the luminous face of the clock said. The moon was full, shining through the window, icy and still. He was awake, lying there staring at the ceiling. He smiled when he saw she was awake too, a warm, unguarded smile she hadn't seen before. She moved on top of him and he was gentle, drawing her hair down until it hung like a tent around them, pulling her head down to kiss her, and afterwards he buried his face between her breasts and murmured, 'Debs, beautiful Debs.'

She woke in the morning alone in the bed. He was making coffee in the small kitchen, and she realized how much his customary daytime face, that relaxed friendliness, acted as a mask to the man behind it. And the mask was back. He was friendly, casual, closed. It was still early. 'Do you need to go home?' he asked. Debbie checked the time. Buttercup would need feeding, but she could phone Jill from work. She shook her head. He took her into college, driving fast and competently, drawing up away from the car park and main entrance, ten minutes later. He didn't say anything until she got out of the car, then he said, 'I'll see you later, OK?'

She didn't know what to think.

He was angry with himself. He hadn't intended to take Debbie home with him – it was as if some kind of automatic pilot had taken over. She wasn't the first woman since Angie. He had women friends like Lynne, women as unattached – and as unwilling to be attached – as he was. Sometimes he got together with somebody for an evening out, a friendly fuck and home. That was the way he wanted it. The last woman he'd spent the night with, spent all night making love to, had been Angie, and he didn't want that with anyone else. The night with Debbie had touched something he thought was safely buried.

She had stood there watching him and he'd put that bloody music on, the quartet that Borodin had written when the composer was newly married and deeply, sensually in love with his young wife. Something about Debbie had made him play it, and then it was as if the music had taken over, wrapped them both in its spell. He could hear it now, and he couldn't stop himself from remembering the way she looked, her gently rounded belly, her small, high tits, the way her face had gone warm and dreamy when he ran his thumbs over her nipples, the way she let him watch her eyes, and the urgent way she had responded to him.

He didn't want it. He really didn't.

Just like all the rest, then. They think they can get away with it, think that no one knows. But he is watching now. She'll know that in time, in his time.

He knows from his past experience that it is easy to move around public buildings as long as you know where you are going and look as though you belong. Most people would think that the best camouflage for this kind of terrain would be the guise of a student. But he knows better. Students belong in groups. A stranger in a group will cause the group to take alarm. There are better ways he can watch his quarry. They see a sparrow in a hedgerow of sparrows, not the shadow of the circling eagle.

And talk, talk, talk in that flat, local voice. Common. He really couldn't be bothered to listen to it all. But the hunter is patient, the hunter waits and observes. And the hunter's patience is always rewarded. Hunters are valuable, hunters serve a purpose. They weed out the weak, the tainted – and the careless – and she was careless. He was not. She mustn't see the noose, the jaws of the trap, the glint of the knife, not until he decides it, not until it is too late. But oh, the surge of triumph – the bag, left behind, ripe for the picking. And if someone should come? He is prepared. The light is gone. He doesn't need it.

77

And then she is there. For a moment, it is as if the hunt is over, the time is now. For a moment . . . To everything there is a season.

It was not the time. He had taken his trophy and gone. Then he had waited. And he knew what she had done.

It's easy to get keys copied — twenty-four hours a day. And the keys will be very useful. Luck? Yes, but he knows how to use luck. There is something else, though, something that can't be ignored. He's just a bit displeased with that one detail. He was noticed. And by someone who could be a nuisance. He'll have to do something about that. He mustn't spoil the ship for a ha'porth of tar.

7

Midday Friday, Lynne Jordan and Dave West were in the offices of Broughton and Partners, Julie Fyfe's employers. Lynne was with Julie's boss. She glanced at her notes. Andrew Thomas, entrepreneur and partner in a thriving company. She looked across the desk at the man facing her, and decided he was also an arsehole. He'd been away after Julie's death, *on business*. 'Talk to him,' Berryman had said. She smiled and said again, 'I need all of the information from Julie's personnel file, Mr Thomas. I'll give you a receipt for anything I take away with me, but you do understand this is urgent.' The files had been slow in coming, and Berryman, and Lynne, wanted to know why.

'Well, Officer,' said Thomas, with a smile that confirmed Lynne's opinion, 'you do understand that I can't release confidential information just on your say-so without consulting my partner.'

'Mr Thomas, I suggest that you do that. This is a murder investigation and I was given an assurance that all of the material would be available to me as soon as I came down this morning.' Lynne was keeping her temper for the moment. Berryman had said that he had some questions for the little shit and she wanted him to jump then, not now. Thomas picked up the phone and dialled.

'Suzy? Get me Peter will you? Thank you so much.' He held the receiver, staring into space, smiling his small, complacent smile. 'Peter! Andrew here . . . How are you? . . . Fine, fine . . . Is it? . . . Is it really . . . Hey!'

Lynne stood up and took the phone from him. 'Is that Mr Broughton?' She identified herself. 'Right, can you arrange with Mr Thomas *now* to release those personnel details for Julie Fyfe? Thank you.' She handed the phone over to Thomas, who took it, listened for a moment, flushed and then hung up.

'Well, Officer, if I'd known you'd talked to *Peter* . . . Come this way. I'll get you the stuff.' He led Lynne into another room where three women were sitting at screens, typing. 'Sandra,' he said to one of them. 'Will you get this lady Julie's personnel file. Will that be all, Officer?'

'For the moment, thank you, Mr Thomas.' Lynne gave him her brief, professional smile. Then she looked at the woman waiting at the desk. 'Did you work with Julie?' she asked.

'Oh, I've already spoken to the police, to one of you, I mean.' The woman seemed nervous, but in Lynne's experience, nervousness wasn't an unusual response from people who had come into contact with crime as witnesses. 'Not all the time; she didn't work in our office. She was Mr Thomas's PA.'

'What did she do on Thursday evenings, to be working so late?'

'Oh, it's part of our small business service. We run training courses and seminars in the evenings. We all work one evening a week. Julie's was Thursday.'

'Did she always travel on the train?' Lynne knew these questions had already been asked, but she found that people often added the significant detail if they were asked again.

Sandra nodded. 'Always.'

'I'm surprised she didn't drive.' Lynne knew the answer again, but she wanted to get the woman relaxed, talking.

'She couldn't drive. She failed her test five times.' Sandra looked smug.

'Wasn't she supposed to have a company car after she got promoted?'

Sandra looked at her screen for a moment and called down a menu. She frowned in concentration, then said, 'Yes, she was a bit sick about that. But Mr Thomas arranged for her to have the money for a travel card – a full card for all round the region.' She turned off the screen. 'I'll get you that file now. It's this way.' She was ushering Lynne towards the door of the office. 'We keep the records down here.'

'Isn't it all on the computer?' Lynne asked, surprised.

'Some of it is, I'll get you all of that in a minute, but the files are kept in here.' She unlocked a door that led into a large walk-in cupboard, and went over to a filing cabinet. She sorted through the keys on the bunch that Thomas had given her, and unlocked it. She started flicking her fingers through the hanging files. 'Here we are – Julie.'

'What was she like, Julie?' Lynne asked, taking the file from her and glancing at the contents.

'She was very nice.'

Don't speak ill of the dead. 'She looked very efficient. Was she good at her job? She'd got a long way in a short time, hadn't she?' Lynne's voice was chatty, indifferent.

Sandra gave Lynne a sideways glance. Lynne went on sorting through the papers in the file. 'She got on well with Mr Thomas,' Sandra conceded.

'Is he one of the partners, Thomas?' Lynne was reading one of the forms in the folder.

Sandra nodded her head, then seeing Lynne wasn't looking said, 'Yes, but he's the junior partner. Mr Broughton, he's the senior partner.'

'Well, that's one way to get on,' Lynne agreed.

'Oh, I didn't mean . . .' Sandra weighed discretion against wanting to have her say. 'It wasn't anything, you know, as far as I know, but she got all the best jobs, the best breaks. She used to be a typist, but she went on this course, and she got to go to these conferences . . . and then they promoted her this August. Then when we got the Small Business of the Year Award, there she was with the bosses in the photograph and the rest of us were all just in the background. It was in the paper, the *Standard*. You couldn't even see me.' She looked at Lynne with indignation. 'We'd all worked, and we did get a bonus and everything, but that picture made it look like it was them, the bosses, and Julie. They should have had us in properly so everyone would know, you know.'

'Did you all feel like that? It doesn't seem very fair.' But Lynne's question had alerted Sandra to the fact that she had perhaps said too much, and she just murmured that it wasn't really anything, it was just the way Mr Broughton and Mr Thomas were. When they went back to the office and Sandra started running information off the computer for Lynne, Lynne saw the disputed photo framed on the wall. It did seem a bit unfair. There in the foreground were Andrew Thomas, a man who must be Peter Broughton and, smiling radiantly between them, was Julie Fyfe. In the background, sitting at three desks, the other women smiled from behind their machines. The head of one, presumably Sandra, was concealed by Julie's elbow. The caption said *Broughton's Winning Team*.

She made a note to tip Berryman off to ask some more questions about Julie Fyfe's relationship with her bosses.

In the car, she asked West how he'd got on with the other women at the firm. 'They didn't like her,' he said. 'They thought something was going on with the boss, that Thomas.'

Lynne nodded. 'That was more or less the impression I got from Sandra. What do you think?'

'She was pretty fit.' West shrugged. 'Could be something, could be nothing. We need to know what was going on, though.' He reached into the glove compartment and fished out a Mars bar. 'Want some? Where are we going now, then?'

'The Varneys'. We're going to talk to Mandy's mum. I want to find out more about these phone calls.' West nodded. They'd discussed it earlier. She pulled out on to the dual carriageway and followed the bypass to the other side of Moreham. As they came off the main road and drove through the mellow stone and tree-lined avenues of what used to be Moreham's wealthy suburb, she said, 'You talk to her, Dave. She doesn't like me – thinks I should be at home looking after my husband or something.'

West, working on his first big murder investigation, was keen to get more experience, be more involved. He liked working with Lynne Jordan. She was willing to let him have a go. The car pulled up outside the neat semi, at one end of a row built among larger Victorian stone houses. The front garden was a neat lawn behind a white fence, overshadowed at one end by the high wall and overhanging evergreens of the next-door garden that tangled in the dark neglect of multiple occupancy. They walked up to the front door and West rang the bell, aware of twitching curtains from the twin semi. A dog yapped furiously. There was a pause, then the door opened on the chain. 'Who is it?' The dog snarled and tried to push its nose through the gap.

Lynne stepped forward with her ID card held up. 'It's DS Jordan and DC West,' she said. 'We phoned earlier.'

'Oh yes.' The voice sounded vague. The door was pushed shut and then opened properly again. Lynne was relieved to see that Mrs Varney was now holding the dog, a small animal that struggled and barked, straining towards the two officers with malign intent in its eyes. Lynne hadn't seen Carol Varney since the murder of her daughter. Then, even in her shock and grief, she had been neat, organized, insisting on making tea and serving it up in matching china, biscuits arranged on doilies. She'd perched on the edge of her chair, well-groomed and in control, talking to the detectives in a carefully modulated voice, while her husband patted her hand and said, 'Now, dear, now, dear,' over and over like a mantra.

Today, she looked untidy. Her hair straggled and darker hair mixed with grey had grown an inch or more from the roots. Her skirt and blouse were slightly rumpled and her eyes were unfocused. There was a faint chemical smell about her. She showed them into the front room. This was as Lynne remembered it, pristine and precisely ordered. Ornaments carefully placed on shelves, a few books strictly marshalled into line, pictures square on the wall, everything sparkling and clean. Lynne wondered how many hours of the day Carol Varney spent washing, vacuuming, dusting. The two officers sat down at her gesture. Lynne nodded to West. He looked over at the woman, uncertain. *Get on with it!* Lynne thought.

'Mrs Varney,' West began. 'We just wanted to go over some of the information you gave us last time we talked to you. It won't take long.' The woman nodded, showing little interest. West waited a moment to see if she'd say anything else. 'Your Mandy' – the woman looked at him for a moment when he said that – 'you said that she'd been getting funny phone calls. Could you tell me a bit more about that? Can you remember when they started, and what happened when a call came through?'

Carol Varney looked blank. Lynne said, 'Did Mandy say anything about the voice, and did she say what he said?'

'Of course she did. I told you. It was that Damien.' She spat the name. 'I told you.'

'Yes, I've got all that.' West looked at his notes. 'Can you remember when the calls started? Was it straight after they split up?'

'Oh no.' Carol Varney was certain. 'It was as soon as they'd got engaged, almost. It was as if he was jealous, or something. Phoning to see if she was in, and then just hanging up when she picked up the phone. Then after they'd broken it off, then he started talking, saying things like he wanted his share of the car, and he wanted his money for the ring.'

'Were all the calls like that? You told us about the ones Damien made when he spoke to your daughter, but were there any others? Did he ever speak to you, or did he ever do anything else?'

Her face was becoming animated now. 'He certainly did. I answered the phone several times and he just hung up. And poor Amanda – she was here alone one evening and the phone was ringing and ringing and he was hanging up as soon as she picked it up. He was doing that right from the time they got engaged, and that went on. She was ever so upset. He often picked on evenings when she was here on her own.'

'Mrs Varney.' West was going carefully now, Lynne was pleased to note. 'How did you know that the hang-up calls were from Damien?'

She looked at him. 'One-four-seven-one,' she said. 'Then I dialled three and I got straight through. I started to give him a piece of my mind, but he put the phone down.'

'I see.' West thought again. 'And did Mandy – Amanda – catch him out the same way?'

'No, he'd got wise to it, hadn't he,' she said. 'There was no number stored, Amanda said, when she tried that. She phoned him to tell him to stop, that first time, but he wasn't answering. She was thinking about going back with him, but I told her, *he's crazy*, and that made her think twice, I can tell you.'

'Thank you.' West put his notebook away. 'That's just cleared up one or two things. If you can think of anything else . . .'

The animation was dying out of her face now. She shook her head.

In the car on the way back to headquarters, Lynne ran over the information Mrs Varney had given them. Mandy's fiancé – ex-fiancé – had been quite open and quite adamant about the phone calls. 'Of course I called,' he had said in his first interview. 'I wanted to get back with her. I was upset. I told her I wanted my stuff if she was going to play silly buggers. I never hung up on her, only if I got that old witch. I'd had enough of talking to *her*.' Then he'd started crying, got angry with himself for showing emotion. He'd been easy to interview, Lynne remembered. She'd been able to wrong-foot him, trip him up, get him rattled – but his story had stayed the same. He didn't have the best alibi in the world, an evening at home, where he lived with his parents, but the details matched and held. His story was convincing. And he did have a cast-iron alibi for the first murder. He'd been in hospital, immobilized with a broken leg. West had managed to get some dates for the evenings Mandy had got the calls. They might try and check lover boy's alibi for those nights, but Lynne's own view was that he hadn't made those calls.

'You reckon it was our man?' West asked. Lynne nodded.

Later that day, Lynne Jordan was going through the files looking at the details of the earlier killings when McCarthy came into the office. He looked depressed, and she raised her eyebrows at him in query. 'The inquest. *Murder by person or persons unknown*. I've been talking to the family,' he said by way of explanation. Lynne nodded.

'Anything?' Lynne paused in her reading.

'Nothing. They didn't know much about her life. She didn't

85

live at home. *She was a good girl,* her mother said.' McCarthy looked at the files on Lynne's desk. 'What are you doing?'

Lynne hesitated. She knew that McCarthy resented her presence on the team, but whether it was because he didn't like women officers or whether it was Lynne herself that he saw as a threat, she wasn't sure. But his attitude was infectious, and she found herself wanting to steal a march on him, wanting to keep ideas to herself until they produced results. That was the kind of attitude that left gaps in an investigation, gaps that the killer could slip through. And the kind of attitude that could foul up promotion chances. She'd seen Berryman watching them at the briefings. She didn't need to play games. She could make her way without that. 'I'm going over the killings again. I'm looking for patterns we might have missed. I'm looking for anything really.'

'Drawn a blank on the previous incident search?' His voice was expressionless, but he looked pleased.

'I'm still working on it,' she said, keeping her own voice neutral. 'This is something else.'

She could see that glint of irritation in his eye, but he sat down at the next desk. 'Let's have a look. If there's anything there, two of us have got a better chance of spotting it than one.'

'OK.' He was right. Lynne tipped her chair back. 'I'll go through what I've found, and you can fill in the details, tell me if you see anything I haven't.' She paused for a moment to get her thoughts clear. 'Right. Lisa Griffin.' She went through the facts of the case. Lisa, the first victim, disappeared on the way back from visiting her parents in Mexborough. She had left her parents' house at half past eight, intending to walk to the station. She had been seen by a neighbour about a hundred yards from the house, and had exchanged greetings. There was another unconfirmed sighting on the bridge across the river, just before the station, and a woman answering her description had been seen going into the station at the appropriate time. She had been found the following morning, dumped on the line a short way outside the station on the way to Denaby, by the embankment. They hadn't been able to identify anyone who'd been at the station at the relevant time. Sunday evenings were not busy.

Berryman's team had questioned the staff on the train Lisa had planned to catch, but the answers had been very unclear. The conductor said that no one had boarded the train at Mexborough, but the record of ticket sales and checks suggested that he hadn't been too meticulous about checking after every station.

Lisa's husband had reported her missing about two hours after she should have arrived home. She had been found hours later by a workman, about six o'clock. She'd died around midnight.

Kate, the second victim, had vanished when she was travelling back from her hometown, Hull, to Sheffield. She had got on the train in Hull – her friends had seen her off – but she hadn't been on the train when it arrived in Sheffield. A friend had been waiting to meet her. They'd planned an evening out. Her body was found near the line that ran through a nature reserve at Balby Carr, south-west of Doncaster. The train had been quite busy and several people remembered seeing Kate. Lynne put the statements from the passengers aside for further scrutiny.

Mandy commuted from Moreham to Conisbrough to work. 'That's not right, for a start,' Steve said. 'No one works in Conisbrough.' This was an exaggeration, but Lynne knew what he meant. Conisbrough was another town that was struggling with the aftermath of recessions that had destroyed the local industries. She thought of the trip she'd taken on the waterbus one summer, along the river to Conisbrough to visit the medieval castle that stood on the east side of the town. Her impression had been of trees and fields, but she knew there was another side, a dying town centre, boarded-up shops, vandalism and a growing drug problem. Mandy had worked there as a clerk in the local school. She hadn't come home one night. She had been found the next day in the cutting where the line ran under the M1 just outside Doncaster.

Lynne thought. The drops were all isolated, not easily accessible from the road, difficult to carry a body, unconscious or dead. Except for . . . She looked across at Steve. 'Does the same thing strike you as strikes me?' she said. 'That the first drop is different?'

He nodded. 'We've talked about that. Why did he leave her so near the station? We've got to assume the others were picked up a fair way from where they were found. Berryman thinks it might be that he didn't realize how much evidence he could leave where he killed them. Then he finds out, and makes sure we don't know. What about the second one, Kate?'

'She must have got off the train.'

'Yes. We talked to her friends. She probably got off at Doncaster. The train waits about five minutes at Doncaster, so she'd jump off, buy herself a coffee to drink on the train, and get back on again.'

Lynne looked at the pile of statements. 'I don't suppose they talked to everyone on the train?'

Steve made a *who can tell* gesture. 'We tracked a lot of them down. I'd put money on it that we haven't seen them all, but these trains are like buses. There's no way of recording the passengers. Not individually.'

Lynne stretched. 'OK, what do we know? For three of the victims, he grabbed them at fairly lonely stations at night, and dumped them some distance from there along the line.'

'You're making assumptions with Julie,' Steve reminded her. 'We don't have a witness can put her at the station, and Moreham isn't like Conisbrough or Mexborough. It's a lot busier.'

'OK,' Lynne conceded, 'but until there's good reason to think otherwise, why don't we assume she went to the station? And Moreham station is just as dead as those others at certain times in the evening. I've been using the train a lot recently.'

Steve gave her a sharp look, but only nodded in grudging agreement. 'Possibly. But we've still got a problem with Kate. Doncaster isn't a quiet station. Never. But no one saw anything. We haven't found one person who saw her there.'

Lynne knew most of this. 'Did her friend raise the alarm? The one who was supposed to meet her in Sheffield?'

McCarthy shook his head. 'She did the journey every

Sunday. She caught the same train and she *always* got off in Doncaster to buy a coffee. She often said she cut it a bit fine. They had an arrangement to meet at the club if the train went without her.'

'Habits,' Lynne said. 'Berryman says he stalks them.'

'She always did the same thing.' McCarthy ran his hand over his chin. He was in need of a shave. 'According to her friends, she'd get on the train in Hull, grab the seat nearest the door. She liked to sit on her own, so she'd take the aisle seat and put her bags on the window seat. Then she'd sleep until the train got into Doncaster. Cup of coffee to wake her up, twenty minutes into Sheffield, and she was ready for a night out.'

'So, what happened?' Lynne said.

Friday night, nine-thirty. Debbie felt like an addict who'd just found out she couldn't do without her fix. She'd found Rob Neave attractive from the time she'd first met him, and he must have been aware of that. She had thought that he liked her, as well. She had wondered, sometimes, what it would be like if he made love to her, a fantasy, out of sequence with her life. Well, she'd lived her fantasy, but it had seemed, almost, like a dream – an unfamiliar, isolated place, a stranger she thought she knew, a sense of danger lurking, a suspension of time. But it had been real and she wanted it to happen again, to move on and develop. And it wasn't going to. What was worse was a sense of loss. Before, he'd been a friend. Now, she wasn't sure that she could count him as that any more. *Let's stay friends,* always seemed to her to be a futile exercise. Sex ruined friendship. She knew that.

He'd phoned her at lunchtime and suggested that they meet. 'We need to talk,' he said. Forewarned is forearmed. They met in a pub ten minutes' walk from the college. He asked her if she wanted to eat, but she wasn't hungry. They had a glass of beer each instead. She knew more or less what he was going to say, so she took the initiative. 'Last night was a mistake, wasn't it?' He nodded, running his hand across his face. He looked ill. The mask was off again, briefly, and the look of tired despair on his face made her want to reach out to him, but she couldn't.

Then he started talking. 'There are some things you need to know, Deborah,' he said. 'Do you know that I'm married . . . used to be married?'

Debbie nodded. 'Yes, I . . . Someone told me.'

'Fucking grapevine,' he said. She hadn't heard him swear before. He seemed angry, not at her, but in a general, unfocused way. He looked at her again, then looked down at the table. 'I'm not good at talking, not like this. She used to make me talk, but I've got out of the habit since . . .' He ran his hand over his face, looking baffled.

'What happened?' Debbie wondered how much bitterness and hurt lay behind his unhappiness. She wasn't ready for his answer.

'No one knows exactly. It was one of those freak accidents, they said. No one's fault. No one should have been killed.'

Debbie was silent for a moment. She should have guessed. 'Your wife was killed,' she said.

'Angie.' He seemed to find it hard to say her name. He picked up a beer mat, turned it round in his hands, looking at it. His voice was toneless. 'And our daughter. Flora. She was six months old.'

Debbie went cold. She hadn't known. She should have known. He went on. 'They should have been all right. They were strapped in. But the car went through a wall and over the edge. They should even have survived that.' He was speaking quite unemotionally, still looking down at the table, his hands occupied with splitting the beer mat in two. 'That makes it worse.' He stopped, and carefully peeled the illustration off the front of the mat in one piece. He looked at it for a moment, then screwed it up and dropped it into the ash tray. Debbie waited. After a moment, he looked at her and there was something in his eyes that made her want to take hold of his hands and stop him. 'There was a fire, you see. They would have been trapped. The people who dealt with it say that they died in the impact or almost, wouldn't have known anything, but no one would tell me for sure, and the reports aren't . . . Flora was still strapped in her chair.

Angie was between the seats. Impact, they told me.' Debbie felt her eyes fill with tears of shock. 'Don't, Deborah,' he said sharply. 'Just . . . don't.'

'I'm . . .' Debbie swallowed her *I'm sorry*. It was inadequate, trite. 'I didn't know.' There didn't seem to be anything to say. She wanted to touch him, to try and show him what she felt that way, but everything about him warned her off.

'I can't do it, Deborah, I can't start anything else. Last night – it should be going somewhere. It can't. This isn't bullshit. You're worth more than one night and goodbye, but I haven't got anything else to offer.'

Debbie took a deep breath. She wanted to argue, to say, *Please* and, *Let's try*. She wanted to prolong this encounter because it was the last one. Oh, she'd see him in college often enough, but those talks in the staff room, a drink together after work, all the things that happened when something seemed possible – those encounters wouldn't happen. He would make sure they didn't. She could feel tears very near the surface. She trod firmly on her emotions. Now was not the time. 'I'm not sorry it happened,' she said. 'I'm just sorry . . .' She shrugged. Her voice was almost right, almost in control. 'Listen, I'd better go. Don't stay away. Keep in touch.' She reached across the table and touched his hand. He squeezed hers briefly and ran his thumb across her fingers. She managed a fairly convincing smile before she left.

Debbie looked at the clock. Nine-forty-five. Time was dragging. She ought to be exhausted, she ought to be able to fall into bed and sleep till morning, but she knew she wouldn't. She needed to turn her mind off, somehow. She stroked Buttercup, who was lying on her knee with her front legs pointing one way and her back legs pointing another. *Hope she doesn't have to get up in a hurry*. The little cat stretched and sank her claws into Debbie's wrist.

Debbie remembered she was going to Goldthorpe the next day, going home. Going home to put flowers on her father's grave. Tears began to prickle her eyes. *Don't get maudlin*. She went upstairs to her bedroom and pulled her briefcase out from under the small table that she used as a desk. She could do some marking. That would soon get her in a mood for sleep. Her keys rattled against the brass catch of the case. She kept them clipped to the little ring that held the catch in place. It was strange. She *never* unclipped her keys. She could have sworn she'd locked the staff room door behind her when she'd gone to her class, and yet the keys had been on her desk. Maybe she could ask Rob . . . *No* . . . she stamped firmly on the thought, and pulled the pile of essays towards her.

The photographs are blurred, dull. Sometimes the pictures dissolve into patterns of shadows, as though his prey is escaping again, eluding him as he hunts them through his landscape. His own pictures are much more satisfactory. If you want a job doing well . . . Black and white, they match the others, but they tell a truth that the others don't. Black and white is perfect. Black and white gives you the shadows of the dark places, the gleam of stuff that oozes and flows, the reality behind the flat images that were all he had before.

Photographs can be poor keepers of the truth. He has another one, a flat, grainy picture, creased and faded. There is a mother, a stepfather and a child. The faces are shadowy and vague. Not the mother's face, which is turned away. He knows that face. That is real. She holds a bunch of flowers, looks towards the stepfather, smiles, but he knows that the mother's smile is for the child. The child is just a pattern in greys, a pattern that could be a bewildered, big-eyed face, confused and afraid behind wire-rimmed glasses.

But now the child is watching, and not seeing. Now the child has shiny tracks down his face. 'Mam . . . ?' The whisper comes from nowhere, fades in the shadows of the roof.

There is another truth that photographs can't tell.

Friday night, ten. Rob Neave was sitting alone in his flat, contemplating getting seriously drunk for the first time in eighteen months. He'd opened the whisky bottle as soon as he had got in, but stopped drinking after one glass, and now he couldn't decide. He picked up a book at random from the table. It was Debbie's book of poetry. He felt a tired anger. He couldn't stay here. He could go to the pub over the road and quietly drink himself into oblivion. The pub he'd been in with Debbie the night before . . . He could see her face as they talked at lunchtime. He hadn't meant to do that to her. Looking for distraction, he turned the radio on. Piano music, one of Chopin's nocturnes. *Angie* . . .

A cold winter's afternoon, a Sunday. Outside, it was frozen and still. The sound of piano music drifted through from the other room. He was sitting in front of the fire, a couple of cans of beer beside him, half an eye on the time. Flora was on his knee, making small complaining noises and kicking her legs. He had been playing with her, making her squeal and laugh, but she was tired now. He lifted her on to his shoulder, rocking her gently, and gradually she became a limp weight against him. He was fascinated by her, her compliance, her dependency. He slid her down on to his lap, into the crook of his arm. Fine, one hand free for opening a beer can and using the TV remote.

He heard the piano in the other room stop, and after a minute, Angie came in. 'What are you doing?' she asked.

'Having a beer, and' – he checked his watch – 'in ten minutes I'm watching the match.' He heard her 'Tch!' of exasperation.

She leant over his shoulder and stroked the fine hair on their daughter's head. He reached backwards and pulled her down, catching her off balance so that she ended up sprawled across his knee. She laughed, and he kissed her, enjoying the feeling of holding his wife and his child in his arms. It had been like that when Angie was pregnant. It hadn't been a particularly easy pregnancy. Towards the end, she had to rest, so they didn't go out, but spent long evenings lying on the bed together, talking, making plans that had seemed like good plans at the time. He still thought of Flora as part of Angie, not yet quite separated from her mother, but becoming so, bit by bit.

Angie was wearing a deep-blue dress, fitted around her waist with a full skirt that had ridden up in her fall. He ran his fingers across the soft skin at the top of her thighs. Perhaps he could give the match a miss. But she sighed and sat up. 'I'm going out, remember? Jean asked me over to look at that piece she's planning to play. Daniel will be there, so I'll take Flora.' She stood up, and leant over to kiss him. 'You spend the afternoon being primitive. Watch the match, drink beer, scratch yourself. We'll see you later.' She scooped Flora up, ignoring her cross wail, and said, 'Come on, lovely, let's get you changed and into your warm coat.'

Ten minutes later, they were gone. He never saw them again.

Berryman told him afterwards that he'd gone berserk when they wouldn't let him see the bodies. He didn't remember that. The car had skidded, it seemed, on black ice at the worst place, that sharp bend where the land dropped away to the woods below. They'd used dental records to identify Angie. He couldn't remember going berserk. He couldn't remember much at all of the days immediately after the accident. There was just that hollow silence, and the dullness of a light going out. It didn't leave him in darkness – he wouldn't have minded the darkness – but all the colours had faded and he was left with the shadows. It was like that time when he was young, twelve, thirteen, something like that, someone had taken him into a cathedral. A huge rose window had glowed above him, and then the sun went in. He could remember the sense of expectant silence, of dark expanses and shades of grey, as if something important had left and wasn't coming back.

Julie Fyfe's funeral was on the Saturday morning. The weather, which had raged and stormed on the night she died, saw her laid to rest with stillness. She was buried in Sheffield, where she was born and where her parents still lived. The cemetery stood at one of the highest points of the city, looking away to the city centre to the east, and across the bare trees of Rivelin Valley to the west. The sky was leaden, uniform grey unchanging into the distance, and the air was ice. Mick Berryman, standing at the cemetery gates, watching the cortege pass through, thought that this bleak burial ground was appropriate for a life ended before it had really begun. What had Julie Fyfe done to have everything taken from her – her lovers, her children, her happiness, her hurt – there was no Julie any more and never would be again.

He watched the mourners at the grave side. Her parents

standing apart from each other, the mother with the calmness of a grief that had gone beyond weeping; her father with that look of helpless bewilderment that Berryman had seen before on other faces. They couldn't help each other. The person they were most used to turning to in grief was deeply enmeshed in something that would never – completely – go away. Other relatives of victims, in the past, had said to him, *Have you got him, will you get him?* as though the apprehension, conviction and punishment might offer some consolation. Berryman wondered if anything could assuage that kind of grief. Maybe it made a difference. He had nothing else to offer them.

After the interment, he went up to the parents, said the things he said on such occasions, tried to reassure them that everything that could be done was being done, that they would be told how the investigation was progressing. Berryman told himself that he would at least try to make sure that they would hear of any arrest before the press did – or at the same time.

He evaded the questions put to him by journalists covering the funeral – *No further developments, still following up leads* – and walked between the gravestones to the far end of the cemetery. He'd brought a flower, a rose. The grave was becoming overgrown now. It didn't look as if anyone tended it. He looked at the headstone. *Angela Kerridge Neave, 1968–1996. Flora Neave, 12th August 1995–23rd February 1996. The sun also rises and the sun goes down.* That was all it said. He put the rose on the grave, and left the cemetery.

8

Lynne Jordan sipped a cup of tea and looked at the young man in front of her. Stuart Griffin, 28, husband of the first victim, Lisa, law-abiding citizen with a well-founded dislike of the police. Or at least of Mick Berryman. 'I'm sorry to trouble you, Mr Griffin,' she said, 'but we're just trying to get a bit more of a fix on the days before your wife –'

He interrupted before she could finish the sentence. 'OK, all right, I said I'd talk to you. What do you want to know?'

'According to your original statement –' Lynne began, but he interrupted again.

'According to my original statement, I didn't kill my wife, I didn't kill Lisa. Fat lot of attention you paid to my original statement then.'

'I'm sorry, Mr Griffin.' Lynne wasn't going to apologize for Berryman's doing his job. 'I know this must be upsetting, but if you could just go over one or two things again, I'll be able to get out of your way.' She flipped through the pages of his statement until she got to the marked section. 'You said your daughter, Karen, talked about *the ugly man* shortly before . . .'

He was frowning at the mention of his daughter, but he said fairly mildly, 'She had some nightmares. Lisa didn't know what it was about, but she said Karen thought he was in her bedroom and had nightmares.'

Lynne thought. 'Did Lisa, or you, have any reason to think she really had seen anyone? Did Lisa see anyone that worried her, or anyone that she didn't know following her or hanging around?'

He sighed. 'You asked me all this at the time. *No*. I don't

96

remember. What I said then will be right. I can't remember now.' He was getting agitated, but what he said agreed with his statement. He hadn't known about anything at the time.

'Can you remember anything else about this ugly man Karen talked about? Did she have any more dreams after her mother . . .' After his originally stopping her, Lynne found it difficult to complete her sentences when they referred to Lisa's murder.

'Of course she bloody did,' he said. 'Her mother was dead. Of course she had bloody dreams.'

Lynne cursed herself. 'I'm sorry, Mr Griffin. I didn't mean like that, I meant specifically about the ugly man.'

'No, not really. I don't remember any more of those.' He looked at the floor, scuffing the pattern on the carpet with his shoe, thinking. Lynne didn't interrupt him. She looked round, waiting. She could remember this room nearly two years ago when they'd first come round, when he reported his wife missing. It had been – not pristine, but glowing with care; paper, cushions and curtains carefully matched, small tables with ruffled cloths and lace overlays, carefully placed ornaments, floor and table lights set to illuminate chosen chairs or pictures. It had been a room someone had created with real love and pride. She'd asked him about it at the time, trying to distract him a bit from his worry. *She'll come back, Mr Griffin, we get a lot of these calls and it's usually a misunderstanding. This is a lovely room.* He'd told her that Lisa sewed. *She did all this* – pride again in his wife who had made all of this for him. Now, the glow was gone. Some of the cloths were still on the tables, but stained and placed unevenly. Other tables had ring marks from cups, sticky marks where a child's fingers had touched. There were dark patches on the settee, dust on the carpet. There was a thin layer of dust over everything.

Stuart Griffin got up abruptly. He went over to a desk that stood in the window, and pulled open the top drawer, rummaged through some papers, pushed the drawer half shut. 'When Karen started having the dreams, Lisa got her to draw pictures, to get it out of her system.' He came back to his seat with a large manila envelope in his hand, and started spreading the contents out on the floor. 'I haven't looked at this for a while,' he said.

Lynne saw a collection of child's drawings, some photographs, a faded newspaper cutting. She picked it up. 'May I?' she said. He nodded, still sorting through the drawings. It was a picture of Stuart Griffin and Lisa – Lynne recognized her because she saw Lisa's picture every day – Lisa looking proud and pretty, with Karen in front of them dressed in a frilly skirt with ribbons in her hair. The caption was *Karen-Can*, and the brief story underneath was about how Karen had won a nursery school fancy-dress competition as a cancan dancer. Lynne looked at the young face of the mother, the beaming, chubby face of the little girl, and felt anger and a sense of weary frustration.

Stuart pulled a drawing out of the pile he was looking through and showed it to Lynne. 'There,' he said. He was holding out a typical child's drawing of a person, a round head with arms coming out of the sides. There were other circles on the head that could have been glasses. Despite the childishness of the drawing, Lynne thought it had a sense of menace, especially the way the figure loomed over the other figure in the drawing, much smaller than the first.

'Is that meant to be her?' Lynne asked. 'Karen?'

'No,' Stuart said, 'that's Lisa, that's Mummy.'

After a moment, Lynne said, 'Can I take this, Mr Griffin?' He nodded. He didn't speak again, just gathered the papers up from the floor into an untidy bundle and took Lynne to the door. 'Thank you,' she said, as she left.

Berryman decided that he wanted Julie Fyfe's boss down at headquarters for the interview. 'Talk him into it, Lynne. I want him off his own territory.' Lynne had taken Dave West with her, and by dint of calling at Andrew Thomas's house when his wife was in, managed to persuade him to come and talk to DCI Berryman at the Morehead offices.

'He couldn't get us out of the house quick enough,' West told Berryman cheerfully. Now Berryman was sitting back in his chair, listening to Lynne gently pressuring the information they wanted out of the man.

'Just tell me again,' she was saying, 'exactly what happened after you promoted Julie.'

Andrew Thomas was starting to look uneasy, realizing that the attractive woman at the other side of the table had a far wider agenda than he had first thought. 'I don't see what that's got to do with her death, Officer. I must say . . .'

Pleased that he was starting to bluster, Lynne smiled gently and said, 'We have to check everything, Mr Thomas, as I'm sure you understand. Now, Julie was promoted in August, according to your records.' He shifted impatiently in his chair. She looked him in the eye. 'You don't have any problems answering these questions, do you?'

'No, of course not. I just don't enjoy having my time wasted.' He must have been in his fifties, Lynne estimated. A bit overweight, a bit unfit. She wondered when he was going to tell her that he played golf with the Chief Constable. She kept on smiling and waited him out. 'Summer. August, yes.'

'Why then?' Lynne looked at her notes.

He looked as if he was going to object again, but thought better of it. 'She was a good worker, wanted to get somewhere. She'd got herself these extra qualifications, so I thought, we thought, that is, that we should encourage her.'

'Which qualification was that?'

'She hadn't actually got it, she'd started it. One of these new things, GNVQ in business studies.' He loosened his collar.

Lynne looked at her notes. 'But she didn't actually start the course until November,' she said.

He waved away an irrelevancy. 'But she had plans, that was the thing.'

Lynne went back to her notes. 'In fact, you had to contact the college and put some pressure on to get them to take her as a late applicant, isn't that right?' He was silent for a minute. 'Mr Thomas?' Lynne prompted.

'Well, yes.' He looked flushed now.

Lynne switched topics. 'I understand that Julie went on a trip for the company, to a conference. Could you tell me something about that?'

He blinked, confused by the change of topic. 'What do

you want to know? It was in September, in London. It was for firms wanting to set up partnerships for a funding programme.'

'How long did the conference go on for?' Lynne knew where this was going, but patiently took it step by step.

'It was just the two days.' He was looking anxious now.

'According to your company's diary, Mr Thomas, Julie was away for a week on that conference.' She let him think through his response, but before he could answer, she said, 'And interestingly, *you* were away at the same time – the twenty-third through to the twenty-ninth.' She waited. She hoped he was just going to tell her now. She didn't want to spend the rest of the afternoon drawing blood from this particular stone. She looked him in the eye and waited.

He looked evasive, gave a half smile and said, 'Well, it's got nothing to do with all this, but Julie and I . . .' The story came out – pretty young clerical officer, susceptible boss, and Julie had done rather well out of the whole thing. He couldn't be so naive, Lynne told herself, as to believe that they could ignore this, accept his word that it had nothing to do with the killing.

They took a break. She and Berryman talked it through in his office. 'What do you think, sir? Could it be a copycat cover-up?'

Berryman shook his head. 'Could be, but it has all the markers for our man. I don't think so, but let's sweat this bastard until we're sure.'

'Will he go on cooperating?'

Berryman smiled grimly. 'If I've got to arrest the bugger, I will. Then let him try and keep his wife in the dark. He'll cooperate.'

Saturday morning, Debbie and her mother walked back from the cemetery into the centre of Goldthorpe. Debbie hadn't been to her father's grave since early summer. She didn't often feel the need – she knew that her father wasn't there. But it seemed important sometimes just to go and stand there, put some flowers in the small metal container on the headstone, read the inscription, and remember him among the quiet of the graves. He came back to her now as her young father. His older, defeated self had been her earlier memory, after he died. She had dreamed, more than once, that she was walking down the road to her house, the house he'd never seen, and he was standing in the window, watching up the road. She'd felt relief in the dream – he wasn't dead – but his face had been so lost and vacant that she had been frightened, had tried to run to the house to see what was wrong.

Her mother, she knew, went to the graveyard once a week, kept the grave clear of weeds, put fresh flowers there. 'Does it help,' she said, suddenly, 'coming to the cemetery?'

Gina didn't answer. Debbie looked at her, and saw that she was thinking. 'He isn't there,' Gina said, after a minute, 'but he isn't anywhere else. I can see him in you, of course. And I can remember him, years of memories. Straight after he died, I used to think he was in the room with me sometimes, I could feel him so clearly, but that's gone now.' She opened her handbag and took out a tissue, then took off her glasses and carefully cleaned the lenses. 'I don't think he's anywhere any more, but I still miss him.'

Debbie squeezed her mother's arm. 'I do too,' she said.

As they walked back through the centre, Gina stopped every few paces to greet friends, catch up on local news, talk to people who'd known Debbie since she was a baby and wanted to catch up on her current life. Debbie smiled and fielded questions about how she was, whether she was courting, how her job was going, why she didn't come back more often, whether she was courting . . . Gina nudged her in the middle of one of these exchanges. 'Here, Debbie,' she said, slipping her a piece of paper. 'Here's the list. Go and get the shopping in.' Debbie escaped.

Goldthorpe was built on either side of one main street, the rows of shops run down and in need of paint and repair. The shops were mostly small – there were none of the big chains in the town. The supermarket was piled high with bargain boxes, tins, jars, the cooling cabinets turned off and used as storage for cut-price goods with strange brand names Debbie didn't recognize. She couldn't find any of the things she wanted.

She went back out on to the main street, trying to get her bearings. It seemed that things changed each time she came back. The old cinema was a carpet warehouse now, selling roll ends, smelling of cut carpet and damp. She went on down the street towards the chemist. The café wafted the smell of steam and boiled milk into her face, and a group of children pushed past her, racketing a skateboard that had seen better days between them. One of them shouted in triumph as he leapt on to the board and flipped it round into the road, steering away from the group, manoeuvring with skilful turns of his hips. The group turned as one and chased the leader back up the road, oblivious of Debbie and any other walkers on the pavement.

There was graffiti – tags mostly – on the walls, and some of the windows above the shops were broken, black and empty. Others were boarded up. Debbie looked up at a flowered curtain that had been left, faded and rotting, hanging half out of one abandoned window. The pavements were a mess of wet leaves, crisp bags, cigarette ends, empty drinks cans. The faces of the people coming towards her seemed unfamiliar, tired, defeated. She watched a young woman – about her own age, it was hard to tell – pushing a pram and pulling a toddler by the arm. The young woman looked blankly ahead of her, a cigarette hanging out of her mouth. She was overweight, and her shoes were trodden down. She wore a shapeless coat hanging open over a faded pink cardigan, her greasy hair flopped into her eyes. The child in the pram was crying, but the woman never looked at it, just pushed on impassively. Her eyes passed over Debbie's briefly, but gave no sign of recognition. Debbie recognized her. She had been in Debbie's class at school, she had been one of the clever ones, like Debbie. Debbie stood as she went past, pretending to look in the window of a junk shop, feeling cold inside. This future had loomed like a pit in front of her, pushing her on to achieve, to escape. Did it also lie in front of the unwary feet of her students – Leanne, Rachel, Sarah?

That evening, Debbie and her mother sat by the fire in her mother's small front room. Gina had bought a neat little terrace, an ideal one-person house, after Debbie's father had died. His redundancy money had still been in the bank, untouched. 'He didn't know what to do with it,' Gina had said at the time. Now she looked at Debbie and said, 'Are you going to tell me about it?'

Debbie flushed. 'About what?' she said, unconvincingly.

'About whatever it is that's making you look like a wet weekend. You've had a face on you all day. You aren't in any kind of trouble, are you?' Her mother's expression indicated exactly what kind of trouble she had in mind.

'Oh. No. No trouble.' She wasn't going to let her mother see that she'd understood her meaning. 'I'm just – it's just a . . .' She wanted to give some kind of truthful explanation, but couldn't think of the right way to put it. She didn't want to go into details, because she hadn't sorted those details out in her own mind yet. 'I started this thing with someone at work, and it went wrong more or less straight away. Nobody's fault, it just . . . well, anyway, that's all it is.'

Her mother waited to see if Debbie was going to say any more. 'Well, I'm always here to talk to, if it helps,' she said after a moment. Debbie shook her head.

Later, they quarrelled amiably over who was going to cook. Debbie lost, and was left to lounge in her chair while her mother made fish and chips. 'You look like a picked chicken,' she said, when Debbie remonstrated at her choice of menu. 'Fish and chips, *proper* fish and chips will do you good. It's no good you being lovesick and pining away.'

They had a glass of wine and spent the evening watching television – Gina was a *Casualty* fan – and talking. 'You'd wonder,' Gina said at one point during the programme, 'how anyone ever survives in that hospital.' A nurse was having hysterics on the shoulder of a consultant, and two doctors were having a row about their deteriorating relationship. Various patients were having cardiac arrests.

'Looks more interesting than City,' Debbie said. Watching television with Gina was entertaining if you weren't too bothered about seeing the programme. Debbie went to bed early and had the best night's sleep she'd had for a week.

*   *   *

The drift of fur against his fingers. It is like that first touch of hair, and his hands want to grip, to twist and pull. But she will detect him in the air, that first note of alarm that could make her wary, make her run. He knows when the right time is for them to see him, when they are at bay, when there is no escape.

He waits in the darkness, and as he waits, he tells himself stories. He knows the stories, knows them well. His stories have bright colours, sharp lines, pictures in his head. He sees her smiling, waiting for him. She doesn't know he is there, but she is waiting. He sees her eyes in the darkness, watching him. He sees her face, and she is fighting, but it is too late to fight. She knows him, now. But the colours are fading, the brightness is going, like her breath, going, gone . . .

And there are other stories.

This is the story of a child, a stepfather and a mother. This story is told on yellowing paper, the letters fading where the paper is folded. **APPALLING CATALOGUE OF CRUELTY.** *These pictures are not bright, the lines are blurred and grainy. The child, big-eyed behind his wire-rimmed glasses, bewildered as children often are, is pictured in a family group, mother, son and new husband. It is a story of beatings, a story of burnings. The mother could have protected her son, but perhaps she had been afraid of her new husband, perhaps, almost certainly, she had been ignorant of the extent of the abuse.*

He can see the yellowing paper in his head, see the words scrolling past his eyes, see them as they slow and come to an end. But the story continues.

The strange thing was, parts of it had been good. The child liked travelling on the train with the stepfather, liked the times when he was sneaked into the cab or watched the furnace being stoked in the red glow by men stripped to the waist. He wanted to do that. He liked watching the cinders fly, and the way the trains flew past houses and yards and he could see women hanging out their washing, children playing in the streets, in the courts, the narrow boats on the canals and the white-hot glow of the metal as they flashed past the great steelworks at night. And if some of the men were cruel sometimes, it was just part of being a man who could swing a huge shovel as though it weighed nothing, who could strip to the waist in the depths of winter. Sometimes it was a cuff across the face that split his lip,

104

sometimes it was a kick, but it was quick and impersonal. Sometimes it wasn't him, it was something else, like the time they threw a cat into the furnace and he watched with horror and fascination.

But that was later. He learnt to be wary when the stepfather came in smelling of that strong, eye-stinging stuff. Sometimes he'd come into the child's room at night, after the mother had gone to bed. The moonlight would shine through the window, reflected in the mirror that stood on the tallboy. He'd pinch out the night light that burned in a saucer beside the bed. The child was scared of the dark. 'Shut up,' he'd say when the child cried. And later, 'Shut up, you little shit, or you'll get what the cat got.'

Then there were the other times. The other men would come to the house. 'He can come with me tonight,' the stepfather would say to the mother.

'Mam . . .' the child would say.

'You be off. You should be grateful. I've never known such a child for looking a gift horse in the mouth.'

And they would go, and he would watch all the things go past and all the stops, but he wouldn't really see them because at the end there would be the dark place. The first time he had cried, and the stepfather had said, 'Don't you look at me like that, you little shit.' It was black and close in there and the smell was terrible. Hands were held over his mouth and round his neck so that he could hardly breathe. The stepfather would say, 'If you tell anybody, you're going into the furnace.' When he got home, the mother would exclaim over the dirt on his clothes, his face, his hands. 'Oh, really,' she'd say, 'can't you keep him clean, Charlie?' and the stepfather would growl, 'Shut up. Stupid cunt.'

When she came in to say good night, she'd pick up his clothes, look at his pants and say, 'Oh, you're too big to make that kind of mess.' He'd say, 'Mam . . .' but she wasn't looking at him, her face was a blank and she went on talking. 'Cleanliness is next to godliness, the child is father to the man . . .' She'd hold her hand over his eyes. 'See no evil,' she'd whisper. He learnt to hide his clothes after he'd been out on one of the special nights. The mother was often in bed when they came back. 'I just seem to feel so tired sometimes,' she'd say, next day.

He doesn't like this story. He tells himself another story, a better one, after the stepfather was gone. The trains. He'd bunk off school *every day and stand and watch the trains, sometimes sneaking rides up and down the local lines. He learnt quickly which trains ran on the line regularly, where they stopped, where they slowed, where they waited. He remembers the cat. He used to go to the pet shop with his money – the mother would always give him money – and buy a mouse. Mice were best because they were small with long tails. One and six, they cost. He had a secret place on the railway where he could light a candle and hold the mouse up by its tail over the flame. He liked watching the way its legs scrabbled and the way it tried to climb up itself. They always died.*

The stepfather did come home again. But the child was no longer there, not really, not any more. The mother took the stepfather back. Let him who is without sin . . . Vengeance is mine. The stepfather fell down the stairs and broke his neck. Fires are better for vermin, but a snare will do, at a pinch.

The cat rubs itself against him. Vermin. But he has more important things to do.

Debbie left Goldthorpe on the Sunday evening, taking the train back to Sheffield. Gina saw her off from the station, despite Debbie's protests. 'It's too cold,' she said. 'Go home, I'm fine.' But her tone lacked conviction. The station was dark and almost deserted, apart from one other traveller who waited in the shadows at the far end of the platform.

'I'm staying here.' Gina wasn't having any argument. 'With that maniac around, I'm not leaving you alone in any station.' She pulled her scarf more tightly round her neck and shivered. 'It is a bit thin,' she conceded.

It was after eight by the time Debbie got back. She called to Buttercup, who usually came running to greet her as she was unlocking the door. She found the cat huddled behind the settee, her place of refuge after a trip to the vet's. Debbie picked her up and stroked her as she walked into the house. 'What's the matter with you, you daft thing?' she said. It felt cold, and the first thing she did was light the gas fire, and stand in front of it, waiting for the chill to leave the room. Buttercup wriggled out of her arms and started stalking up and down, demanding food. 'You've been fed,' Debbie said severely. Her neighbour, Jill, was very good about feeding Buttercup when Debbie was away.

The house felt strange, as though she'd been away a lot longer than one night. Debbie looked around. Her diary was on the table – surely she'd put that away before she left. She didn't write much personal in it, but she didn't want Jill reading it. She looked round the room again. The drawer where she kept her photographs wasn't properly shut. Perhaps Jill had been having a nosy. She was a bit curious about Debbie, and kept an eye on the comings and goings. That was what was making the house feel strange. Things had been disturbed, shifted, and they were out of order. Debbie was annoyed, but she didn't want to confront Jill. She didn't want a row with her neighbour, and if the price for a peaceful relationship, and having someone nearby to feed Buttercup, was a bit of prying, she'd tolerate it – but she'd lock everything away next time. That would be enough of a hint.

When she went back to work on Monday, she felt a lot better. She breezed through her Monday morning class, helped along by the students' insistence that in the last week before Christmas, they couldn't be expected to do any serious work. She came out of the classroom at the end of the morning, her hair festooned with Silly String that the students were aerosoling all over the college, a bundle of Christmas cards in her hand, and the cheery farewells of the students, who wouldn't see her again until after Christmas, ringing in her ears. Perhaps Christmas would be bearable after all.

In the afternoon, her A-level group were disinclined for work. They nagged her about assessments, and seemed distracted. She'd been half expecting this and was surprised they had turned up at all, but the only absence was, surprisingly, Sarah. She gave them a quiz, as a gesture to Christmas, and for some reason this bit of frivolity helped to buoy up her spirits. At the end of the class, she went back to the staff room feeling better than she had for a long time. She was sorry that Sarah hadn't been there, and wondered what had happened to her. She didn't usually miss classes.

Her good spirits gave her the courage to phone Rob Neave

to ask him about her keys – maybe he'd found them and left them on her desk, or something. Maybe she'd dropped them at his flat . . . she veered her mind away from dangerous ground. However, when she phoned his number, it was answered by Andrea, the clerical assistant. 'He isn't here,' she said. 'I'm not expecting him in until next week.' The way her high spirits plummeted warned her that making contact was a bad idea. She'd been using the keys as an excuse to phone, she might as well admit it. It was probably just as well he was away now until after the college closed, and she wouldn't see him again until after Christmas. She couldn't always protect herself from being hurt, but she could make some effort to avoid it.

She planned to put in an hour's work before she went home, and got out her marking folder, that seemed to increase in size each time she looked at it. She was just settling down to work, when the phone rang, the long ring that indicated an internal call. Maybe Rob *was* in, maybe Andrea had told him . . . She picked up the phone, heard the shake in her voice as she tried to control her breathing, but the phone went dead. Debbie was angry with herself for hoping, so that the pang of disappointment was all the stronger. What if it had been him? What would he have said to make any difference? The phone rang again, and she made herself wait, let it ring a couple of times before she picked it up. 'Hello, Deborah Sykes.' Again, it went dead. She shook her head impatiently. Her hard-won recovery seemed false and empty, and a feeling of depression and anxiety began to creep over her. Suddenly, the thought of marking seemed intolerable. She was going home. She stuffed the folder of work into her bag, pulled on her coat and left, closing the staff-room door on the ringing phone.

Tim Godber wanted to be a journalist – not someone who did a bit of freelancing, but ultimately a columnist on a national. And the first step into that career was a writer's job on a national. The short cut to that was a big story, one that would get his name known where it mattered. OK, so he wrote stories for the poxy little local paper, but that wasn't good enough. He was in the middle of a big story now, right on the doorstep, and he couldn't work out how to use it. Strangler stories were being written up by everyone – human interest angles, psychological angles, local-colour angles – *The killer who stalks the streets of a shattered metropolis* – but these didn't need his particular local knowledge. He'd tried insinuating himself into Mick Berryman's circle. They had some contacts in common, but Berryman was keeping a distance from the press, and Tim had a feeling his story about Debbie had queered his pitch. He hadn't realized that that bastard Neave had Berryman in his pocket. There was something going on with Neave and Debbie, he was certain of it, and he intended making it his business to find out.

He fantasized for a few minutes about getting lucky, about finding the Strangler, being in on the next kill – not *in* on it, of course, but maybe to be the person the Strangler decided to contact, things like, *The next one will be . . . They missed me this time . . . I am God's messenger.* He could see the photographs – him looking serious and concerned, sitting by his phone, his articles on the screen of his word processor. He did have one important contact. He *knew* Debbie had seen the Strangler. All his journalist's instincts told him that. And since his story, the killer had seen Debbie. He'd pay attention to his press. They always did. Tim needed a high-profile association with Debbie in a way that would bring him to the attention of the killer. How . . . He began to plan what he would write when he – a journalist – led the police to the Strangler.

Actually, Tim thought, he needed a better nickname. 'The Strangler' was boring and utilitarian. He began playing with names for when he could write his big story. The Eye Guy, the Orb Man, Vision Express – no, he'd never get that past the legal team – something catchy but gruesome and scary. He'd made a bad mistake falling out with Debbie. He'd better start sweet-talking her. She'd been looking a bit down in the mouth lately.

He headed towards the cubbyhole she shared with Louise Hatfield, wondering if a bit of professional discussion might not be a starting point. A student was hanging around near the staff room, the lanky, dishwater blonde who'd been in his media group for a while. She was standing outside the door, chewing the nail of one finger, looking indecisive. He caught her eye and smiled. 'Hello' – he racked his brains – 'Sarah. You look a bit lost.' When she turned to look at him, he saw that she had a bruise on the side of her face, and a swollen lip. She looked as if she'd walked into a left hook.

She smiled back, not quite meeting his eyes. 'I was looking for Debbie. I couldn't get to class this afternoon and I needed to see her,' she said, after a moment. She looked a bit tense, a bit nervous.

He was pretty sure this was one of Debbie's lame ducks. *Get into the good books!* He smiled again, injecting a bit of ruefulness this time. 'Me too. Isn't she in?' The girl shook her head, and backed off as though she was planning to leave. Tim stopped her. 'Do you want me to give her a message?' This would be the opportunity he needed to talk to Debbie. *Come on, love, give me a message for Miss.*

'It's nothing . . .' It was obviously something, and Tim had a feeling she wanted to tell someone. Well, he wasn't a journalist – even if it was only freelance – for nothing. He hoped it wasn't going to be some tale of personal angst involving the marks on her face.

'It doesn't look like nothing to me, Sarah. Come and have a cup of coffee and tell me about it.' He smiled warmly, trying to catch her eye, knowing that a lot of the students thought he was attractive, and when she went a bit pink, he thought, *Yes* and looked at her with reassurance and concern.

He took her back to his room – it was nearer, quieter, but with enough people around not to cause any problems – and bought her a Coke from the machine. He was expecting a sad tale about a violent boyfriend, or a violent father, but in fact it was more useful than he could have dreamed. He listened with quiet sympathy as she told her story about the man she'd seen watching Debbie round the college one day last week. 'He was following her, I'm sure. I kept seeing him. I waited to tell Debbie, but . . .' Tim's heart was beating faster. *This was it! How to use it, how to keep it safe . . .*

'Which man? Start again at the beginning and tell me the whole story.' He listened as Sarah told him about the man in the blue overalls she had seen watching Debbie as she walked round the college.

'I was worried. I waited to tell her, but . . .'

'What did he look like, this man?' Tim kept his voice gently concerned, but not alarmed. He listened as she described what she could remember. She'd *thought* he was a caretaker. One she didn't know. But he wasn't working, he was only pretending to work. Big – solid, not tall – glasses, thick glasses. Nothing more. She hadn't been able to see him very well – he'd kept his distance.

Now Tim had to do his stuff well. He tried to keep the chuckle out of his voice, then he let it become more obvious, then he laughed out loud, watching the girl flush with confusion. 'I'm sorry,' he said. 'You were quite right to be worried, but it's nothing. We've got a quality-assurance audit going on, that's all, and they follow you round watching everything you do. One of the auditors, he thinks he's on a building site, wears these stupid clothes – I had him after me a couple of days ago. Debbie'll laugh herself silly when I tell her . . .' *Right*. The girl's flush had deepened into one of mortification. He gave her a tolerant, understanding look. 'You don't want me to say anything,' he said, gently. 'Look, it was an understandable mistake' – again that not-quite-suppressed laughter – 'but if you don't want me to tell anyone, I won't.'

By the time she went, she was expressing gratitude that she had met Tim before she met Debbie. She also let slip that she'd waited for Debbie outside college that evening, but that Debbie had left with 'that security man'. *Gotcha!* Tim had the cards now. He needed to think how to play them.

Sarah set off home. She had time tonight to get back, have something to eat and sit down for a while before she went out to work. She worked her finances out in her head. If she could give her dad forty pounds this week, he would be able to get the things for Christmas Day. That would leave her with enough money to buy a present for Lee, something for her dad, and something for Nick. That would give her a reason to phone him. She bit at her lip. They'd had a row

111

at Adam's party – more than a row. He'd been late meeting her, and Adam had seen her when she was waiting in a corner by the door. She frowned, remembering. Adam had been drunk, and he'd given her a kiss – a kind of birthday thing. It hadn't meant anything. Only . . . Nick had arrived then. He'd been angry. He hadn't meant to hit her, she was certain, but he'd just been so angry. She should have thought. He hadn't given her a chance to explain, but if she phoned him about his Christmas present, maybe he'd listen. She was working lunchtime on the twenty-fourth, but she could buy him something on her way home, and still have time to do the turkey – if she got it the day before it should be thawed by then – and the potatoes.

The bus station was busy with the throng of Christmas shoppers. There was no one at her stop when she got there, which meant a bus must have just left. She checked her watch. Fifteen minutes to the next one.

Her mind whirled off on to everything they needed and she decided she'd better write a list. Perhaps she ought to do the shopping herself. She chewed her finger anxiously. Her dad would take the car, but he didn't like being told what to get, and then there wouldn't be everything on the day, and then there'd be a row . . . If she took a bit more time off college she could do a lot during the week. She could go in the morning, get into work for twelve and then take everything home after. That would do. And her dad wouldn't mind getting the beer. She shifted uneasily. Someone was standing behind her in the queue. There was a sour, unwashed smell. She moved forward a bit to get away from it.

Her bus pulled into the stop and she got on, still thinking. She was vaguely aware of the bulk of the man behind her as he pushed on to the bus. She kept her eyes fixed on her hands as he moved away from the conductor, praying he wouldn't sit near her, but he disappeared up the stairs.

Night time. A time to wait and watch. He turns off the overhead light, and presses a switch beside the track. The lights sparkle all over his landscape, streetlights, station lights, signal lights. It's so beautiful. He runs the train towards the edge of his layout, the place where the lines end abruptly, before the freight yards start. He hasn't included the freight yards. But his mind lingers around them, lingers in the place that isn't there.

The freight train speeds through Moreham station, the announcement of its coming only a thrumming of the tracks and a singing in the wire fence. Its weight and its power hold the travellers still, its rhythms pounding them as they wait, watching as it fades into the distance.

The stepfather is gone, now. The mother's face is turned away, and the child crouches in a corner, making himself small, making himself not there. 'Sharper than a serpent's tooth . . .' She does not look at the child. 'Spare the rod . . .' But the mother doesn't twist, pull, hurt. There is another dark place, cold, hard, damp. 'Until you learn . . . Out of my sight . . .' The beast lurks in the shadows, waiting to take the child away, swallow it up. The child knows the beast is there. He closes his eyes and lets the darkness take him. The stepfather comes through the door as the child lies there, waiting. The night light flickers by the bed. The stepfather pinches it out. Shiny tracks on the child's face, clear in the moonlight. The mother's face is blank and turned away. She smiles, smiles at the stepfather, frozen in the picture. 'Mam . . . ?' A voice in the darkness. The beast reaches out and draws the child in. He doesn't know that voice. There are no voices in the darkness, not now, not any more.

9

Friday had been enough for Neave. After seeing Debbie in the pub he'd gone along to the personnel department and told them that he needed to take a week's leave as a matter of urgency. As a non-teaching member of staff, he could take his annual leave when he chose. This last-minute decision wouldn't be popular, but he wasn't worried. He knew he'd be leaving soon. The events of the week had decided him. He'd take up Morton's offer of a partnership in Newcastle. He'd hand his notice in as soon as he got back. That decision which had been nagging at the back of his mind for days, made itself easily, and the way he felt told him it was the right decision. He could get on with the business in hand. He knew that the college was in wind-down mode for Christmas, and all the arrangements for the last week were in place and sorted. He put a note for the head caretaker in the internal mail, and left. Nine o'clock Saturday morning he was driving north.

His original idea had been to get to the sea by the quickest route, spend a few days on the coast, but the low mud cliffs of Hornsea and Withersea, the flat Humberside landscape, were not what he wanted. He headed north and further north, and finally stopped on the rocky coast of Northumberland. He spent Saturday and Sunday there, driving up the coast a way, walking along the cliffs to the ruins of Dunstanburgh Castle, walking along the beach on the rocky shoreline of Budle Bay, watching the grey waves of the North Sea wash on the sands, and listening to the cries of the sea birds as they wheeled in the air high above him. He stayed in a hotel close to the sea, and at night, he could hear the sounds of the waves breaking endlessly on the

114

shore, the gentle monotony carrying him into sleep. He didn't dream.

After two days, he felt restless, in need of something more remote, wilder, and he headed north again, crossing the border and arriving eventually at the high cliffs of St Abbs Head. He found a room at a rambling guesthouse at Coldingham Sands. 'We don't usually get visitors at this time of year,' his landlady said with a friendly smile, but she left him to his own devices, just serving up substantial breakfasts that he didn't want. The resident dog, a black labrador with voracious jaws, became an invisible companion in the dining room, mopping up the food he would otherwise have left.

He walked along cliff paths above sheer, dizzying drops to the sea below. One afternoon, he parked the car on a lane near a farm and walked down a field that went from flat to steep, and from steep to precipitous as the path approached the cliff edge. Where they met, the path hung at an angle above a two-hundred-foot drop where the waves foamed and sucked at the cliff foot. He stood there for a while, watching the rise and fall of the sea. He knew that there was one solution that was here in front of him, one way out of the whole pointless mess. He was tired with it all, exhausted. He stood there for a long time, watching the sea.

The path continued, narrow and treacherous, leading down to a rocky promontory where the ruins of a castle stood. He thought for a bit about the reasons for building a castle at the sea edge, here where the landscape formed a fortress far more impenetrable than anything people could create. From where he stood he could see along the coastline, rocky and bleak. As he looked, he realized he could see heads in the water bobbing among the waves. Seals. He stayed and watched them for an hour, then because the light was starting to go, he headed back along the path. It was time to leave.

He got back to Moreham on Monday, two days before Christmas. The college was closed for Christmas week, but his mind slotted back into the grooves of work, and he realized he'd missed something important. The implications of that Thursday night weren't just those personal ones that he'd – let's be honest here – run away from. Getting distracted by

Debbie meant that he hadn't paid attention to the incident that triggered the whole bloody mess – an intruder on the long staircase. A possible intruder on the long staircase. He was trying to work out what could have happened to frighten Debbie – and he hadn't even bothered to ask her about it – not properly. *Try thinking with your brain next time, Neave.*

The college may have been closed, but he had access to it, and the caretakers were in every day anyway. He could go and have a look. He parked in the empty car park and let himself in through the main entrance of the Broome building. Les Walker and Dave were moving filing cabinets out of the lift. There was someone working with them that he didn't recognize. He stopped to talk to Dave and pick up any important news. 'Good holiday?' Dave asked.

Neave shrugged. 'It wasn't really a holiday.' He didn't feel like elaborating. 'New staff?'

'Yeah, he started last week. Replacement for Steve Benson. Temp from the agency.' Neave was annoyed. The turnover among unskilled staff was high, and there were always unfamiliar faces working in the college. In theory, he should be informed before anyone was set on. In practice, it rarely happened with temporary or casual staff. It was just another headache. They discussed details of the running of the college over the Christmas period, then Neave headed up the stairs for the IT suite. It was locked up, and when he opened the door, the empty silence made him uneasy. The room smelt unfamiliar, unused. The light from the windows was dim in the winter afternoon, and he had to turn on the lights.

He crossed the room to the old fire door and opened it. He tried to remember what Debbie had said. 'The door blew shut.'

There was no draught, though it was windy outside. OK. He moved one of the heavy boxes that were stored on the landing so that it would prevent the door from closing completely, then he went down the stairs to the door at the bottom. It was locked on a Yale lock, and the bolts were pulled across. He drew the bolts, which moved easily and silently, and opened the outside door. A swirl of air eddied round him, and the door two landings up slammed against the box holding it open.

116

It had been dark. When he'd opened the door in response to Debbie's frantic calls it had been like opening the door into a black pit. No wonder she'd been frightened. The light hadn't been working. He remembered that. It must have been working when Debbie brought her students on to the stairs – she wouldn't have taken them down to the bottom in the dark. He knew the switch was faulty, that if someone turned the light off at the bottom, it wouldn't work from the top switch, but it wasn't working at all now. The repair job was probably on someone's schedule, low priority. He looked up at the light. The fitting looked strange. By going back up the stairs a short way, he could reach the bulb. He took it out of the light, slipped it into his pocket, and shone his torch on the fitting. It had been damaged, the wires pulled loose. It was useless, and probably dangerous. And that wasn't accidental damage.

So there had been someone there, someone who'd made sure the light wasn't working, someone who'd opened the bottom door and caused the draught that made the upper door slam shut. Someone who'd terrified the level-headed Deborah. Who? And what was that person doing on the long staircase? He picked up the phone and dialled Berryman's number. He was tied up until after Christmas. They arranged to meet on the twenty-seventh. 'I'll tell you,' Berryman said. 'Two kids under three and the in-laws coming, I'd change places with you tomorrow.'

Neave could hear Berryman's pause as he realized what he'd said, and quickly finalized the details. 'Friday, then, the Broomegate, eightish.'

Christmas meant celebration. Debbie tried. She went to parties and came home early. She went clubbing with friends and left halfway through the evening. Fiona, her close friend from university days, was exasperated and concerned. 'What is it? Post-term stress disorder? Come on, Debbie, it's Christmas!' Debbie couldn't understand why she had lost all her capacity for enjoying herself. It couldn't all be to do with Rob. It had been a bad term – hard work and insecurity, the incident at the station, Tim Godber's article, that strange sense of menace she still hadn't managed to throw off, and, OK, Rob. *Pull yourself together, woman.*

She tried again. That evening, she went clubbing with Fiona and Brian, another university friend. She felt leaden and tired. After a couple of hours, she was ready to go, and told the group, now expanded to eight, that she was going for a taxi.

Brian came out of the club to wait with her. Debbie almost protested, but when she was outside in the dark, with jostling groups of young men shoving each other along the pavement, shouts and screams in the distance and the sound of breaking glass, she was glad of the company. Brian put his hands in his pockets and hunched himself against the cold, watching out for a taxi. 'What's wrong, Debbie?' he said after a minute.

Debbie shook her head. It was too complicated to explain. Brian didn't push it, and they waited in silence until a taxi came. Debbie gave him a quick kiss and jumped in, elbowing her way past two queue-jumpers. 'Have a good Christmas,' she said.

'I doubt it,' he said, with a mournful look, and waved goodbye.

Debbie paid the taxi fare – five pounds she could ill afford – and let herself into the house. It felt cold. Buttercup was behind the settee again, and seemed anxious and nervous when Debbie coaxed her out, twining round the chair legs, her eyes wide and alert. Debbie picked her up. There was a strange silence in the house, as though some loud noise had just stopped, leaving that ear-ringing sense of emptiness. Debbie frowned. It was odd. There was something not right. She went into the kitchen and opened the fridge door to get Buttercup some milk. That was when she realized what the strange silence was. The fridge was switched off. The sound of the motor was pretty constant, as it was an old fridge and not very efficient. She couldn't understand it. How had she managed to do that? She pressed the switch and the fridge hummed into life, rattling the bottles standing on it. It must have been off all evening. She checked the stuff in the freezing compartment, but it still seemed frozen solid – odd, as she'd been out for at least three hours. Thank God for cold weather. She went to the phone to check on her last caller. Gina sometimes phoned just before she went to bed, but whoever had called left no number recorded.

Christmas Eve found Debbie at Goldthorpe, rushing around the market for last-minute things Gina had forgotten. 'We don't need to go the whole hog,' Debbie protested when she realized that Gina planned a full traditional Christmas. 'There's just the two of us.'

'All the more reason to make it special.' Gina was making bread sauce and the kitchen was filled with the smell of cloves and onion. 'Anyway, you might have brought someone with you, so I had to be ready.' Debbie recognized a flanking manoeuvre and ignored it. 'And Jean and David are coming on Boxing Day so they'll want cold turkey.'

'So we cook it on Christmas Day so they can have it cold on Boxing Day. Mum . . .' Gina hurried back to the kitchen to take mince pies out of the oven. 'Mum!' Debbie said in exasperation as she saw the racks of pies her mother had made.

'You can carp, miss,' said Gina. 'Half of Goldthorpe will be round for mince pies and Christmas cake next week. Now. It's eight o'clock. Let's have a glass of sherry.'

Debbie and her mother sat in the cosy front room lit by the tree lights and talked. Debbie remembered Christmases when she was a child, the sheer magic and excitement of it, the spicy fragrance of the kitchen, the lights on the tree, the mysterious pile of presents waiting to be opened on the day, her father, as excited as she was, helping her with the letter to Santa, and the empty stocking at her feet as she went to bed that was always knobbly and full when she woke up in the morning. Thinking about it, Debbie felt relaxed and happy for the first time in what seemed like an age.

She poured herself another sherry and offered one to Gina. 'No, not for me. You drink more than you should, you know, Debbie.'

'Not that much,' Debbie protested, thinking Gina was probably right. 'It's just that you don't drink enough.'

'A sherry at Christmas and my nightcap,' Gina agreed. She had solved her insomnia problems years ago with a measure of rum in a cup of cocoa, and this was still part of her nightly ritual. Before she sat down in the evening, she would put the milk in the pan, and cocoa, sugar, milk and rum mixed to a cream in her cup ready for her to go to bed.

Christmas Day, Debbie made a morning visit to her father's grave, taking Christmas roses. 'I'm in a mess, Dad,' she said, as she arranged the flowers, breaking off the stems and putting them into the small container on the headstone. 'Something's wrong and I don't know what it is.' She didn't know what she expected. Her father wasn't there. When she got back, Gina had dinner in the oven, and Debbie's present was on the table waiting to be opened. It was a dress in a fine deep-blue jersey that Gina had made.

'You'll look lovely in that,' Gina said. 'It's just your colour. It matches your eyes. As soon as I saw that material I knew it was just the thing for a dress for you.' Gina also gave her a bottle of whisky – from Santa, the label said.

'I thought you said I drink too much,' Debbie said, looking at the bottle.

'Yes, but it makes you easy to buy for.' Gina was opening a box of chocolates from her neighbour. 'You know,' she said, looking round the room, 'I do like Christmas.'

That evening, Gina said, 'You're still upset, aren't you, love?' She was knitting by the fire. She always seemed to have some project on the go. Debbie couldn't remember seeing her mother sit down without some work in her hands.

Debbie sighed and nodded. There wasn't a lot of point in trying to keep the whole thing from Gina. She'd certainly find out eventually. She needed to talk about it anyway. She gave her the bare bones of the story, and waited for her mother's comment.

'He lost his wife and child together? Poor man.' Gina was shocked. 'Well, I wouldn't pay too much attention to what he says he wants and what he doesn't. He's probably not in his right mind.' She thought about it. 'Mind you, I'm not saying it's something you'd want to get involved in.' She was silent for a minute as she negotiated a tricky section of the pattern.

'I don't think I've got much choice,' said Debbie. 'He's made it clear what he wants. Or what he doesn't want, more to the point.'

'Which one does he talk about most? Or miss the most? The woman or the baby?'

Debbie was surprised by the question, but she had no trouble answering it. 'His wife,' she said.

'Sounds like a man who hasn't had too much love in his life.' Gina stopped knitting and pushed the needles through the ball of wool. 'He's likely to be trouble, Debbie. Keep your eyes open. Well, I'm ready for bed now, I'll just go and do my nightcap and then I'll be off.' She came back a few minutes later carrying a cup from which the mingled smell of chocolate and rum drifted. 'Don't sit up too late, you look tired.'

Debbie laughed. 'Mum, I'm twenty-six.'

'Yes, and I'm still your mother, so don't forget that.' She gave Debbie a hug and a kiss, and headed up the narrow staircase. Debbie sat up a bit later, thinking about what Gina had said. She was probably right. She had wondered herself how easy it would be to have a relationship with someone who had experienced what Rob had experienced. She thought, as well, that there must be something else. He never talked about his childhood, never mentioned parents or family, kept himself secret and safe behind that mask. Gina was almost certainly right, but it didn't help Debbie a bit.

Sarah put down her pen for the fifth time, and went to the door of the living room. 'Make us a cup of tea, love,' her father said from his chair in front of the television.

'Can't Lee? I'm writing my essay.' Sarah's brother was sitting on the floor pushing buttons on his new playstation. He looked up at Sarah's words.

'Can't make tea,' he said.

'Yeah, love, you do it, he can't do it right.' Her father smiled affably. Sarah started to protest again, but saw his eyes start to narrow, so she picked up his cup from the floor and went back into the kitchen. The sink was still full of the dirty dishes, and the table was a cluttered mess. She had her books and papers on one corner that she'd cleared, hoping to get her essay for

Debbie finished. It had to be done for when term started, and she was working all week.

She put the kettle on, and tried to hold the thread in her mind. She had come up with a good idea, and had been trying to follow it through the poem, something about the different ways the poet created a sense of fear and menace . . . no, she'd lost it. She poured water into the teapot. Her father liked his tea made in a pot. He was pleased with her this evening. She'd made sausage and chips for tea and he liked that, and she'd done a fruit pie, using that pie filling that he liked, with custard. 'That was smashing, that, love. You're turning into a right good cook.' She wondered what to do with the cold turkey. He wouldn't eat that. Maybe she and Lee could have it in sandwiches.

But after tea it had been, 'Where's the telly guide, love?'; 'Take our Lee out, he's driving me mad'; 'Bring us the paper', as she sat at the table and tried to work on her essay. It was always like that, he just didn't understand about college. She poured the tea, added milk and sugar and stirred it. She took it through to her father. 'Thanks, love,' he said absently, his eyes on the screen. Soon, in about half an hour, she'd have to go to work, and the kitchen still wasn't done. With a sigh, she put her books away and started running water into the sink.

Nick was meeting her after work. She'd phoned him about the present, as she'd planned. He'd been pleased, had been nice, he'd even apologized for the Friday night. *You shouldn't get me jealous*, he'd said, and she'd felt – somehow – flattered. He'd agreed to meet her. She could give him his Christmas present. It was wrapped and ready in her handbag. It would have been nice if she could have given it to him on Christmas Day, but – she tried to imagine Nick and her dad together. She frowned, worried. Her thoughts were interrupted by her father's shout. 'Shut the door, Sarah, I can't hear my programme for that racket!' She pushed the door shut, and began clearing the table.

Half an hour later, she hurried out of the house towards her bus stop. It was dark and, as usual, half the streetlights weren't working, though Christmas lights shone in the windows of the houses. She could hear someone on the pavement behind her, some way back. She looked round, but she couldn't see anyone. She waited at the stop, checking her watch. The buses were often late at the moment, with the holiday, but it came into view up the hill, more or less on time. As she paid her fare, someone who'd been waiting in the shadows by the wall got on. She got that whiff of unwashed body again. She looked round as she went to her seat, but whoever it was was disappearing up the stairs.

Berryman was waiting at the bar of the Broomegate Tavern, on Friday evening, as he and Neave had arranged. He used it more than the Grindstone these days. The town centre pubs were too full of people he knew professionally to be relaxing places to go to often. He wanted Neave's thoughts on some of the material that Lynne Jordan had brought in. She'd come up with some interesting stuff. As to whether it would be useful or not . . . . Berryman was getting tired of having that feeling that the investigation was about to break, and then finding they were down another blind alley. He was certain that the answer lay somewhere in the memories of the relatives, the people who'd lived with the victims before they died. It was up to him, to his team, to spot the important facts and start following them. He was downing his second pint by the time Neave came through the door.

The pub was noisy and busy at the end of Christmas week, but they found a table in an inaccessible corner where they were able to talk. Neave asked about the investigation and listened without comment as Berryman ran through the latest developments. After a minute, he said, 'You think he does stalk them, then?'

Berryman nodded. 'Two reasons. One: he's never been seen doing a pick-up. He can't be that bloody lucky all the time. He must be able to choose his time and his place. Two: it's possible that some of the victims were being followed by someone or phoned by someone. Lisa' – Berryman almost always referred to the women by their first names now. He felt as if he knew them – 'her little girl started talking about an *ugly man*, just in the few weeks before her mum was killed. *Something* frightened her. She drew a picture as well. There's

123

something about it . . . And Mandy, she was getting phone calls. Her mum said it was the boyfriend, but it wasn't, not all of them – we've checked. I've got Lynne Jordan working on the others now. You know Lynne?'

'You asked me that last time.' Neave was noncommittal. He didn't think it was any of Berryman's business. Lynne was a very independent woman. 'OK, I've got something you might find interesting then.' He told Berryman about Debbie's experience in the college and his own findings when he went to investigate. He watched as Berryman's face darkened.

'Why the fuck –' he began, but Neave interrupted him.

'OK, I know, but I'm telling you now.'

Berryman began pushing for details, and Neave ran through the events of the Thursday evening, and his search of the staircase the Monday before Christmas. 'You didn't see anyone or hear anyone? But someone had unlocked that door from the inside?' Berryman thought. 'And the damage to the light – it's the fitting, not the bulb? And the Sykes woman went back to your place . . .' Berryman wasn't making much of it, but there was something in his voice, 'And you haven't talked to her since?'

'Not since the Friday. We didn't talk about the staircase.'

'Her briefcase, was anything missing?'

'She didn't mention anything.'

'Did she check?'

'Not straight away, not while she was with me.'

'And she hasn't missed anything since?'

'She hasn't said anything.' Neave was aware that Debbie couldn't have told him anything anyway, so he added, 'I went away on the Saturday. She hasn't seen me.'

Berryman thought about it. 'You think this could be our man?' Neave shrugged. 'Why?' persisted Berryman. 'Why would he be after anyone now? It's too soon. And why would he be at the bottom of that staircase? I'll tell you something, I can't think of a better way of getting a few computers out of that building. There's been trouble with pilfering before at that place. It's that door that opens on to the back lane, isn't it, by the car park?' Neave nodded. 'Have you checked your own people? Sounds like an inside job to me. Down the fire escape, out the back door, put the bolts back later. Whoever it was was probably shitting himself when half the bloody college starts playing around the fire escapes. An intruder on a staircase, that's not stalking.'

Neave had thought about that. He knew that Berryman could be right, couldn't think of any convincing reasons why he should be wrong. Except . . . Berryman emptied his glass. 'Want another?' he said.

'My round.' Neave went up to the bar. The barmaid, a tall blonde, smiled timidly at him and he realized he'd seen her around the college. She must be a student. She had a fading bruise on her cheek and her lip was slightly swollen. He ordered the drinks and smiled back as he gave her the money. She went pink and slopped the beer over the side of the glasses.

'Sorry,' she said.

'OK, love. Going to top them up a bit?' Neave looked at the level in the glasses which was distinctly lower than the line now. She went even pinker, and carefully pulled more beer into each. He looked at her face as she was concentrating on the level in the glasses. *Not your problem, Neave.* He winked at her and took the drinks back to his table. Berryman had been thinking.

'Look. I'll get someone up to the college to have a look. See what we can pick up. Did you touch that light fitting?' Neave shook his head. 'I'll need convincing that it's anything much, but I will make sure it's looked into. Anything else?'

Neave took a piece of paper from his wallet and gave it to Berryman. 'I had a look at the attendance that evening. Those are the students who were in that room. Most were gone before seven, but there are a few stayed later, and these stayed to the end.' He pointed to names by a signing-out time of nine o'clock.

Berryman looked at it. 'Sarah Peterson. Richard Fury. A. Mellors. Right, I'll get someone to talk to them once the college is open again. It won't hurt to talk to the Sykes woman again – Steve's already talked to her, but I'll send someone round. And I might need something from you, depending

125

on what we come up with.' He waved Neave's protest down. 'Just be glad you're not working for me any more. Fucking a witness gets you a disciplinary, these days.'

Sarah loaded glasses into the dishwasher, and looked at the clock. Nearly eleven-thirty and she was nowhere near finished. She was worried. She had seen the security man from college, and she wanted to ask him about the man following Debbie. She'd felt a lot better after talking to Tim Godber, but through the week a feeling of unease had been growing, and she wasn't sure any more. She'd seen the man, and Tim's explanation just didn't seem right. The security man, he'd know what to do. She waited for him to come back to the bar, but as the evening wore on, he didn't, and she couldn't get out to talk to him. The landlady, Maggie, who usually came behind the bar to help when it was busy, was in bed with flu, and the other evening bar staff, Jacquie and Pete, were as rushed as Sarah, and there was no time for anyone to take a break.

Nick should have been here by now. He'd said eleven. She looked at the clock again. Tony came round behind the bar. 'All right there, Sarah? How are you getting back? Want a taxi?'

Sarah shook her head. 'Nick's meeting me,' she said, pulling another load of glasses across the bar.

'He'll get locked out if he doesn't get a move on.' Tony was watching the last of the customers leaving the pub. 'Good night. Good night. Right, Pete, get that door closed and let's get finished.'

Jacquie dumped two ash trays on the bar. 'That's about it, Sarah. Want any help over there?'

The pub was empty now, and Sarah was loading the last of the glasses into the machine.

'Want a drink?' Tony and Pete, the barman, couldn't wait to see the customers off the premises, but often stayed late in the end having a drink after doors.

'Nick'll be waiting,' Sarah apologized.

'OK.' Tony never asked Nick to join these late sessions, though he sometimes asked Jacquie's boyfriend Dave. 'You get off, Sarah, I'll finish up here. Go out the back, I've locked up now.'

Sarah went and got her coat, looked in the mirror, rubbed some more concealer over the fading bruise and dragged a comb through her hair. She wanted to take more time, but she didn't dare leave Nick waiting any longer. She hurried out of the back door and round to the front of the pub where he'd be waiting. There was no one there. She looked up and down the road. It was empty, apart from a man waiting in the shadows at the bus stop opposite. She chewed her finger, wondering what to do. Nick had said eleven. 'I'll come at eleven. Make sure you've got a drink in for me. And try to finish on time, I don't want to be hanging around all evening.' She looked at her watch again. It was gone eleven-forty-five. He wouldn't be coming now. Her eyes began to prickle.

She could go back into the pub, phone for a taxi, but all the doors were locked. She'd have to ring the bell and that would wake Maggie, and maybe the kids. Tony would see her looking red-eyed and she would feel a fool. She chewed her fingernail again, undecided. There was a phone box up the road. If it was working, she could phone a taxi from there. Then she remembered. She didn't have enough money for a taxi. She looked at her watch again. If she could just get across to Headlands Road, she could catch the late bus. She'd caught it before. If she went round by the road, she'd miss it, but she could cut across the footpath to the bridge and be there in five minutes.

The footpath was busy during the day, a stretch of green in an urban landscape where the land dipped down between high walls to a bridge over a stream. The banks of the stream were overgrown with shrubs and trees, and the ground could be treacherous underfoot. Most of the path was in darkness, though there was a streetlight at the other end, just before it rejoined the main road, but the moon was bright. Sarah shivered. It was starting to get cold.

She crossed the road and went down the steps at the beginning of the gennel that led down to the bridge. If she walked quickly, it wouldn't take her five minutes. She began to speed up her steps. The wind was getting up, and the clouds were starting to blow across the sky, drifting across the face of the moon. The path faded into darkness.

Sarah slipped through the shadows, following the path down. The moon was appearing and disappearing behind the clouds that raced across it. She looked behind her. The path wasn't lit, but she thought she saw something moving further back behind her in the dark. Her heart lurched and began to beat more quickly. *Don't be stupid*, she admonished herself. She'd think about something else, about her essay, remember her ideas about the poem. She'd been reading it, trying to get the essay right for Debbie.

> *Like one that on a lonesome road*
> *Doth walk in fear and dread*

Sarah quickened her pace, her breath catching in her throat. She didn't want to think about the poem now. The bushes were higher around the path, meeting above her. A branch brushed against her hair and her heart leapt. Where was the bridge, where was the light? It couldn't be far now. The path ahead was shadowy. She didn't look back. There was only darkness behind.

> *And having once turned round, walks on*
> *And turns no more his head*

She wished she'd stuck to the road now. There was a cold wind that blew against her face, making her shiver. She wrapped her coat tighter round herself, but the shivering wouldn't stop. The wind was moving the bushes now, making a soughing sound, and a rustling as though some large animal was moving in the undergrowth. Her steps quickened until she was almost running.

> *Because he knows a frightful fiend*
> *Doth close behind him tread*

She made a sound somewhere between a sob and a laugh. She could write a good essay for Debbie about the poem tomorrow. The stream was ahead now, she could feel the extra coldness in the air, the dampness of a place that never got the sun. Where was the light? Of course, you couldn't see it until you were over the bridge. The wind rushed through the undergrowth, drowning out the sound of her breathing, and blasted into her face, almost knocking her off her feet. She staggered and regained her balance, gasping. She had to go on. The road was only just over the next rise. She could see the gleam of water between the banks, the bridge. Just across that and then she would be able to see the light, the road. The damp smell of the river was disgusting. It was rank and fetid in her nostrils. It didn't usually smell like that after rain, it smelt like that in the summer when the water ran low.

A cloud crossed the moon and the bridge was in darkness. So black it seemed almost solid. The smell was strong now, sharp and nauseating. Sarah's feet felt like lead. She stepped on to the bridge, and the darkness solidified in front of her. The smell was overwhelming, and cold hands gripped her round the throat and pulled her into it.

10

Debbie stayed in Goldthorpe until Monday. Fiona was having a party that evening, and she felt in more of a party mood than she had done before Christmas. She left in the middle of the morning, persuading Gina that there was no need to come and see her off at the station at that time of day. It was cold but bright and sunny, and she felt her spirits lift as she walked down the road, turning and waving to Gina at the corner.

Even the station, with its grimy concrete functionalism, couldn't spoil her mood, and she began to look forward to the evening. She also, she admitted it to herself, began to look forward to the start of term when she could get back to the students, and back to her colleagues. She felt a bit of a twinge when she thought about seeing Rob, but told herself that the sooner they could re-establish a friendly relationship the easier that would get. She wasn't going to think about it, anyway. As she stood on the platform waiting for the train, she looked up at the sky which was blue and cloudless. Life was good, on the whole it was very good. Even though it was cold, she could feel the sun warming her face, and she smiled.

The journey back took her through countryside and towns and villages. Sometimes she was looking out on fields white with frost, and sometimes she was looking into snatches of people's lives – a little boy wobbling on a new bike in his garden, a woman hanging out washing in the sun, a group of children skateboarding on the pavement. In the bright frost, even the industrial dereliction looked less raw, less ugly. The signs of decay and neglect – the dumped rubbish

130

and the abandoned cars – were covered with the shimmering of frost. *Christmas decorations,* Debbie thought. *Even here, there are Christmas decorations.* As the train pulled into Sheffield station, she collected her things and joined the queue for the doors, to give herself the illusion of speed. She wanted to be home.

She nipped into the newsagent's at the station to buy a paper. She was queuing to pay for her *Guardian* when a photograph on the front of the local paper caught her eye. She picked it up and looked more closely, looked at the headline, read the first lines of the story again, feeling, after that first thump of her heart that had almost brought her to her knees, cold, feeling nothing, feeling that strange blankness she remembered feeling when her father died. Sarah Peterson stared back at her from the front page of the paper, smiling, the photograph bringing out her muted prettiness. *It's a good picture, Debbie* . . . The headline said: *Moreham student killed.* The article was short. Sarah's body had been found on Friday – there must have been something in yesterday's paper. The police said that she wasn't a victim of the railway strangler. A man was helping police with their enquiries.

'Are you paying for that?' The checkout girl was looking at Debbie with irritation.

Debbie stared at her. 'Oh. Yes.' She scrabbled for her purse, and fumbled with her change as the queue shifted restlessly behind her. Mindlessly, she crossed the road outside the station, climbed the hill that ran up beside what used to be the poly, and walked through the subway under the dual carriageway that split the city centre in two. The homeless man who sat at the far end of the subway was there as usual. Debbie stared at him blankly as she went past, only realizing later that she hadn't stopped as she usually did to say hello and give him a pound.

The city centre was full of people. They all seemed to be rushing towards Debbie, making her stop, sidestep, veer off her path. She still wanted to get home. The bright light made everything look stark and ugly. She wanted to shut her door behind her and try to think about what had happened.

She let herself into the house, absently greeting Buttercup, who brought her a catnip mouse by way of a welcome home, and dumped her coat and bags on the chair. She went into the kitchen and put the kettle on. When the tea was ready, she took a cup into the front room, sat down and took the paper out of her bag. She read the article again. She was finding it hard to believe. *Sarah!* Sad, inoffensive Sarah, who wanted to do well, who wanted to please. Why would anyone kill Sarah? She looked at the paper again. *A man is helping police with their enquiries.* She went upstairs and got her briefcase out. There was a folder of marking from the A-level group. Sarah had handed an essay in on – Debbie thought back – not the last week, Sarah had missed the last class – the Friday before. She flicked through the work waiting to be marked – Rachel, Chris, Leanne – there was a surprise – Kirsty, Sarah – there it was. She looked at Sarah's last essay, an essay on symbolism in Coleridge's 'Rime of the Ancient Mariner'.

The rhyme of the ancient mariner was written by Samuel Taylor Coleridge and it is about a man who shoots an albatross. He tells a wedding guest about it. Coleridge uses a lot of symbolism in this poem, for example . . .

Debbie's eyes felt sore and she blinked rapidly. She had wanted Sarah's last essay to be good. She read on. It was an unstructured mixture of narrative, comments Debbie recognized as her own, quoted back to her almost word for word, some quotations from the poem that had marginal relevance. Then at the end, Sarah said: *The mariner is all right in the end. He gets home but he has to tell his story to people. But the albatross is still dead and it fell into the sea. No one really remembers it.* Strange fruit that discussion had borne – Sarah's original thought, poorly expressed, but her own. There wouldn't be any more. The phone rang and she hurried downstairs. It was Louise. 'Have you heard the news?' she said. Debbie told her about buying the paper at the station. 'I can't believe it,' Louise said. 'I saw the girl in college at the end of term. She was having a heart to heart with Tim Godber.'

'With Tim? She doesn't know Tim. When was that?'

'It was Monday. Late Monday. I know because I was just coming out of one of those meetings with Davis, and I was in a foul temper. Debbie, you must be feeling awful. I didn't

really know the girl, but you'd taken her under your wing.'
Louise was concerned.

'That's odd. She wasn't in class that Monday. Listen, Louise, do you know anything else? It didn't say much in the paper, except it sounds as if they've got someone already. I just can't understand it.' Debbie thought back to that Monday. She'd gone home early. What had Sarah come into college for?

Louise, as usual, knew a lot. 'It's the boyfriend, they say. A nasty bit of work, and a bit of a bully. Apparently he beat her up just before Christmas. The students were full of it. Mind you, I know the father, and he's just as bad. Poor Sarah. They found her on that bit of wasteland down by the river, you know, up the top of Broomegate.'

Debbie knew the path. It was a pleasant place in summer, an unexpected patch of green in the middle of rows of Victorian terraces, not unlike the area where Debbie lived. But it would be a lonely and intimidating place in winter, in the dark – a lonely place to die.

She was standing by the phone wondering what to do next, when the doorbell rang.

Lynne Jordan had only been in Sheffield for four years, but she knew enough now to come to the back door of terraces that opened on to the street. She rang the bell and waited with West to see if there was anyone in. This was their second visit. They had called round earlier in the day, and were just making a second call on the off-chance as they were passing. Berryman had filled her in on the details of Neave's story, and she was feeling distinctly irritated with him – with both of them, actually. Berryman for sending her on a wild-goose chase, and Neave for his long and unexplained – by him – silence. She was about to press the bell again when there was the rattle of a key and the door opened.

Lynne smiled. 'Deborah Sykes?' she said, and when the woman who'd opened the door nodded, she introduced herself and West. 'Could we talk to you?' she asked.

The woman, Deborah Sykes, looked a bit blank, as though her mind was on something else, but she stepped back and invited them in. Lynne looked at her closely as Deborah led them through the kitchen into the front room and asked them to sit down. Small-boned, pale. Dark, pre-Raphaelite hair. 'Would you like a cup of tea, or something?' A quiet voice, local. Another of Neave's faerie children. Lynne, who had planned to be an English teacher herself, until she'd realized what a mug's game it was, had met Neave's wife a few times and had nicknamed her – for private consumption only – La belle dame sans merci. It had proven all too prophetic. She had seen Neave, caught in some bleak wasteland of the mind, become a hollow shadow of the man he used to be, the man she had met and liked when she first joined the Moreham force. *Oh, what can ail thee, knight-at-arms?* The words drifted through her mind. Deborah Sykes was speaking again. 'Is this about Sarah?'

'Sarah?' Lynne asked.

'Sarah Peterson. The girl . . .'

'The Christmas girl,' West said.

Lynne remembered that the young girl killed post-Christmas had been a student at City College. 'No, it isn't about Sarah. Did you know her?'

'Yes. She was a student of mine.' Head down, hair obscuring face. She was upset.

Lynne tried to make her voice gentle. 'I'm sorry. This isn't a good time, but I really do need to talk to you.' She wasn't expecting to find anything interesting – neither she nor Berryman were convinced by Neave's interpretation of the college break-in – but if there was anything, then it would probably be easier to find out while the woman was distracted by this death.

'It's OK. It's just that it's been a bit of a shock. You don't expect . . .'

'No, of course not. I want to talk to you about Thursday.' She checked her notes. 'Thursday the twelfth. The evening of Thursday the twelfth.' She kept her face towards her notes, but she saw the woman flush. 'We know there may have been some kind of break-in at the college. Could you just tell me what happened?' She made some notes while Deborah talked. 'So you didn't see anyone?' she confirmed, as the story came to an end.

'No, but Rob, Rob Neave, said the door was unbolted. If there was anyone, they got out the bottom.'

'You said you heard footsteps. Are you certain about that?' Lynne was trying to work out how much she could rely on this woman's story.

Deborah Sykes flashed her a sudden smile, and Lynne warmed to her. 'I was at the time, but I'd just been on those stairs frightening the students with ghost stories. I'm not usually that nervous, I don't usually hear things in the dark, but I was as well set up for it as I could have been. I certainly heard *something*. I didn't imagine that.'

A sensible woman after all. Lynne was getting on to the tricky bit now. 'You left your bag at the bottom of the stairs. Was anything missing from it when you found it?'

Deborah paused for a minute, then shook her head. 'No, there was only my purse, really. Not that there was much in it. But, no, nothing was missing.'

'Did you check straight away?'

'Not at once, no.' She didn't expand, and Lynne gave her nine out of ten for tact.

'When did you check? When you got home?'

'I didn't go home. I spent the night with a friend. But I would have noticed in the morning if anything was missing.'

Full marks. Lynne was amused, and decided that she didn't need to tease out that final bit of information. She looked at Deborah thoughtfully. 'Since that article appeared in the paper . . .' She saw Deborah flush at this new topic, another one that was clearly difficult for her. 'Have you had any unusual phone calls, thought that anyone was following you, anything at all that made you feel uneasy?'

Deborah shook her head. 'The other detective . . .' She reached for the name.

'Steve McCarthy?' Lynne supplied

Deborah nodded. 'I think so. He asked me all of this. Is there any reason to . . . ?'

'Look, Deborah, this is purely routine. But you were identified as someone who saw the Strangler. I think we told you at the time to be careful.'

Deborah pulled a face. 'I didn't see anything useful, that's

the stupid thing. I was so angry when that article appeared.'
She looked at Lynne, who nodded. Deborah Sykes didn't
strike her as an attention seeker.

'And you're not aware of anything unusual, anything at
all?'

'Only visits from the police telling me to be careful.'

Lynne laughed and put her notebook away. 'I don't think
you need to worry too much, Deborah, but there's no harm
in playing safe.' She got up to go. 'If there's anything else
you remember, or if anything happens to bother you, you
can contact me on this number.'

Deborah took the card she was holding out. 'Who told you
about that Thursday?'

'It was reported,' Lynne said vaguely. 'We thought it needed
checking.' She assumed that Deborah knew exactly who had
talked to Berryman. But there was nothing here that pointed
to the killer.

*Vermin. Fire and snares are what you use for vermin. It is important
to protect the creature you hunt, keep it safe and sleek and ready
for the chase, for the blooding – blood that is warm and alive,
not cold and dead – and for the kill. He sits at his layout and
broods for a moment over the scene. He pushes a lever. A train
pulls slowly into Moreham station and then stops. Can he repeat
himself? Moreham would be easiest. He pushes the lever again and
manipulates the points. The train moves out of Moreham and on
through Mexborough, Conisbrough, Doncaster, Kirk Sandall, Goole
. . . more difficult. He needs to think.*

*He's been very successful so far, though he knows the dangers of
complacency. 'Don't count your chickens,' his mother used to say.
A hunt is never successful until the kill – the trophy taken and the
hunter safely home. Still, a successful beginning is a good omen for
a successful end. The skilled hunter follows the spoor of his prey,
knows where it is and where it is going, knows the best time and
the best place to set the trap and spring it. The skilled hunter can
find his prey anywhere and can follow it wherever it tries to hide.*

*And he now has some formidable weapons in his armoury. A
bunch of keys, some labelled in his handwriting, some not, yet.
Some photocopied pages from a diary, going back some months.*

July 20th – Department party, 7.30, Drama studio. Got off with TG!!! July 30th – Mum's, 12.30. Shopping. NB buy black top for tonight. November 5th – Brian, Chris et al, bonfire party at Katy's. 10th RN in pub!!! 11th December, DS McCarthy ... *Dates of holidays, dates of meetings, phone numbers and addresses.*

He presses buttons on the control panel again, and again the trains start to move, all in a time, all in a pattern. He closes his eyes, and he can hear their rattle against the lines, the echo of their horns as they cut the darkness and are gone. And they leave the darkness behind them. He knows the dark places, knows them well. And so will she, soon, in good time.

Moreham, then

11

With Christmas safely out of the way, Neave was in a position to do something about Pete Morton's offer. They'd discussed it briefly when he'd decided to jack it in at City. Going into partnership in a security business wasn't exactly what he'd had in mind, but Morton had talked about getting into the investigation business as well when Neave phoned him. 'There's a lot of cross-over. There's a firm of solicitors that always comes to me now – because they know I get results – and I'm advising some big companies. It isn't the sleaze side of the business, it isn't bashing kids up in nightclubs, it's good work and it's good money.' It sounded interesting. It was time he got out of Moreham. He should have left two years ago.

He almost missed the paper. He didn't usually bother with the local, and the story, if it had made the nationals, hadn't made a splash. It was as if eighteen-year-old women were murdered every day. Well, they probably were. It was the photograph that caught his eye, though he didn't recognize it at once. He read the story, thinking at first that it was the Strangler again. He looked at the girl in the picture and remembered her – the girl behind the bar at the Broomegate. Killed later that night. He ran the evening through his mind, trying to remember faces in the pub, people she might have talked to, when the name snagged his memory. He pulled out his wallet and flicked through the miscellaneous bits of paper in the back. Yes. He checked the list of names. He thought he had remembered it right. Sarah Peterson, the student who had signed out of the IT centre last thing on that Thursday night, one of the students Berryman was going to talk to.

He dialled Berryman's number, but he was in a meeting. He left a message for Berryman to phone, then paced the room restlessly trying to decide what to do. He went to the phone again, and this time dialled Lynne Jordan's number – her mobile. When she answered he could hear traffic noise. She was out somewhere. 'Lynne,' he said.

'Oh. Hi, how are you? You've caught me bang outside the bus station, I can't hear a thing.' She sounded cheerful enough.

'Listen, Lynne, have you got some time? Can you meet me? In about an hour?'

There was a pause while she thought. 'Make it a bit later. I'm off at three – well, I'm not but I'm checking some stuff in the library, so I expect I can give you a few minutes.'

They arranged to meet in the coffee bar of the library building. Neave checked the time – half past one. He felt edgy and impatient. He made himself a bacon sandwich and ate it pacing up and down waiting for Berryman to get back to him. When there was no call by two-thirty, he remembered that Berryman had the number of his mobile, and went out to meet Lynne.

The coffee bar was one of those with plastic-stacking chairs and a pervasive smell of steam and stale cloths. He was unenthusiastically stirring sugar into a cup of pale-beige coffee when Lynne came through the door, her short brown hair sparkling with rain drops and her face flushed with the cold. She waved and went to the counter to get a drink. Wiser than Neave, she came back with a Coke. She looked at his cup. 'Christ, Neave, what died in there?' He was pleased to see her and didn't try to keep the smile off his face. She grinned back at him. 'So. What's the hurry? What's on fire?'

He felt anxiety press down on him again, and he rubbed his hand over his face. 'Nothing, I hope. Listen, this Sarah Peterson killing . . .' He saw her frown, but he quickly ran through his conversation with Berryman, and the fact that Berryman had agreed to have her interviewed about the Thursday break-in. 'It's too much of a coincidence, Lynne. Does he know it's the same girl?'

Lynne looked at him. 'I know about the Thursday thing.

139

Berryman sent me round to talk to the Sykes woman about it.' She paused, thinking. 'As far as I know, no one talked to the Peterson girl. Berryman knows who she is. But it doesn't get us any further.'

'Someone killed her.'

'Yes. And we were on the blocks waiting to go as soon as we heard. But it didn't look right, and the postmortem confirmed it. It wasn't a strangler killing. Or it wasn't *the* Strangler. It looks as though it was the boyfriend. She went out of the pub to meet him, in a hurry because he'd got locked out. They'd had a row a week or two before – her friends talked about it. She was always turning up at college with bruises, black eyes, things like that.' She gestured her distaste.

'That's not enough.'

'I agree. It would put him in the frame, but that's all. The thing is, he was there, that's the point. He came hammering on the pub door, got a flea in his ear from the landlord and went off after her breathing fire. Then he lied about it when they picked him up. There doesn't seem much doubt.'

'Is that definite? Are they going to charge him?'

Lynne wasn't sure. 'They will, when they can. They're still questioning him – he's cooperating.'

'If they're so bloody sure, why hasn't he been charged?' Neave was insistent.

'Christ, Neave, I don't know. It's not my case.'

'Forensics?'

'Not much, I heard. Can't be, or they would have charged him. It's early days. They won't have that information yet.' Lynne sipped her Coke and pulled a face. Neave changed tack.

'So what did Deborah say?'

Lynne gave him the gist of Debbie's account. 'There's no reason for anyone to have been down there, anyone who was looking for her. And there's no sign of anything else. We've warned her, Neave, she knows she's got to be careful. At the moment, I don't see what else we can do.'

He shook his head. 'It's too much of a coincidence, the Peterson girl getting killed.'

Lynne let her irritation show. 'I agree it's a coincidence.

We're keeping an eye on it, I told you. I don't like coincidences. What else do you want us to do?'

The comeback was quick. 'More than you're doing at the moment!'

Lynne knew when to go in hard. It was one of the qualities that made her a good officer. 'Everyone walks on egg shells with you, Neave. They think you can't cope with things because of what happened to Angie and the baby. You're panicking because you got involved with this woman, so you think she's going to die. You think she's going to be murdered. And Berryman listens to you because you used to be a good copper. *Used to be*. Now you're getting in the way.' That made him more angry, she could see that. He'd gone white and his face looked tense. She hadn't particularly wanted to upset him, but it had to be said, and no one but her had the balls to say it. She looked away and lifted her glass to her mouth.

For a moment she thought he was going to walk out. She was aware of him making a conscious effort to calm down. 'OK. Sorry. You're right. Only – I think there is something going on. Look, I'll be getting off. You've got work to do.' But his tone didn't mean *sorry* at all. She didn't think he was going to forgive her for that one.

When Lynne arrived back at the incident room, Steve McCarthy was at his desk going through a pile of statements. 'Anything interesting?' she said. Her encounter with Neave had left her feeling depressed, and she wanted some distraction.

He didn't look at her. 'Statements from passengers on Kate Claremont's train. I'm trying to answer that question.' When she didn't respond, he glanced across. 'Where did Kate get off the train?' he reminded her.

Lynne looked over his shoulder. 'Have you found anything?'

'I'm not sure. Look, we've been assuming that she got off at Doncaster, right?' Lynne nodded. 'We've got her friends' statement that says she often did that. But look at these.' He pushed some sheets of paper towards Lynne. 'Those are all people who mention seeing Kate on the train. We know she got on at Hull. Her friends saw the train off. Several people say they saw her, anyway. This guy' – he waved a statement at Lynne – 'saw her when he got on at Ferriby. Someone here gets on at Goole. He saw her. This woman got out at Thorne North. She said she had to lift her bag down over a woman who was asleep. That was Kate – same seat, same description. That's it. No one saw her after that.'

Lynne looked at the map. 'Well, the next station is Doncaster, so that would fit.'

'No,' McCarthy said. 'It was a slow train. It would have stopped at Kirk Sandall. Look.'

'Why would she get out there?' Lynne looked at the station on the edge of the – what? Village? Small town? It looked like a nondescript place. Why would someone like Kate get off the train at Kirk Sandall. 'Suppose she did? Where does that get us?'

'It solves the Doncaster problem. He doesn't take them from busy stations.'

'OK, but it's still guesswork. There's nothing that tells me she did anything different from normal.'

'Something did happen, though. There was a delay.' He looked at Lynne to see if she was with him. She listened, without saying anything. 'I checked with the conductor's statement. He says there was a short delay – couple of minutes – because one of the doors got stuck – it wouldn't shut. We know something odd happened on that journey, and that's the only thing I've been able to find. I'm going back through the statements to see if there's anything else happened there. Something that made Kate get off the train.'

Lynne was hooked. 'I'll give you a hand.' He nodded, and passed across a pile of papers. They settled down to read.

Lynne was trying to concentrate on yet another account of the journey from Hull to Sheffield – this one from a Thorne to Doncaster traveller – when McCarthy's voice interrupted her. She picked up the suppressed excitement in his tone. 'Lynne!' She swivelled her chair round, still holding the statement she was reading in her hand. 'Listen to this.' He began reading. '"When we stopped at Sandall I thought they called Doncaster and I got off, but it wasn't so I got on again."

142

That guy was sitting in the seat in front of Kate's.' He looked at Lynne.

'Kate thought it was Doncaster? Someone tricked her? How?'

McCarthy leant towards her. 'Think about it, Lynne. Kate's next to the door. She always grabbed a seat by the door, her friends said. An airline seat, by the door, next to the aisle, her bags on the window seat. She'd have a sleep and jump out at Doncaster to get a drink and a paper.'

'And he knew that . . .' Lynne thought. 'Someone calls "Doncaster", she wakes up and it's dark . . . Could he be sure she'd fall for it?'

'I'd say it was a good bet. She had to move quickly to get off and on again in five minutes at Doncaster. She was probably tuned for waking up then, and hearing the word must have jolted her out of sleep. She was probably on automatic pilot.'

Lynne went over to the map and looked at the pins marking the places where the bodies had been found, and the places where the women were last seen. If McCarthy was right, it would be the only pick-up beyond Doncaster. She looked at Kirk Sandall, and she looked at the small lake east of Balby Carr where Kate had been found. Then her eyes went back to the map again. 'Steve!' she said. 'Look at this!'

Now Neave wasn't sure. He was angry with her, but trusted Lynne's judgement – more in some ways than he trusted Berryman's. He *was* basing all his suspicions on very little. He wasn't sure what to do next, and that feeling of uncertainty was something he wasn't used to. He could go and talk to Debbie, find out exactly what was going on from her perspective. But Lynne had done that, and said that nothing was going on. He was reluctant to seek Debbie out. It would open things up that he hoped were closed. He planned to keep out of her way as far as possible when term started, but if he did need to talk to her, it would be better in the college.

He went into work after he left Lynne. He needed something to distract him. The college was very quiet. The caretaking staff were in, but the students and teaching staff wouldn't be back until after the New Year. The quiet, the silent corridors and classrooms suited his mood. He walked the college, checking it over, getting a feel for it. The North building, which housed most of the administrative staff, was the busiest. He stopped and talked to the receptionist for a while, fielded questions about his Christmas and found out what had been happening in his absence. She talked a bit about the dead student, but in a detached way. She hadn't known the girl. 'It brings it close to home, though, doesn't it?' she said. Neave nodded agreement, though in fact he didn't think it did come close to home. When it came close to home . . .

The Moore building was like a graveyard. He met no one on his walk, and the small office that served as a reception area was locked and empty. He wondered why the building was even open and made a note to check if it should be kept locked until the teaching staff were back.

The long, high-ceilinged corridors of the Broome building reminded him of Debbie. He could see her walking briskly through the imposing gloom, laughing with the students, telling ghost stories with wide-eyed conviction. He'd come across her with one of her classes, and had listened from a discreet distance as she told a story – some nonsense about mysterious figures walking into locked rooms – to a fascinated and silent group. She'd make an excellent con-artist. He remembered her white-faced terror locked on the long staircase. He stopped his mind there, but went on up to the IT suite to look at the staircase again.

He was surprised to find the receptionist at her desk, working at her VDU. She looked up when he came in, apparently as surprised as he was. 'Oh, hello,' she said. 'Did you have a good Christmas?'

'Hello' – he did a quick mental trawl and came up with her name – 'Sheila. I didn't expect to find anyone here.'

'If I don't get this paperwork done when it's quiet, I don't get it done at all,' she explained. 'Did you want to work in here? I'm not going to disturb you, am I?'

'No, not at all. You might be able to help me with something. Can you show me the attendance log for the twelfth

of December, the evening? I want the last hour and a half.'
He'd already seen the log, but he wanted to look at it again.
'Were you on duty that night?'

Sheila shook her head, then said, 'Hang on, yes, I was. I
did that night because someone was off ill.'

'I know it's some time ago, but you notice things, Sheila.
Tell me what you can remember about the people who were
in here on that Thursday.' He showed her the attendance
sheet and she went through the details of the students she
could remember, but she didn't know a lot of the evening
attendees.

She ran her finger down the list, trying to remember
each student. 'He just came in to leave some work . . . I
don't remember him . . . she had an appointment with David
Matthews . . . then this girl, Sarah, she was here till the end.
That's about it, I think.' The name didn't seem to register
with her.

'Did anyone come in late, towards the end?'

She frowned, thinking, then her face brightened as she
remembered. 'Debbie Sykes brought some students in about
eight, eight-fifteen. They went through the fire door – they
weren't using the machines.'

'Anyone after Deborah?' That memory of Debbie was
good, it would help Sheila to pinpoint the evening in
her mind. She shook her head. No one after Debbie. He
talked her through the system for using the room, booking
people in and out, keeping an eye on who had access to the
equipment. It was a vanilla system, but it seemed to work.
'You don't book me in when I come in,' he said. 'Is that
policy?'

'Oh, we don't book in the staff. Well, the teaching staff we
do, but the technicians and the caretakers are in and out all
the time. We don't book them in.'

He had to be careful now, make sure she gave him an
accurate answer. 'Can you remember if anyone like that came
in on that Thursday? Say, after Deborah Sykes brought her
students in?'

She thought again. 'I wouldn't really notice, if they didn't
stop to talk. I think one of the caretakers might have come

in.' She closed her eyes, trying to picture it. 'I really can't remember,' she said, shaking her head apologetically.

'Thanks, Sheila, that's helpful. Let me know if you remember anything else.'

She smiled at him. 'Is there a problem? I mean, was there a problem?'

No point in alarming anyone. 'No, I'm just taking a look at some of these rooms. I don't think it's a good idea that you're alone in here of an evening, for one thing.'

She nodded and leant across the desk confidentially. She lowered her voice. 'I don't usually work evenings, but Elaine says they used to get all sorts coming in at one time. It's been better since they've closed off some of the entrances. But it isn't very nice. You've got no back-up if there's trouble.'

He hesitated. 'I'll see what I can do,' he promised. 'I'm just going to have a look at the fire escape, OK?' She gave him a quick smile and turned back to her screen.

The long staircase looked as though no one had opened the door since he'd been through it before Christmas. The broken light fitting still dangled unrepaired. He wondered if Berryman had kept his promise about getting the light fitting checked. Neave thought for a minute. If the person who'd damaged the light was a standard student vandal, there'd be prints on the fitting. If it was someone else, then the fitting would probably be wiped clean. He needed to know that at least.

Berryman looked at the map that Lynne was showing him. 'McCarthy thinks that Kate may have got off the train here,' she said, pointing to Kirk Sandall. 'Now look.' She ran her finger along the line west of Kirk Sandall, and down a freight line that ran off it. The freight line ran south-west past the mine at Armthorpe, past Bessacar and then joined up with another freight line just by the lake where Kate's body had been found.

McCarthy leaned over the map. 'And look, sir,' he said, leaning forward round Lynne. 'Here – Mandy.' Berryman looked where he was pointing, at the freight line branching off close to the spot where the killer had left the remains of

Amanda Varney. 'And,' McCarthy went on, 'look at the siding near Rawmarsh. Freight lines run off the junction there.'

'It can't be a coincidence.' Lynne stood back from the map. 'We think this man could be a driver for one of the freight companies, and he's using those trains to move around the tracks.'

'OK.' Berryman could buy that. 'That's worth following up. But there's still Lisa, remember. And you haven't solved the main problem. He can't be driving those trains and killing women at stations at the same time, right? A train isn't something you can park up for half an hour until you need it again.' He looked at them. 'Come on, this has to be something. Think. What is he doing?' Lynne shook her head in baffled frustration.

'Right. You two get on to the freight companies now. Any that run traffic along these lines. You want times and dates, and you want employees – anyone who'd know the schedules.'

The start of term came with a change in the weather. From the freezing cold of December, January brought grey skies and rain. The day barely got light and progressed in grey dullness until what light there was faded into the late-afternoon darkness. The weather seemed to have affected the mood of the people coming back to City. The students, who normally provided the noise, the colour and the light, were dull and apathetic – either sullen and uncooperative or oppressed by work. They caught the more general feeling of darkness that hung about the college with the knowledge that one of their number had died, had been murdered, within a mile or two of the college doors.

As Debbie walked towards the Broome building, she looked up at the dark windows watching her, and was reminded of that sense of menace that had haunted her last term. She was glad to collide with Louise, who was struggling up the steps with boxes, bags and a briefcase. 'Holiday work,' she explained breathlessly, 'in case I ran out of things to do.' Debbie took one of the boxes and a couple of bags, and pushed open one of the double doors into the building with her shoulder. They dumped their burden on the table that stood in the entrance hall.

'I knew I shouldn't have tried to bring that lot in all at once,' Louise conceded, looking at the pile. 'I just couldn't face two trips to the car park. It's my day for the top car park,' she added.

'You should have asked one of the caretakers. Come on, let's get it along to the staff room.' Debbie balanced one of the bags on top of a box.

'There was only Les, and I didn't want to be responsible for the hernia.' Louise looked over Debbie's shoulder. 'Salvation. Rob, you'll give us a hand with these, won't you?'

Debbie was unprepared. She turned round and saw him standing in the entrance. He gave her a neutral smile and looked at Louise. 'I wouldn't worry too much about Les getting a hernia. He makes sure he's at no risk. Where do you want them?'

'Staff room for the moment, thanks. Did you have a good Christmas?' Louise began to sort the stuff into bags and boxes.

'I'll go and open up the staff room.' Debbie grabbed a couple of bags and fled. When her eyes had met Rob's, briefly, she had had a sudden memory of his eyes looking into hers in the firelight, and had felt herself going red. She was sitting at her desk looking at her post by the time he came through the door with the boxes, followed by Louise who was carrying the bags and her briefcase. He put them down on Louise's desk.

'That's fine, thanks,' Louise said. 'I'll sort them at lunchtime. So, what's new in City, then?' She took off her coat and unwound the scarf from round her neck.

'Same old stuff. I can't stay, I've got a meeting.' He gave Debbie a quick nod of acknowledgement and was gone. Debbie stared fixedly at her post, waiting for Louise's comment.

'Well . . .' Louise hung up her coat. 'So who's been rattling *his* cage?'

'He's probably just busy,' Debbie said, staring blankly at the memo in her hand.

148

'Probably,' Louise agreed. 'By the way, that's just an out-of-date Happy Christmas wish from our principal.' Debbie looked at her. 'You seemed to be riveted by it, that's all.' Louise raised an eyebrow at her and turned to her own post.

Debbie finished going through the pile on her desk. There was very little that was important, apart from a memo summoning all the staff to a meeting in the North building lecture theatre that lunchtime. There was another memo from Peter Davis, expressing *deep regret about the recent tragedy* and taking the opportunity to remind the staff that they were contractually bound not to talk to the press without the principal's express permission. It also gave the date and time of the funeral. *Staff who worked with this student may attend if they have no teaching obligations at this time. A representative from the college will be in attendance.* Debbie didn't care about timetables. She was going anyway. She heard Louise's snort of derision and looked across. 'He's got the soul of a tax accountant,' Louise said. '*If they have no teaching obligations,* my arse. You want to go, don't you, Debbie?'

'Yes. Of course.' Debbie was glad she was going to have Louise's support.

'Well, go. Let's not make an official thing about it if you *are* teaching then. I'll sort something out on the QT. Have you got the memo about the full staff meeting at lunchtime?'

Debbie nodded. 'What do you think it's about?' It was unusual for a principal's meeting to be called at the beginning of the winter term. He usually confined them to the beginning of the academic year, when the staff were assembled for a routine pep talk and what Louise described as an orgy of management self-congratulation.

'Bad news, I should think.' Louise frowned. 'I haven't heard anything, but I think the union is calling a meeting for later.'

Debbie shelved that problem and pulled out her teaching file, wondering what to do with the A-level group that morning. It didn't seem right to carry on as usual, but they couldn't spend two and a half hours talking about Sarah. She decided that they'd go on with 'The Rime of the Ancient Mariner'. They'd nearly finished the poem, and the sense of peace and resolution that the ending gave would be appropriate. They had their exam all too soon. They needed to work.

In the event, they were subdued, did what Debbie asked them, worked, but were unresponsive, as though the spark of interest that always made this group so lively and unpredictable had gone. Debbie could understand that. She'd said a bit about Sarah at the beginning of the session, but after break she said, 'Listen, I want to send some flowers from the class, not just from me. Who wants to put their name on the card?' She'd bought a card at the weekend. She got it out of her bag and circulated it round the group for them to sign their names and write messages. She'd already decided that the class was over for the morning, and when they'd written the card and made contributions for the flowers, she set them some reading and told them they could go.

Leanne hung back briefly. 'Sarah was looking for you at the end of term. She said there was something she had to tell you.' She looked a question at Debbie.

'I didn't see her.' Debbie shook her head in confusion. Leanne shrugged her shoulders and followed Rachel and Adam down the corridor. Debbie locked the classroom door and walked down the long corridor, dim in the winter light. For a moment, she had a feeling that someone was behind her, but when she turned round, the corridor was empty.

The lecture theatre filled up with people. The light on the tiers of seating was dim compared with the bright light on the stage with its lecterns and screen. Debbie came in with Louise, and they looked for places to sit among the two hundred or so people who worked at the college in different capacities. Most faces looked apprehensive or gloomy. Debbie saw Tim Godber sitting near the back at the end of a row, where he could make a quick getaway. He waved to her, and gestured urgently that she should go and sit with him. She ignored him. If Tim had something to say to her, he could come over and say it. She and Louise went across to sit behind Trish. 'What's going on?' Louise asked. Trish always knew.

Louise had been right. It was bad news. Funding was

down, costs were up and it looked as though redundancies were inevitable.

Debbie found it hard to concentrate on what the principal was saying. She didn't want to think about the implications for her own life of losing her job. She listened enough to find out that there was an anticipated month of restructuring before decisions would be made, redundancy notices issued and appeals heard. She'd better start applying for jobs. There was very little chance of work in South Yorkshire. She'd have to move. What about her house? At least houses like hers were still selling. How long would it take to get a job? Most jobs were for a September start. What could she do in the meantime?

The people around her began to move, and she realized that the meeting was over. There was a babble of voices as people began to discuss the implications of what was happening. Someone touched her arm and she jumped. She looked behind her. Tim Godber was signalling to her to wait outside the theatre for him. Maybe it was important. Maybe it was something about Sarah. He'd seen her in the last week, when Debbie hadn't.

He caught up with her in the North canteen. 'Have you got time for a coffee?' He looked a bit apologetic, a bit uncertain. Debbie's inconvenient soft-heartedness was aroused.

'I'm not sure. What did you want to see me about?'

'Do I need a reason?' He smiled tentatively. 'I want to apologize.'

That did sound like bullshit, but Debbie couldn't bring herself to snub him when he was making the effort, and agreed to a coffee. 'I've only got about fifteen minutes, though.'

They sat down at one of the tables. The room was large with a tiled, floor and tended to echo. Conversation was difficult unless you sat close to the person you were talking to. Debbie opted for shouting, and pushed her chair back a bit as Tim moved his forward. She was reflecting on the potential for farce if she and Tim ended up in a chase and retreat round the table, but he acknowledged her unspoken wish and instead leant forward across the table towards her. 'I really am sorry, Debbie,' he said. 'I just saw a story and went for it. I wanted to apologize at the time, but I didn't know how.'

'*Sorry* usually does it quite well.' Debbie wasn't letting him get away with that.

'Yes, OK. Don't be hard, Debbie, it doesn't suit you. You sound like your gorgon-lady colleague.'

Debbie was torn between being offended on Louise's behalf and reflecting that Louise would be pleased to know that Tim thought she was a gorgon. 'OK, you've apologized. I accept your apology. Is that all?'

She could tell that she'd annoyed him, but he kept his temper. 'I wanted to say how sorry I am about your student, Sarah. I didn't really know her – but I used to teach her. She was in my media group last year. For a while.'

'Louise said she was talking to you at the end of last term,' Debbie said. She was surprised when Tim looked taken aback. It seemed a strange reaction. Maybe Louise had got it wrong – or maybe it was just that he didn't like Louise. 'She didn't come to class, you see, and I wondered if she was looking for me.'

Tim was staring into his cup, frowning. He looked up. 'No, no, it was nothing really. Well, she was looking for you to tell you why she'd missed her class. She was worried you'd be angry with her, so I just said some soothing words about what a nice person you were.'

That last bit *was* bullshit. Debbie was surprised that Sarah had been worried enough to come into college. She'd missed classes before. All the students did from time to time. Debbie rarely got heavy with them about it – she understood the pressure they were under. 'Is that all she wanted?'

'All she told me about,' Tim said lightly. 'I'm not saying there wasn't something else, but if there was, she didn't tell me.'

That would fit. If there had been something worrying Sarah, she would have to talk to someone she trusted. It had taken Debbie the best part of two years to win Sarah's trust – she wouldn't be likely to confide in Tim. Debbie shook her head. It was a mystery and one she'd like to solve – she felt that she had somehow let Sarah down. Perhaps she'd talked to the other students. She looked across at Tim. 'Did she seem upset, worried?'

'No, not really. She just wanted to let you know about the class.'

That didn't seem right. Tim had said that Sarah *was* worried. A strand of Debbie's hair had escaped from its mooring, and she twisted it round her fingers. There was nothing she could do for now. She changed the subject. 'What about the meeting? What do you make of it?'

'Oh, it's the usual. Give them the option of getting it wrong or getting it right, and they'll go for getting it wrong every time. It's no skin off my nose. My work's expanding here. If they try to make me redundant, they'll be in trouble. I've got plans, anyway.'

'I've got to go.' Debbie had had enough of Tim. She picked up her bag and stood up. He jumped to his feet.

'I'll come across with you,' he said. Debbie couldn't think of any way to refuse. His staff room was in the same building as hers. As they waited to cross the road, Debbie saw Rob crossing from the other side. He saw her and gave her that same rather closed smile. Debbie glanced at Tim and caught him looking at her speculatively. She felt her face going red again. *Shit*. As they were going up the steps into the Broome building, Tim said, 'Fancy a drink sometime?'

'No.' Debbie was certain about that. She didn't want to get into a discussion about it, and she didn't want to be emollient about it. 'I'm teaching now. Bye, Tim.'

Well, it could have gone better, but it could certainly have gone worse. He'd established that he and Debbie were talking to each other again. Now he had to get round her prickliness and hostility. He'd hoped for an evening over a few glasses of wine, maybe a club or some food afterwards, reinstate their on-again off-again relationship. Tim wasn't too worried. He could charm Debbie again. Now for the other problems. He should have been ready for that question about the Peterson girl. Trust that eagle-eyed cow to spot him! And what was the situation with Debbie and Neave? The encounter outside the college didn't look too friendly. With a bit of luck it, whatever it was, was over – if it had been anything in the first place.

He sat at his desk and thought. He *wanted* that big story. Berryman could cut him out, but he had something real, something that no one but he knew. Someone was following Debbie, and he had a good idea who that someone was. He'd planned to talk to the Peterson girl again, but she'd got herself killed. He'd been worried about that at first, worried that the Strangler had got her. When it turned out to be the boyfriend and he'd had a fright for nothing, he'd been angry. Of course, it was a terrible tragedy, but he hadn't been sure how long his stopper would have worked. She couldn't have been too bright to have fallen for it in the first place, and she was bound to have mentioned the whole thing to somebody soon. Well, she wouldn't now. But he needed more information, he needed something that would stand up before he could write his story. He'd show Berryman up. He imagined his headline. *Blunderman bungles in Strangler killings.*

Tim hadn't wasted his Christmas. He'd spent a lot of time with a computer friend, and a lot of time trawling round some not-so-public files. The result of that was he'd met up with – more by good judgement than luck – a clerk who worked for the local police, one who worked with Berryman's team, to be exact. He hadn't said anything to her yet about the case, but he was planning to work round to it that night, ask her how things were going after they'd had a few drinks, see how she responded. She was plain, plump, quiet. He was reasonably confident she'd give him what he wanted. He smiled. It should be easy.

The first days back after a break were always difficult, but this particular start of term had been worse than most. By Wednesday, Louise and Debbie were exhausted, and in an almost unspoken agreement, they ended the day at six o'clock in a wine bar in the town centre. 'Dan says I'm turning into an alcoholic,' Louise said gloomily. 'He's probably right.'

'That's what my mum says,' Debbie agreed. 'Oh, God, what a week. I saw the A-level group on Monday. I didn't know what to say to them.'

154

They talked about Sarah for a while, but Debbie was relieved when the topic changed to the problems at City.

'You really do need to move on,' Louise advised her. 'Even if your job was safe – and you don't need me to tell you what's happening – you'll stagnate here. You need to expand your experience, get some management responsibility, go somewhere where they'll appreciate you.'

'I know.' Debbie was beginning to realize this. 'I just hate the thought of leaving. I've got a house, friends, a life – I'm happy here.'

'It's none of my business, but you don't seem too happy at the moment.' Louise looked at her. 'You've been down for a while, and at the end of last term you looked really low. I can probably put a name to the problem, as well. Rob Neave, right?'

Debbie felt herself going red. 'Is it that obvious?' she said, angry with herself.

Louise raised an eyebrow. 'I may not be a counsellor for Relate,' she said, 'but when two people who seemed to be getting on fine suddenly grow two left feet in each other's company, then I draw my own conclusions.' She looked at Debbie and added more seriously, 'I hope you know what you're doing.' Debbie stared into her wine glass. 'You can tell me to mind my own business,' Louise added. 'Probably will. But I'm worried about you.'

Debbie sighed. 'I did start something with Rob, but it sort of stopped before it really got anywhere. It was just the wrong set of circumstances at the wrong time, or it never would have happened.'

'Oh, I expect it would,' said Louise. 'It's been a disaster waiting to happen for weeks. Look, in my capacity as nosy friend and line manager, I've been asking a few questions and calling in a bit of old gossip.' She stopped Debbie's protest with a look. 'You probably think you don't want to know, but you should. Rob Neave, he's a lovely man, I grant you that, but he's had a rough life. He's quite damaged, I think.'

'I know about his wife and his little girl,' Debbie said. 'He told me. That was why . . .'

Louise nodded. 'I'd kind of worked that out,' she said.

'There's a bit more, if you want me to tell you.' Reluctantly, Debbie nodded. 'Well, for a start, he was brought up in a series of children's homes, which isn't the best background to have. Not that I'm blaming him for that, you understand. But I talked to Claire – she's married to someone who used to work with him. Apparently her husband and Neave, they used to hang out together, did all the usual man stuff, women, booze, you know. Claire said that all the women fancied Neave, but she thought he was a cold-hearted bastard. That was before she and Mick were married – she was just a clerical officer, a civilian, but she saw a lot.'

'That was ages ago,' Debbie said.

'Oh, yes,' Louise agreed. 'I'm just giving you some background. Well, it seems that all this changed when Neave met his wife. He was bowled over, Claire said. He stopped going out, stopped going to the pub with the lads, stopped socializing with his colleagues. It's an important thing in the police – a kind of mutual-support thing. You tend to stick to your own, so that didn't go down too well. Claire said that it was fine by her – it slowed Mick down enough for her to grab him on his way past – but it caused a bit of resentment.'

'I know he hasn't got over it yet. I don't think he ever will.' Debbie was thinking about his face as he talked to her in the pub that Friday.

'Claire showed me this. I asked if I could borrow it.' Louise got an envelope out of her bag. 'It was taken just over two years ago.' She took a photograph out of the envelope and passed it over to Debbie. It showed a couple on a beach. It looked like one of those fine days of early winter, because the light was brilliant, sparkling off the sea, but the sun was low in the sky and the couple were wearing gloves and scarves. The man was standing behind the woman with his arms round her waist, laughing at something behind the camera. She was leaning back against him, one hand shielding her eyes, obscuring them with a band of shadow. The bright light seemed to have bleached all the colour from her, except for her hair which was a red-gold blaze. Debbie tried to get some sense of the woman's face, but there was nothing to see, just shadows. Rob Neave and his wife. He looked so young, so happy. Louise took it from her. 'Just two years ago, and it changed him that much,' she said. 'Do you see what I mean?'

Debbie did. She looked at Louise, waiting. Louise took the picture back, looked at it again and went on, 'He wasn't equipped to cope with any of it, I shouldn't think, poor bastard. You don't learn a lot about relationships in a children's home. What you learn is how to survive. Which is just about what he's doing.' She looked pointedly at Debbie. 'You've got to survive as well.' She put the photograph back into the envelope. 'You wouldn't believe the problems I had getting that lot out of Claire without her cottoning on why I wanted it. When I asked for the photograph I think she thought I was after him myself.'

Debbie had to know. 'What was she like? His wife, I mean.'

'I don't know. I never met her. I was never in that crowd. I just know Claire. Claire didn't like her – said she was arty, bohemian. Not Claire's type, in other words. She was a musician. Played the violin, I think, and very well by all accounts. She was in her last year at university when she met Rob. Mick described her as weird, but he didn't define his terms. I don't know what he thought about her, apart from that. One thing Claire did say, she was beautiful.'

Strangely, that bit hurt. Debbie could cope with the idea that this woman had been talented and artistic in ways that she herself was not, but the idea of her being beautiful was harder.

'I'm pathetic,' she told Louise. 'I'm jealous of her. She's dead, her child's dead and I'm jealous.'

'You're human.' Louise had no patience with self-castigation. 'What, specifically, are you jealous of? That he was in love with her? At least it shows he's capable of it, and I can tell you, Claire never thought he was before.'

Debbie pulled a face. 'That she was beautiful, actually,' she said. 'I told you I was pathetic.'

'Yes, you are, but it's par for the course. I'd be at a bit of a loss if you were going green about her musicianship, but her being beautiful shouldn't present you with any problems.' Louise looked at Debbie for a moment. 'I'm not trying to interfere. I just think you need to know what you're getting into.'

'I don't think there's anything to get into any more.' Debbie sighed. 'I told you, it's over before it really began.'

'Oh, I wouldn't bank on that,' said Louise.

Gina Sykes sat in front of her fire, reading the paper. The house felt unbearably quiet. Some nights it seemed empty, then she would put on some music, turn on the television, to give the illusion of company. Tonight, though, the quietness disturbed her. It was a waiting kind of silence. She didn't like it. She kept looking over her shoulder, thinking someone had come in through the door. She looked at the clock. It was midnight. Maybe she should just go to bed. The stuff for her nightcap was all set out in the kitchen, the cup with the cocoa mixed to a cream with a little milk and a measure of rum, the milk in the saucepan waiting to be heated. She liked to drink her cocoa in bed then read until she felt sleepy. She lit the gas under the milk and watched to make sure it didn't boil. The taste of boiled milk spoiled the taste of the cocoa. Just as the milk began to foam, she poured it over the cocoa in her cup, stirring it to make it dissolve. The smell of the alcohol was very strong. She liked the smell of rum. It reminded her of Christmas.

Christmases with Gerry, and with Debbie when she was little. Debbie used to love Christmas. It had been the same every Christmas morning, the excited whisper from the bedroom door – *has he been yet, has he been?* – and Gerry's groan of despair as he looked at the clock. She remembered the war of attrition – *has he been now?* – at carefully calculated intervals until the required permission to open the stocking had been obtained. Debbie loved presents, she still did. Gina nodded. The new dress had been just right for Debbie. That blue was the perfect colour.

She put her drink on a tray along with her book and tea things for the morning, then she went up to her bedroom. She lay in bed, sipping her nightcap and turning the pages of her book in a distracted way. She was still thinking about Debbie. This man – Gina felt uneasy about him. Was it that

158

that was making Debbie so unhappy? Was it the problems at work? Her mind wandered on. She sipped her drink. She'd certainly had a generous hand with the rum bottle tonight, or perhaps she hadn't made the cocoa quite strong enough. She finished it. She really ought to go and clean her teeth, but she felt so drowsy that she couldn't be bothered. She felt quite tipsy, in fact. She turned the light off and drifted into sleep.

Then she was wide awake. She reached instinctively, as she always did when she woke suddenly, to Gerry's side of the bed, but of course he wasn't there. What had woken her? Her head ached and swam, as though she'd had a bottle of rum, not one drink. She listened. There was a noise from the other bedroom, from the room Debbie slept in when she stayed. Gina frowned. Had Debbie stayed? She shook her head to clear it. No, of course she hadn't. She heard the noise again, like – she couldn't identify it, rhythmic, quiet but quite distinct. She was too fuddled to feel afraid. She swung her legs over the side of the bed and pushed her feet into her slippers. Her eyes wouldn't focus properly. Quietly, using the light from the lamppost outside her window, she crossed the narrow landing at the top of the stairs, pushed the door of the other bedroom open and turned on the light.

He was kneeling on the floor by the bed. He had those photographs of Debbie when they were on holiday, the ones in the bikini, his trousers were open, he was . . . His face turned towards her. His expression, slack and vacant, changed to one of anger and surprise. Gina took a breath as he got quickly to his feet, and before she could speak or move his fist slammed into the side of her head.

He's angry. He's taken risks to use this key, and now he's been found, been seen and . . . And he hasn't found anything useful. He thought he'd tipped enough vodka into the milk to knock her out for the night. He looks at the unconscious woman on the stairs. She's drunk and disgusting. Will she remember? He can't take the risk. He bundles the photographs back into the drawer where he found them and snaps off the light. He looks at the staircase, precipitous and narrow as they always are in these houses. Small and skimped.

159

Like mother, like daughter. She's halfway down the stairs. He goes down and looks at her. Though he's bruised her he hasn't broken the skin, and her hair is thick enough to conceal the fact that she was hit with a fist — luck, but use it. She moans. He's breathing faster now. He doesn't like to be rushed, not if he hasn't planned things. Think. He knows what he's got to do. He knows how to do this. He reaches for her . . .

She rolls the rest of the way down the stairs, and yes, her head hangs loose. He follows. He feels her pulse. Faint, racing, going, going . . . It excites him. It reminds him of a hunt. But now is not the time.

He waits until he's certain she's dead. Some people might have panicked, but the hunter knows how to deal with the unexpected. Has he left any traces? Few, if any. Will they even look? He checks his watch. One-thirty. He decides to leave it as it is. He knows when to stay and when to go. He slips out of the back door, pulling it shut behind him, double locking it on the Yale. He can't think of a way to bolt it. It's a dark, starless night. No one is likely to see him, but he stays in the unlit gennel until he is some way from the house.

12
_____

Late on Thursday afternoon, Debbie was trying to interest her tutorial group in planning their university applications. She always felt at a low ebb at this time, knowing that she still had several hours of work ahead of her and wouldn't be home until gone ten. She was organizing the group into subject areas, when Sheila, the departmental secretary, came to the classroom door. Debbie broke off what she was saying and, slightly puzzled, went over to Sheila. 'Hang on a minute,' she said to her class, and the low murmur of chat that had been annoying her rose as the students realized they had an unofficial break.

Sheila said, 'Sorry to disturb you, but can you go to Peter Davis's room?'

Debbie was surprised that Sheila had interrupted her tutorial for that. 'Yes, sure, tell him I'll be along in' – she checked her watch – 'half an hour, if I haven't killed this lot before then.'

'No, he wants you to come now. He said to send your students across to the library.' Sheila gestured to indicate that she didn't know what was going on.

'OK.' Debbie thought hard. She hadn't done anything to warrant a summons like this – _leave your class_ was serious. She wondered if she ought to take her union rep. with her. 'OK,' she said again, more loudly this time. 'Something's come up and we're going to have to finish early.' She ignored the ironic cheer that went up. 'I want you to go over to the library and spend the rest of the session with the UCAS handbooks. I want _everyone_ to have a shortlist of institutions by next week.' She heard Matthew Price saying to Darren Wilde,

'Wormwood Scrubs, Strangeways, Wakefield High Security,' and, reflecting that he was probably right, Debbie hurried up the stairs to the head of department's office.

As she stepped through the door, she saw Peter Davis, Louise and two police officers. She stared for a minute, then her stomach lurched as the significance of this hit home. 'What's wrong?' she said. Her voice seemed to come from far away, but she felt very calm, very detached.

'Miss Sykes?' One of the officers, a woman, came forward. 'I'm afraid I have some bad news for you about your mother, Gina Sykes. There's been an accident . . .'

Debbie knew then that Gina was dead. She nodded. She felt very cold, and everything was crystal clear. 'What happened?'

The policewoman said something about a fall, something about a neighbour and an ambulance, some other things that Debbie listened to, nodded at and didn't take in. She understood that her mother had been dead by the time they got her to the hospital. 'I must go,' she said, 'to the hospital, I must see her.'

The policewoman took her arm. 'Are you up to it? We'll take you.' She was quiet, efficient. Debbie was glad of that.

Louise said, 'I'll come with you, Debbie. Don't worry, I'll come along and do whatever's necessary.' Debbie nodded again. She needed Louise's good sense here. Peter Davis was saying something about being sorry, not to worry about her classes, fluttering around nervously in the background. She walked out of the office, the WPC still holding her arm. She was surprised to find she needed the support. Louise was behind her. 'I'll get your things, Debbie, and follow on in the car. I'll be at the hospital soon.' She checked with the other officer: 'Moreham General?'

As they came down the stairs, she saw Rob Neave stepping out of the lift, his eyes widening with surprise as he witnessed the scene. Debbie was aware of Louise stopping, talking to him, as she went down the stairs with the woman still holding her arm, the man following behind. *It must look as though I've been arrested.* Debbie found this funny and wanted to giggle for a moment. Nothing seemed real. It all seemed very far away.

162

She heard Louise's footsteps hurrying on the stairs. 'I'll be there,' Louise called, and ran towards the staff room.

At the hospital, things seemed to start moving more quickly, people came and went, talked to her, asked her questions. The policewoman said something about identifying the body. She said, *Yes. Yes.* Someone gave her a cup of tea. A nurse was standing beside her. 'Are you sure you're ready now?' she asked. Debbie nodded, and went down a corridor with her. There was a lift and more doors, then she was standing by a bed with a sheeted figure on it.

If her horny feet protrude, they come
to show how cold she is, and dumb

The words flashed into Debbie's mind. 'Let be be finale of seem. The only emperor is the emperor of ice cream.' She didn't realize she'd spoken aloud until she saw the nurse looking at her. 'It's a poem,' she said. The nurse nodded, still watching her. Then she carefully pulled back the sheet from the face on the bed, and time lurched into place.

Debbie had been thinking about her mother, about the days they had spent together over Christmas, about the book she had given her for Christmas, about how she had liked it; and she had been thinking about her mother being dead, and the thoughts didn't seem to gel but ran on parallel lines in her mind. She looked at the face. It was waxy-white, blue-tinged around the lips. The jaw hung slackly, the eyes were half closed and vacant. Her hair, her rich dark curls, looked dull and lifeless. Lifeless. Of course. It was her mother, and yet she couldn't imagine anything less like her mother. She would have to write to the phone company to tell them not to worry about the faulty line. She would have to . . . Her mind ground to a halt. She didn't know what to do next.

The policewoman was standing beside Debbie. 'Is this your mother, Mrs Gina Sykes?' she asked quietly.

'Yes,' Debbie said.

Then she was in the car with Louise. She remembered talking to a man, someone from the police, a nurse said, who was telling her what happened. She couldn't understand much.

'It looks as though your mother got up in the night and fell down the stairs. Did she always have a drink before she went to bed?'

'She often had cocoa with a tot of rum,' Debbie said.

'She maybe overdid it a bit,' the man said. He didn't seem to hear what Debbie was saying. 'We're looking into it, Miss Sykes, but it looks like an accident, a tragic accident.'

'What did he mean?' Debbie asked Louise later in the car.

'I think he thought she was drunk,' Louise said.

It was dark by the time they got to Debbie's house. 'Do you want to come back with me for the night?' Louise asked. 'You're welcome to our spare room. I'd stay here, but I can't get in touch with Dan to let him know.' The house was cold. Louise went over to the fire to light it.

'No, leave it,' Debbie said.

Louise looked at her. 'OK,' she said after a moment. 'Let me get you something. You look awful. You're white as a sheet.'

'Just . . . I'd like a large whisky. There's a bottle in the cupboard.' Gina's Christmas present to Debbie. Gina never got drunk. Louise got the bottle out and poured two drinks.

'What about tonight?' Louise asked again.

Debbie looked round her. She wanted to be at home, not anywhere else. She didn't want to wake up in a strange bed, have to cope with Dan's embarrassed sympathy. She wanted to be alone and think about her mother, and about her father. What would he have thought? How would he have coped with it? She felt angry with him for not being here. She needed him. 'I really think I'd rather stay here. Thanks.'

Louise was concerned. 'Are you sure that's a good idea? Look, I can stay anyway. I'll get in touch with Dan later. He'll be back after midnight. I'll phone him then. Or I'll get a neighbour to leave a note.'

'No, really, I want to be on my own. I really do, Louise.' Debbie was determined, and Louise gave in reluctantly.

'Well, all right, but have another drink and then get your-self off to bed. Get enough of this inside you to knock you out for tonight. I'll phone in the morning.' She filled Debbie's glass again then began to gather her things together. 'I'll phone . . .' she said, and stopped for a moment. 'I'll phone you in the morning.'

Debbie waited until she was gone, then sat down. Being alone had seemed important, but now she couldn't remember what it was she wanted to do. She drained her glass and filled it again. She picked it up and walked through to the kitchen, swallowing half the contents in one gulp. She could feel it starting to warm her now. Her face felt wet, and she realized she was crying. She didn't feel as though she was crying. The tears just seemed to run down her face. She went back into the middle room and put her glass down on the table. It was empty. She looked at it and wondered if she should drink any more, then she filled her glass again.

The house felt dark and silent. Being alone didn't seem like such a good idea any more. She ought to go to bed, Louise was right, but she didn't want to go up the stairs into that dark emptiness. Except it wasn't emptiness. There was something up there waiting for her. Things that watched her. Dark things that jumped out of shadows, Sarah on her lonely path, her mother on the dark stairway. There was a pattern that she couldn't quite see. She drank the whisky and poured more into her glass. Maybe if she turned the light on – but she didn't want to do that, be in the glare, in the view, while things peered at her from the dark outside. She could close the curtains, but then they would know she was there. It was very cold. She sat in the chair and drank more whisky, drawing her legs up under herself for warmth. She sat there shivering, staring into the darkness.

Some time later – how much later she couldn't really tell – the doorbell rang. Debbie shook her head to clear it, and stood up, staggering a bit as she found her feet. It was hard in the dark. The bell rang again. 'Coming, I'm coming,' she mumbled. It was cold. The fire wasn't lit. She went into the kitchen and squinted at the door. 'Who is it?' It didn't come out too clearly. She realized that tears were running down her face again, and brushed them away.

'Rob. Rob Neave. Let me in.'

She stood there for a moment trying to think, then she

took the key off the hook by the door, and tried to put it in the key hole. She missed the first couple of times, but got the door open on the third try. She stood in the doorway blinking, as he stepped round her into the kitchen and closed the door behind him. 'Rob,' she said. 'Did you know . . . how did you know . . .' She couldn't work out how to say it.

'Louise told me you were on your own. I don't think that's a good idea. Come on, Debs, come and sit down.' He steered her back into the middle room, sat her down in a chair and passed her the box of tissues. She realized she was crying again, and ineffectually mopped her face. 'I brought something to drink, but I don't think you need it.'

He lit the fire and went out of the room. She heard his feet on the path and a car door slam. He came back a few moments later with a travel rug which he wrapped round her shoulders. 'It's cold in here. You're frozen.' Debbie tried to say something, but nothing coherent came out. She could hear him moving round the room, drawing the curtains and closing the door. The haunted emptiness felt further away now. She was so tired.

She closed her eyes and leant back in the chair, feeling the warmth of the fire and the blanket wrapped round her. She dropped into blackness and then she was wide awake again and she saw her mother's face, the mouth gaping, the lips tinged blue. 'Is this your mother, Mrs Gina Sykes?' *Yes, yes, yes!* Her eyes snapped open and she was in her own house again, someone moving behind her in the kitchen, the overhead light off. Who was it? Louise? No, she'd sent Louise away.

Rob came through from the kitchen. He looked at her. 'I thought you might need this tonight.' He smiled at her, holding her hot-water bottle.

'Rob,' she said. There was something she wanted to ask him, but she couldn't remember what it was.

'Come on.' He helped her to stand up. 'It's gone midnight. You need to try and get some sleep.' Get some sleep. She was afraid of being asleep. He was guiding her over towards the stairs. 'Come on, Debs, you need to lie down.' He was right, she did. She couldn't stand up. He looked at the whisky bottle as he steered her past the small table with her photographs on. 'Did you drink all that tonight?' She shook her head. She didn't know. She couldn't remember. She tried to turn back to get Gina's photograph but he was firmly guiding her towards the stairs. 'Hold on to the rail, Debs.' He came up the stairs beside her, one arm supporting her against the handrail, holding her arm with his other hand. She could feel that clearly.

Then she was lying on her bed, the room spinning. 'Oh, God.' She sat up. 'I'm going to be sick.' He held her head over the wastebin as she threw up. 'Pure whisky,' he said. 'You'll be better for that tomorrow.'

'Sorry, I'm sorry.' She was shivering, her teeth chattering.

'Drink this.' He was holding her hands round a cool glass. She sipped the water, feeling the nausea subsiding a bit. 'Try and drink some more, Debs. As much as you can. You're going to feel like shit in the morning.' She didn't care. She felt tears running down her face again, then she was lying down and it was too warm. She threw the covers off, and someone put them back over her again and then the room started spinning, slowly then more quickly, then she was falling into the blackness and she wasn't there any more.

13

Debbie felt terrible. Her head ached and she felt sick. There had been a brief moment of warmth and comfort, and then she was awake with a sense of dread lurking behind the sheer physical misery. She'd been drunk. Something terrible had happened. She struggled into a sitting position, holding her head to stop it from pounding itself apart. Saliva rushed into her mouth, and she just made it into the bathroom before she threw up. She thought it was over, then the nausea hit her again and she was left hanging over the toilet bowl, dry retching, a disgusting taste in her mouth and an acid burn in her throat. She slumped on to the floor, supporting herself on the seat, breathing deeply, waiting for the sickness and headache to retreat. She knew what had happened now. She was mourning her mother collapsed on the bathroom floor after drinking herself into oblivion. Gina, she reflected, would not have been surprised. *I want my mum!*

She got a grip on her emotions. Everyone said that crying was good for you, crying got it – whatever *it* was – out of your system. After her father had died, it seemed to Debbie that all crying did was make your eyes swell, your nose red and your face wet. It didn't make you feel any better. She took stock. It was late morning – she'd slept for a long time. She was wearing a T-shirt and pants. She vaguely remembered someone had put her to bed. She wasn't sure if she remembered who it was, or if she was remembering a dream. She stood under the shower, letting the water wake and refresh her. A cold shower was supposed to be good for a hangover, but she felt bad enough as it was. The warmth of the water was comforting. She wrapped her hair in a towel,

168

pulled on a clean sweatshirt and a pair of jeans and went downstairs.

The fire was lit and turned low. Rob was sitting in front of it flicking through the pages of her *Othello*. He looked at her appraisingly and said, 'Bad?'

Debbie nodded. 'Did you stay last night?'

'Spent the night in this chair.' He smiled, but his eyes looked tired and he was unshaven.

She didn't know what to say. 'Thank you. For coming round, I mean. I got really drunk. I'm sorry.'

He shrugged. 'Best thing to do. Louise was worried about you. She was right. You shouldn't have been alone. Do you want something to eat?' Debbie shuddered and he grinned sympathetically. 'Thought not. Look, I've been monitoring the phone. Louise called – I said you were still asleep. She'll phone later. The police want to talk to you. They're coming round this afternoon unless you aren't up to it.' Debbie looked at him. 'I'd talk to them as soon as you can,' he said.

'I don't know.' Debbie felt a sense of bewildered desolation coming over her. 'I don't know what I want to do. I don't know what I should do.'

He stood up. 'Have a cup of tea, take something for the hangover.' That wasn't what she meant, but it seemed like good advice, so she nodded when he offered to make her one, and sank down into the other chair. Her glass and the whisky bottle had gone. He'd presumably put those away. Buttercup was comatose on the rug in front of the fire, so Rob must have fed her. Her eyes skidded away from the photographs on the table. She'd look at those later. Her eyes felt wet again, and she dug her nails into the palms of her hands. Crying did no good.

At the briefing that morning, Lynne rather tentatively brought up the Deborah Sykes connection again. 'Can I just check what we did with that?' she asked.

'I got someone to look at the staircase in the college,' Berryman said. 'There wasn't anything that looked like our man, unless you count a damaged light fitting. There were no prints worth taking. I still have to say – if there was anyone on those stairs, it was someone after something in the college. I've talked to their security,' he added, reflecting that a chat over a pint probably counted, and Neave knew what to do anyway.

He moved on. 'I've still got a watching brief on the student who was killed, but as you know, it doesn't look like one of ours. Lynne, why did you ask that?' He was interested in Lynne's opinion. She had a good instinct.

'It's just that there's been another death associated with Deborah Sykes.' Lynne was uncertain. 'It came through on the bulletin this morning. A Gina Sykes died in a fall over in Goldthorpe. They found her on Thursday afternoon, but it happened the night before. I checked. She's Deborah Sykes's mother.' She shrugged, indicating that she couldn't take it any further.

There was a stirring of interest. 'Is Peter Cave on that one?' Berryman was trying to remember who was based at Goldthorpe.

'Bit of a Jonah, this Deborah,' McCarthy murmured in Lynne's ear.

'I'll contact him, let him know we may have a connection. Lynne, you talked to her. Was there anything, anything at all – phone calls, someone following her, *anything?*'

Lynne shook her head. 'I asked her specifically. And Steve warned her.'

McCarthy nodded. 'She wasn't aware of anything. I told her to watch out, to be careful.'

Berryman scowled in frustration. 'OK. Next?'

Other teams reported back. They were still doing some follow-ups on the house-to-house, and still trying to talk to some of Julie Fyfe's contacts. 'We've lost a neighbour,' someone said. 'She moved in November. Rebecca Wilcox. She's emigrated, gone to Australia. That's where she went when she left.'

Berryman checked the notes. 'She left on the twentieth, right? When did she leave the country?'

'The twenty-first. I'm still trying to track down an address.'

Berryman thought. 'She's about Julie's age, isn't she? I'll get the Melbourne people on it. We need someone to talk to her. OK. Anything else?' No one had anything new to report. Lynne's team were talking to the freight companies, looking at schedules, trying to find any significant details for the nights of the killings. 'It's difficult getting to the drivers,' she told the team. 'They work different hours. So far, we've drawn a blank, but there are a lot more people to talk to.'

'Hurry it up,' Berryman said. 'Put more people on if you have to. I don't need to tell you how important this is.' He looked at McCarthy. 'Get on to the Goldthorpe people. Tell them why we're interested. Make sure we're in close contact.' Lynne returned to her desk, thinking about the Goldthorpe connection and laying odds with herself how long it would be before Neave contacted her.

Neave wasn't sure about the best way to play this. He could go to Berryman, try to get some information from him. He could try Lynne Jordan. She'd listen, and she'd probably be willing to give him some of the details. Was she still pissed off with him, though? She hadn't tried to contact him, but after the library incident, that was hardly surprising. She'd be busy as well. Berryman was working his team into the ground, he knew that.

He picked up his phone and keyed in Lynne's number.

She answered almost straight away, and didn't seem surprised to hear from him. He explained what he wanted, quickly. He wondered about apologizing for the long silence, but decided against it. 'You've got a cheek, Neave,' she said, when he'd finished. 'You're still on this after everything I said to you? And now you're asking me to tread on Pete Cave's toes because some old biddy got drunk and fell downstairs?'

'Yeah, OK, I shouldn't have asked. There isn't anyone else to ask though. Lynne, I really need this. It's important.'

'It may come as a surprise to you, but we're already on to it. There's no obvious connection, but we're not stupid enough not to look.'

There was a moment's silence. 'OK. Sorry. I didn't exactly convince you last time.'

'You haven't this time. It's an outside chance, but we are looking, all right?'

171

'Thanks, Lynne. One more thing. Let me know what *you* think about it when you've seen the file. Let me know if it looks right to you.'

.'OK.' She sounded resigned. 'Where can I get this to you? Do you want to meet up somewhere?'

'That's a bit difficult at the moment, Lynne. Give me a ring when you've got something, and we'll take it from there. OK?'

'Christ, Neave, you really owe me for this. I'll phone you.' She hung up. Lynne didn't mess about with see-yous and goodbyes. He wondered if she was really angry with him. He didn't think so – a bit pissed off, but he couldn't blame her for that.

He'd made some excuses and left Debbie's when he'd seen the police car pull up outside. He wanted to talk to Lynne before he talked to Debbie about her mother, and he wanted Debbie to talk to the team looking into Gina Sykes's death without his interference. He knew from his own experience of that kind of work that if there was anything problematic about it, Debbie would be seen as a potential suspect. He ran his hand across his face and grimaced. He needed a shave. He needed to decide what to do, as well.

He'd better call in to the college briefly. He'd phoned to say he was working off-site, which was true enough as far as it went, but a brief appearance would be a good idea. Not that it was too important. He was leaving at the end of the month.

There was nothing to keep him at City. He collected his post, told Andrea to phone him if anything urgent came up, and was heading back to his car when his phone rang. It was Berryman wanting to see him at once. 'I want you in here to tell me exactly why you're fucking around with Pete Cave's Goldthorpe case.'

Neave debated telling Berryman that he wasn't working for him any more, but decided he'd be better cooperating, and arrived at Berryman's office twenty minutes later. Berryman already knew the details of Gina Sykes's death. What he wanted to know was Neave's involvement. 'I've followed up everything you've given me, and it's come out nowhere,' he said. 'We aren't ignoring it, but it's not a first priority. If there's anything wrong with the Goldthorpe thing, Pete Cave will let us know. They're investigating it, right? They don't need you treading on their toes. *We* don't need you treading on our toes. Oh, and don't ask Lynne Jordan to do your dirty work for you.'

Neave waited for Berryman to finish. 'OK,' he said mildly. 'But what's the thinking on the Goldthorpe case? Is there a problem?'

He watched as Berryman swung between apoplexy and the old ties from the days they had worked together. He knew which one would win. Berryman still trusted his judgement. 'It looks like an accident,' he said after a moment. 'The postmortem says she was drunk. Her blood alcohol was high. No sign of a break-in, no sign of a struggle, nothing the neighbours noticed. Your girlfriend seems to be well alibied – not by you or I wouldn't be talking to you now – so, it isn't closed yet, but it looks pretty straightforward.'

Neave thought. On the face of it, it looked convincing. But he wanted to get out there himself, see what he felt when he saw the scene of the death. He would be clearer in his own mind then what had, and what had not, happened. 'When will the house be available?' He saw Berryman's expression. 'Deborah wanted to know,' he lied.

'I don't know. Soon, I expect. I'm doing what I can, OK? And that's because I do trust your judgement, though I'm not sure you're in a condition to be judging anything clearly at the moment.' There was a knock at the door, and Lynne Jordan put her head into the room.

'The report from the lab's come back, sir,' she said. She glanced in Neave's direction, and when Berryman started rummaging in his desk drawer, she waggled her eyebrows and pulled a face. Neave grinned. She mouthed, *My room*, and held up five fingers.

Berryman looked up and said, 'Have you got the file? I had it in here yesterday.'

'Yes, sir, I put it back with the others. Shall I get it for you?'

'Put it on my desk. And give me the report.' He held his

hand out. Lynne passed the report over to him and left. Berryman looked at Neave. 'Well, that's it,' he said. 'That's all I can tell you. If you can give me anything else . . .' He shrugged. Neave nodded, and left. He'd been lucky to get that much, he knew. He'd go and see what Lynne wanted.

Lynne was sitting at a desk in the room she shared with three other officers. It was a small room, crowded with desks, filing cabinets, a coat stand getting in the way of the door. She smiled when she saw Neave and pulled open her desk drawer. 'Sorry if I dropped you in it with Berryman,' she said, not sounding particularly sorry. 'Any joy?' She pulled some folders out of the drawer and began spreading the contents over the desk top.

Neave shrugged. 'It all depends what's going on. How are you doing on the Strangler cases?'

'We aren't. If there's another one and we don't get him quick, heads will roll. That's official, and one of them will be Berryman's. Look. I want to show you this. This might convince you. These are the four victims.' She showed him the pictures of the women. 'Nothing that strikes you about them except they're all young, right? He doesn't go after blondes or brunettes specifically, or small women, or fat women – just young women. Now look at these.' She spread out the pictures of the bodies. 'There, you can see a pattern. He does the same things to each one, right? What you can't see is on the report.' Neave looked, observing the mutilations, the extent of the bruising round the necks, the evidence of sexual attack, the incidental damage – bruising and lacerations to the bodies. The pictures were horrible, the reports were worse, and his stomach felt uneasy. He'd forgotten what it could be like. 'There was none of that in the Peterson case or the Sykes case. Peterson was strangled, but it was manual strangulation – the killer wore gloves. No mutilation, no sexual assault and the body was found near where she was killed. The pathologist is quite clear – no significant similarities. Sykes – it looks like an accident. Something disturbed her and made her get up, but she fell downstairs after she'd had too many. Loads of people do it, but they're usually luckier.'

Neave could see all of that and he'd argued these points

174

with himself. Killers like the Strangler worked to a pattern. They might change their MO, but the mutilations, the sexual attack – that would stay. That was what it was all about. He couldn't get away from the facts. The Strangler wasn't ready to kill again and he didn't kill like this. But he still felt uneasy. He flicked through the file contents again. 'If I'm right, then these two, Peterson and Sykes, were just convenience killings. They weren't the real thing. Peterson might have seen her. Berryman was going to interview her. Sykes – what if he broke into her house?' He saw Lynne's expression. 'OK, I know there wasn't a break-in. And I don't know why he would have done. But I don't like it.'

Lynne came round the desk and looked over his shoulder at the files. 'It's all a bit tenuous at the moment, though, isn't it?' She began taking bits of paper out and looking at them. Neave saw a newspaper cutting – *Karen-Can* – and a cutting of the Small Business of the Year Awards. 'I just want to check something,' Lynne said. 'Look, I'll keep an eye on things. I'll let you know what's going down, OK?' She packed up the files again, and tucked them under her arm as she made for the door. Neave followed her.

Neave decided to go back to Debbie's. She'd put on a brave face earlier, but she'd looked pale and sick. She'd probably be feeling lousy after the events of the day. He knew what came with the territory of violent death. He'd need to make sure she wasn't on her own tonight – he could take her round to a friend's, something like that. His mind wouldn't focus on the problem, so he thought instead about the death of the student, and the intruder on the stairs. Was he adding one and one and one and coming up with six and a half? Had Lynne been right in her analysis of his motives? He still felt angry about that conversation, so maybe she'd struck a nerve. He just didn't know any more. He called in at his flat for a shave and to change his clothes. He was on his way out when he stopped, went back and put some overnight things into a bag. Just in case, just for an emergency.

It was getting dark by the time he knocked on her door. Debbie seemed pleased to see him. She looked better than she had last night, but she didn't look well. She was pale and red-eyed; her hair, normally so meticulously constrained, was pulled off her face in a tangled mass and held with a band twisted round it. He followed her into the middle room. The phone was unplugged and there was a wallet of photographs spilled across the table. 'They were here for ages,' she said, referring to the police who had arrived as he was leaving earlier in the day. 'And the phone has been ringing and ringing.' She twisted her neck back against her hand, trying to relieve the tension.

'Who's been phoning?' He was alert.

'Mum's friends. The local paper. My friends. I got fed up in the end.' She looked at the photographs on the table. 'I was just . . .' Her voice tailed off.

He picked them up and looked at them. A woman with Debbie's gypsy curls, holding the hand of a little girl. They were both squinting in the sunlight. A young man with the same little girl, more recognizably a young Debbie in this picture. Here she was again, held between both adults, all smiling at the camera. He didn't understand about families. He'd had one for such a short time. He looked at the photo of Debbie and her father again, a young man looking at his daughter with delighted pride. Would he have been like that with Flora? She had been such a mystery to him. He felt the familiar ache of loss again, not for Angie this time, but for the daughter he'd never really had a chance to know, and should have known. He looked up. Debbie was watching him. He reached for a topic. 'Have you had something to eat?'

She shook her head. 'I'm not hungry.'

He looked at her. 'I'll get you something. You'll feel better if you have something to eat.' She didn't object, so he went into the kitchen. He wanted to be away from her until the moment passed. He looked in the fridge, in the cupboards. 'There isn't much,' he called. 'I'll make you a sandwich to be going on with, OK?' He gently fielded the insistent cat that had materialized under his feet, and looked at the bread. It was fresh enough for a sandwich, and there was some cheese. That would do for the moment.

Debbie came and stood in the door of the kitchen, watching

him. The cat stood on its back legs and patted her knee. She picked it up and held it against her shoulder. 'Thank you for coming back,' she said, tentatively. She picked up some cheese from the worktop and fed it to the cat. 'She likes cheese,' she said.

He kept his eyes on what he was doing. He wasn't surprised she hadn't eaten. He could remember how quickly appetite could sicken – he'd thrown out more food, almost untouched, in the weeks after Angie died . . . It was probably the alcohol that had kept him alive. He thought about the doorstep specials that Lynne liked to make at the end of an evening – crisp bacon, melting brie, lettuce, barely contained in a hot roll. Something like that would do Debbie good. She had lost weight recently. He'd been shocked at her thinness as he'd half carried her up the stairs last night. He looked across at her, registering late what she had said. 'It's OK,' he said, keeping his voice neutral.

She put the cat down, and absently picked hairs off her shirt. 'You didn't have to.'

'I wanted to.' He cut the sandwich in half, put it on a plate, pulled a stool out from under the worktop and sat Debbie down on it. 'Now eat that.'

'Aren't you having anything?' She pulled a bit of bread off the sandwich and put it in her mouth.

'I've eaten. I'll get something later.' He watched her as she toyed with the sandwich, clearly not hungry, but not wanting to offend him by leaving it. A couple of times she started to say something, then stopped. He took pity on her after she'd eaten half, and said, 'Leave it if you're not hungry. Have something more a bit later on.'

She dropped her pretence of trying to eat. 'You know how it feels, don't you?' she said.

'None better.' He meant it to be light, but it came out with some bitterness.

'I'm sorry,' she said, 'I didn't mean to . . .'

He tried to think of something to say to smooth the moment over, to get back on to the impersonal, the practical, but his mind was blank. She stood up. 'Are you planning on staying here tonight?' She wasn't looking at his face, but down at her hands where she was twisting a ring round and round her finger.

He had to make a decision. 'I don't think you should be on your own.' His voice sounded OK to him, practical, helpful. 'I could take you over to a friend's.'

'No, I want to stay here. I want you to stay here.' Debbie took a deep breath. 'What I mean is, you don't have to sleep in that chair, you know. There's plenty of room in my bed. If you want.'

She forced the decision on to him. The trouble was, he knew what he wanted to do, had known since he packed that bag. He looked at her in silence for a moment. She still didn't meet his eyes but kept on twisting the ring on her finger. 'I'm a bad bet,' he said. He put his hand out towards her and lifted a strand of hair, tucking it behind her ear. 'Deborah . . .' he began. She caught his hand and held it against her face.

She did look at him now. 'Just for now,' she said. 'Just for the moment. Let's not think about the rest.' She needed the comfort, like he did. A great wash of fatigue flooded over him. He put his arms round her and buried his face in the soft mass of her hair. He thought about the cliffs at St Abbs Head, the two-hundred-foot drop to the waves foaming on the rocks, and wondered if this wasn't another kind of forgetting.

The mother smiles and smiles. He smoothes the picture with his hand. The moon through the window turns her face into light and shadows. He waits, quiet, still as the searching eyes drift past him, pause, waver . . . and are gone.

Quiet and still. He stares at the picture through thick lenses, his large frame stooped over. The night wind rattles the trees, and a hunter's moon fills his window with its cold light.

Debbie lay in bed and floated in and out of sleep, tired, wanting to drift away, wanting to hold on to the last hours for a bit longer. Beside her, Rob was asleep. She could feel his breathing, slow and regular. She felt warm, languorous, and though her grief was still there, the sharp edge of it was blunted. She could let it float deeper in her mind without having to push it down and struggle until it burst painfully out. She turned over and he slipped his arm round her waist, pulling her close into his warmth, murmuring something in her ear, slow and relaxed now as he had been urgent and insistent before.

He had held her on the bed, stroking her, kissing her, touching her with his hands and with his mouth, asking her to tell him, no, insisting that she tell him, what felt good, how it felt, if she liked it. 'Tell me,' he whispered, and, 'That's good, isn't it, you like that,' and she did, and she told him that she did until she couldn't speak any more. She wondered if she should feel guilty, but she thought that Gina would understand, would probably approve. Such moments were for the living, and Debbie knew, for the first time in her life, that she would surely die.

14

Debbie woke early. She slipped out of bed carefully, not wanting to wake Rob, and went downstairs. She made herself a cup of tea and fed Buttercup who, with a cat's facility for recognizing an opportunity, had materialized under her feet, mewing and twining. She sat in the kitchen, pulling her dressing gown round her for warmth, and drank the tea, blowing on it to cool it. It was just six, and still dark. She turned on the radio and listened to the early news. She felt strangely blank. It was as if she was inside a cocoon. There was a pressing sense of urgency, but it was outside of her, close to her but not touching her. She stared at the tiles on the kitchen wall. White, plain ceramic, the grouting starting to stain a bit. They needed cleaning. *Plain white is best for tiles*, Gina used to say. The tiles in the kitchen at Goldthorpe were white. The tiles in the old house, the one Debbie had lived in for most of her life, had been blue. She could remember them. Deep blue, and every now and then a yellow flower. Debbie used to think the flower was a fire, blue tiles with fires in, the glaze crazing with age. Her father kept saying he would put on new tiles. He never did. Gina had put the tiles in at Goldthorpe. She'd shown Debbie how to do it. *Get the tiles straight*, she said, *don't worry about the wall. That'll never be straight.* She'd been right, too. Debbie smiled, then shook herself. She'd almost dropped off, and now her tea was cold.

She looked at the clock. Quarter to seven. She made a fresh pot, put it on a tray with cups and a jug of milk, and took it upstairs.

Rob was still asleep. She stood in the doorway for a moment, watching him. Strangely, he looked older when he was sleeping, as though the persona he presented to the world was a younger man, maybe a younger version of himself. Maybe he went back, or tried to go back, to the attractive, careless young man Louise had described, who was Rob Neave before he met – her mind tripped on the name – before he met Angie.

She put the tray down beside the bed, and he woke up. He looked blank for a moment, then seemed to take everything in, the room, Debbie sitting on the bed. He looked at his watch, muttered, 'Christ!' and rubbed a hand across his eyes. 'You've finished me, Sykes,' he said. 'I'm normally up and off by this time.' He grinned at her and she felt her face grow warm. He sat up, leaning against the pillows, and took the cup she was holding out to him. He put his arm round her and she leant back against the pillows beside him. It felt comfortable, companionable. They lay there in silence for a few minutes, then he looked at her, and this time his face was serious. 'Listen, Debs, there's something I've got to talk to you about.'

Debbie felt something cold clutch at her stomach, and told herself angrily not to be so stupid. They'd had an agreement. He was still looking at her. 'Think carefully,' he said. 'The past few weeks. Have you noticed anyone following you, any strange phone calls, anyone hanging around? Anything?' This was unexpected, and Debbie just stared at him for a moment. He waited, still watching. He was serious, he wanted an answer.

'No . . .' She thought about it. Was that strictly true? She remembered the feeling of menace that had haunted her the last few weeks of term – but that was just a feeling and it had gone, vanished with the new term. 'No,' she said again, more positively. 'Why?' She remembered the policewoman who had come round, who had asked her similar questions, and felt herself going cold.

'That Thursday,' he said. 'You thought you heard some-one on the stairs. I began to wonder, when I got back, what was going on that night. That person you saw at the station – he's never been accounted for. And that newspaper article – whoever was there may have seen that. I talked to the senior officer – Berryman – and to someone else I know . . .'

'Detective Sergeant Jordan?' Debbie asked.

'Yes.' He looked at his cup and put it down. 'No one could see a connection. I thought they were right, so I left it. Then that student was killed, and now . . .'

'How does Sarah fit in?' But Debbie could remember that sense of a pattern that she had felt, drunk on whisky, alone, after her mother had died.

'She was there that night, in the IT workshop. She might have seen someone going on to the stairs. Berryman was planning to interview her.' He ran his hand over his face. 'I just don't know,' he said again.

Debbie closed her eyes. 'She came looking for me, at the end of term.' The sense of dread, the chill, gnawing anxiety, began to break through the cocoon. 'Do you think . . . ?' She felt overcome with weariness. *I don't want to talk about this!* She tried again. 'And you think, my mother . . . ?'

'I don't know what to think,' Rob said after a moment, watching her. 'There's nothing concrete to make the links. Sarah's boyfriend – everything points to him. Your mother – at the moment, it looks just like what it seems – an accident.' He tightened his arm round her shoulders and ran his hand over her hair. 'But there's no harm in playing safe. Just – be a bit careful. Until it's over, one way or another, don't travel on your own when the trains are empty. Don't wait at the station unless it's busy. Try to have someone with you. Don't follow a pattern – change your times and your ways of travelling.'

'But if you're right,' Debbie said, the cold feeling settling more heavily on her, 'it's my fault what happened. If it hadn't been for me . . .'

He sighed. 'Look, it's not unusual to feel like that,' he said. 'I know, I've heard it before, but it's just a distraction. It keeps you from thinking about the real things. Whatever happened, you didn't do it. Don't be stupid, Debs.'

She was quiet for a minute. She could see what he meant, but it didn't entirely change the way she felt. She did feel responsible for Gina's accident. Sarah had wanted to talk to her and she hadn't been there. Logic and feelings . . .

182

they weren't always compatible. Maybe he thought they were.

The next few days she drifted. There were things to be done, and she did them. She went out to Goldthorpe to check her mother's house for the investigating officers. They asked her if anything was missing, if anything was out of place. She checked Gina's few valuables, her jewellery, her china, her television – everything was there. There was really very little. Gina had disposed of so much when she left the home she'd shared with her husband. She talked them through Gina's nightly routine, her daily routine, her friends, her work. There didn't seem to be anything that contradicted the obvious facts – Gina had drunk too much and had fallen downstairs. She had obviously gone to bed – her empty cup had been on the bedside table, her book – her Christmas present from Debbie – on the floor beside the bed, the bed covers thrown back. The only slight variation from her routine was that the bolts on the back door were open, though the door had been locked – double locked, which argued strongly against a break-in. DI Cave asked Debbie if anyone apart from herself had keys to the house. No one did. He gently reminded Debbie, largely by the questions he asked, that she wasn't really familiar with her mother's routine any more. Debbie's insistence that Gina didn't drink – and she *knew* her mother didn't drink – was clearly contradicted by the evidence. The postmortem analysis showed a blood alcohol level that was equivalent to about five single measures. Not enough to make her roaring drunk, but more than enough to make her tipsy, unsteady.

Rob stayed. Each morning when he left, he asked her if he should come back that night, and she always said, 'Yes.' They didn't talk about anything beyond that day. It was as if they were both taking literally Debbie's original restriction – *just for now.* She was living, she knew, in a cocoon of unreality. Real life – work, friends, grieving for her mother – lurked a few days away, but she shut it out of her mind.

Lynne Jordan was aware of the man's eyes on her legs. He wasn't trying to conceal it, in fact, he seemed to want Lynne

183

to notice, he was so blatant. She assumed it wasn't an inept pick-up technique. He had been arrogant – the word *insolent* slipped into her mind – from the beginning of the interview. She made herself a mental picture of him in nappies, sitting in a playpen. 'So this delivery takes place every month?' she asked.

'No, love,' he said, with exaggerated patience. 'At the end of the months they order. That's not every month.'

'I see.' He was looking at her legs again. Well, she was damned if she was going to pull her skirt down, or show him she was embarrassed in any way. *Pathetic creep.* 'But these orders go in some way ahead?'

'It's a contract,' he said, in that same tone. 'It's all arranged in advance.'

Lynne made a note to look at the contracts, deliberately uncrossed her legs then crossed them again high up so that her skirt pulled tight against her thigh. She flashed a brilliant smile at the man, patent in its insincerity, leant forward and said, 'Tell me about the delivery on the fifth.' The night that Julie died. He looked a bit uncomfortable. She waited for a moment then flashed the smile again. 'Is there a problem, Mr . . .' She made a point of looking at her notes, though in fact she could remember his name. 'Mr Glenn.'

'I took the train down, we unloaded, I came back.' He was trying to win back the initiative.

Lynne gave him his own tone of exaggerated patience. 'I meant in a little more detail, Mr . . . Glenn. I need your route, and I need to know if you saw anything unusual, out of the ordinary that night.' She felt tired.

'Well, what kind of thing?' She told herself he wasn't being deliberately obstructive. He was just stupid.

'Did you see anyone on the line or by the line? Did you stop anywhere? Did anything happen that didn't usually happen, that you remember?'

'Look, *love,*' he said. 'You don't just stop a freight train, you know. You don't pick up passengers, you don't stop at stations. You only stop if the signal's against you.'

'And was it?' Lynne wondered if there was any reason she could justify fingering him to Berryman as a suspect, arrange for a very unpleasant twenty-four hours for him. *Probably not.*

'The signal? Only at Moreham. There's a train goes through at twenty-three-thirty, so they stop you at Moreham.'

Lynne was alert. She sent her mind back to the postmortem report on Julie. *Time of death around midnight . . .* 'They always stop you at Moreham?'

'Trains run to timetables,' he said. 'If it's there once it'll be there again.' Now, at last, Lynne knew where to start looking.

Reality settled around Debbie the day of the inquest. To her, it was some kind of weird formality that had nothing to do with her mother, but she wanted it to be over, to provide some kind of ending. She had insisted to the police investigating Gina's death that her mother hadn't been drunk, though the results of the postmortem clearly contradicted her. She felt as though this point alone had destroyed her credibility, and she was seen as the daughter who wasn't prepared to admit to any faults in her mother.

Apparently, Gina's behaviour had been normal in the days before she died. She hadn't been working on the Wednesday, but there had been nothing remarkable in her manner at work the day before. On the Wednesday, the last day of her life, she had seen her neighbours, gone shopping. She'd been to visit her husband's grave that afternoon. A friend had met her coming back at around six, six-thirty, and had said she seemed a bit subdued. Rob told Debbie that the verdict would almost certainly be accidental death.

In the event, it was inconclusive. The police said they had an ongoing investigation, and everything was postponed, held in abeyance. Rob met her, driving away quickly from the front of the court house, before anyone could talk to her. Debbie felt the cocoon around her crumbling away, leaving her with an unfocused fear, a sense of something horrible, something unknown, and for the first time since the day of her mother's death, she wept.

Rob pulled up in a lay-by once they were outside the town, and waited. He wound the window down, letting the cold air blow through the car, leaning his arm on the edge of the door. He didn't say anything, but watched the winter landscape as she got herself under control.

Debbie blew her nose and mopped at her wet eyes with a wad of tissues. Crying didn't help. 'What does it mean? What's left to investigate?' she said, after a moment. Her voice caught and she bit down hard on her lip.

Rob shook his head. 'I don't know. It doesn't mean they've found anything to make that link. It just means they haven't finished, haven't written it off.' He was leaning both arms on the steering wheel now, looking at her. 'Let's go out there. To your mother's house. Let's see what we can find.'

Debbie swallowed. Her stomach felt uneasy. She hadn't been back to the Goldthorpe house since her visit with the police, when it had seemed more like a stage set than the house she knew so well. Rob sat quietly, waiting for her to make a decision. 'Yes. All right. Let's do that.' He nodded and swung the car round to head back the way they had come.

The road to the Dearne Valley, the old mining area, was a strange mix of old industry, new industry, small pit villages and mining communities and some countryside as beautiful as that in the well-travelled and well-protected Peak District to the west. But the countryside was becoming scarred with new roads; the old deep pits were being replaced by strip mining, mining that laid the land waste and paid poorly. Debbie was glad, all the same, to be travelling this route by road, not train. When she arrived in Goldthorpe on the train, Gina had often been on the platform waiting for her, a stroll round the market planned, or a curiosity in the local junk shop to see. Goldthorpe approached by road had nothing to do with Gina.

The house looked dark and abandoned, as though it had been empty far longer than a week. Debbie, seeing the curtains in the next-door house twitch, let herself in through the front door. The smell that greeted her was both familiar and strange. She could recognize the faint, spicy smell that she had always associated with home when she was a child, and had come to associate with this house. It was overlaid with a smell of cold and the faint smell of damp of a house that had

186

been empty and unheated for a while. Already it was starting to feel uninhabited, as though the imprint of her mother was fading.

Rob looked at the place with the eyes of a policeman, which Debbie found chilling and disconcerting. He looked at both of the doors and asked Debbie about Gina's usual method for locking up at night. 'The door wasn't bolted,' he said, 'but they put that down to the booze in the end.' He frowned. He seemed to be worried about more than the result of the inquest. Debbie stood in the front room, looking at the familiar things and wondering what to do with them.

Neave checked the kitchen and looked again at access to the back of the house. It would have been very easy for someone to get in unseen. There was no evidence to show that someone had. He looked at the door. The bolts were stiff. The Yale was a good one that would double lock. He checked his memory. It had been double locked when Gina Sykes was found. Would she bother with those stiff bolts as well?

He went into the front room and checked the bottles in the sideboard. There was only sherry. The rum was in the kitchen, standing openly by the cooker. He looked in the kitchen cupboards. He nearly missed it. At the back of one cupboard, tucked away behind some cookery books, was a 35cl bottle of vodka. It had a price label, pristine and new, from one of the large supermarkets. It was more than half empty. He frowned, and called to Debbie, who was in the other room. 'What did your mother drink?'

'Rum,' she called back.

'What did you drink when you were here?'

'Sherry, usually. Wine, if I bought some. Why?'

'Nothing.' The problem was, who'd hidden the vodka? If Gina Sykes was a secret drinker, then the openly admitted bottle of rum in the kitchen and the hidden bottle of vodka would be a pattern he'd expect to find. He looked at the price label on the rum. It looked faded, old. It came from an off-licence, he recognized the name of the chain. He was pretty sure there was one in Goldthorpe. He could check. He knew, though, that the supermarket the vodka came from didn't

187

have a Goldthorpe branch. The nearest one would probably be Mexborough. Another part of an expected pattern – don't buy the drink at your local shops. If Gina Sykes had been a secret drinker, would Debbie know?

Debbie wandered round the house. Everything was just as Gina had left it, a book on the table by the sofa, the TV guide open to the day she died. She felt a welling up of desolation and wanted to walk out of the house, leave it, ask someone to come in and take everything away.

The china cabinet. There was the good tea service that had never, to Debbie's knowledge, been used. It had been a wedding present. She wondered what to do with it. If she took it, it would be broken within a year, unless she kept it unused for another several decades, until her own child, or friends or distant relations looked at it in the same bemusement that she looked at it now. Perhaps she could give it away. The only things she wanted at the moment were the photographs, the record of their life together as a family, a small collection that Gina had kept in a drawer in the spare room.

She went upstairs, looking at the steep, angled stairway that could, it was true, be lethal to someone who fell. In Gina's bedroom, clothes were neatly placed over her chair, and the bedding was thrown back as though someone had just got up. Debbie's Christmas book lay on the floor, face down.

She pushed open the door of the bedroom where she had slept when she stayed here. The bed was made up, but unused. She went over to the chest where the photographs were kept, and opened the top drawer. A photograph slid off the top of the pile. Debbie grabbed for it and missed, dislodging a few more. A wallet of photographs had been left spilling out in the top of the drawer. Gina must have been looking at them, put them away in a hurry. Debbie frowned. Gina didn't brood over the photographs the way Debbie sometimes did. Which ones had she been looking at? The ones of that last holiday in Ireland, the last holiday they'd taken together as a family, visiting Caitlin. There was her father outside Caitlin's house, squinting in the sunlight. Debbie had a sudden, sharp picture of her mother going to visit his grave, then coming back to the empty house, looking at photos of her dead husband. Her eyes felt hot, heavy.

She picked the photograph up that had fallen on to the floor, and something caught her eye. Under the chest of drawers – another photo. She reached and pulled it out. It was from the same batch, Debbie in that bikini that should have got her arrested. The photo looked crushed, bent. She put out her hand to flatten it out, then withdrew it. It was there again, that cold sense of dread and menace, as though something alien was watching her.

15

Lynne Jordan sat at the desk in the archives of the *Moreham Standard* and fast-forwarded the microfilm through the viewer. Pages of newsprint shot past her eyes. She slowed it down a little, trying to see dates as they crossed the screen. There! She stopped the film, then slowly wound it back a couple of pages. There was the picture and the article – the Griffins with their daughter. The headline, *Karen-Can*, and the short article. It was exactly the same as the cutting she had seen when she talked to Stuart Griffin that last time. She made a note of the date of the article and pressed the print button. She rewound the spool of film and put it back in its box, then checked her notes again. The more recent issues weren't on film yet, but the issue she wanted might be. She looked at the dates on the boxes – yes. She took the last box from the shelf and wound it on to the viewer. Again she fast-forwarded the film, slowing it down as she thought she was getting near the date she wanted. She checked a date on the screen – too far. She rewound a few pages, and there it was – *Broughton's Winning Team*. She printed it off and checked the date against her notes. Right.

Now for the difficult bit. She went back to the boxes of film, and went back through the dates until she had three boxes for checking. She sighed, loaded the first one in the machine and pressed the forward button. The pages of newsprint flowed past. She got to the end of the reel without stopping it. She knew she'd lost her concentration. She rewound the reel and went through it again. Still nothing. Backwards or forwards? She checked her dates again, and went and got another box from the shelf. Earlier issues. She went through the same process with this film, but this time, on the second run-through, she stopped the film and looked closely at an article and photograph. Kate's face was small but recognizable as she looked challengingly at the elegant man in the picture with her. The headline was, *Sheffield Students in Protest to Minister*, and the caption of the photo read, *NUS rep. Katherine Claremont hands a petition to Education spokesman in Sheffield today.* Yes! She felt the tension beginning. Now for the next one. 'Come on, Mandy,' she said. 'Show me where you are.'

The next hour was frustrating. Her eyes were aching from staring at the screen, and she was finding it harder and harder to keep up the level of concentration necessary to select possible pictures as they flowed past her eyes. Maybe a picture wasn't necessary? Maybe a mention in an article . . . ? No, it had to be a picture. She rubbed her face with her hands and thought. She'd gone back six months – that was surely too far. Had she missed it? It was possible, but she'd been through these films three times. She was wasting time. *Think, woman!*

She went back to her notes on Mandy. Amanda Varney, 21. A clerk in a small firm. Nothing memorable or newsworthy there. Lived at home with her mother, kept a dog. Had the dog done anything interesting? She made a note. Single. She had been engaged, had broken it off. Boyfriend upset. There had been the phone calls. Lynne thought about this. There wasn't anything there to attract press interest. She tapped her thumbnail against her teeth. Would it be quicker to go and talk to Mandy's mum again, or would it be better to keep plugging on with the film for another hour or so? When was Mandy's birthday? No, it was almost nine months before her death. Too long, probably. But something was nagging at Lynne now. She sat quietly, letting her mind work. Yes. When did Mandy get engaged? February, two months before she died. What had her mother said about a photograph? Lynne went back to her rolls of microfilm, and got out the one that covered the late winter. These photos were smaller, so she ran the pages more slowly through the machine. And there it was. In the local news, the photograph that Mrs Varney said was so good. There were photographs of six couples under the headline, *True Lovers Love the Spring!* There was Mandy, smiling prettily at a nondescript youth beside her. It *was* a good photograph.

It surely couldn't be a coincidence. Each of the victims had had their picture published in the local newspaper shortly before they died. Lisa's was six weeks almost exactly. The gap was a bit longer with Kate – just over seven weeks. Mandy's engagement was announced on the eighteenth of March. She was killed six weeks later. But the pattern didn't continue. The story about Broughton's appeared on the thirteenth of August. Julie was killed in early December, almost seventeen weeks later. Why the discrepancy? Lynne collected her things and prepared to go back to the station. Her weariness was gone now, and an adrenaline surge was running through her. Maybe this was the breakthrough they needed.

The adrenaline carried her into Berryman's office, where, to her annoyance, she found Steve McCarthy discussing the information that had come in from the recent house-to-house enquiries. Berryman looked at her. 'Lynne?' He didn't sound in a mood to be interrupted.

'Sorry, sir, but this is important. It's . . .' She pulled out her folder of photocopies. 'I was looking at the files again and something came up.' She spread the pictures over the desk, pointing to the dates she'd marked on each one. She felt the atmosphere in the room change as they realized what she was showing them.

'How do these link up?' Berryman heard her through and wanted her ideas, now. 'Is it just the local paper, or is there another connection?'

'I don't know.' Lynne had thought about this. 'There aren't any similarities that we haven't found already, but . . .'

'Photographers? Journalists?'

'I'm checking on that. The stories were written by different people. The photographer angle – one of the pictures was sent in by a relative.' She pointed to Mandy's engagement picture. 'The others I need to check out.'

'Send one of your team. Get them to talk to everyone involved in those stories.' Berryman pressed his fingers against his forehead. He thought for a moment and looked at Lynne and McCarthy again. 'Are we missing anything here?'

After a moment, McCarthy said, 'Deborah Sykes.' Lynne cursed herself. She'd been too tied up in the past, too cock-a-hoop at finding this connection. She hadn't been thinking ahead. And McCarthy had got there first. Deborah's picture, about five weeks ago. *I saw the face of the Strangler.*

Berryman looked at them. 'What do you think?' he said.

Lynne and McCarthy exchanged glances. 'It's early for the next one,' Lynne said slowly, talking it through. 'I wouldn't want to pin everything on that – he's broken his pattern already. But . . . We know with Lisa and with Mandy, the stalking started almost straight after the pictures went in the papers. I've checked,' she added, in response to Berryman's unspoken comment. 'Lisa's diary, she wrote about Karen's "nightmares". They started within a couple of days of the picture appearing. Mandy's boyfriend didn't make all those calls, not the early ones. When I talked to Deborah, I asked her about phone calls, people following her, anything odd, out of place. There wasn't anything.'

'But then her mother . . .' McCarthy sounded as unsure as Lynne felt.

'It's out of the pattern. Why? No other families were bothered. Only if they lived with the victim. I don't know.' She shook her head, looking at Berryman.

'I'll get back to Pete Cave,' he said. 'He'll keep his team on alert, look again. What's happening with the Peterson case?'

'They charged the boyfriend. Manders says he's coming apart, thinks he might confess, go for manslaughter, sudden loss of control.' McCarthy had been liaising with the team investigating Sarah Peterson's death.

Berryman nodded. 'Maybe they need to look again. Get on to them, Steve. What about the Sykes woman? Someone's going to have to talk to her again. I don't want this photograph thing getting out though.'

'She seems to have Rob Neave in residence at the moment,' Lynne said, aware of a surprised glance from McCarthy. She felt irritated at the efficiency of the gossip machine. 'He'll keep an eye on things.'

Berryman grunted in bad-tempered agreement. 'He'll get up my nose as well. OK, she's in good hands. But get someone to go and talk to her. I'll get in touch with Cave.'

The new possibilities of a connection with the recent killings was the first thing Berryman discussed at the day's briefing. He could see the same frustration in the eyes of his team as he felt himself. It was all too nebulous, and it all needed checking, tying in or finally eliminating.

Lynne Jordan had better news for them. Finding the photographs had been the result of a flash of insight. The work with the freight companies had involved Lynne and Dave West in hours of painstaking work, interviewing, coordinating interviews, coordinating information that came in, and it had paid off. 'What we found,' Lynne was saying, trying to avoid looking at the rather sour smile on McCarthy's face, 'was that trains stopped at signals, freight trains, on the relevant nights. We can get that information for those dates because they were stops for scheduled trains. Anyone who knew the schedules would know about them. And these stops all occurred within an hour of the estimated times of death.' She went over to the map. 'Here – Julie. A train went through Moreham station at eleven-thirty. It stopped just before the station because something was due to go across higher up the line. Here – Kate. A train comes off the main line on to the freight line at Kirk Sandall, two hours after she vanished, if Steve is right. It was stopped at the signal here. There's another train that goes through Conisbrough at the right time for Mandy. It waits just before the cutting for the InterCity. The clincher for me is this one.' She indicated a page on the report. 'A train was supposed to go through Mexborough the night Lisa died. It usually does. But it was delayed at the last minute – they had a breakdown. It actually went through about two hours late – and so it didn't stop at the signals like it would have done at the normal time.'

There was silence as the team absorbed what she was saying. McCarthy frowned. 'You're saying we've got a hitch-hiker?'

194

'Yes, only he doesn't ask.' Lynne was wary of McCarthy's response, but he only nodded.

'They're dead when he puts them on the train?' That was Curran, a member of McCarthy's team.

'I'm assuming so,' said Lynne.

'It's a hell of a job,' McCarthy said, 'lifting a body from the line on to one of those trucks.'

'Yes.' That had got in the way of Lynne's thinking at first. 'But this is another thing. They were trains with either flatbed trucks, or some flatbed trucks. It can be done. Dave and I experimented.' She grinned reluctantly at the laughter that greeted this. 'A strong lad like Dave,' she went on, 'can lift someone of my size on to one of those things. Then it would just be a case of getting on himself and holding on. He could use a strap or a hook if he needed to.'

'And getting off?' Berryman knew Lynne's thoughts, but he wanted the rest of the team to have them. 'Another stop?'

'I don't think so, sir, not necessarily. If you look at the drop places, there're bends, signals, obstructions. The drivers go fairly slowly at those points, slowly enough for someone to risk jumping.'

'Push the body off with him and he'd have a soft landing anyway,' West added. There was silence as they thought about the postmortem injuries that the pathologist attributed to a possible fall.

'OK,' said Berryman. 'If this is right, then he's got to know those schedules like the back of his hand, and he's got to know those routes. Who are we looking for?'

'Freight company employee, ex-freight company employee. Railtrack employee, ex-Railtrack employee.' McCarthy pulled an expressive face. 'Trainspotter, or some other kind of anorak.'

'It's not that bad,' said Berryman, thinking it was bad enough. 'He's local – or he's got local connections. We've got a profile, but remember, it's only suggestions. Don't ignore a possible because he doesn't profile right. Physically, we have evidence to suggest he's strong. He's got to be to do it, and the Sykes woman said the man she saw was big. He might wear glasses. We've got the picture that Lisa's daughter drew.

Lynne, Steve, I want both of you on this. I want some names. OK. Any questions?'

It was over a week after her mother's death that Debbie went back to work. The world of the college carried on as normal and Debbie was seamlessly incorporated into the routine of teaching, marking, meetings. The A-level class were pleased to see Debbie. That was partly because they had had Louise to teach them while she was off, and Louise was a notorious dragon with her classes. But it was also, Debbie realized, that they liked her, enjoyed the work they did with her, and felt in sympathy with her.

'OK,' she said, signalling the beginning of the class, 'let's just go over the timetable again. Your exam is in June. I want your coursework in at the end of the month.' She looked up as groans arose from various parts of the room. 'And I know some of you are going to have trouble with that deadline, so start working *now*, please. We've got one more book to do – *The Handmaid's Tale* – so if you haven't started reading it, get on with it. I've got some handout material here on theocracies, religious states, that I'd like you to have read by Monday. We should have plenty of time for revision at the end.' She could feel herself slipping back into harness, feel the control of knowing what she was doing, and knowing she would do it well. She was looking forward to the next few weeks.

The initial seeing of people was difficult, because they all wanted to say how sorry they were about her mother. They were embarrassed by bereavement, and Debbie didn't really know what to say to them. She was always glad when the necessary ritual was over. She was aware of some people who ducked into empty rooms when they saw her coming, avoided her eye when they met, couldn't bring themselves to mention the unmentionable. She didn't let it worry her.

To her surprise, Tim Godber wasn't one of these. She didn't see him until the Monday of her first full week back, the last week in January. Her morning class had been no ordeal. The students came from another course, felt no allegiance to Debbie and were probably unaware of what had happened. She took them briskly through some exam practice, and reminded them about the deadline for finishing their coursework. She was on auto pilot.

At midday, she went back to the staff room. Her desk was awash with paper. Louise had tried to sort and organize it so that it wouldn't present her with too daunting a pile on her return, but there was still a lot to get through. She put the marking from her morning class into the folder for attention at the weekend, and was trying to sort the paperwork into degrees of urgency, when Tim came into the staff room. 'Debbie,' he said.

She wasn't too pleased to see him. 'Hi, Tim. If you're looking for Louise she's in a meeting.'

'I wanted to see you. I just wanted to say how sorry I was about your mother.'

That was nice of him, to come down specially. Debbie nodded her acknowledgement. 'Thanks, Tim. It was a terrible shock. Everyone's been really good, though.'

'Is there anything I can do?' He looked at her anxiously, apparently sincere. It seemed to matter to him.

'No, everything's dealt with, thank you. But thanks for the offer.' Debbie thought he looked downcast at her refusal. Maybe he saw this as a way of making up for the article.

'Are you OK for company in the evenings? Are you getting out? Let me take you out for a drink.' He smiled hopefully at her, giving her that mock-hangdog look he used to give her when apologizing for minor misdemeanours.

'Oh.' Debbie's alarm bells rang. She didn't want to offend him, but she didn't want to go anywhere with him. 'Thanks,' she said, after too long a pause, 'but I'm really busy at the moment. Some other time, maybe?'

He looked a bit put out, but took it with grace. 'OK. Will you let me buy you lunch, then?'

Debbie laughed. He was persistent, but she genuinely couldn't go. 'I've got far too much to do,' she said. He seemed happier with this and hung around for a few more minutes, chatting, before he left. Debbie returned to her pile of paper. What would happen, she wondered, if she put the lot in the bin.

Tim Godber was in the administration section of City College, talking to Jean Glossop, the personnel officer. They got on well, and she was a useful contact to cultivate. Despite his confident words, he was by no means certain that his job was secure, and he was putting a few safety lines in place. 'I'm thinking of reducing my contract, anyway,' he was saying, as he managed to pull the talk round to the topic of the college crisis. Jean could be indiscreet, but she didn't take kindly to being pumped. Tim knew from previous experience that he'd have to offer her opportunities, and then she might tell him things he needed to know.

'Oh?' Jean was filing some staff records. 'Why is that, Tim? We'll miss you.'

'I've got so much freelance work. It's time I made the decision, really.' An exaggeration, but one that could be usefully passed back to management. Human nature tended to want to keep what was valued elsewhere. 'Either I'm a journalist, or I'm a teacher. At heart, I think I'm a teacher, but you've got to go where the work is.'

'That's true.' Jean looked depressed, and it occurred to Tim that her job might be on the line as well. She seemed to be one of a large crowd in the college whose job was to move paper around. He couldn't see that the place would run any less smoothly without her.

He smiled at her. 'Well, whatever happens, *you'll* be all right.'

'What makes you say that?' The look she gave him made him wonder if he'd overplayed his hand.

He made himself look surprised. 'Personnel. The college can't manage without a proper personnel officer.'

'Oh, can't they?' She went back to her filing.

'Jean? You're not at risk, are you? I'm sorry, I didn't know. I've been going on about my job, and you . . .' He wondered whether to put his arm round her, but decided that might complicate things too much. They were well established as friends.

'Oh, I don't know. I'm just worried. Everyone else seems to be getting out, and I don't know if I could find such a well-paid job anywhere else. Well, not round here.' She closed the filing cabinet, and stared out of the window. She looked a bit pink around the eyes. 'With the kids, it's so difficult. It's just my salary, you see. I don't see how I could manage on less.'

Tim forced himself to listen patiently and make soothing noises as she gave him the single-parent lament. He'd get her back on track in a minute. After she'd mopped her eyes and apologized, he patted her on the shoulder. 'Coffee,' he said. 'I'll make you a cup.' He turned the kettle on, and took two cups from the tray. 'But you don't know?' he asked. 'You haven't seen anything definite.'

'Oh, no.' She blew her nose. 'They're playing their cards very close to their chests. I know that they're looking at the teaching staff in humanities – but don't worry, Tim, they want to expand your GNVQ work.'

He poured water in the cups. 'Sugar?'

'Put one of those sweeteners in. Thanks.' She took the cup from him and smiled gratefully. 'Really, Tim, I do think you're safe. You don't have to give up teaching if you don't want to.'

'Well, that's a relief.' Tim mulled this over. If he could keep his full-time salary for another year, he could build up his freelance work to the point when he could opt out. If he never saw another student again, it would be too soon as far as he was concerned.

Jean was still talking. 'It just got me down, you saying you were going. Trish Allen, she's off, and Rob Neave . . .'

Tim became alert. 'I didn't know about Trish,' he said, carefully. 'I'm not surprised, though. She's been looking for work in higher education for a while. I'd heard about Rob Neave. Where is it he's going, again? I've forgotten.'

'He didn't say much. You know what he's like. I didn't know he'd told anybody. He's got a job in Newcastle.' Jean sipped her coffee. 'He's off in a couple of weeks.'

'Oh, yes.' Tim waited a moment, but there was nothing else. 'I heard a rumour that Debbie Sykes was off as well, but she hasn't said anything to me.'

Jean looked surprised. 'Well, she hasn't handed in her notice. I think she's had some job applications in because they took up reference from Barnsley, but then there was that awful business with her mother.'

'Well,' Tim said, 'I can't see Debbie moving away from South Yorkshire.' His visit to personnel had been more useful than he expected. He looked at his watch. 'I'd better be off. Keep hanging in there, right?' He closed the door on Jean's grateful smile.

He'd got rid of his class that morning, given them an unofficial reading break. He found that he could get away with that sometimes, as long as he didn't overdo it. No one had caught him yet.

He'd been out with Lizzie, his plump police clerk a time or two, and it had proven very rewarding. He was about, he hoped, to reap some of those rewards today. The other rewards had been worth it as well. Like a lot of women who thought they were unattractive, she was very appreciative of sexual attention and was an enthusiastic and inventive lover. Tim rather liked plump women, though supermodel waifs were better for his image.

It was his talks with Lizzie that had sent him to the archives at the local paper. He had no trouble as a well-established freelance in getting access to these. Lizzie was discreet, and rarely talked about her job. He'd managed to get this information by talking about the female DS on the Strangler case, Lynne Jordan. As he suspected, Jordan wasn't too popular with the clerks. Tim had met her once in his role as a journalist and found her bossy and overbearing. Lizzie had said something about her coming back with some photographs looking pleased with herself. He'd teased Lizzie – *It'll be pornography for the senior officers, a bit of bondage for Berryman* – and she'd let slip that the photographs came from the local paper.

The next stage had been chatting up the librarian in the archives, who'd told him, in response to a lucky question, which microfilm copies had been taken. She didn't say that it was the police that had them, but Tim was pretty sure from the dates that this was what Jordan was so pleased about. He went to the shelves to see what was missing, and now he was here in the local library looking to see what had got her so worked up.

It took him a couple of hours, but when he finished, he felt a prickle of excitement run up his back. He'd done the same count that Lynne Jordan had done, he knew what kind of time scale was operating. He had copies of the photographs now: *Karen-Can*; *Broughton's Winning Team*; *Sheffield Students in Protest to Minister*; *True Lovers Love the Spring!* He puzzled over the discrepancy with Julie Fyfe's photograph. The other pictures had appeared about six to eight weeks before the killing. Why the gap?

He had one more picture. It was dated from six weeks earlier. He thought that Lynne Jordan might not have realized the significance of that last one – but then she didn't have the information he had. He looked at it. Debbie smiled. *I saw the face of the Strangler.* 'I know you did, sweetheart,' he murmured to himself.

Neave had some decisions to make, and he didn't want to make them. His quixotic dash to Debbie when Louise had phoned him had surprised him. He had done it almost instinctively – if he'd thought about it, he would have foreseen the consequences. And done what? The same, probably. And now they'd been effectively living together for the past fortnight. He could feel the tendrils of dependency – his own, not hers – creeping through him. He found himself thinking about her when he wasn't with her, the way she looked, the way she felt, the things she said. He was starting to need to be with her – and he didn't want that.

His mind skipped on to another problem, and he opened his desk drawer. The crumpled photograph of a teenage girl in a bikini. He'd put it into a plastic wallet, but Debbie had handled it, and so had he before she'd told him where she'd found it, why she was showing it to him. He ran his hand over his face, trying to concentrate. He should have passed it over to Berryman, but – a drawer with photographs spilling out, a woman who may have been upset, an unnoticed photograph on the floor, trodden on, kicked under a piece of furniture. It didn't mean anything. He could imagine what Berryman would say. He put the wallet back in the drawer. He'd drop it off later. He paused, as a thought struck him. Protocol. He'd better go through Cave. Right, he'd drop it off at Goldthorpe tomorrow.

He pulled his mind back. His plans were made. He was leaving City in a fortnight, and he had about four weeks' grace before he had to be up in Newcastle permanently. He had to disentangle himself, he had to tell her, and he had to make sure that someone was watching out for her, someone who took the – admittedly tenuous – threat seriously. He'd been there, watching, waiting. There had been no sign of anyone, any threat, any danger. Still, he wouldn't feel confident that Debbie was safe until the Strangler was caught, or until he'd shown in the only way he could that Debbie was not his target.

He'd start the process of disentanglement by going back to his flat tonight instead of staying with her. He was giving her a lift home, but they'd agreed for the rest of the week she would just make sure she had someone to travel with if she went on the train. Enough of the staff at City used the train for that not to be a problem. It was important to get out of the pattern of staying with her every night. Thursday nights were different. Neave knew the station weekday evenings. It was deserted. The commuters travelled between five and six, the shoppers during the day and early evening. People from Moreham wanting a night out in Sheffield travelled between eight and nine. No one travelled at half past nine from Moreham to Sheffield. Thursday night, he would take her home. And then . . . ? He ran his hand over his face. It was all a mess. He didn't know what to do.

Now it was starting to come together, Tim realized he needed to do some careful planning. What did he want from this? He wanted his story, he wanted to show everyone, in the scoop of the decade, that he'd got there before Berryman. He knew who the Strangler's next victim was to be. The problem was, how could he write his story? He needed proof that Debbie was being stalked by the killer, and his only proof – well, his only evidence – had gone. He couldn't have used that anyway. The fact he'd kept it quiet wouldn't have sat too well with the heroic image he planned to cut for himself. He thought about the headlines – he enjoyed putting himself in headlines – *Journalist Jousts with Death*. He needed to witness the stalker, he needed to get close enough to Debbie to watch, but not so close that the Strangler would be aware of him. He frowned, running the permutations through his mind. Where and when was the Strangler likely to attack? Obviously, the station. That made Thursday nights a high-risk time. Would the Strangler watch Debbie at the station? He was bound to. He needed to know her movements.

That reminded him of another complication. He'd been in his car in the car park the other day, and she'd come out of the college with Neave. Tim had watched as she got into Neave's car, watched the way they talked, looked at each other, watched as the car had swung out of the car park. He'd got it wrong when he'd thought there was nothing going on. And it was going to get in the way of his story. If Debbie changed her pattern, if she stopped going on the train, if she stopped to-ing and fro-ing predictably . . . He'd have to do something about that.

Debbie needed to be back on the train. She wouldn't travel alone. Something told him that she was wary, something had made her wary. Right, *he* had to be the one taking her to the station, and then . . . He began to devise plans for the way he could be with Debbie but not visibly so, be there to observe, to photograph – *that* would be a story – to get the last bit he needed to write his piece. He began composing the article. *Brave journalist, Tim Godber* – would *Timothy* sound better, more serious? – *risked his life to save* . . . That was the rub, though. Suppose, just suppose, the Strangler attacked Debbie. Lizzie had given him as much information as she could. She was indignant when he told her that Berryman was cutting him out of the loop. Tim knew that the investigation suggested that the Strangler was a big man, strong. He'd need to cover his bases.

Keep back, in the shadows. And if the killer was there, if the killer was waiting? Tim would have his phone – *999, woman*

203

being attacked at the station. With a bit of luck, the Strangler wouldn't spot him, but if he did . . .

He looked at the can of Mace. He'd get into trouble for having it, but would anyone prosecute him – dare prosecute him – the brave journalist who'd been the only one looking out for the Strangler's next victim? Who'd been abandoned by Berryman – and by Neave? He could see the pictures, see the headlines. *Barnsley Ace Beats the Strangler.* He'd be a hero.

And save Debbie. She'd be grateful for that.

At the morning briefing, there was an atmosphere of tension. The investigation seemed to be moving, but it was the slow, imperceptible movement of routine and paperwork, and they had followed that route before into dead ends. 'What progress?' Steve McCarthy asked, echoing the fatigue of the team.

Berryman looked at him thoughtfully. 'It depends what you call progress, Steve. We've got fingerprints that are likely to be his. We've got a line on the way he's finding them, we've got a good indication that he *is* stalking them. We're getting some kind of a timetable. We think we know how he's moving them round the track, and that's given us somewhere to look for him. That's not an actual name and address, I'll grant you that. You going to tell us that?'

'No, sir.' McCarthy flushed and avoided Lynne Jordan's eye. The rest of the team waited in case Berryman had any more to say.

'How's the check on the freight companies going?'

'We've got people on it round the clock. We're starting to get names for possibles. It's going to be a massive interview job.' Berryman knew that. McCarthy ran through some of the names he'd got. 'These were all in the right place at the right time – there's no more than that to go on. They're familiar with the right schedules, they're local and they weren't at work on the dates in question. None of them have got form. We won't know any more until we talk to them. We're starting today. These are people who are still working. I've only just got the lists of ex-employees.' Everyone knew about the redundancies. Everyone knew how long those lists would be.

'How far back have you gone?'

'Five years.'

'What details have you got?' Berryman was sure that employee records wouldn't hold the information they were looking for.

'We've got people standing by to look up background information. For any that look likely. Then we'll start on the unlikely ones.' His gesture indicated the size of the task.

'OK. There's a whole team to do the initial sorting, Steve. Keep at it. You don't need me to tell you how important it is. Right, any questions? Yes, Dave?'

Dave West flicked through his notebook. 'How are we using the time-scale information?'

Berryman went over the timing again, pointing out the dates on the photos that had appeared in the newspaper, and the six-to-eight-week time gap between the picture and the killing. 'We're looking at intervals of seven months, six months and then eight months. We'd look for another killing from May onwards, if the timing is an important factor. Which means that women appearing in photographs in the *Moreham Standard* from the end of February are potential victims. The break in the pattern worries me, though. Why didn't he go after Julie Fyfe in September? Everything we've found says that he should have done.'

'Maybe he couldn't.' McCarthy leaned back in his chair.

'We know she was away for the crucial week,' Berryman said. 'With her boss. What we don't know is why, after that, he waited another ten weeks. And why he changed his time. Is the last week in the month important, or is it just convenient?' They'd asked this question before. Was it a work pattern, a shift worker who had free time around the end of the month? Did something happen that made the killings easier then? No one had come up with anything that looked promising.

'No one seems to know much about her,' said Lynne, going back to Julie. 'She wasn't particularly friendly with anyone at work . . .'

'Except Thomas,' West interrupted.

'If you want to call that friendly,' said Lynne. 'And he

couldn't tell us much about her life. It's that sort of detail we want to find out about that ten weeks.'

'How much can we rely on him to stick to this timing pattern?' This was West again.

Berryman shook his head. 'We can't. We don't have enough information. The expert opinion is that he's satisfied his needs for a certain length of time after a killing. Then he needs to do it again, and he needs the whole of the ritual. The stalking is part of it. But the expected pattern is for the intervals between the killings to get shorter. We haven't got that. I want someone looking into this timing thing with Julie Fyfe. Talk to the people at Broughton's. We need to know if there's anything in that ten weeks that tells us why the killer left her alone.'

He runs the trains forward and back, forward and back. He feels resentful, angry.

It's so near the time, so near, and she's changed. First she wasn't there, and now she is there, she's never alone. He's been watching, but careful, hidden, from a distance. Forward and back, forward and back. He's had to do it before, change his plans. But the hare has never escaped the hound. He won't let this one go . . . There's so little time. But . . . if at first . . . He's put so much time, so much effort into this hunt. Everything is ready, everything is right. He looks at the picture and twists the pins that secure it to the board, one where each eye used to be, one where the mouth is. Then he looks at the calendar. The moon will be gone, the sky will be dark and with luck – and isn't he always lucky – cloudy, the night she should be at the station on her own. If she won't come to him, he knows where to find her. It has to be right. It will be right.

16

It was strange to be on her own in the house. Debbie had been a bit disconcerted when Rob had seen her home, and then announced his intention of going back to his flat. 'I've got a lot of stuff to sort out,' he said vaguely. Debbie hadn't objected. She felt disadvantaged by the fact that in her contacts with him, she was the needy one, the helpless one. First she had been trapped and terrified by – what? By whatever had been on the stairs. That episode confused her now, and she was coming round to the idea that she had imagined it. But whatever had happened, she'd done a classic damsel in distress, and the erotic charge from that had propelled them – fortunately or unfortunately, she couldn't tell – into bed. Then she had been alone and grieving. She was more grateful than she could say for Rob's help, but she knew that gratitude and neediness were not good bases for a relationship, and she knew – or she thought – that she wanted the relationship. She needed to change the balance of things.

So she'd smiled more cheerfully than she'd felt and said, 'OK, I'll see you at work tomorrow.' He'd hesitated for a moment before he'd left, started to say something, then stopped.

'Right. I'll see you tomorrow, Debs.' And he'd given her a quick hug and gone, leaving her feeling a bit uncertain, a bit uneasy. *Pull yourself together, Deborah!* She went round the house, drawing curtains and picking up bits and pieces that had been left lying around, looking at the house with new eyes. Buttercup materialized at her feet, rubbing against her legs and trying to trip her up.

'Oh, so I'll do now, will I,' Debbie said tartly, picking the animal up. Buttercup twisted in her arms and positioned herself across Debbie's shoulder, purring loudly. 'Fickle, fickle,' Debbie chided her. When Rob was there, Buttercup, with that infallible feline instinct for the cat hater – or at least the indifferent to cats, Debbie amended – followed him round, jumped on to his knee, gazed into his eyes with quivering whiskers and breathy purrs, in a shameless display of adoration. And it worked. For cats, it damn well worked. He'd moved from pushing the little cat away, to ignoring her, to stroking her and finally to adopting Debbie's habit of talking to her. *You see?* Buttercup seemed to be saying, looking at Debbie with benign contempt. *It's easy.*

'It's all very well,' Debbie continued the argument. 'But I've got my pride which *you* most certainly have not.' Buttercup purred even louder and rubbed her furry cheek against Debbie's face. Holding the animal in her arms, Debbie completed her tour of the house, and wondered what to do with the evening. Give Fiona a ring? Or Brian? Or both of them? She decided that she didn't feel like company, but she felt nervous about spending the evening on her own. This would be the first time since that evening after Gina's death. She decided she needed a lot to do. The marking in her briefcase nagged at her conscience. If she did it this evening, she might get some time free at the weekend.

But once she was upstairs at her desk, she began to feel nervous, uneasy. The thought of the dark rooms below her made her edgy. Had she locked the doors? Drawn the curtains? In the silence, she began to imagine she could hear someone moving outside the house – or was it inside, downstairs, in the darkness? She found herself standing in the bedroom doorway, waiting, listening.

There was a sudden clatter, and Buttercup shot past her, tail erect, fur fluffed out. Debbie let out the breath she didn't realize she'd been holding. Cats. She'd been frightened by cats. After that, she decided work was out of the question. She settled down in front of the television downstairs. But she checked all the doors and left the lights on.

Steve McCarthy and Ian Curran were looking through the

records and tag ends that were the last remains of Julie's life when Lynne came back to the office. The records consisted of statements from workmates, friends, family, the details from the postmortem, the scene-of-crime details and pictures. The tag ends consisted of the clothes she had been wearing and possessions that had been with her when she died. Lynne stopped to ask them if they wanted a hand. She wanted to review the Fyfe killing. McCarthy was working his way methodically through the statements. Curran, young and less inured to the violence that the job threw him up against, was finding it hard to come to terms with the death of such a young, and such a pretty, woman. Such a death, as well. His eyes kept wandering back to the postmortem photographs. McCarthy glanced at Lynne suspiciously, but gestured towards the box of Julie's possessions. 'We haven't looked at those yet,' he said. Lynne wanted to look at the statements, but started going through the contents of the handbag again – a purse, an address book, a diary – all being painstakingly followed up. Lynne opened the purse – a bit of cash, her travel pass with nearly a year to run, a library card for the college, an organ donor card. There was an irony, Lynne thought.

Curran was helping McCarthy with the statements. 'There isn't much from her neighbours,' he said.

McCarthy said, 'She hadn't lived there long. And her neighbours were new.' He looked at the others. 'She moved in at the beginning of April. The neighbours, the ones next door, didn't move in until the end of November. So they won't have had much time to get to know each other.'

'Who lived there before?'

McCarthy flicked through the details. 'Rebecca Wilcox. Same age as Julie.'

'Did anyone talk to her?' A young woman was more likely to attract Julie's confidences than the middle-aged couple who rented the house now.

McCarthy was still looking. 'I'm trying to remember, there was something . . . yes. She emigrated. She's gone to Australia. Berryman's been trying to get a contact for her.'

Lynne was thinking. Why that ten-week gap? There was

209

something she wasn't connecting. McCarthy was on to it too. He was staring blankly at the desk, caught by the moment. *She was away in September. She'd moved. She'd been promoted. Her neighbour moved.* Lynne went back to the purse she'd been looking at. The travel pass, a one-year pass, to be renewed on the thirtieth of November the following year. She looked at the other two. 'She'd just bought a travel pass,' she said, 'or she'd just renewed one.' She and McCarthy looked at each other, then Lynne reached for the phone as McCarthy whipped open the file. Curran looked baffled.

Lynne was still hanging on, waiting for the clerk from travel office records to phone her back, when McCarthy waved a piece of paper at her. She raised her eyebrows at him and he gave her the thumbs-up. Then the phone rang. 'Yes, that's right, Fyfe, yes. That's the address. She did? And the date? Thank you.' She looked at them. 'Julie's travel pass ran out at the end of September. She didn't get it renewed again until the middle of November. But the woman I talked to at Broughton's said they gave her a travel card as part of the package when she was promoted.'

McCarthy held out the receipt he'd found in the file. 'It's here. She paid for a ten-month pass.'

Lynne was thinking. 'They gave her the money, that's what they said. They gave her a year's worth, and she paid for ten months.' They looked at each other.

'She wasn't travelling on the train for those ten weeks,' said McCarthy. 'And bang goes her travel pattern.'

'But he waits,' Lynne said, 'because he knows she'll go back.' Berryman was right, she thought, he does stalk them.

One of the things that Debbie noticed on her return to work was that the feeling of menace and foreboding around the college that had disturbed her was definitely gone. Maybe, now that something really bad had happened, she didn't need to feel any sense of danger. The real had overtaken the imaginary.

After her morning class, she went back to the staff room, hoping to see Louise. They'd agreed to have a talk over sandwiches and coffee. However, when she got there, Tim

Godber was sitting at her desk, and Louise's chair was empty. 'Hi,' he greeted her. 'Louise asked me to tell you that she's got a meeting with Pete Davis this lunchtime. As message bearer, I thought I'd hang around and see if there was a coffee in it.'

Debbie thought quickly. 'Thanks, Tim, but I said I'd meet someone. I'm running a bit late as it is. Help yourself to coffee.'

He stayed put, watching her as she put her books and folders away. 'Making the most of it?' he asked.

'What do you mean?' There was something in his voice she didn't like.

'Oh, come on, Debbie, it's not a secret, you know. You and the SAS, or whatever he is.'

Debbie felt her face go red. 'It's none of your business, Tim,' she said, trying to keep the anger out of her voice.

'Of course not. Did I say a word? I just thought you were making the most of it before he goes. Good luck to you.'

Debbie froze. 'Before he goes?' She looked directly at Tim and thought for a moment she saw triumph in his eyes.

'Well, he's off in a fortnight, isn't he? Off to the wilds of Newcastle or somewhere, I thought. Or have I got it wrong?' Now he was talking casually, as though this was something widely known.

Debbie felt cold all over. *Rob leaving? Going to Newcastle?* She could feel Tim's eyes on her, measuring the effect of his words. Her mouth was dry. She felt as though something had thumped her hard in the stomach. *Say something!* 'I didn't think it was common knowledge,' she said, her voice sounding strange even to her ears.

'Oh, it's been around for a while,' Tim said, breezily.

Debbie sorted her marking into her Friday folder, concentrating on what she was doing. 'Word gets around,' she managed, after a moment. She looked at him quickly, and caught an expression of satisfaction on his face. That was it. She couldn't stand Tim's company any more. 'I've got to go. I'm late. I'll have to lock up.' She waited impatiently as he unwound himself from her chair and wandered towards the door.

'See you, Debbie,' he said cheerfully as he left.

Debbie sat down in the chair he'd vacated. She felt a deep anger against Tim, and, though she tried to pretend it wasn't there, she was starting to feel it against Rob as well. He'd left her wide open to that. He should have told her. There was no point in hanging around. She needed to talk to him, and she needed to talk to him now. If she spent all afternoon brooding about this, she'd be good for nothing. She tried telling herself that Tim had probably got hold of the wrong end of the stick, or that he was just being malicious, but she knew he was telling the truth. He never passed on information unless he was sure about it.

She looked at the clock. She had an hour before her next class. Time to go and find Rob. She crossed the road to the Moore building, and went along the corridor to his office, a small room off the larger office where Andrea and the reception staff worked. Andrea was at her desk, and gave Debbie a blank stare as she walked through. Rob's door was open, and he was sitting at his desk, drumming his fingers as he read something on the screen in front of him. The desk top was empty, apart from a folder that was open next to the keyboard. He hit a button and the screen display changed. She tapped her fingers on the open door to let him know she was there. He looked pleased to see her. 'Debs!' He gestured to a chair and stood up to push the door shut behind her. 'Are you OK?' He closed the folder and put it to one side. 'Paperwork. It's what I hate about this job.' He waited for her to tell him why she was there.

'Yes. Me too.' She managed a smile. She didn't want a row. If he was going, that was his right. They'd made no commitment – *just for now*, she'd said it. But he should have told her. 'Listen, there's no easy way to say this. Is it right that you're leaving City in a couple of weeks and going to work in Newcastle?'

His face immediately went blank. He tapped a couple of buttons on the keyboard and said, 'Yes, more or less. I'm going to Newcastle in about a month.' He wasn't looking at her.

'That means it's . . . There never was any chance of any future in it, was there?' Her voice sounded calm, the way she wanted it to, but she could feel anger under the surface.

212

He studied the screen for a moment. She waited. 'I should have told you,' he said.

'Yes.' Debbie twisted a rogue tendril of hair round her finger. Her anger was starting to bubble up now, but whether it was with Tim, or with Rob for leaving her vulnerable to Tim's malice, or with herself for being such a fool, she didn't know. Her voice sounded sharp in her ears. 'I wish you had. I had to hear it from Tim Godber.' He looked surprised, but didn't say anything. 'Who else knows?' Debbie persisted, at the same time telling herself, *Stop it, stop being angry.* 'Everyone apart from me, I assume.'

'No one,' he said, calmly. 'No one should know. I handed my notice in to personnel before Christmas.' He looked at her. 'Debs, we agreed . . .'

She felt the anger build up. 'I know what we agreed. That doesn't give you a licence to treat me like shit. That doesn't give you a licence to lie to me.' She wanted to shake him out of his calm – he had no right!

His eyes narrowed. 'I didn't lie to you, Deborah.'

That had got to him. 'You weren't exactly truthful, though, were you? Did you think it wasn't relevant, something I didn't need to know? Something else for you to be so bloody secretive about?' She stood up. She was going to start crying in a minute, and she was damned if she was going to let him see that. 'I'm going.' She turned to the door, but he grabbed her arm and pulled her back.

'Listen, for Christ's sake, will you?' He was close to her, looking at her, and they were both silent for a moment. The anger that had built up exploded. She shouted incoherently and lashed out at him. He let go of her, and put his hand up to protect himself. She grabbed his arms and tried to shake him, digging her nails into his skin, saying, *'Bastard, bastard, lying bastard!'* He fended her off easily and held her away from him. His face was white with anger. She tried to pull her hands free, but he was holding her wrists too tightly. 'Just stop it, Deborah, just fucking stop it!'

Debbie waited, tense, breathing hard. He reached for the door behind her. For a moment she thought he was going to open it and push her through, but she heard the key turn as he locked it. 'Just shut up,' he said. She took a breath but he pushed her up against the wall, closing her mouth with his. He pushed her skirt up around her waist, slipping her pants aside. She felt his fingers inside her and pulled her head back, gasping, but he pressed his mouth down on hers again. The anger had become something else. His feet edged her feet apart, then his thighs were between hers, spreading her wider as he lifted her slightly. He slipped his fingers out of her and fumbled for a moment with his belt, then she could feel him guiding his penis into her, hard and deep. Her legs would hardly hold her and she gripped his shoulders. He slipped his arms round her and down, supporting her weight, and she wrapped her legs round him, digging her nails into his back, wanting to mark him, to hurt him, not wanting him to stop until she felt the warmth exploding inside her.

The anger had gone. He let her slide down gently, keeping his arms round her, supporting her against the wall. She pressed her face against his neck. 'Debs . . .' he said. 'Oh, God, I'm so sorry . . .' The dead weariness was back, the expression of tired despair she remembered from weeks ago when he'd talked to her in the pub about his wife and his daughter. 'I'm sorry, Debs.' She wasn't certain what he was apologizing for. 'I've got to get away – I should have done it months ago.' He closed his eyes. 'I've got to make a clean break. I'm going crazy here. Angie and Flora, they're like burdens I have to drag round with me. Angie would have hated that, she would have given me six kinds of hell. I have to get away.'

'Albatrosses,' Debbie said. He looked at her.

'I'm here for the next month,' he said.

She sighed. It was tempting, but as Louise had said, she needed to survive as well. 'I can't. I couldn't stand it knowing you were leaving.' And she knew that once he was gone, he wouldn't come back.

His face tensed and he started to say something, then stopped. There was silence for a moment. Then he nodded slowly in acknowledgement of her decision. 'I'll miss you, Debs.' He touched her face. 'Listen. Don't forget I'm here. Call me if you need me.'

'Yes,' she said. 'I will.' But they both knew she wouldn't. Clinically, briskly, she straightened her clothes, tidied her hair. She didn't look at him. She wasn't sure what she wanted to see. Ten minutes later, she was walking through the outer office, aware of Andrea looking at her with curiosity.

So that was that. As Debbie packed her stuff away at the end of the day, she wondered what she was going to do. Work? That seemed a thin and unreliable comfort. Talk to her mother? That was gone. She didn't want to think about her mother. When she was a child, she couldn't imagine anything worse than her parents dying. Her life felt anchorless, pointless, grey. *Pull yourself together, Deborah!*

Louise breezed in, carrying a pile of textbooks. 'I'm keeping these in here,' she said, indicating the books. 'They're walking off the shelves of the stockroom. It's my fault. I haven't got time, so I say – Go and help yourselves – and then I don't know where they've gone.' She looked at Debbie. 'Are you OK? You look awful.'

'I'm just tired.' Debbie managed a smile. 'It's worse than I thought, coming back.'

'Take more time if you need it.' Louise was concerned.

'No. I need something to do.' The thought of being at home all day horrified her. 'I'm just tired,' she said again. She pulled her briefcase from under the desk, then remembered. 'Louise, I need a lift back on Thursday night. If I can't find anyone else, could you . . . ?'

'Of course, no problem. Dan's out, so I'll come back and pick you up. Don't bother looking for anyone else. I'll do it.'

Thank God for friends, Debbie thought. She decided to give Fiona a ring and see if she wanted to come round for a drink. She needed to talk.

Fiona's hair was the colour of ripe strawberries. She sorted through Debbie's tape collection and found some guitar music. 'It's a bit folky for me,' she said. 'Haven't you got any decent jazz?' They had their usual music argument, Debbie trying hard to sound as though she minded. Talk seemed awkward, halting, until Fiona said, 'What's wrong, Debbie? You look awful.'

Debbie tried to be evasive, but Fiona persisted. 'Brian keeps threatening to descend. He's really worried about you. You've gone into hibernation since . . . well, we've hardly seen you, really. He only let me come round on my own because I said I'd be able to get you to talk more easily.'

Debbie realized she wanted to talk about it. She told Fiona about Rob, about the footsteps on the stairs, about his wife and baby, about how he'd supported her through Gina's death, about his worry for her safety, about how he was just walking out on her without a word. 'We agreed,' she said, 'we'd just take it in the short term. He didn't make any promises. But I did think he'd tell me what he was doing.'

'Maybe he was going to,' Fiona said, after a moment.

'I don't know.' Debbie shook her head. 'It's just – he knew he was going right from the start, and he didn't say anything. I told him I didn't want to see him again.'

'Maybe it's best. If he can't . . .' Fiona shook her head.

Debbie sighed. 'I suppose I was fooling myself that it would go somewhere. I don't know.'

Fiona, who had been thinking a bit more about Debbie's account, said, 'Just go back a minute. He thought *what*?' She listened with obvious alarm as Debbie explained. 'Someone's stalking you? The *Strangler* is stalking you? Debbie . . .'

'No. I don't know.' Debbie had her own confusions and doubts. 'Rob was worried. Because of that article, and because of one or two other things. He just thought I ought to be careful.'

'Well, he's right about that.' Fiona wasn't completely reassured. 'Why don't you go to the police?'

'Rob did. He told them everything but they didn't think there was anything in it. And Rob said that they were right – there wasn't really. He just felt it. He said it was his police-man's instinct.'

'He's a policeman?' Fiona might as well have said, *He's Pol Pot?*

'He used to be,' Debbie said, not wanting to get drawn into one of Fiona's discussions of the fascist state.

'The main thing is, you've got to be careful. Don't forget that Brian's got a car. You know he'd give you a lift any time if you needed it.'

Debbie realized how little in the past few weeks she'd talked to the people she used to – still did – care about. She felt guilty, selfish. Maybe she was better off without Rob, if that was what he did to her. 'I can't start asking him to run me around. He's got better things to do. Don't worry. I am being careful. I've got lifts sorted out for my late night.'

'I'll tell you what I do.' Fiona reached over for her rucksack. 'I always have this in my pocket or in my bag.' She rummaged round and produced a thin, rectangular piece of plastic. 'Look, it's like a Stanley knife, only you can slide the blade up and down.' She showed Debbie how the cutting part consisted of a series of razor blades that could be broken off one by one and discarded. 'Anyone tries anything with me, they'll get one of those in them. Here, take this. I've got more. Put it in your coat pocket.'

'Isn't it illegal?' Debbie asked.

'Probably. Oh, not to own one. They're perfectly legitimate tools. It probably is to carry one around. If I get caught, I'm going to play dumb. *Oh, I* wondered *what I'd done with that!* Might work.'

Debbie laughed. After Fiona had gone, she picked up the knife and slid the blade up and down. It was wickedly sharp. She couldn't imagine attacking anyone with it but she dropped it into the pocket of her mac.

He should have been feeling relieved. It should have been a weight off his mind. Instead, he was restless, jumpy, unable to settle to any of the things he ought to have been doing. He tried to focus his mind on the sheaf of paper Pete Morton had sent him, but each time he read to the end of a page, he realized he hadn't taken any of it in. He was tired. That must be it. He hadn't had a lot of sleep this last two weeks. Though this was the first time he'd felt weary, or jumpy, or unsettled.

She'd been right to be angry. He'd done the one thing that could be construed as a violation of their informal,

217

no-strings arrangement – of course she'd been angry. He hadn't been able to think straight. He should have let her do what she so clearly wanted to do – smack him in the teeth – but instead he'd screwed her up against the office wall, excited beyond caution or fairness. Then she'd said goodbye and that had hurt. He hadn't expected to feel like that, and he hadn't known what to say. He thought he knew his own mind. And now, instead of feeling relieved, instead of getting on with what needed to be done, he couldn't stop thinking about her.

He'd got to the end of the page again and he still had no idea of what he'd just read. Angrily, he jammed the papers back into the folder and picked up his jacket. He was going out for a drink.

Something had been nagging in the back of Lynne's mind ever since the briefing, when Berryman told them the Melbourne police had managed to contact Rebecca Wilcox. 'I've got a copy of her statement that I want you to look at. The important thing I can see is that she did give Julie a lift into work for the period we're interested in. She says that Julie asked her to keep it quiet. She used to drop her off on Station Road.' There had been a sense of a minor puzzle being ticked off as solved, but Lynne had felt something jump in her mind. She hadn't been able to pin the thought down, so in the end she'd left it, knowing from past experience that it would come back, and now something was tantalizing her with that *on the tip of my tongue* feeling. The Strangler had waited. He'd broken his pattern to wait for his victim. She closed her eyes. There was something important there. She almost had it . . . The phone rang, breaking her concentration, and she felt the pattern escape, elude her and vanish. *Shit!* She picked up the receiver. It was West to say he was bringing a set of files up.

Wednesday was a grey day, cloudy and dull with the threat of rain. The weather forecast predicted stormy days ahead. It was typical end-of-January weather. Debbie was an automaton who took herself into work, delivered her classes and

218

collapsed into her chair in the staff room during breaks. She couldn't make herself do anything she didn't have to do, and was becoming uneasily aware of the bulging marking folder that was getting fuller and fuller as deadlines came nearer. She'd do it tomorrow. She'd do it at the weekend.

She stayed in the staff room that lunchtime as she didn't want to risk running into Rob in the canteen, or into Tim, for that matter. She was listlessly taking a sandwich apart and wondering what had happened to her appetite, when Louise came through the door, weighed down by a large pile of folders. She dumped them on her desk, looked at Debbie and said, 'Coursework folders. English language. Half each, swap next week?' She and Debbie had to mark, and agree marks, for the work the A-level English students had done towards their qualification. It was a demanding process, and Debbie drooped at the prospect.

'With a bit of luck,' she said, 'I'll be made redundant.'

'Don't even joke about it.' Louise looked at the pile of work. 'Incidentally, I've just had Rob Neave giving me earache about you.'

Debbie paid close attention to her sandwich. 'Oh yes?'

'He wanted to know how you were getting home on Thursday. I told him to ask you and he went all evasive on me. First time I've ever seen that man at a loss for words. What have you done to him, Debbie?'

'Did you tell him you were giving me a lift?' Debbie tried to keep her voice light, but she knew it sounded toneless.

'Yes.' Louise looked at her for a moment, then changed the subject. 'Let's sort out a timetable for this marking. If we know what we're doing and when we're doing it, it'll be a lot easier.'

Relieved, Debbie got out her diary, and Louise neatly and efficiently sliced their time into milestones and deadlines. 'Right,' she said when they'd finished. 'You haven't got a class this afternoon, you haven't got any coursework marking to do because I know when you've got to do that. You're leaving. You can go home, you can go shopping – buy yourself a book, buy yourself a new dress – you can go to the gym. But get yourself out of here and give yourself a treat.'

Debbie felt tears pricking at the back of her eyes for a moment, and had to pretend to sort things on her desk. 'OK,' she said after a moment. 'Thanks.'

She took Louise's advice and bought herself a book, then went home and ran a deep bath. She poured bath essence in until the bubbles came over the side of the tub. She forgot to shut the bathroom door, so she had to put up with Buttercup who tightroped along the edge of the bath, mewing anxiously, then spent the rest of the hour that Debbie soaked herself sitting on the taps trying to catch the drips. At seven o'clock, Debbie decided on oblivion, took a couple of sleeping pills and went to bed. She was vaguely aware of the phone ringing as she drifted into sleep, but she couldn't be bothered to do anything about it.

Neave put the phone down and wondered what to do. He'd dialled Debbie's number on an impulse, and he wasn't sure what he had planned to say to her. He'd been in a foul mood all day, and when he'd reduced Andrea to tears he decided it was time to go. 'I'm not in tomorrow,' he told Andrea, ignoring the *Thank God* she mouthed at her screen. 'I've got to see those people in Manchester. I'll be in on Friday, but phone me if anything urgent comes up.' He knew he ought to apologize for upsetting her, but the fact was, he wasn't sorry. He wanted to upset someone.

He hadn't slept well last night, and when he did sleep, he had vivid, unpleasant dreams in which he had to be somewhere urgently, to find something urgently, but kept getting distracted and delayed. He'd woken up sweating with anxiety, and had reached out to put his arms round Debbie. And there was no one there. It had taken him back to those mornings when he had reached out for Angie, and had had to realize that she wasn't there, would never be there again. He'd felt tears filling his eyes and clogging his nose, and he'd leapt out of bed and under the shower, turning the water on full blast and cold.

The gnawing worm of anxiety had stayed with him all day, finally causing him to shout at Andrea when it turned out that some of the work he needed for tomorrow wasn't done.

He would have to do something about this. Whatever was happening with him and Debbie, it was unfinished business and he needed to talk to her again. He'd go round to her house when he got back from Manchester. When she got back from her evening class, he amended.

He turns off the lights. It's done. He has been distracted, side-tracked – this has been the most difficult, the most arduous hunt – but everything is in place now, everything ready. She will be waiting for him – he knows it.

'Shut up, you little shit, or you'll get what the cat got.'

Whisper, whisper in the darkness. The trees are blowing in the wind. The child is afraid of the dark. But the hunter is not afraid. Hunters know the dark places, take them, use them, make them their own.

Lynne Jordan was checking through the latest names from the search through rail employees. As Berryman said, it was a massive task, and even with the new people, they were still understaffed. Lynne wondered how many people the Strangler had kept pinned down over the past two years. Berryman had set the search up so that more experienced officers would be looking at the most likely candidates, and looking at them first. She was looking for trigger events – what had happened to set the killer off? Previous convictions – anything that might suggest an escalating pattern of behaviour. Though, as Berryman pointed out, a lot of what they were looking for may never have come to light.

She felt pulled in ten different directions. She wanted to follow up on the photographs. Something was still nagging her mind about the timing. She was sure they'd missed something, and it was close, like it was on the tip of her tongue. But she agreed with Berryman – if they could find a name, they could short-circuit the whole process. The other questions could be answered later.

She was reading through a folder on one David Nathen. She was tired and it was hard to concentrate. Nathen had certainly had the cards stacked against him. Prostitute mother, alcoholic father, series of 'stepfathers'. A background that contained violence and disruption. One of the 'stepfathers' had died in suspicious circumstances. Some evidence of abuse – but nothing that had come to court. Mother dead, now. No information about that – she wanted dates and details. Nathen had been made redundant from his job as a driver four years ago. Would redundancy be sufficient trigger to set him off? Lynne had a sudden vision of the whole of South Yorkshire filled with serial killers. Tired, she was tired. No previous convictions, not known to the police. Too many queries. She put the folder into the growing pile for further checking.

The next one was a William Stringer. Another redundancy, an engineer. Background not so obviously a problem as Nathen's. His mother was single when he was born – had married a few years later – not the father? She made a note to check. The husband had died in an accident over twenty-five years ago – no recent trauma there – mother died three years ago. It looked as though Stringer had lived with his mother. Would her death do it? Would that have set him off? How had she died? *Damn!* The information wasn't there. Another one for more checking. Anything else? Why had Stringer's name come forward as a possible? She made a note to ask the person who'd pulled the file out.

She moved on to the next one.

The problem with sleeping pills, Debbie decided, was that they left you dull and muddle-headed the next day. She had woken up late, and pulled herself out of bed feeling sluggish and unrested. Her Thursday morning students were a demanding group – adults who were working for university entrance. They worked hard, and expected the teaching staff to work hard as well. Usually, Debbie enjoyed this group and found them stimulating. This morning, she felt she could barely cope. She would have to pull herself together. She couldn't go on like this.

She was walking towards the staff room at break when she saw Tim coming down the corridor towards her. It was too late to turn back, so she nodded at him and prepared to walk past. He stopped her with a hand on her arm. She shook him off. 'Yes?' She knew she sounded impatient, and she didn't care.

He raised his eyebrows at her tone of voice, but said, 'I was just wondering if you wanted a lift back. It is your late night, isn't it? I could run you home afterwards if you want.'

That was nice of him. He lived in Barnsley, the opposite direction from Sheffield. She was ashamed of her bad temper. 'That's kind of you, Tim,' she said, more warmly than she felt, 'but there's no need. Louise is giving me a lift back.'

He looked surprised. 'She doesn't work late on Thursdays.'

Debbie explained. 'She's coming back to pick me up.'

'Let me do it,' he said. 'It'll save Louise a journey.'

Debbie really didn't want his company, and didn't want to be obliged to him. She would probably have to argue about not inviting him in, and even though he was being very nice at the moment, Tim, when crossed, could be vicious. She just wasn't up to it. 'No, thanks a lot. We've arranged a get-together after work.' That was a lie. She'd have to tip Louise off about that. 'But thanks, really.'

'Oh, well, just thought I'd offer.' He didn't seem too put out. 'You can't be too careful these days.' He gave her a wave, and turned back towards his own staff room. Relieved, Debbie headed towards a cup of coffee, but got caught by a student before she made it back to her room, and spent the rest of her break talking through an essay.

Tim sat at his computer screen and racked his brains. This was his big career break if he could just make it come right. At nine o'clock tonight, he must be the one officially taking Debbie home, and she had to be going on the train. She had to re-establish her pattern, and then he could watch and wait.

OK, he had to plan a two-line attack. He had to get Louise out of the picture, and then he had to put himself in. He had an idea, but he needed some more information. He checked his watch. Lunchtime. He picked up the phone.

'Hi, is that Louise –
—It's Tim Godber –
—Listen, I need to talk to you about a timetable glitch –
—I know, I *know*, it's engineering –

—It's a bit complicated. Have you got a few minutes if I
come over –
—What time are you leaving –
—Fine. See you then. Bye –'
OK, he knew when she was leaving. He had to make sure
she wouldn't be coming back, or – his idea began to form –
he had to make sure her car wouldn't be coming back. Or
wouldn't be leaving in the first place.

It was late in the afternoon. Lynne had spent most of her shift
sorting and eliminating names. You could spend days, even
in this time of computer records, jumping from one archive
to the next, Lynne reflected, as she tracked names through
the systems. In some ways, it had been a useful session. She
had managed to eliminate three of the five names on her
list. David Nathen was proving elusive. He was no longer at
the address last recorded for him, and wasn't on the electoral
roll. She'd tried various other databases and records, where
Berryman had cleared the obstacles and had people standing
by, and drawn a blank. Other people were looking for him. He
had run up debts at the address she had, and then moved on.
No forwarding address, no police records, nothing she could
find – yet – through his health records. Had he vanished
deliberately, and if so, had he vanished for a good reason?
Their man – he surely needed a secure address, a place to
work from. He could hardly be a random killer wandering
the streets – could he? For a moment, Lynne's convictions
about all the careful patterns they had identified wavered.
Were they imposing patterns on the random actions of a
madman? Once more, that tantalizing feeling of *something*
nagged at her mind. She sat quietly, waiting for it to come
to her, but her mind remained stubbornly blank. OK, she'd
reached a dead end with Nathen. Start again tomorrow –
get some people foot-slogging on his trail. She looked at her
watch. She was off at eight. She'd just see what she could
pull up on Stringer, and then call it a night.

Louise slammed her car door and headed disgustedly back
into the college. She was on the phone when Debbie came

into the staff room for her break. She waited until Louise finished and looked at her in enquiry. 'It's the car,' Louise said. 'It won't start. I've phoned the AA, but I've no idea when they'll get here. I don't know if it's something they can fix tonight.' She looked harassed. 'Listen, Debbie, if they can't, I'm not going to be able to give you a lift. Have you got enough money for a taxi?'

Debbie pulled a face. 'That'll cost a fortune! I'll think of something.'

Louise sighed. 'You'll do more than that, or I'll stay in college and walk you home. Now, what are you going to do?'

The door opened behind her. 'Hi, Debbie, Louise, have you got a minute?' Tim Godber stuck his head round the door. Debbie groaned to herself. He was the last person she wanted to see. Louise brightened.

'Tim. You've got your car here, haven't you?' She ignored Debbie's frantic signals. He nodded. 'Listen, Debbie really needs a lift back to Sheffield tonight. She mustn't go on the train on her own.'

'Of course not,' Tim agreed. He looked over at Debbie. 'Do you want a lift? The offer still stands. I've got a load of work to do, so I can stay here till nine and get it out of the way. It'll do me good, but I'd like to get straight off then, if that's OK with you.' He smiled rather apologetically in Debbie's direction. Louise looked pointedly at her.

'Thanks, Tim.' Debbie had no choice. It did solve a problem. She tried to sound more grateful. 'Thanks a lot, really.'

'I'll meet you here at nine, then. Listen, I wanted to talk to you anyway about Matt – in your tutorial group?' Debbie nodded. 'I'll tell you about it in the car on the way back. See you. See you, Louise.'

Debbie and Louise looked at each other. 'I know,' Louise said after a moment. 'If my car's fixed, I can still give you a lift, but you've got something sorted for if it isn't.'

Debbie nodded. 'It had to be Tim Godber, though. If you knew how much I didn't want to spend any time with Tim Big Gob at the moment . . .'

'Stop complaining,' ordered Louise. 'It's a lift.' Debbie

couldn't think of anything else to say, so she gave Louise a grudging smile, and got her sandwiches out of her bag.

Berryman picked up his files and stretched. 'I'm going home,' he said to Dave West, who was typing a report into the computer in the outer office. 'We've got visitors. I'm a dead man if I'm not home on time.' West grinned sympathetically. His girlfriend had a lot to say about the amount of time he spent at work these days. 'Phone me if anything comes in.' He went out of his office, pulling on his coat. He was tired. What he really wanted to do was sit in the pub, have a few beers, a chat with some of the lads, just a chance to relax for a couple of hours. But Claire had a right to a social life too. He supposed. He looked round the door of the main office, and was pleased to see Lynne Jordan there, going through files on the computer and making notes. 'I'm off now, Lynne,' he said.

'About time.' She didn't look up. 'You've been living here these past few days.'

'Guests.' Berryman's face was tellingly blank, and Lynne grimaced. 'Phone me if anything, and I mean *anything*, goes down.'

'Yes, sir.'

He felt himself relax a bit. He knew he could rely on Lynne to make the right decisions. 'Who's on tonight?' Lynne ran through the list of people on duty. As usual, it was too few for the workload, but it was a good team. He checked his watch. If he left now, he could have a quick pint in the Grindstone before he went home.

Tim typed the last line, saved the report on to disc, and slipped it into his briefcase. He ran the whole thing through in his mind again. The only flaw had been that Debbie had broken her pattern recently, being driven into work and home again by Neave, who'd been behaving like her own personal Rottweiler. Still, that seemed to be sorted, now. Tim gave himself a mental handshake and reviewed his plan. His car needed to break down, just like Louise's had. The thing was, should he really disable it, or should he just tell Debbie it wasn't working? Would she think it was too much of a coincidence? Not if his car had been vandalized like Louise's – shockingly – had been. Did he have to make the supreme sacrifice and cut his own petrol line? No, he could get away with just taking off the distributor cap. If he had to try the car in her presence, it genuinely wouldn't start. After all, he could always pick it up later if nothing happened.

Lynne checked her watch. She should have been off nearly an hour ago, but she wanted to get the information about Stringer off the systems. She wanted more information about his mother's death. Could that have been the trigger event? She had snarled up originally when she'd looked for his mother under *Stringer*. The name was different, *Howard*. So her son had kept his original name. Important? Hard to tell. Each bit of information generated another bit of information. The fax hummed and spilled out more paper. Three sheets. Lynne picked them up and read through them. OK, so Susan Howard had died – in an accident, a house fire. Died of smoke inhalation. She frowned. Presumably, there had been no cause for worry – there was a short article from the local paper about the inquest. *Coroner warns of dangers of smoking in bed.* But something tugged at her memory. She looked at the record again. That was it! Stringer's father had died in an accident as well. Nature unspecified. Too many coincidences. Something else to look up. *Leave it until tomorrow?* It was tempting, but there was just a chance that there would still be someone there . . . Lynne sighed and picked up the phone.

When Debbie came out of the staff room, Tim was waiting for her, looking a bit apologetic, a bit worried. She managed a smile. After all, he was doing her a favour. 'Debbie.' He looked more worried. 'My car, I was just up there putting my stuff in. It won't start. I think it's been vandalized, like Louise's.'

'Oh, God. I didn't know Louise's car had been vandalized.' Debbie felt depressed. 'What did they do?'

'They cut the fuel lines. Apparently it's the way you help yourself to petrol these days. Because of locking petrol caps,' he added in response to Debbie's look of incomprehension.

Debbie felt guilty. 'All because you waited for me,' she said. 'I'm sorry, Tim.' That was obviously the right thing to say, because he looked pleased. She *was* sorry.

'I expect they did me the same time they did Louise,' he said, easily. 'Don't worry, Debbie.'

'Have you phoned the AA, or whoever you do phone?'

'Oh, yes, but they can't come for ages. Look, I think you'd better go on the train or you won't get back till midnight. I'll walk to the station with you, see you on the train. I tell you what, I'll even come back on the train with you.' He looked a bit evasive. Debbie wondered what lay behind that offer. Whatever it was, she wasn't playing.

'Thanks, Tim. There's no need for that. Just seeing me on to the train will be fine.' She put her bag down and began pulling on her coat. 'I'm ready to go. I brought all my stuff along to the classroom. I don't suppose there's the same rush now. What are you going to do about the car?'

'I'll leave it here tonight.' He looked a bit put out. It must be a great end to the day for him, having to wait for her and then his car packing in on him. 'I can get a taxi from across the bridge. Look, Debbie, we've got a bit of time. Let's go to that pub opposite the station and have a drink.'

Lynne took another mouthful of coffee. She pulled a face – *cold!* The caffeine was starting to make her feel jittery. It was getting late, and she was – more and more – tempted to leave it. The clerk at the records office had already stayed on way past his usual time. But there was a pressing sense of urgency she couldn't account for, along with that nagging feeling of something left, something missed. She had a picture of mountains of paper, the vital piece hidden in the piles, as they searched frantically through. She looked at the fax. *Come on!*

Steve McCarthy was over the other side of the room, talking to two of the women who were working on the employee files. He looked across at Lynne, and came over. 'Cath says you're working on some of the people they pulled up yesterday,' he said. Lynne nodded. 'Anything?' Just as Lynne was

228

about to answer, the fax hummed quietly and papers glided into the tray. Lynne looked at the sender's address, and felt relief. This was her stuff. She could read it and go.

'Last lot coming through and then I'm finished.' She thought back to his question. 'I don't know. There's a couple I'm still chasing up – this odd character who seems to have gone missing, about three years ago. I've lost him in the records. And there's this one I'm waiting for now . . .' She was reading as she spoke.

'If we hit lucky, we could be winding this up in a couple of days, but have you seen . . .' McCarthy stopped talking, looking at Lynne's face.

'Steve . . .' A chill was creeping up Lynne's body, a feeling of things missed, a feeling of events rushing past her too fast to stop now. 'This one, William Stringer – his father – his stepfather – died in an accident when Stringer was fourteen. He fell downstairs, Steve. He was drunk, he fell downstairs and broke his neck.'

The rain was heavier now. Tim tried to draw Debbie under his umbrella, but she pulled away and wrapped her scarf round her head. Before they reached the crossing to the station, the rain had penetrated her mac. She could feel her blouse damp against her shoulders, and the icy cut of the wind. All she needed to do was get on the goddamn train. Once she was in Sheffield, she could get a taxi home, fall into a hot bath, forget about today. And yesterday. And the day before.

Tim checked his watch. 'We've got loads of time. It's only ten past. Let's have that drink.' They were passing the pub that he'd mentioned earlier.

Debbie wasn't enthusiastic. She didn't want to socialize with Tim any more than she had to. She just wanted to be home, but the choice seemed to be between the windy platform or the warmth of a pub. 'OK,' she said.

McCarthy hung up the phone he'd just used to call Berryman and looked across at Lynne, who was holding the other phone, drumming her fingers on the desk. Her face was tense. 'He's coming in,' he said to her as he hung up. She put her

229

phone down slowly. 'He wants us to contact Deborah Sykes.'
Lynne shook her head. She'd just tried Deborah's number.
A feeling of roller-coasting disaster was rising up inside her.
Deborah Sykes. Deborah Sykes and Thursdays. Hadn't it been
a Thursday . . . ? She worked late on Thursdays. That's why
she'd been at the station that stormy night when Julie Fyfe
had been abducted and killed.

And now, too late, that last piece of the jigsaw fell into place.
Of course! The timing, the shortening interval. The timing *did*
matter, it *was* important, but so was the chosen victim. He was
prepared to wait until she made herself vulnerable again. He
must have known a lot about her to have known that all he
had to do was wait. Careful and meticulous. But he didn't
have to break his *overall* pattern. If he kept to his original
pattern then he should be due to kill again four months from
the end of September. Which brought them to the end of
January. This week.

Lynne listened to the rain lashing against the window, and
realized that she'd got it all horribly, horribly wrong.

Neave tried Debbie's number. It was only twenty past, but if
the roads were clear, she and Louise could be back by now.
He could do the Moreham to Sheffield run in fifteen minutes
outside of rush hour. There was no reply. He banged the
phone down in frustration. She might not go home. She
might go back to Louise's. He'd give it five minutes and try
there. He had to talk to her.

Debbie insisted on buying the drinks, and toyed with her
beer while her mind drifted. She should have known. Her
mother had warned her, Louise had warned her, Rob had
bloody warned her, but she hadn't listened. Tim was saying
something. She pulled herself back to the present. 'I said,
"Penny for them,"' he said.

'Oh. Sorry. It's nothing. I was miles away.' She checked
her watch. Nine-twenty. When she got back, she'd take one
of those sleeping pills. She hadn't needed them before. Not
until Tuesday happened. Rob had proven far more efficacious
than any sleeping pills. She was angry with herself. She'd

cured herself once, and she'd gone and walked right back into it again, like a heroin smoker subjecting herself to cold turkey and then going out and mainlining. *Idiot, idiot, idiot.*

Tim touched her hand and she jumped. 'I'm having trouble keeping your attention,' he said. His voice sounded a bit sulky. He didn't like to be ignored, she remembered. She tried to concentrate. He was doing her a favour, after all.

With an effort, Debbie said, 'So how's the journalism business these days? Are you doing any more newspaper work?'

He smiled, looking rather pleased with himself, and said, 'I think I might have something pretty good going down soon. With a bit of luck, I'll be saying goodbye to dear old City before it says goodbye to me.'

'Do you think they're planning to do that?' At the moment, Debbie really didn't care.

'Oh, yes, they've got their list. I think the first redundancy notices will be going out any day now. Mind you, I don't think I'm on it.' Debbie presumed Tim was right. He had enough contacts in the personnel department. *I expect I am though.* She looked at her watch again. Almost half past.

She drained her glass. 'We'd better think about moving.' She waited impatiently while Tim finished his drink. 'Come on,' she said, 'I'll miss it.'

They were leaving the pub with a comfortable five minutes to spare when Tim said, 'Sorry, Debbie, I'm going to have to nip in here for a pee. You go on over. I'll just be a couple of minutes,' and he'd gone before she could say anything. Great. Well, she wasn't waiting. She walked out of the pub and across the road towards the station. It was still raining, even more heavily now. The cold penetrated her damp clothes. A car shot past as she reached the other side of the road, soaking her with dirty water as it raced through a puddle.

Berryman was there by twenty-five to. The team had been called in, and they ran through the implications of what they'd got. 'Right,' Berryman said. 'Lynne's tried to contact the Sykes woman. There's no reply. That doesn't mean anything, but we've got to find out where she is. I've sent a car to her house, and someone's gone up to the college to find out when she left. A car's gone to the station to look out for her there. Anything else?'

Lynne remembered, with a feeling of relief. 'Neave.'

'His phone's engaged. I've got someone trying. And someone's gone to his flat. He's been keeping an eye on her, so there's a good chance she's with him. If she is, she's safe. But we don't know that – we can't assume it.' He looked up at the waiting team. 'Our first priority is to find Deborah Sykes. What we do have to assume is that she's in danger *now* from the Strangler.' His eyes moved to the board, to the photographs, the eyeless faces and mutilated bodies of four women he'd failed so far. Not another. Please.

Neave tried Debbie's number again. Still no reply. He checked his watch. Maybe they had gone back to Louise's. Debbie probably felt like some company tonight. It was gone half past. They should be back by now. He tried Louise's number. She answered on the third ring.

'Oh, hi, Rob. No, Debbie isn't here, I didn't give her a lift in the end.' Louise explained the changes in the arrangement. 'I don't think you need to worry. Tim's reliable in his own way, and Debbie knows better than to take risks.'

He thought about it for a moment. 'She should be back by now. Would she have gone anywhere with him? Or anywhere else?'

Louise was pretty sure. 'I can't see her going anywhere with Tim Godber. And she doesn't usually go out after her night class. Have you two –'

He interrupted her. 'Have you got his number? Can you phone and check?'

Louise picked up the urgency in his voice. 'Do you want to phone?'

'No, I'm going to give City a ring. The caretakers will still be there. I'm going to find out if anyone saw them leave.'

The phone call only made him more uneasy. No one knew when, or even if, Debbie had left. Tim Godber's car was still in the car park, with a note on the windscreen saying it had broken down. Louise phoned back. 'There's no reply from Tim's,' she said.

Neave checked his watch. 'She might be on the train. It gets in at about nine-fifty. I'm going down to meet it.'

The station was dark, the ticket office closed, and the screen announcing arrivals and departures was out of action. Debbie's anger carried her past the ticket office, down the ramp and on to the platform. Then she stopped. The platform was dark and empty, the waiting room a locked black box. The rain drummed on the canopy above her head. A feeling of uneasiness began to grow. The opposite platform was empty too. The Doncaster train must have gone. There wasn't another train from that platform for nearly an hour – no one would come now. She looked at her watch. *Come on, Tim!* She couldn't go back up to the station entrance and wait for him. She might miss the train. It was late already. The flickering zigzag of the screen caught her eye. She let her gaze travel upwards beyond the screen to the girders and canopy above. She had noticed it before she became aware of it. The platform was dark. The light. Where was the light? Suddenly, she felt cold, felt her legs turn weak and cold. Slowly, knowing what she was going to see, slowly, because she didn't want to see it, she looked towards the ramp.

Nothing. She drew a breath, shaky with relief. Then a hand reached from behind her and clamped over her mouth.

17

Tim gave it five minutes – just enough time to establish that Debbie was on her own – then he headed towards the door of the pub. 'Hey, Tim,' a voice hailed him. It was one of the reporters from the *Moreham Standard*. He gave the man a friendly wave and mouthed, *Got to go*. The man came on over to him and gripped his arm. 'Just to tell you,' he said, 'there's some work coming up that's right up your street. You'll need to talk to Steve, though. Have you got his number?'

Tim shook his head. 'Look, I'm on something really important now. I've got to run, but I'll get on to that tomorrow. Thanks.'

'Don't leave it,' the man said. He looked a bit offended at Tim's lack of interest.

'I won't,' Tim promised. 'I'll be in touch first thing, OK?' Hiding his impatience, Tim smiled his thanks and moved towards the door again. He was almost there, when a sudden influx of people jammed into the pub. As he tried to push through, he was held back. 'Let them through, mate,' a voice said, as a man carrying a bulky piece of equipment backed through the door. Frustrated, he watched as they manoeuvred what looked like some kind of sound system into the pub.

'I've got a train to catch,' he said to the man who was holding his arm. He checked his watch. Ten minutes.

'Sorry, mate,' the man said, cheerfully. 'We're in now. Let this guy through, Dave. He's got a train to catch.' Tim pushed through the door. The road was a stream of fast-moving traffic. More busy than he ever remembered seeing it. He looked back up the road. He could run up to the crossing, wait for the lights, or would that take longer than waiting for a gap. He looked at his watch again. Fifteen minutes. *Christ!* The traffic slowed a bit and he launched himself off the kerb and wove in and out of the cars, ignoring the shouts and the sound of horns. 'Get out the fucking road,' a voice bellowed at him as a car almost ran him down. He was across. He ran into the station. Which platform? He never used the station. The screen was down. He looked round. *Platform One for all stations to Sheffield.* He raced round the corner, and there in front of him was a long ramp on to platform one. The dark of the platform waited for him at the bottom of the ramp, and Tim came to a sudden halt.

Down there, down in the darkness, who was waiting for him? All at once, it was real, really happening, not part of the story he was writing in his mind. His rational brain said that there was nothing to worry about, Debbie would be waiting, or her train would have gone, but something else, some other instinct, was making the hairs rise on his scalp, his senses come alert. He reached into his pocket for the phone, made sure it was set as he pressed himself against the wall and moved cautiously on to the ramp. He had the canister in his other hand, his finger on the button, not worried now, at this moment, if anyone saw it or not. He edged his way down as more of the platform came into view. His heart was thumping and his stomach clenched with tension. Slowly, slowly, he moved on to the platform, letting his breath out in a sudden release. Empty. No sign of Debbie. He looked across the line, breathing hard. No one there. He felt himself relax. The train had probably gone with a well-pissed-off Debbie on board.

He looked round. The platform was dark. He began to feel uneasy. Anything could be hiding in the shadows. He kept the canister in his hand as he walked up to one end of the platform and peered into the concrete space under the ramp. Nothing. He stood up and wondered what to do next. Assume Debbie had got the train? How could he make sure? He'd be lucky if she was home in half an hour. He could start phoning then. Call the police? Oh, yes, make a total fool of himself, lose his story. Find out if the train had gone? He could phone the enquiry line. They might tell him. He stood there indecisively, hearing, but not really hearing, the sound of sirens.

The giants were after her. She ran, but her legs were slow and heavy. She was in a tunnel, and voices followed her, echoing and strange. Debbie's giants were evil and dangerous, and one was coming through the night to get her. But it was only a bad dream, she would wake up soon. She could feel her head on the pillow, though it felt cold and hard, and her throat hurt so that she couldn't swallow. There was a smell of decay. She tried to turn her head away from it. There was a choking, rasping sound that she realized was her own breathing, and then she was conscious again.

She was in blackness. She was lying on something hard and gritty. It was cold and wet. There was a trickling sound, hollow and echoing, and the air around her had a sour smell, a smell of drains and sewers. Her face was pressed against the cold, gritty surface. She found it difficult to breathe. She moved her head, and it jerked as the support under it vanished and the roaring sound became louder. There was empty space beneath her. She tried to move her arms, but her hands were held fast behind her. Tears of panic filled her eyes, and for a moment her nose clogged up and she couldn't breathe. There was something across her mouth and she was choking. She blew out through her nose, and it cleared. For a moment she lay there breathing, not daring to move in case she choked again. Then her mind began to work.

She pulled her head back from the edge, and cautiously rolled on to her back. Her hands felt crushed. She swallowed and the pain in her throat made her moan. There was a small, lighter patch in the pitch blackness, above her, within reach if her hands were free. Water dripped through it on to her face. The trickling sound was water running, close to her head, but there was also the roaring sound of running water away in the distance. She could remember the cold terror she felt when the hand had pressed over her face. She could remember something pulling tight round her throat and the lights exploding in her eyes. She didn't know why she was still alive. Then the terror kicked in again. She was still alive because it wasn't the end, it was just the beginning. A fit of shaking seized her and she seemed to hang in darkness with no up, no down, no end.

Berryman listened to the radio for a moment, his face tightening. 'We've got a problem,' he said to the waiting group. 'West and McCarthy went to the station. Deborah Sykes vanished after leaving the pub – the Old Bridge. The man who was supposed to be keeping an eye on her – he says she left the pub to go to the station. West found him on the platform but he can't get much more out of him than that. He says he saw her last about twenty minutes ago.' He looked at Lynne and shook his head at her unspoken question. It hadn't been Neave with Debbie.

'Could she be on the train? Did she catch the train?' Lynne, looking for a way out.

Berryman shook his head. 'They've checked. That train was cancelled. There hasn't been a train through Moreham station in that direction for about forty minutes. I've got someone checking the train that went through the other way, but I don't think she'll be on that. Come on, we're going out there, and we're going to look. We'll assume the worst. If we're lucky, she'll turn up tomorrow after a night at the boyfriend's. If we're unlucky . . .' He didn't finish. 'So, if it is our man, we know whereabouts he got her. We go and look and we find everybody we can who was anywhere around. We check that station from end to end. We check the area, we track down every car. And we don't assume she's dead. He might have got her, but he doesn't kill them at once. We could be in time.'

Lynne thought about the other women, about being alive with the Strangler, about living with your eyes scraped out of your head, about living with the memories, and wondered if they'd be doing Deborah any favours if they didn't find her very, very soon.

The night makes black, angular shapes. The line stretches ahead like a silver ladder, shining coldly in the darkness. He moves in the shadows. He can feel that bubble of glee inside him that escapes from his mouth in a thin giggle. It makes his breathing uneven, and he tells himself he must be in control, not relax, not yet. He feels the stickiness of his hands inside the gloves, and it reminds him. He breathes hard and giggles again, rubs his fingers together to simulate the feel of soft flesh, pressing, squeezing . . . The feel of hair between his fingers, that first touch, soft, gentle, to make her look at him, make her eyes shine wetly in the darkness, shiny tracks on her face.

He feels hot, hard at his core. This one has cost him, this one must make it worth every difficult moment, every worry, every second of frustration. She will learn she made some bad mistakes. He fingers the instrument in his pocket, feeling its steel rigidity, the sharpness of its edge. He can remember the power of the moment. Next to it, the whispered touch of the silk scarf. The bubble of glee rises up again and a high giggle escapes. He is nearly there. He can feel himself start to breathe more heavily. He stops for a moment and looks at the sky, rubbing himself in anticipation. Soon. Here.

There was a scraping sound above her head. She was suddenly alert, frozen in the darkness. A whisper. *Deborah Sykes.* Her eyes strained. She couldn't see the lighter patch now. Again, the whisper. *Deborah Sykes* and a high-pitched giggle, quickly suppressed. Footsteps, muffled but close, grating like boots on gravel. A whisper again, babbling, excited, hard to follow . . . *see no evil . . . little shit . . . cunt, get your . . . big boy like you,* then that giggle again, like a child's, gleeful and cruel. Debbie felt her heart thudding, tried to pull enough air in through her nostrils, felt her chest tightening, stifled, suffocating. She had to free her mouth. She had to breathe. She struggled against the tape for a moment, then forced herself to be calm, pushed the air out of her chest and breathed in slowly and deeply. Then out. In. Out.

The sounds, the scraping sound, the whispers, the giggling, they had come from above her. She pulled herself into a sitting position, and looked up. She could see the lighter patch again now, just above her head. Then it was obscured, and the whispering and the grating sound began again as something moved in the darkness above her.

She was still wearing her mac. It was sodden, confining, but she was still wearing it. She heard Fiona's voice in her mind. *Anyone tries anything with me, they get one of those in them.* The knife! Was it still in the pocket? Her wrists were crossed and firmly bound, but she could move her arms, and her hands, though stiff and cramped, could move a bit. She gripped the fabric of her coat, and began pulling the pocket towards her hands. Which pocket? She worked her fingers into the first one. Nothing, just some paper. Perhaps he'd found it, taken it? She began working the fabric the other way, until she could get her hands into the second pocket. Her breath was coming faster and she couldn't stop the panicky moaning noises as she breathed. She could feel it! Feel the flat, rectangular shape of the knife.

Scraping above her, and heavy breathing like someone making an effort. She forced herself not to rush. If she dropped the knife now . . . Water – rain, she realized – was falling on her head. She could see a lighter strip widening above her, as though someone were sliding a lid off a box. The sound of water still echoed around her. She didn't know where the drop was, but the distant roaring made it sound like a long way down. It was hard to manoeuvre so that the blade was against the binding on her wrists, and she cut herself, feeling the handle become warm and sticky. She couldn't breathe. Then her wrists were loosening, she could work her hands free, pulled her right hand free and, wincing with the pain in her shoulder, brought it round to the front of her body, then the left hand, clutching the knife all the time. Then the gap above her was obscured as something bulky filled it and she heard the giggling again.

Neave beat his fists against the steering wheel in frustration. He'd arrived at the station to find, after minutes of waiting for someone on the enquiry desk to check, that Debbie's train had been cancelled. He'd tried Berryman's number. The line was transferred. DCI Berryman was busy, couldn't come to the phone. He tried Lynne's number. Her phone was switched off.

He didn't know what to do. He could drive to Moreham, see

if she was still at the station. She had someone with her. He kept telling himself that. She wasn't alone, she had someone with her, she should be all right. But he couldn't stop the feeling of unease that was getting stronger, making it harder to concentrate, to make decisions. He rubbed his hand over his face. *Think, Neave!* There were three possibilities. She was at Moreham station waiting for the next train. Tim Godber was probably with her. Or she'd gone off somewhere with Tim Godber – for a drink, maybe back to his flat. He didn't want to think that, but she was angry, upset. It was possible. At least she'd be safe. Or something had gone wrong and . . . He felt that welling up of emotion again, of rage and frustration and something else he couldn't put a name to. He trod hard on his feelings. He was good at that. *Think.* Right, if she was at the station, or if . . . *Think!* He needed to be at Moreham. The other option he couldn't do anything about until tomorrow. He could shelve that. He needed to be at Moreham.

Then he remembered, with a cold clarity, the photograph still in the wallet, still in his desk drawer. Now, he could see it – now it was too late. He'd known – hadn't he, really? – it couldn't have been Gina Sykes's foot that had carelessly crushed that picture, kicked it out of sight. And he'd waited, hesitated, worried – and finally forgotten. In his mind, he heard the scream of tyres on an icy road, the crash of a car going through the low wall and rolling, tumbling down the steep edge. He heard the first crackle of the flames and could smell the smoke as it twined through the fumes of spilled petrol. *Angie* . . . But it was too late.

He switched the ignition on, and was just preparing to pull out of the station forecourt when his phone rang. He wanted to ignore it, but it could be Louise, it could be Debbie, who'd know he'd been ringing. He picked it up.

It was Lynne. 'You didn't hear this from me,' she said, 'but you'd better get out to Moreham station as fast as you can.' He listened to what she had to say, then spun the wheel and headed north.

For a moment, Debbie watched herself watching the figure squeezing through the opening above her. Something reached down and touched her hair, then pushed against her face, cold and clammy. She tried to scream, but only a thin, high sound escaped through the gag. Her nose clogged and she choked. She heard that giggle again, and again something brushed her face. She felt something touch, cold and slug-like against her screwed-shut eyes. Then the paralysis broke and she realized she could move. She gripped the knife tightly, and the next time the touch came on her face, she cut and slashed at the thing touching her. It snagged the knife, almost jerking it from her hand until the blade snapped, releasing it. She pushed the blade up a notch. And slashed again. There was a grunt from above her. She pressed herself back against the wall and stared up through the darkness. The bulk was still there. Another whisper, harsher. *Deborah Sykes.* Her eyes were becoming accustomed to the dark and she could see more in the small amount of light the gap let in. He'd reached down with his hand before. Now he was swinging his legs over the edge, climbing into the pit with her.

She gripped the knife with both hands and ripped it down the leg, pushing to send it in deep. The blade broke against the fabric. Something warm spattered on to her face. He kicked out at her, catching her shoulder and sending her sprawling above the drop. She rolled back and slashed out at his leg again, choking for air. As he drew his leg back, she ripped the tape from around her mouth and screamed. Not loud enough. She didn't know if anyone could hear her, if there was anyone to hear her. She slashed out with the knife again, and again the leg swung out of the way. She took a deep breath and screamed as loudly as she could. Then he was pulling his leg back over the edge. She could see the shape of his head looking down at her. Again the whisper, *Deborah Sykes.* Then the gap was narrowing, it was getting darker. *No . . .* There was the grating sound again, and something closed over the gap above her, leaving her in the dark. Sobbing with terror, Debbie reached up and put her hands against the underside, which was metal. She pushed. It wouldn't shift. She pushed up at it again, trying to use the whole force of her body, but her legs were trembling with cold and shock, and she could feel the strength running out of them. It wouldn't move. She was trapped, alone in the dark. She could feel blood from her hand running down her arm, and she felt cold and weak. The trembling in her legs got worse and she realized she would fall, maybe fall off the edge into the unknown drop where the water gushed. She dropped to her knees, still clutching the knife, and shook with terror.

Tim sat in the back of the dark patrol car and gnawed at his knuckle. It had happened too soon, too quickly – he'd missed it! He'd missed it by minutes. He could have seen it, he could have been a hero, and now he was having to explain things to two Plods, while all the action was going on elsewhere. He'd told them, *My car broke down, I got held up in the pub, I don't know where she is.* They didn't believe him, he could tell. He peered through the rain. He could just see two other cars, blue lights flashing, people getting out and milling round in the rain. Had they found her? He tried his door. It wouldn't open from the inside, of course. He needed to get out, get down on the platform, watch what was going on. He hammered on the car window, trying to attract the attention of one of the officers.

It seemed like an age, but it must have been only seconds, when water started splashing more heavily on to Debbie's face, and she began to control her panic. She had to get out of here by herself. There was no one else to help her. She sat up and tried to get an idea of where she was, of what surrounded her. The smell of wet decay was still in her nostrils, but the water that fell on her face was clean, smelled of the air. Rain. She had a better idea of where she was, now. She was on a ledge just under the lid that sealed the pit – she suddenly realized where she was. She was under one of the covers that let into the inspection pit for the storm drains. The storm drains by the track? She didn't know. She didn't know how long she'd been there, how long she'd been unconscious. The track drains must empty into the river. The drop would take the water down. If she could get down there, she might be able to get out. Then what? Drown in the river? It was deep, dirty and fast-flowing. Better that than wait.

The cold was beginning to overcome her. She shook uncontrollably and her hands and feet felt numb. Her gloves had vanished – they would have been useless in this wet, anyway. Her feet were soaked, frozen beyond the point of pain. At least she was still wearing her shoes, heavy and wet than they were. She would need their protection. She could get rid of them if she made it to the river. Up or down. She had to get out. If he came back he would kill her. If he didn't come back, she would die of cold like an animal in a trap. No one would find her here.

She reached up again and tried to move the cover from the opening to the drain. It wouldn't shift. The effort started her hand bleeding again. She edged towards the drop, sat with her legs dangling over and felt with her feet. She could feel something in the side – rungs. People were meant to climb up and down here. The thought of people, ordinary people, made the dark place seem less threatening, less unknown.

She clutched the knife in one frozen hand, rolled over and began to inch herself over the edge, feeling with her feet for the rungs. It was difficult to tell when she had found them as she was losing the feeling in her legs. She found hand grips and began her descent into darkness. The roar of the water seemed louder, faster, and the stench of decay was stronger. This time it reminded her of the night she was trapped on the stairs, that same sickening smell. How far down did the drop go? She wasn't sure how long her hands would grip. She climbed down further, and reached out with her foot, feeling for the bottom.

Then the whispered babble – *none so blind . . . cunt . . . see no evil, see no . . .* and something gripped her ankle with unbelievable strength and pulled.

And then the heavens opened. The rain fell in sheets, filling the gutters in seconds, running over the suddenly full drains. Roads became rivers, drain covers exploded as the pressure of the water burst through. Moreham centre became a torrent as the water flowed across the drains and poured through the precinct, washing away the accumulations of rubbish that danced and swirled in the eddies and flows.

Neave's car swerved as his wheels aquaplaned on the flooded road. He cursed and slowed down, the chunk, chunk of the windscreen wipers speeding up as they battled ineffectually with the torrent.

The police car slammed to a halt outside Moreham station, and Lynne leapt out, closely followed by Berryman. The rain cut through Lynne's clothes, soaking her to the skin in the few seconds it took her to get under the shelter of the station canopy. The ground was running with water, backing up from the overloaded drains to start pooling in front of the ticket office.

The platform was awash, the line starting to flood as the rain teemed down. It was dark, the rain turning the view up and down the track to black nothingness. The drumming on the canopy was a roar, drowning out all other sound.

In the centre of Moreham, the security cameras caught a young man, dressed for summer, riding an improvised surf board through the flooded precinct.

The rivers rose. The Porter, running through the west of Sheffield, changed from a gentle beck to a fast-running torrent as it rose over its banks and spread across the finger of green that ran from the countryside into the heart of the city. Paths and grass disappeared under a sudden influx of tributary rivers that gradually joined into one racing mass of water.

In Moreham, the rush of the river became a roar as it rose higher up its concrete banks, washing away the green track beside it, flattening out the weir, rising and rising, covering the exits from the storm drains, backing the water up and up.

Her hands, already weak with cold, lost their grip. The knife slipped through her fingers and clattered into darkness. She clutched frantically at the rungs, scraping her face against the wall as she slipped and fell. Her head cracked against the side of the shaft. It wasn't a long drop, and she lay stunned and winded in the fast-flowing stream at the bottom, hearing that mad giggle. She could see the light through the grating of the storm drain far above her. The darkness around her was dank and rotten. Water was flowing underneath her. She must be in the pipe that led to the river. So near! Her breath came in great sobs. She smelt his closeness and lifted her hands to protect herself, rolling over as his heaviness landed on top of her, taking the force of his weight on her ribs rather than her stomach. She felt something snap inside her. She doubled up with pain, aware of his hands pulling at her, but unable to do anything but reach for the air that had been crushed out of her lungs. Her hands grabbed at the side of the shaft, searching for the rungs of the ladder, but finding only wet brick or stone. She was lost, disorientated. Her breathing drowned out other sounds, a gasping, sobbing rasp. Her hands found the rungs, and she reached up, gasping at the stabbing pain in her chest, then hands grabbed her hair and pulled her back and down.

Lynne looked along the track. She'd looked at the maps so many times, she could picture them in her mind. She knew that the track and the river ran close together a short way down the line back in the direction of Sheffield. She shouted her plans in Berryman's ear, and he nodded. Calling to West and McCarthy, she set off down the line, the light from her torch barely penetrating the rain. The downpour was easing off slightly. Lynne was glad of that because the water next to the track was almost over the tops of her shoes. She had boots in the car, she remembered, too late.

Her light shone on the track ahead. She moved it from side to side. She didn't know what she expected to see, didn't know what she was looking for. Her mind was running over the timings. Tim Godber had lost sight of Deborah for about twenty minutes. In that time, someone had to subdue her and get her out of sight. Out of the station and into a car? It was possible, but other people were looking for that. Somewhere in the station? Berryman was there with Curran and Barraclough. Down the line? Possibly, and she was here. Up the line, there was no one, but others were arriving by the minute and Lynne was gambling now, working the odds.

*   *   *

245

Debbie's strength was nearly gone. A cold heaviness was weighing her down, a resignation that made her struggles slow and ineffectual, a grip round her throat that made her voice a thin and feeble whisper. She could hear a monotonous chant, a litany of obscenities that whispered and echoed around the dark, telling her what she was, telling her what he was going to do. The fear was something detached from her, something distant, abstract. She knew she was going to die. She wanted it to happen soon, to get the stench of him out of her nostrils, the feel of him away from her body. She could see the faint light high above her, and her mind drifted away to sunlight and blue skies and clouds on summer days. She was walking in the woods near Goldthorpe with Gina, the woods of her childhood, the ones she knew so well . . . but there was something wrong. The cool shadows under the trees beckoned. Something was waiting for them, something terrible, something dangerous. She turned to Gina to tell her to keep away, and she heard her mother's voice: *Fight!* And she pushed with all her remaining strength, twisting her body, throwing off the weight that was pinning her to the ground. Her hands reached out, and one hit against the cold metal of a rung. A lifeline that she gripped on to as she felt him lurch towards her in the blackness, knowing that that was it, that was all she had, she had no more.

Then there was a rush of water up the pipe, river water, she could smell its filth. The water filled the pipe and almost washed her away, flooded her nose and mouth, making her gasp and retch, but she hung on to the rung and the water pushed her up the shaft as it began to rise. She felt something grab at her feet again, this time from under the water, this time with a frantic grasp, and she slipped again, her head hitting against the rungs as she fell back into the water.

Arms round her waist, gripping her tightly. Something pressing into her stomach. Blackness, swirling darkness, her chest tight, her heart hammering. Air. She had to breathe. She couldn't pull herself free, couldn't get her head above the water. She kicked madly, and in her panic her mouth opened and she breathed the filth of the river into her lungs.

*　　*　　*

246

The dark place, and the beast is waiting. The mother's face is turned away – the child holds her, grips her, presses his head into the folds of her skirt. Mam! . . . Out of my sight . . . Out of my sight . . . She pushes him deeper into the dark. The child is locked into it – he struggles but he can't escape. Shiny tracks on his face, in the moonlight . . . But there is no light. Just the darkness and the beast, and the child drifts away . . . Mam . . . Mam . . . Whispering in the darkness, in the emptiness, gone . . .

Lynne played her torch over the gravel by the track, and then up against the wire fence that separated the track from the river path. The fence was intact, as it had been all the way along. She shone her torch further. No sign of any break. Was there anything here, anything at all, apart from the closeness to the river? Her light travelled over the raised storm drain for the second time before it registered and she went over to look. There was something lying across the cover. Her eye caught sight of something on the ground, and she shone the torch on it. A glove, a woman's knitted glove, soaked by the rain. Could have been there for ages, but . . . She called to McCarthy, who was shining his torch into the undergrowth. He and West ran over. She directed their attention with the light of her torch. McCarthy shone his torch at the drain, and said something. She couldn't hear, but he grabbed her arm and pointed. Lying across the cover was a heavy iron bar. The water pooled underneath it looked dark – rust? Dirt? Lynne looked closer. As she shone her torch on it, the colour changed. Blood?

West was looking at the fence, and called. Behind the shrub, the wire was pulled away at the bottom, leaving a gap easily large enough for an adult to get through. There were stains on the wire. She thought. *Quickly, woman!* 'Get Berryman!' she shouted to West. 'Quick.' Her gestures transmitted any of the message the storm obscured. She turned to McCarthy, pointed to the cover of the drain. 'Help me get this thing open.' It took two of them to shift the heavy bar holding the cover down.

They were dragging the cover off with an improvised lever as Berryman ran up with Curran. Lynne shone her torch

247

inside. A ledge, just about four feet below the opening, and a deep dark shaft. There were dark stains on the ledge, and something that looked like crumpled paper. She shone her torch down the shaft. Water, just a few feet down, dirty and stinking, and . . . something floating, weed, rags, no, hair, a woman's long hair, a woman was under the water in the shaft.

Neave could see the cars by the station, the blue lights flashing, the officers keeping back the small crowd that had gathered even in the appalling weather. He ran up to the entrance. One of the officers was someone he knew. He couldn't remember the name. 'They phoned me,' he said.

The man looked doubtful, but didn't try to stop him as he pushed through. He sprinted down the ramp. He could see lights along the line, bobbing as though the people carrying them were running. He ran on, wiping the rain out of his eyes. The lights grouped ahead of him, stopped, but seemed to be getting no nearer. Then he was there. The rain was slowing now, and he could see them clearly, the men working in the open drain, Lynne and Berryman standing to one side, Berryman talking urgently into his radio, the light of the signal hanging like a green eye above them. He looked back up the track and saw the figure of Tim Godber on the bridge, watching, hands raised to his face. *Flash!* Lynne turned. She came and stood with Neave and they watched together as West and McCarthy lifted the lifeless body of Deborah Sykes on to the ground by the track.

18

Berryman was tired – more tired than he could remember being. It was a mess. Loose ends flapping around, and no way to tie half of them up quickly. They'd searched the drain after the river level dropped. They'd found the body of a man down there. He wore blue overalls that had ripped on the sleeve and caught on a broken rung set into the wall of the inspection pit. He had cuts – they looked as though they'd been inflicted with a knife – on his hands and legs, but he'd almost certainly drowned, hooked on the metal as the river flooded in. The postmortem would confirm it. There was nothing on him to identify him. Lynne's late – almost too late – findings about William Stringer would give them a starting point, and Berryman hoped, a finishing point, at last.

They'd inspected the river outfalls from the storm drains. They were fitted with grilles to stop people going into them, but one had been tampered with, the bolts holding it cut through and replaced. It made an easy entrance and exit to and from the track side.

He pressed his hands over his eyes, trying to keep himself awake. The scene by the track came vividly into his mind again – the torchlight catching the rain, reflecting on the wet gravel, illuminating the woman on the ground, her face grey, tinged with blue; illuminating the figures of McCarthy and Curran, trying to hold on to any spark of life that was left. He was cursing himself inside – *too late, too late* – aware of Neave, frozen beside him. He remembered the sound of running feet as the paramedics arrived, he could see them crouched over the body on the ground, and then the words – *OK, OK, that's it, she's still with us.* And the scene began to move again.

He sighed and reached for the phone.

A light, unbearably bright, a harsh, metallic voice, cutting in and out. DEB-ah -orAH. Everything ached. A sharp, chemical smell. Something moaned. —AKE up! COME ON, De— Blackness.

The light. Things clattering near her head. The pain. She tried to say something and gagged and choked on an obstruction in her throat. 'It's all right, Deborah. Just lie still. You're in hospital,' as the obstruction was pulled away. Voices in the background. *I think that's it . . . Is she . . . Early to say . . .* She tried to move, but hands pressed on her shoulders. 'Just stay where you are, Deborah. Keep still. You're fine. You're in hospital.'

That's stupid. I can't be fine. I can't move.

Gina put down her knitting. *It's all in the head*, she said, smiling. But there was someone behind her. She wanted to warn her mother, *Look out!* but her throat hurt too much. She sank back on to the pillow. The tunnel was rushing past her, she was being swept down and away by the water. She was trapped. She would never get out, get away. *Deborah Sykes*, Gina said, nodding her head thoughtfully. *Half-hourly obs*. She was walking away. She didn't know Debbie was trapped, didn't know that a giant was chasing her through the tunnels. She crashed into the pain. Someone was moaning. Blackness.

A moment of clarity. She was lying flat on a bed. Her head hurt more than anything she'd ever felt, an icy, gripping pain. Her arms felt cold and heavy. The room was dimly lit, and there was a faint humming sound. A terrible sense of desolation. She could see the drip stand above her and the line running down from it. She couldn't turn her head. Someone was holding her hand. She moved her eyes. Rob was sitting beside the bed, his arms resting on the cover, one hand holding hers, one hand supporting his head which drooped forward. She squeezed his hand. He leaned quickly towards her. She tried to smile, but it didn't feel as though it worked. He looked across the bed, at someone or something she couldn't see, then she was walking down the corridor behind a tall bulky figure. She couldn't get past. She could see Rob walking ahead, away into the distance. He wouldn't turn round. *I shouldn't expect too much at the moment*, Gina was smiling again. *Mum*, Debbie wanted to say, *I was trapped and I couldn't get out*, but the words wouldn't come. She felt tears trickling down the side of her face, into her hair, her ears. Someone wiped them away. She drifted off into darkness.

Berryman was reading the folder on William Stringer that Lynne had given him, expanded now with more details that had come through in response to her requests. The death of Charles Howard, Stringer's stepfather, the death of a violent man with a history of alcoholism, hadn't attracted much attention. Berryman got the impression of a cursory investigation coupled with a *good riddance*. If they'd suspected anything, they'd suspected the wife. *If we'd had these facts* . . . He went through the case in his mind again. Was there any way they could have come up with this name earlier? With hindsight, probably. In the maze of confusion they'd been working in? Probably not. And the Goldthorpe link. Gina Sykes's death. Berryman wasn't a man to castigate himself needlessly, but – should they have seen the link earlier?

They *had* seen it – that was the point. Had they done enough? It was tenuous, it was being investigated, and Deborah Sykes, warned and watched, should have been safe. What series of mischances had put her alone on the station platform? *That* was what should never have happened. He remembered Neave's haunted face, and wondered if he was going to be able to ask him the question. Why hadn't he been there?

Lynne Jordan came in, carrying a cup and a sheaf of papers. 'Coffee, sir,' she said, putting a cup in front of him. 'You looked like you needed it.' She put a piece of paper in front of him. He read it.

'Right, we've got a match with the fingerprints. He's the one who left those prints on Lisa's bag. They're checking the other stuff now. We need a positive identification. Have you got a current address for Stringer?'

'We're checking.' There were other things she needed to know. 'Any news about Deborah?'

Berryman shook his head. 'I've left Curran there for the moment. The medics said she wasn't likely to come round properly tonight, and even if she does, she won't be fit to talk to us.'

Lynne had been at the hospital for a while but hadn't heard the doctors' verdict. 'Is she going to be all right?'

'They think so. They wouldn't commit themselves, of course. She was in a bad way – concussion, hypothermia, broken ribs, cuts and bruises, shock. No skull fracture, though. Anyone who's taken on board as much of the Morebrook as she has is going to need watching, but apparently there was less muck in the storm drain – it was rain water rather than river water. No, it's wait and see.'

The house was large, a three-storey Victorian terrace. The small front garden was overgrown, a tangle of dead vegetation twining through the railings, a dark funereal shrub obstructing the gate. The low wall leaned outwards, pushed by roots and the weight of the damp earth. The windows looked on to the road, black and empty. The downstairs front was empty – no furniture, bare boards, when Lynne peered in through the sagging bay.

They went round the back, which showed signs of habitation, signs of exit and entry. Rubbish bins overflowed on to the sparse, muddy grass and broken asphalt. The light from the moon streamed down from a sky that was now clear, but an iron fire escape from the next house in the row cast a shadow over the yard. There was a smell of damp and decay. A curtain was pulled across one of the basement windows, and Berryman knocked at the door. There was no response. He tried again, and then signalled to Lynne as he heard footsteps and the rattling of a key in the door.

A young man, naked apart from a towel wrapped round his waist, stood blinking at them. He smelt of beer, and a frowsty mixture of alcohol, cigarettes and unwashed bodies hung in the doorway. He seemed confused, half asleep. Lynne showed her card. 'William Stringer?' But she already knew the answer. This man was too young. He shook his head and gestured towards the stairs. He said he was a lodger, had lived there for just under a year. He was planning to move on. He didn't like it here, didn't like Stringer, his landlord. A minute convinced them that this man knew nothing. West stayed with him, and they continued through the house, up the stairs from the basement, into the entrance hall.

Bare boards and peeling wallpaper, the smell of damp and emptiness. Lynne tried the light switch. Nothing. She shone her torch round. There were rooms to either side of the front door, and a room behind them at the end of the corridor. Empty, apparently long empty, and neglected. McCarthy indicated the stairs, and they went up, Lynne slightly ahead, shining her torch off the walls and ceiling. The stairs led to a landing with three doors off it. McCarthy pushed the door to his right open. A bathroom. The light worked in here. The bulb was bare. A damp towel lay on the floor. The bath was not boxed in. There were rust stains round the plug hole where the tap dripped. The basin and the wall above it – no mirror – were spattered with white flecks. There was a sour smell of damp cloth, overlaid with a faint, sweet smell.

The room to the left was a small room that overlooked the front of the house. It was dusty and empty. The last room showed signs of habitation. A bed, a chair, a rug in front of a two-bar electric fire. There were shelves against one wall with piles of magazines, some books. Lynne looked at them. They were railway magazines, mostly, going back over several years. A few pornographic magazines that Lynne thought were probably imported. She flicked through the pages – women tied and chained, exposed, helpless, flesh bulging against tight bonds. Penetrations with sharp heavy implements. Pain and screaming, simulated or real. It was evidence. She looked at McCarthy. His face registered distaste.

Lynne looked at the shelves again. Underneath them, folded against the wall, was a loft ladder. Their eyes went up to the trap door in the ceiling.

There was something clinical, sterile about the way the light bounced off the white walls, that contradicted the heavy, sweet smell of decay that pervaded the loft. It made the investigating team recoil as they arrived, made Berryman shake his head in disgust. It caught at Lynne's throat and made her gag, but her eyes were drawn and held by the perfection of the railway, the miniature landscape that was laid out in front of her. The minute tracks ran between carefully sculpted hills and valleys, platforms and stations meticulously replicated, waterways, bridges and roads appearing and disappearing as they impinged on the line. A child's toy, a plaything, become a playground for a monster. She thought about the labyrinth and the minotaur, the young women who were pursued to their deaths through the maze where the monster lived and fed.

He had known his playground well, had known the entrances and exits, had enticed his victims into his game of hide and seek. She heard a whistle of amazement from McCarthy behind her. 'A train anorak. A fucking train anorak.' She left him to marvel over the models.

She moved round the room, touching nothing, looking. She saw the computer with its pages of print-outs – timetables, freight schedules, dates, places, notes. She saw the overalls hanging against the wall, stained and stiffened, the pockets distorted. The smell was stronger here. She was glad, later, that it was other people who had to look closely at them, analyse the stains, empty the pockets.

She saw the file of newspaper clippings. She looked at the board that hung on the wall above the entrance to the loft. It was the first thing she had seen as she had climbed through the trap door. Lisa, Kate, Mandy, Julie stared back at her, their mutilated pictures somehow more shocking than the pictures she saw every day in the incident room. And at the end of the row, Deborah Sykes, her picture almost torn to shreds where the sharp pins had been pulled through it.

In the days that followed, there were loose ends to sort out. William James Stringer was the Strangler, and the Strangler was dead. Berryman doubted that the coroner would record anything other than accidental death against his name. The loft, which the newspapers used as a Bluebeard's chamber to hang their stories on, gave up some secrets. The file that

254

Lynne had seen, consisting mostly of newspaper cuttings, filled in some of the gaps in the story. It began with a birth certificate, that telling certificate that marked disgrace in those days, not so very long ago. Lynne wondered why Susan Stringer had kept her son. Had she loved him? She must have done, surely. Then, records of a marriage. Susan Stringer and Charles Howard. Howard was a local celebrity, a minor name on the boxing circuit. A newspaper photograph of the bride and groom, Susan Stringer smiling adoringly up at the face of her husband to be. A small child was half obscured by the edge of the frame. Records of work. Trains. Howard was a driver, and someone had recorded the schedules he worked, the routes he followed, the run from the freight yards to the docks at Hull at the end of each month.

A newspaper report, a case of child cruelty. A depressingly familiar story of beatings, burnings, neglect. A mother who denied her son had been hurt by anyone. *He's careless, he falls.* Her ignorance admonished but excused, his cruelty punished by a short prison sentence. Lynne wondered what cruelties were unknown and unspoken behind the routine indignation of the reports. Another cutting, this one almost falling to pieces – *Darnall monster dies.* The death of the stepfather. And then, many years later, the death of the mother. *Local woman dies in blaze.* William Stringer had lived quietly with his mother, it seemed, until her death when he was forty-five. The psychologist put his late eruption into psychosis down to this. She had held him in a state of arrested development, the psychologist speculated, until her death, when he finally broke free.

Cuttings recorded the deaths of each of the victims, all reports into the developing investigation, carefully and chronologically placed, including the pictures of the victims as they had appeared in the paper where he first saw them. Lisa, smiling lovingly at her husband, Karen in the foreground, Kate smiling triumphantly at the Education Secretary, Mandy casting a fiancée's loving look at Damien Hastings, Julie's smile at Andrew Thomas – *Broughton's Winning Team* – understand-able, to those in the know. And Debbie, whose smile was directed at someone who wasn't even in the picture. Each one an echo of Susan Stringer's smile at her bridegroom, her smile turned away from the child half cut away from the frame?

There, also, in due order, were the deaths of Sarah Peterson and Gina Sykes. Written under their names, in one of the few personal records that Stringer left, was the word *Vermin*. A bunch of keys, carefully labelled, lay beside the file.

The world that Debbie woke up to was a different one from the one she'd left. A procession of people came to see her at the hospital. Berryman came, with Lynne Jordan. She wasn't sure if this was an official visit or not. He asked her some questions, but didn't push her when she said she couldn't remember something. 'If anything comes back . . .' he said. He asked her about her keys, how they could have come into the killer's possession, and she remembered the morning she had found them slung carelessly on her desk, as though someone had thrown them contemptuously down – and hadn't wanted to think about what that meant. They told her that her mother, and Sarah, had both been victims. Debbie knew that she had led the killer to them, unwitting, unintentional though it had been. 'It wasn't your fault,' Berryman had said, seeing the expression on her face. He was a kind man. The papers were full of the story for the first few days. The staff tried to keep them away from her, but it was impossible, really.

She had no job. The redundancy notice had landed on her mat, posted on Friday morning before the news of the attack got out. Debbie rather thought they would have held off, if they had known. Louise brought it in to her on the third day of her hospital stay. She didn't care.

Tim Godber was a hero. His story appeared on the front page of the national that was now employing him. His picture, of the track pointing like an arrow, the group frozen underneath the eye of the signal light, the two men by the open pit lifting a limp figure with a lolling head, had been printed in every paper in the country. She'd looked at it once, and never wanted to see it again. The nurse said he'd come to the hospital, wanted to see her, but she'd told them to send him away.

She thought about going home. But her house seemed like a stranger's in her mind – the familiar furniture, the bits and pieces, the pictures and colours that had meant so much to her were just – nothing. He'd been there, he'd seen her things, he'd touched them. She didn't feel revulsion, just distance. Louise had tried to reassure her. 'I've been round and really cleaned the place up,' she had said. 'Not that it needed it, but you know . . .' Debbie could almost smell the lemon and lavender, the polish and bleach with which Louise had tried to obliterate him. Louise. Debbie smiled briefly. Lovely Louise, rallying round, supporting her, trying to put the pieces back together again, not realizing there weren't any pieces to put together. Debbie didn't feel broken, only changed. No, not changed – touched, spoiled, contaminated. She thought of the photographs on the table. Gina's serious face above her graduation gown, her father's proud smile at the little girl holding the trophy, his older, blurred face already fading into memory. And another face – she saw Sarah's eyes watching her through a tangle of hair. Gone, all touched, contaminated and destroyed. The house would be cold after standing empty. The cold felt right. Cold stopped things from germinating, taking root, growing. She couldn't go home. There was nowhere to go.

There was still a lot they didn't know. Stringer had been a solitary man. Their enquiries identified no friends, and few acquaintances. The men he had worked with had few memories of him – he was *a quiet man*, he was *a loner*. One of them said, *He knew more about these railways than anyone I've ever met. He loved them.* His lodger hardly saw him, living in the flat in the basement. He collected the rent and that was all. He'd bought the house with the insurance money from his mother's death, and his redundancy. After his redundancy, he seemed to have made a living from renting the basement of the house he had bought. He wrote articles for model makers that were published in some special-interest magazines. Back issues had suddenly become collectors' items.

And then there were the questions that would probably never be answered. Berryman doubted they would have

257

been answerable even if William Stringer was still alive. *What makes a man stalk, mutilate and kill?* They had something of his story now, but there had to be another part, the bit they didn't know, the bit that was lost. Some dark part of his mind? Some cruelty that can't be ignored or forgotten? The desires of an evil man? Berryman didn't know the answer, and didn't want to know it. It was over. Let it lie. He looked at the clock. Nearly ten. God knows when he'd get home. There was a tap on the door, and Lynne Jordan came in. 'There's just me and Steve left now, sir,' she said.

Berryman sighed. 'I don't think there's much left to be done tonight. Anything new?'

'Do you need to talk to Deborah Sykes again?' Berryman shook his head. 'She's out of hospital. They discharged her today. She's gone away for a couple of weeks. Rob Neave's taken her up north somewhere.'

Berryman grinned. 'Miserable sod. What's wrong with Tenerife?' He flicked through the papers on his desk. 'Is she OK? No permanent damage?'

'Who's to tell?' Lynne shrugged.

Berryman pushed the last pile of papers back into the file. 'Right. I'm leaving this until tomorrow.' He stood up and picked up his coat, a big man, heavily built. He was going home to his family, but Lynne thought he looked lonely.

'Good night, sir,' she said. She went back into the main office. She felt lonely too. The desks were empty now, the incident room being wound down. Steve McCarthy looked across at her, his thin face weary. Lynne waited for the irritation that usually crossed his face when he saw her. Instead, he smiled. She responded with a friendly nod. 'You ready for off, then, Steve?'

He rubbed his face in a gesture that reminded her sharply of Neave. 'I'm calling in for a drink first,' he said. 'I need one. How about you?'

Lynne thought for a moment. 'Sounds good.' She paused. Was this a wise move or not? Probably not, but what the hell. 'First round on me.' She had a fridge full of beer at her